"CONNOLLY WRITES LIKE A POET ABOUT TERRIBLE HORRORS. . . . HIS WORDS SING."

—Houston Chonicle

Critical acclaim for #1 international bestselling author John Connolly's thrillers

BAD MEN

"Powerful. . . . Connolly has quickly and decisively established himself as a unique voice."

—Michael Connelly, bestselling author of *The Narrows*

"Terrifying. . . . Think Thomas Harris by way of Stephen King. . . . Not for the faint of heart."

—*Publishers Weekly*

"A supernatural chiller. . . . A stylish darkness sucks you under."

—*Kirkus Reviews*

"An honest-to-goodness fright fest. . . . Connolly takes the chills to a new level."

—*Denver Rocky Mountain News*

"Totally compelling."

—*St. Petersburg Times* (FL)

"A violent, bloody, page-turning thriller."

—*The Sunday Oregonian* (Portland, OR)

"The plot, approach, even the setting, will hold great appeal for Stephen King fans, as well as for the legions of followers Connolly has earned with his previous award-winning work."

—*Times-Picayune* (New Orleans, LA)

"FEW CRIME WRITERS CAN CONJURE UP MENACE AND CHILL AS JOHN CONNOLLY. . . ."

—The Toronto Sun

THE WHITE ROAD

"Darkly brilliant, spellbinding, and disturbing."

—Harlan Coben

"You don't want to miss a word of this near-perfect story."

—*Denver Rocky Mountain News*

"The malevolence here is almost palpable."

—*Publishers Weekly* (starred review)

"[A] complex, compelling read."

—*Times-Picayune* (New Orleans, LA)

"Connolly . . . depicts an America that chills to the bone."

—*Library Journal*

THE KILLING KIND

"Unfolds with the force and logic of a nightmare."

—*The Washington Post*

"Connolly has that rare ability to hit you head-on with a great crime story while giving you goosebumps in the process."

—*Clarion Ledger* (Jackson, MS)

"More than a great detective story. . . . A deep character study about loss, reparation, and revenge."

—*Denver Rocky Mountain News*

“[CONNOLLY] COMBINES BEAUTIFUL LANGUAGE WITH HORRIFYING IMAGES TO CREATE GRIPPING NOVELS OF SUSPENSE.”
—Mystery Review

DARK HOLLOW

“*Dark Hollow* is the real deal.”

—*People*

“Grim, hard-edged, and compulsively readable.”

—*Publishers Weekly*

“Filled with tension and menace and peopled by some fascinating characters.”

—*The Toronto Sun*

EVERY DEAD THING

“Terrific. . . . A complex tale as riveting and chilling as *The Silence of the Lambs* and *Kiss the Girls*.”

—*San Francisco Examiner*

“Stunning. . . . *Every Dead Thing* ensnares us in its very first pages and speeds us through a harrowing plot to a riveting climax.”

—Jeffery Deaver, *New York Times* bestselling author of *Garden of Beasts*

“A spellbinding book . . . holds the reader fast in a comfortless stranglehold.”

—*Los Angeles Times*

“A multilayered work that draws the reader ever deeper into an abyss of pain and madness. Compelling . . . filled with fascinating characters and motivations, blending horror, compulsion, and fear.”

—*The Dallas Morning News*

Also by John Connolly

Every Dead Thing
Dark Hollow
The Killing Kind
The White Road
Nocturnes

BAD MEN

JOHN CONNOLLY

POCKET STAR BOOKS
New York London Toronto Sydney

This book is a work of fiction. Names, characters, places and incidents are products of the author's imagination or are used fictitiously. Any resemblance to actual events or locales or persons, living or dead, is entirely coincidental.

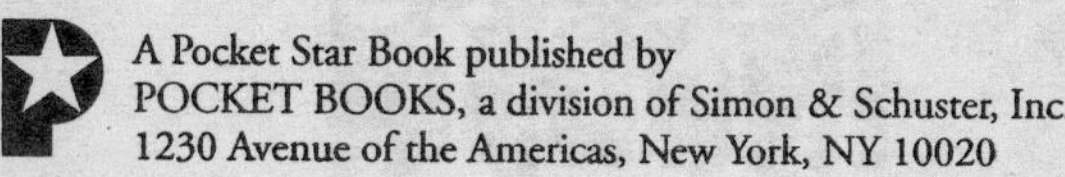

A Pocket Star Book published by
POCKET BOOKS, a division of Simon & Schuster, Inc.
1230 Avenue of the Americas, New York, NY 10020

Originally published in hardcover in 2004 by Atria Books

ISBN: 0-7434-8785-0

First Pocket Books paperback printing May 2005

10 9 8 7 6 5 4 3 2 1

Cover art and design by Jae Song

For information regarding special discounts for bulk purchases, please contact Simon & Schuster Special Sales at 1-800-456-6798 or business@simonandschuster.com

Manufactured in the United States of America

PROLOGUE

. . . they are not towers but giants. They stand in the well
from the navel down; and stationed round its bank
they mount guard on the final pit of Hell.

—Dante Alighieri, *Inferno,* canto 31

Moloch dreams.

In the darkness of a Virginia prison cell, he stirs like an old demon goaded by memories of its lost humanity. The dream presses upon him once more, the First Dream, for in it lies his beginning, and his end.

In the dream, he is standing on the verge of a dense forest and a smell clings to his clothing, the scent of animal fat and saltwater. There is a weight at his right hand: a musket, its rough leather strap hanging almost to the ground. On his belt there is a knife, and a powder horn, and a bag of shot. The crossing was difficult, for the sea was wild and the waves broke upon them with the force of a great hand. They lost a man on the journey to the island, drowned when one of the bark canoes capsized, and a pair of muskets and a leather bag filled with powder and shot descended with him beneath the waves. They cannot afford to lose weapons. They are hunted men, even as they are become hunters themselves this night. It is the year of our Lord 1693.

Moloch, twisting on his bunk three centuries after the time of his dream, drifts between sleeping and wakefulness for an instant before he is drawn back into this world of images once again, slowly submerging, sinking deeper and deeper, like a man drowning in recollection, for the dream is not new, and its coming is by now expected when he lays his head upon the pillow and at last surrenders himself to its hold, his heartbeat loud in his ears, blood pumping.

And blood flowing.

He is aware, in the brief moment that he breaks the surface of his uneasy rest, that he has killed before, and will kill again. A conflation of reverie and reality occurs, for Moloch has slain in both dream and wakefulness, although now the distinction between the two realms has grown indistinct.

This is a dream.

This is not a dream.

This is. This was.

There is sand beneath his feet. Behind him, the canoes have been drawn up onto the shore and there are men around him, awaiting his command to move. They are twelve in total. He raises a hand to them and the whites follow him into the woods, the Indians breaking off and sprinting ahead of them. One of them glances back at him, and he sees that the native's face is pitted and scarred, one ear missing, a consequence of mutilation at the hands of his own people.

Wabanaki. A Wabanaki mercenary, an outcast. The Indian

wears his skins with the hair turned inward, in accordance with the demands of the winter season.

"Tanto," says the native, speaking the name of the god of ill will. The foul weather, the drowning, perhaps even the fact that he is here in this place, surrounded by hated white men, all are ascribable to the actions of the bad god. The Wabanaki is called Crow by the other men. They do not know his tribal name, although it is said that he was once a great man among his people, the son of a chief, a sagamore, and that he would have become chief himself had he not been exiled by them. Moloch does not reply, and the native follows his fellow scouts into the woods without another word.

Later, when he awakes, Moloch will wonder once more at how he knows these things (for the dream has been coming more frequently in recent months, and in ever greater detail). He knows that he does not trust the natives. There are three of them, the Wabanaki and two Mi'kmaq with a price on their heads back at Fort Anne, vicious men who have pledged themselves to him in return for alcohol and weapons and the promise of rape. They are useful for now, but he feels uneasy around them. They are despised by their own people, and they are intelligent enough to realize that the men to whom they have attached themselves despise them too.

In his dream, Moloch decides that they will have to be killed after their work here is done.

From the trees ahead comes the sound of a brief scuffle, and moments later the Wabanaki mercenary emerges. There is a boy in his arms, no more than fifteen years of age. He is struggling against his captor's grasp, his cries stifled by the native's large hand. His feet kick impotently at the air. One of the Mi'kmaq follows, holding the boy's musket. He has been apprehended before he can fire off a warning shot.

Moloch approaches, and the boy stops kicking as he recognizes the face before him. He shakes his head, and tries to utter words. The native releases his hand from the boy's mouth but keeps a knife pressed to his throat so that he does not cry out. His tongue freed, the boy finds that he has nothing to say, for there is nothing that can be said. No words can prevent what is about to occur. Instead, his breath plumes whitely in the cold night air, as if his essence were already departing his body, his soul fleeing the pain of what his physical being is about to endure.

Moloch reaches out and grips the boy's face in his hands.

"Robert Littlejohn," he says. "Did they tell you to keep watch for me?"

Robert Littlejohn does not respond. Moloch can feel him trembling beneath his hand. He is surprised that they have maintained even this level of vigilance for so long. After all, it has been many months since his enforced departure.

It strikes Moloch that they must fear him a great deal.

"Still, they must think themselves safe if they leave only a child to watch the western approaches to Sanctuary." He eases his grip on the boy's skin, and caresses it gently with his fingertips.

"You are a brave boy, Robert."

He stands and nods at the Indian, and the Wabanaki draws the knife across the boy's throat, gripping him by the hair to pull his head back so that the blade will have easier passage. Moloch steps back to avoid the arterial spray, but continues to stare into the boy's eyes as the life leaves them. In his dream, Moloch is disappointed by the nature of the boy's passing. There is no fear in his eyes, although the boy must surely have been terrified during his last seconds on this earth. Instead, Moloch sees only a promise, unspoken and yet to be fulfilled.

When the boy is dead, the Wabanaki carries him to the rocks above the beach and casts him into the sea. His body sinks from view.

"We move on," says Moloch. They ascend to the forest, their footfalls carefully placed, avoiding fallen branches that might snap loudly and alert the dogs. It is bitterly cold, and snow begins to fall, driven into their faces by the harsh wind, but Moloch knows this place, even without the scouts to guide him.

Ahead of them, a Mi'kmaq raises his hand and the party halts. Of the other natives, there is no sign. Silently, Moloch creeps up to the guide's side. He points straight ahead. Moloch can see nothing for a time, until the tobacco glows briefly red as the sentry takes a long draw. A shadow grows behind him, and the man's body arcs against the hilt of the knife. The pipe falls to the ground, shedding red ash on the dirt and dying with a hiss upon the newly fallen snow.

Suddenly the barking begins and one of the settlers' beasts, more wolf than hound, breaks through a patch of scrub and bears down upon a figure to Moloch's left. It leaps, and then there is a gunshot and the dog bucks and twists in midair, dying with a yelp and falling on a patch of stony ground. Now the men are emerging from the cover of the woods and there are voices calling and women shouting and children crying. Moloch raises his musket at a settler who appears as a silhouette in the doorway of one of the cabins, the dying embers of the fire within making him an easy target. It is Alden Stanley, a fisherman like the savior he so adores. Moloch pulls the trigger and Alden Stanley is briefly lost in a cloud of sparks and smoke. When it clears, Moloch glimpses Stanley's feet twitching in the open doorway until finally they grow still. He sees more knives appear, and short-handled axes are drawn as his men move in for close-quarters combat, but there is little fight in these people. They have been caught unawares, convinced of their safety in this remote place, content with only a single sleepy guard and a boy on a rock, and the men are upon them before they even have a chance to load their weapons. The settlers outnumber their attackers by three to one, but that will make no difference to the outcome. Already, they are beaten. Soon, his men will pick their victims from among the surviving women and young girls, before they too are dispatched. Moloch sees one man, Barone, already in pursuit of a little girl of five or six, with pretty blond hair. She is wearing a loose ivory gown; its folds hang like wings from her raised arms. Moloch knows her name. As he watches, Barone catches her by the hair and pulls her to him.

Even in his dream, Moloch feels no urge to intervene.

A woman is running, making for the interior, and he moves off in pursuit of her. She is easy to track, her progress noisy, until the stones and roots begin to take their toll on her bare feet, tearing at her soles and heels and slowing her down. He moves ahead of her and cuts into her path, so that she is still looking back toward the slaughter when he emerges from his cover, the pale light filtering through the branches casting his shadow across her features.

And when she sees him, her fear increases, but he recognizes the anger there too, and the hatred.

"You," she says. "You brought them here."

His right hand lashes out, catching her across the face and sending her sprawling on the ground. There is blood on her mouth as she tries to rise. Then he is on top of her, pushing her nightdress up over her thighs and belly. She strikes at him with her fists, but he throws aside his gun and holds her arms over her head with his left hand. His right hand fumbles at his belt, and she hears the sound of steel upon leather as the knife is unsheathed.

"I told you I'd return," he whispers. "I told you I'd be back."

Then he leans in closer to her, his mouth almost touching her lips.

"Know me, wife."

In the moonlight the blade flashes, and in his dream Moloch begins his work.

So Moloch sleeps, believing that he dreams; and far to the north, on the island of his visions, Sylvie Lauter opens her eyes.

It is January, centuries after the events of which Moloch dreams, and the world is skewed. It rests at an angle, as if the physical reality has somehow come to resemble Sylvie's perception of it. It has always appeared canted to her, in a way, always off-kilter. She has never quite fit into it. At school, she has found a place with the other outcasts, the ones with the dyed hair and downcast eyes. They give her some sense of belonging, even as they reject the concept of belonging as somehow unsound. None of them belongs. The world will not have them.

But now that world is altered. Trees grow diagonally, and a doorway has opened to reveal the night sky. She reaches out to touch it, but her view is obscured by a spider's web. She tries to focus and sees the starburst shatter in the glass. She blinks.

There is blood on her fingers, and blood on her face.

And then the pain comes. There is a great pressure on her legs, and a terrible ache in her chest. To breathe is to be constricted by nails. She attempts to swallow and tastes copper on her tongue. With her right hand she wipes the blood from her eyes and clears her vision.

The hood of the car is crumpled inward, wrapped around the trunk of the oak tree in a twisted embrace. Her legs are lost amid the wreckage of the dashboard and the workings of the engine. She remembers the moment when the car veered out of control on the slope. The night rewinds for her. The crash itself is a jumble of sights and noises. She recalls feeling strangely calm as the car struck a great shard of sloping concrete, the front lifting as the passenger side of the vehicle left the ground. She remembers branches and green leaves filling the windshield; the dull sound of the impact; a grunt from Wayne that reminded her of the sound he makes when he is puzzled, which is often, or when he climaxes, which is often too. Now rewind again, and she and Wayne are on the edge of the man-made slope, the former site of the old gun emplacements and army bunkers, ready to freewheel down the incline. Now she is breaking into the garage, and watching Wayne steal the car. Now she is on her back upon a mattress, and Wayne is making love to her. He makes love badly, but still he is her Wayne.

Wayne.

She turns to her left and calls his name, but no sound comes. She again forms the word with her lips, and manages a whisper.

"Wayne."

Wayne is dead. His eyes are half closed, staring lazily at her. There is blood around his mouth, and the steering column is lost in his chest.

"Wayne."

She begins to cry.

When she opens her eyes, there are lights before her. Help, she thinks. Help is coming. The lights hover around the windshield and the damaged hood. The interior of the car glows with a diffused illumination as one of them passes overhead, and she wonders at how they can move in that way.

"Help me," she says.

A single light draws closer, nearing the open window to her right, and she can at last see the form behind it. The shape is hunched, and cloaked with leaves and wood and mud and darkness. It smells of damp earth. It lifts its head to her, and in the strange half-light that filters from the lamp in its hand, Sylvie registers gray skin, and dark eyes like oil bubbles, and torn, bloodless lips, and knows that she is soon to join Wayne, that they will travel together into the world beyond this one, and that at last she will find a place where she fits into the great pattern that has remained hidden from her for so long. She is not yet frightened. She simply wants the pain to end.

"Please," she says to the dead woman at the windshield, but the woman retreats and Sylvie has a sense that she is afraid, that there is something here that even the dead fear. The other lights also begin to recede and Sylvie extends an imploring hand.

"Don't go," she says. "Don't leave me alone."

But she is not alone.

A hissing sound comes from close by, and a figure floats beside her at the other side of the glass. It is smaller than the woman, and it holds no light in its hands. Its hair is white in the moonlight, and is so long and bedraggled that it almost entirely covers its face. It moves nearer as Sylvie feels a wave of tiredness wash over her. She hears herself moan. Her mouth opens as she tries to speak, and she no longer has the strength to close it again.

The figure at the window presses itself against the car. Its hands, with their small, gray fingers, clutch the top of the glass, trying to force it farther down. Sylvie's vision is dimmed once more, obscured by blood and tears, but she can see that it is a little girl who is trying to enter the car, to join her in her agony.

"Honey," Sylvie whispers.

Sylvie tries to move and the pain surges through her with the force of a jolt of electricity. It hurts her to turn her head to the right, so she can see the girl only from the corner of her eye. Momentarily, Sylvie's mind clears. If she can feel pain, then she is still alive. If she is alive, then there is hope. All else is just the imaginings of a mind driven to the edge by trauma and distress.

The woman with the light was not dead.

The child is not floating in the air.

Sylvie feels something brush against her cheek. It hovers before her eyes and its wings make a dull clicking noise as it strikes the windows and roof of the car. It is a gray moth. There are others nearby. She senses them on her skin and in her hair.

"Honey," she says, haltingly, her hand striking feebly at the insects. "Get help. Go get your mommy or your daddy. Tell them the lady needs help." Her eyes flutter closed. Sylvie is fading now. She is dying. She was mistaken. There is no hope.

But the child does not leave. Instead, she leans into the car, forcing her body through the narrow gap between the window and the door, head first, then shoulders. The hissing grows louder. Sylvie feels a coldness at her brow, brushing across her cheeks, coming at last to rest upon her lips. There are more moths now, the sound of them louder and louder in her ears, like a scattering of applause. The child is bringing them. They are somehow a part of her. The coldness against her mouth grows in intensity. Sylvie opens her eyes and the child's face is near her own, her hand stroking Sylvie's forehead.

"No—"

And then fingers begin to probe at her lips, pushing against her teeth, and she can feel old skin crumbling like dust against her tongue. Sylvie thinks instinctively of the moths, of how one of the insects might feel in her mouth. The fingers are deep inside her, touching, probing, gripping, trying desperately to get at the warmth of her, the life within. She struggles against them and tries to scream, but the thin hand muffles her voice. The child's face is close to her own now, but there is still no detail. It is a blur, a painting left out in the rain, the shades running, blending into one another. Only the eyes remain clear, black and hungry, jealous of life.

The hand withdraws, and now the child's mouth is against her own, forcing it open with her tongue and teeth, and Sylvie tastes earth and dead leaves and dark, filthy water. She tries to push the child away and feels the old bones beneath the cloak of vegetation and rough, rotted clothing.

Now it is as if her last energies are being drawn from her by the phantom child; a dying girl, being preyed upon by a dead girl.

A Gray Girl.

The child is hungry, so very hungry. Sylvie digs her hands into the child's scalp and her nails rake across her hair and skin. She tries to force her away, but the child is gripping her neck, holding her mouth against her own. She sees other vague shapes crowding behind, their lights gathering, drawn by the intensity of the Gray Girl's hunger, although they do not share her appetites and are still kept back by their fear of her.

Then, suddenly, the child's mouth is no longer against hers, and the feel of the bones is gone. The lights are departing, and other lights are replacing them, these harsher than before, shedding true illumination. A man approaches her, and she thinks that she recognizes him from somewhere. He speaks her name:

"Sylvie? Sylvie?"

She hears sirens approaching.

"Stay," she whispers. She takes hold of his arm and draws him to her.

"Stay," she repeats. "They'll come back."

"Who?" he says.

"The dead ones," she says. "The little girl."

She tries to spit the taste of the child from her mouth, and dust and blood dribble onto her chin. She begins to shake, and the man tries to hold her and comfort her, but she will not be comforted.

"They were dead," she says, "but they had lights. Why do the dead need light?"

And the world turns to darkness, and she is finally given the answer that she seeks.

The waves break on the shores of the island. Most of the houses are dark. No cars move on Island Avenue, the community's main street. Later, when morning comes, the postmaster, Larry Amerling, will be at his desk, waiting for the mail boat to bring the first delivery of the day. Sam Tucker will open the Casco Bay Market and lay out the day's baking of doughnuts and croissants and pastries. He will fill the coffee urns and greet by name those who drop in to fill up their travel cups before they take the ferry into Portland. Later, Nancy and Linda Tooker will open up the Dutch Diner for its traditional seven hours of business—seven until two, seven days a week—and those who can afford a more leisurely approach to life will wander down for breakfast and a little gossip, eating scrambled eggs and bacon as they look out of the windows and onto the little landing where Archie Thorson's ferry arrives and departs with reasonable regularity and slightly less reasonable punctuality. As midday comes, Jeb Burris will transfer his attentions from the Black Duck Motel to the Rudder Bar, although in winter neither business places great demands upon his time. Thursday to Saturday, Good Eats, the island's sole restaurant, opens for dinner, and Dale Zimmer, the chef and owner, will be down at the landing negotiating prices for lobster and fish. Trucks will leave Jaffe Construction, the island's biggest employer (with a total of twenty employees), to deal with Covey Jaffe's current slate of jobs, ranging from house construction to boat repair, Covey being a man who prides himself on the flexibility of his workforce. This being early January, school is still out, so Dutch Island Elementary remains closed, and the older kids will not be taking up space on the ferry to the mainland schools. Instead, some of them will be thinking up new ways to make mischief, new places in which to smoke pot and screw, preferably far from the eyes of their parents or the police. Most will not yet know of the deaths of Wayne Cady and Sylvie Lauter, and when they learn of the accident the next morning, and its impact sinks in, there may be fears of reprisals from the adult community in the form of parental constraints and increased police vigilance. But in the first moments there will be only shock and tears; boys will remember how they lusted after Sylvie Lauter, and girls will recall with something like affection Wayne Cady's adolescent fumblings. Bottles will be raised in secret, and young men and women will make their pilgrimages to the Cady and Lauter houses, standing in embarrassed silence as their elders hug one another in open grief.

But for now, the only light that burns on Island Avenue, with the exception of the island's twelve (count 'em) street lamps, can be found in the Dutch Island Municipal Building, home to the fire department, the library, and the police department. A man sits slumped in a chair in the small office that constitutes the home of Dutch Island's police force. His name is Sherman Lockwood, and he is one of the policemen from Portland on permanent roster for island duty. He still has Sylvie Lauter's blood on his hands and his uniform, and glass from the shattered windshield of the car is caught in the treads of his boots. A cup of coffee lies cold before him. He wants to cry, but he will hold it inside until he returns to the mainland, where he will awaken his still-sleeping wife by pressing his face to her skin and holding her tightly as the sobs shudder through him. He has a daughter Sylvie Lauter's age, and his greatest nightmare is that someday he may be forced to look upon her as he looked upon Sylvie this night, the promise that her life held now given the lie by her death. He holds out his hand, and the light from the desk lamp shows up the blood still caught beneath his nails and in the wrinkles of his knuckles. He could go back to the bathroom and try to remove the last traces of her, but the porcelain sink is speckled with red and he thinks that if he looks upon those marks, he will lose control of himself. And so Sherman balls his hands into fists, eases them into the pockets of his jacket, and tries to stop his body from trembling.

Through the window, Sherman can see a great shape silhouetted against the stars. It is the figure of a man, a man perhaps eighteen inches taller than he is, a man immeasurably stronger, and immeasurably sadder, than Sherman. Sherman is not a native of Dutch Island. He was born and raised in Biddeford, a little south of Portland, and he and his wife still live there, along with their two children. The loss of Sylvie Lauter and her boyfriend, Wayne, is terrible and painful to him, but he has not watched them grow as the man beyond the window has. Sherman is not a part of this tightly knit community. He is an outsider, and it will always be this way.

And yet the giant too is an outsider. His great bulk, his awkwardness, the memories of too many taunts delivered, too many whispers endured have made him one. He was born here and he will die here without ever truly believing that he belongs. Sherman decides that he will join the giant in a moment. Not just yet, though.

Not just yet.

The giant's head is slightly raised, as if he can still hear the sound of the Portland Fire Department boat departing, taking the bodies of Sylvie and Wayne back to the mainland for autopsy. In a couple of days' time, the islanders will gather at the main cemetery to watch the coffins as they are lowered silently into the ground. Sylvie and Wayne will be buried close by each other after a joint service out of the island's little Baptist church. Much of the entire winter population will gather, along with media and relatives and friends from the mainland. Five hundred people will walk from the church to the cemetery, and afterward there will be coffee and sandwiches at the American Legion post, with maybe something a little stronger for those who need it most.

And the giant will be among the mourners, and he will grieve with them, and he will wonder.

For he has been told the girl's last words, and he feels unaccountably afraid.

The dead ones.

They were dead, but they had lights.

Why do the dead need light?

But for now the island is quiet once again. It is Dutch Island on the maps, a tiny oval one-and-a-half-hour's ferry ride from Portland, far out in Casco Bay on the margin of the outer ring of islands. It is Dutch Island to those who have only recently come here to live, for the island has attracted its share of new residents who no longer wish to stay, or can no longer afford to stay, on the mainland. It is Dutch Island to the reporters who will cover the funeral; Dutch Island to the legislators who will determine its future; Dutch Island to the real estate salesmen driving up property prices; and Dutch Island to the summer visitors who come to its shores each year for a day, a week, a month, without ever really understanding its true nature.

But others still speak of it by its old name, the name the first settlers, the people of Moloch's dream, gave to it before they were slaughtered. They called it Sanctuary, and the island is still Sanctuary to Larry Amerling, and Sam Tucker, and old Thorson, and a handful of others, but usually only when they speak of it among themselves; and they say its name with a kind of reverence, and perhaps just a hint of fear.

It is Sanctuary to the giant too, for his father told him of its history, just as his father told it to him, and similarly back and back again, far into the lost generations of the giant's family. Few outsiders know this, but the giant owns whole sections of the island, bought by his family when nobody wanted to own this land, when even the state was turning down the opportunity to buy islands in Casco Bay. Their stewardship of the land is one of the reasons the island remains unspoiled, and why its heritage is so diligently protected, its memories so carefully stored. The giant knows that the island is special and so he calls it Sanctuary, like all those who recognize their duty toward this place.

And perhaps it is still Sanctuary also to the young boy who stands amid the breaking waves at Pine Cove, staring out to sea. He does not appear to heed the cold, and the force of the waves does not make him rock back on his heels when they break, nor threaten to suck his feet from their anchorage beneath the surface. His clothes are rough cotton, apart from the heavy cowhide jacket that his mother made for him, hand-stitching it by the fire while he watched patiently, day after day.

The boy's face is very pale, and his eyes are dark and empty. He feels as though he has awakened from a long sleep. He brushes his fingers gently against the bruises on his face, where the grip of the man left its imprint upon him, then touches the memory of the wound on his throat left by the passage of the knife. His fingertips are heavily grooved, as if by time spent in the water.

For the boy, as for the island, there is no past; there is only the eternal present. He looks behind him, and sees movement in the forest, the shapes drifting among the trees. Their wait is almost over, just as his unspoken promise is about to be fulfilled.

He turns back to the sea and resumes his unblinking watch upon the waiting world beyond.

THE FIRST DAY

They asked again what was my name,
They asked again what was my name.
And two were dead before they could move,
Two were dead before they could move.
I said, "That's my name. That's my name,
If you please . . ."

—"Outlaw Song" (traditional)

CHAPTER ONE

The giant knelt down and watched the gull's beak open and close. The bird's neck was twisted at an unnatural angle and in its single visible eye he saw himself reflected and distorted, his brow shrunken, his nose huge and bulging, his mouth tiny and lost in the folds of his chin. He hung suspended in the blackness of the bird's pupil, a pale moon pendent in a dark, starless sky, and his pain and that of the gull were one. A dry beech leaf fell from a branch above and performed joyful cartwheels across the grass, tumbling tip over stem as the wind carried it away, almost touching the gull's feathers as it passed. The bird, lost in its agony, paid it no heed. Above its head, the giant's hand hovered, the promise of mortality and mercy in its grasp.

"What's wrong with it?" said the boy. He had just turned six, and had been living on the island for almost a year. In all that time, he had yet to see a dying animal, until now.

"Its neck is broken," said the giant.

The wind rolling in off the Atlantic tousled his hair and

flattened his jacket against his back. Within sight of where he squatted, the eastern shore of the island began its steep descent to the ocean. There were rocks down there, but no beach. The old painter, Giacomelli, kept a boat in the shelter of a glade close by the shore, although he used it only occasionally. In the summer, when the sea was calmer, he could sometimes be seen out on the water, a line trailing from the boat. The giant wasn't sure if Giacomelli, or Jack, as most islanders called him, ever caught anything, but then he guessed that catching things wasn't the point for Jack. The painter rarely even bothered to bait the hooks, and if a fish was foolish enough to impale itself on a barb, Jack would usually unhook it and cast it back into the sea, assuming he even noticed the tug on the line. Fishing was merely his alibi, an excuse to take the boat out on the waves. The old man was always making sketches while the line dangled unthreateningly, his hand working quickly with charcoals as he added another perspective to his seemingly endless series of representations of the landscape.

There weren't too many people living over on this side of the island. It was too exposed for some. Sheep sorrel, horseweed, and highbush blackberry colonized patches of waste or open ground, but mostly it was just trees, the island's forest petering out as it drew closer to the cliffs. In fact, this was maybe the closest thing to a concentration of houses over on the eastern shore: the boy and his mother in one, Jack in another, Bonnie Claeson just over the rise to the north, and a sprinkling of others within reasonable walking distance. The view was good, though, as long as one didn't mind looking at empty sea.

The boy's voice called him back.

"Can you help it? Can you make it better?"

"No," said the giant. He wondered how the bird had ended

up here, lying in the middle of a patch of lawn with its neck broken. He thought he saw its open beak move feebly, and its tiny tongue flick at the grass. It might have been attacked by an animal or another bird, although there were no marks upon it. The giant looked around but could see no other signs of life. No gulls glided. There were no starlings, no chickadees. There was only this single, dying gull, alone of its kind.

The boy knelt down and stretched out a finger to prod the bird, but the giant's hand caught it before it could make contact, engulfing it in his palm.

"Don't do that," he said.

The boy looked at him. There was no pity in his face, thought the giant. There was only curiosity. But if there was not pity, then neither was there understanding. The boy was just too young to understand, and that was why the giant loved him.

"Why?" said the boy. "Why can't I touch it?"

"Because it is in pain, and you will only increase that pain by touching it."

The boy considered this.

"Can you make the pain go away?"

"Yes," said the giant.

"Then do it."

The giant reached down with both hands, placing his left hand like a shell above the body of the gull, and the thumb and forefinger of his right hand at either side of its neck.

"I think maybe you should look away," he told the boy.

The boy shook his head. Instead, his eyes were focused on the giant's hands and the soft, warm body of the bird enclosed within their ambit.

"I have to do this," said the giant. His thumb and forefinger moved in unison, gripping the bird's neck and simultaneously pulling and twisting. The gull's head was wrenched one hundred and eighty degrees, and its pain was brought to an end.

Instantly, the boy began to cry.

"What did you do?" he wailed. "What did you do?"

The giant rose and made as if to grip the boy's shoulder, but the boy backed away from him, fearful now of the power in those great hands.

"I put it out of its misery," said the giant. He was already realizing his mistake in euthanizing the bird while the boy was watching, but he had no experience in dealing with one so young. "It was the only thing that I could do."

"No, you killed it. You killed it!"

The giant's hand retreated.

"Yes," he said. "I did. It was in pain and it could not be saved. Sometimes, all that you can do is take away the pain."

But the boy was already running back to the house, back to his mother, and the wind carried his cries to the giant as he stood on their neatly trimmed lawn. Gently, he cupped the dead gull in his right hand and carried it away to the treeline, where he dug a small hole with the edge of a stone and covered the little thing in earth and leaves, placing the stone at last upon the mound. When he rose again, the boy's mother was walking toward him across the lawn, the boy clinging to her, shielded by her body.

"I didn't know you were out here," she said. She was trying to smile, both embarrassed and alarmed by her son's distress.

"I was passing," said the giant. "I thought I'd drop in, see how you were. Then I saw Danny crouching on the grass, and went over to see what was the matter. There was a gull, a dying gull. I—"

The boy interrupted.

"What did you do with it?"

His cheeks were streaked with the marks of his tears and his grubby-fingered efforts to wipe them away.

The giant looked down upon him. "I buried it," he said. "Over there. I marked the place with a stone."

The boy released his hold upon his mother and walked toward the trees, his eyes grave with suspicion, as if he were convinced that the giant had somehow spirited the bird away for his own dark ends. When his eyes found the stone he stood before the gull's resting place, his hands hanging loosely by his sides. With the tip of his right foot he tested the earth, half hoping to reveal a small swath of feathers, darkened with dirt now like a discarded wedding gown, but the giant had buried the bird deep and no trace of it was made visible to him.

"It couldn't be saved?" asked his mother.

"No," said the giant. "Its neck was broken."

She spotted the boy and saw what he was doing. "Danny, come away from there."

He walked back to her, still refusing to look the giant in the eye, until he was once again by his mother's side. Her arm gripped the shoulder of the boy, and she pulled him closer to her.

"There was nothing anybody could do, Danny. The bird was sick. Joe did the right thing."

Then, in a whisper to the giant, she added: "I wish he hadn't seen you kill it. You maybe should have waited until he was gone."

The giant reddened at the chastisement. "I'm sorry," he said.

The woman smiled to herself as she tried to comfort both boy and man simultaneously. He is so big, so strong, she thought, and yet he is made awkward and small by the sorrow of a little boy and his feelings for the boy's mother. This is a strange position in which to find myself, circling this huge man as he circles me, almost—but not quite—touching. It took him so long, so long . . .

"He's still young," she said reassuringly. "He'll learn, in time."

"Yes," said the giant. "I guess he will."

He grinned ruefully, briefly exposing the gaps between his teeth. Then, suddenly conscious that he was revealing them, he allowed the smile to die. He squatted down so that his face was level with that of the boy.

"Good-bye, Danny," he said.

The boy was still looking toward the grave of the gull and did not respond.

The giant turned to the woman. "Good-bye, Marianne. Are we still okay for dinner?"

"Sure," she said. "Bonnie's going to look after Danny for the evening."

He almost smiled again.

"Say good-bye to Officer Dupree, Danny," said the woman as the giant prepared to leave. "Say good-bye to Joe."

But the boy only turned his face away, burying himself in the folds of her skirt.

"I don't want you to go with him," he said. "And I don't want to stay with Bonnie."

"Hush," was all his mother could say.

And the giant named Joe Dupree strode toward his Explorer, dirt beneath his nails and the warmth of the bird still palpable on the palm of his hand. Had there been any strangers around to see his face, the sadness upon it would have given them pause. But to the natives on the island, the look upon the huge policeman's face would have seemed as familiar as the sound of breaking waves or the sight of dead fish upon the shore.

After all, he was not called Melancholy Joe for nothing.

He was born huge. His mother would often joke that, had Joe Dupree been a girl, he could almost have given birth to her. They had been forced to cut him out of her, and, well, that was that as far as Eloise Dupree having more children was concerned. She was almost forty by the time her son was born, and both she and her husband were content to remain a one-child family.

The boy grew and grew. For a time, they feared that he was suffering from acromegaly, the ailment of giants, and that their beloved son would be taken from them at an early age, his life span halved or even quartered by the disease. Old Doc Bruder, who was then not so old, sent them to a specialist, who conducted tests before reassuring them that their boy was not acromegalous. True, there were risks associated with his size later in life: cardiovascular disease, arthritis, respiratory problems. Some form of chemical intervention could be considered at a later stage, but he advised them to wait and see.

Joe Dupree continued to grow. He towered over his classmates in elementary school and in high school. Desks were too small, chairs too uncomfortable. He stood out from his peers like the seed of a great tree dropped in the wrong part of the forest, forced to survive amid alder and holly, its strangeness apparent to even the most casual of glances. Older boys baited him, treating him like a handicapped oddity. When he tried to strike back at them, they overwhelmed him with numbers and guile. Even the sporting arena offered him no comfort. He had bulk to go with his size, but it was without grace or skill. His was not an immensity and strength that could be put to use in any competition. He lacked the instincts necessary as much as the abilities. His great body was a burden on the football field and a liability in the wrestling circle. He seemed destined to spend his life either falling over or getting up again.

By the time he was eighteen, Joe Dupree had topped out at over seven feet, two inches and weighed over 360 pounds. His mass was a millstone in every way. He was intelligent, yet it was assumed by his peers that he was stupid because of how he looked. Instead of proving them wrong, he became what they perceived. He was the freak, the freak from the island (for it was his upbringing on the island that doomed him, as much as anything else; already he was an outsider to the kids from Portland, who thought little of the islanders to begin with, even those of normal size). He retreated into himself, and after high school took a job on the island driving for Covey Jaffe. It was only when the time of his father's retirement drew near that Dupree joined the Portland PD, his size almost an impediment to his acceptance until his family's history in the department was taken into account. When his father at last retired, it seemed natural that Joe Dupree should take over his role as the island's resident policeman, assisted by the existing roster of cops from the mainland.

Dupree's father had died three years earlier, six months after Eloise had passed away. His father had simply proved unable to live without her. There was no other possible reason for the sudden decline in his health, despite the opinions of doctors and specialists. They had been together for forty-seven years, living in a modest house on this most remote of the inhabited islands, a profoundly enamored couple secure in the center of a close community. Dupree missed them both deeply, his father in particular, for he was forced to travel the same paths, to drive the same roads, to greet the same people, to wear the same uniform as the old man once had. There was a link between the two generations that could not be sundered, and he strengthened it with every day that he worked.

In his darkest moments, Dupree would recall his childhood, and his father telling him tales from legend and from the Bible: of Goliath, who stood over six cubits; of King Og of Bashan's bed, which was nine cubits long; of the giants of Greek myth, the sons of heaven and earth, who were slain by the Olympians and buried under the earth, their remains creating the mountains of the world; of the Titans, parents of the gods; of Agrius the Untamable, born fully mature and clad in the armor of battle, who waged war on the gods of Olympus after the Titans' defeat; and of Aurgelmir, of Norse myth, who was the first being, the father of the giants who followed, and whose body was used to make the very earth itself. Neither deities nor lesser spirits, the giants were beings out of time, and gods and men decreed that they should be destroyed.

Dupree understood his father's purpose: to make him feel special, part of some great heritage, a gift from the gods, maybe even from God himself. He told his son stories of Pecos Bill, of Paul Bunyan, of the army of giants raised by Frederick the Great. It was all part of his great effort to give his son some comfort. It had not worked, for the Bible contained no stories of laughing girls and mocking boys, and the giants of myth were felled by weapons and wars, not words and enforced isolation. Yet he loved his father for trying.

Dupree looked back at Marianne Elliot's house. Danny had already gone inside, but his mother was standing on the doorstep, watching the dark sea and the white plumes upon it, like shards of sunlight glimpsed through stormy skies. He tried to recall how often he had encountered her in this fashion. At first he had thought her hypnotized by the sea, as those who came to the island from away sometimes became, unfamiliar as they were with its rhythms. But once or twice he had caught her unawares and had been struck by the absence of peace in her face. Instead, her expression was one of concern, even fear. He wondered if she had lost someone to the sea yet still found herself somehow bound to it, like the widows of drowned fishermen unwilling to leave the side of the great grave that refuses to relinquish their loved ones to them. Then she seemed to realize that he was watching her, for she turned to him, raised her hand in farewell, and followed her son indoors.

Dupree started the Explorer's engine and drove toward the coast road, heading east along it. The road did not make a full circuit of the island. There were areas to the northwest, at Stepping Stone Hill, and southwest down by Hunger Cove, that were virtually inaccessible by car, but since nobody lived in those areas, the absence of roads was no great burden. Still, each spring Dupree would lead a group of volunteers over to Stepping Stone and Hunger and they would cut back the trees and brush that had begun to colonize the dirt trails leading down to the sea, just in case access was ever needed from the main road. It was a tiresome job, but far less irksome than having to build a new trail in a few years' time, or being forced to hack a way through in the event of an emergency.

About seven hundred people lived on the island year-round, a figure that tripled, at least, during the summer months. The island was large, five miles long and almost two miles wide, one of over 750 islands, islets, and exposed ridges scattered throughout the two-hundred-square-mile vastness of Casco Bay. It was bigger and more populous than its nearest rival, Great Chebeague, but its size meant that most people still lived in relative seclusion, apart from the community that had built up around the main ferry landing, known only as the Cove. The population increased during the summer, but not to the same extent as on the other Casco Bay islands nearer the mainland, like Peaks or Chebeague or Long Island, for Dutch lay much farther to the east, and was more exposed than the rest. In winter, only the old families remained. Their history was entwined with that of the island, and their names had echoed around its woods for hundreds of years: Amerling and Tooker, Houghton and Hall, Doughty and Dupree.

The heat was turned up high in the Explorer, for it was fiercely cold, even for January. There was talk of storms coming, and Thorson, the ferry captain, had posted a warning of possible suspension of the ferry services over the coming week. Already, Dupree had been forced to break up some heated arguments that had arisen at the ferry landing over accusations of excessive timidity on Thorson's part. It was hard for occasional visitors to the island to understand the importance of the ferry link to year-round residents. Casco Bay Ferries, which ran regular services to a number of the islands, did not do so to Dutch Island due to the distances involved and the relative paucity of passengers, although its mail boat did make daily stops. Thorson's family had been providers of the island's ferry service for over seventy years, taking kids over to high school, students to college, grandparents to visit grandchildren, workers to their offices, patients to the hospital, boyfriends to their girlfriends, children to aged parents who had been consigned to homes . . . the list was endless. If you needed to buy a new TV, you parked down in the lot by the ferry, climbed onboard with a hand trolley, headed over to Circuit City, then used a bus or a cab to get your new TV back to the dock in time for Thorson to help you bring it home again. That also counted for stoves, machine parts, new tires, medicines, ammunition, new clothes for the kids, toys for Christmas, and just about any other item that you cared to mention, apart from the general foodstuffs available in the Casco Bay Market. Thorson's ferry was mainly a people carrier. For larger purchases, like a new car or a piece of serious farm equipment, Covey Jaffe had a construction ferry that could be hired out, but without Thorson's ferry to take care of all the little day-to-day things, life on the island would go from occasionally difficult to damn near impossible. Whether or not to run the ferry in the face of a storm warning was Thorson's call, but Dupree figured he'd talk to the old man over the next day or two and maybe remind him that where the ferry was concerned, being overcautious was nearly as bad as being reckless.

Dupree made some casual calls along the way, checking on older residents, following up on complaints, handing out gentle warnings to errant teenagers, and examining the summer residences of the wealthy to make sure that the doors and windows remained intact and that nobody had taken it into his mind to redistribute some of their wealth to more deserving causes. It was the usual island routine, and he loved it. Despite the rotation schedule—twenty-four hours on, twenty-four hours off, twenty-four hours on, followed by five days off—Dupree worked almost as much unpaid overtime as he did scheduled hours. It was unavoidable when he lived on the island and could be approached after church or in the store, or even while he was tending his garden or fixing his roof. It was the way things ran on the island. Formalities were for funerals.

On his way back to town, Dupree paused by an old lookout tower, one of a chain of towers built during World War II across the islands of Casco Bay. The utility companies had taken to using some of them as storage facilities or as sites for their equipment, but not this one. Now the door to the tower was open, the chain that held it closed lying in a coil on its topmost step. The towers attracted the local kids like sugar drawing flies, since they offered sheltered and relatively remote sites in which to experiment with booze, drugs, and, frequently, one another. Dupree was convinced that the origins of a number of local unwanted pregnancies could be traced to the shady corners of these towers.

He parked the Explorer and took his big Maglite from beneath the seat, then headed through the short grass toward the steps to the tower. It was one of the smaller constructs built close to the shore, barely three stories high, and its usefulness as a lookout post was virtually negated by the growth of the surrounding trees. Still, Joe was curious to see that some of those trees had been crudely cut back, their branches broken at the ends.

The policeman paused at the base of the steps and listened. No noise came from within, but he felt uneasy. It was, he thought, becoming his natural state. Over these last few weeks, he had become increasingly uncomfortable as he conducted his patrols of the island that had been his home for almost forty years. It seemed to him that it was different, but when he had tried to explain it to Lockwood, the older cop had simply laughed it off.

"You been spending too long out here, Joe. You need to take a trip back to civilization once in a while. You're getting spooked."

Lockwood might have been right in advising Joe to spend more time away from the island, but he was wrong about the nature of his partner's unease. Others, like Larry Amerling the postmaster, had expressed to Joe a sense that all was not well on Dutch Island lately, although when they spoke about such things, they used the old name.

They called it Sanctuary.

There had been . . . *incidents:* repeated break-ins at the central lookout tower, involving the destruction of even the strongest lock and chain Dupree could find, and the surge in plant growth on the pathways leading to the Site (and in winter, mind, when all that usually grew was darkness and icicles). Nobody visited the old massacre location during the winter anyway, but if the paths became overgrown, then it would be a hell of a job revealing them again when spring came.

And then there was the accident one week before, the one that had killed Wayne Cady instantly and Sylvie Lauter a little more slowly. The accident bothered Dupree more than anything else. He had been behind Lockwood as the girl spoke her last words about lights and the dead, and Dupree recalled words once spoken by his own father.

"Sometimes, there's no grave deep enough to bury a bad death."

He looked to the south and thought that he could distinguish gaps in the trees: the circle of marsh and bog that marked the approach to the Site. He had not visited it in many months. Perhaps it was now time to return.

From inside the tower came a low, scraping noise. Dupree undid the clasp on his holster and laid his hand on the butt of his Smith & Wesson. He stood to one side of the doorway and called out a warning.

"Police. You want to come out of there right now, y'hear."

The sound came again. There were footsteps, and a voice, low and nasal, said:

"It's okay, Joe Dupree. It's okay, Joe Dupree. It's me, Joe Dupree. Me, Richie."

Joe stepped back as Richie Claeson appeared at the base of the tower's main staircase, sunlight shining through the single filthy window on that level casting a soft glow over his features.

"Richie, come on out now," said Joe. He felt the tension release from his shoulders.

What was I afraid of? Why did I have my hand on my gun?

Richie appeared in the doorway, grinning. Twenty-five, and with a mental age of maybe eight. He liked to roam the island, driving his mother to distraction, but nothing had ever happened to him, and, Joe suspected, nothing ever would. Richie probably knew the island better than almost anybody, and it held no terrors for him. During the warm summer months, he even occasionally slept out beneath the stars. Nobody bothered him much, except maybe the local smart-asses when they'd had a drink or two and were trying to impress their girls.

"Hello, Joe Dupree," said Richie. "How are you?"

"I'm good, thanks. Richie, I told you before about keeping out of these towers."

The grin on the face of the boy-man never faded.

"I know, Joe Dupree. Stay out of the towers. I know."

"Yeah, well if you know, then what were you doing in there?"

"It was open, Joe Dupree. The tower was open. I went in to take a look. I like looking."

Dupree knelt down and examined the chain. The padlock was open, but when he tested the lock by trying to close it, it wouldn't catch, instead sliding in and out of the hole with a soft click.

"And you didn't do this?"

"No, Joe Dupree. It was open. I went in to take a look."

He would have to come back out here with a new lock, Dupree figured. The kids would probably just break it again, but he had to make the effort. He closed the tower door, then wrapped the chain around the handle to give the impression that it was locked. It would have to do, for now.

"Come on, Richie. I'll give you a ride home."

He handed the Maglite to the handicapped man and watched with a smile as he shined the light upon the trees and the top of the tower.

"Light," said Richie. "I'm making lights, like the others."

Dupree stopped.

"What others, Richie?"

Richie looked at him, and grinned.

"The others, in the woods."

Danny grabbed a can of soda from the refrigerator and wandered down to his mother's bedroom. Pieces of paper lay spread out on the bed before her, as she kneeled on the carpet and tried to sort through them. She had that expression on her face, the one she got when they went over to Portland on the ferry and she had to go into the bank or the car place.

"You okay, honey?" she asked when she noticed him standing beside her.

He nodded.

She sat back on her heels and looked at him seriously.

"Joe had to do what he did, you know? It was the kindest thing for that gull."

Danny didn't respond, but his face darkened slightly.

"I'm heading over to Jack's house," he said.

He saw the scowl start to form, and his face grew darker still.

"What?" he said.

"That old man—," she began, but he cut her off.

"He's my friend."

"Danny, I know that, but he . . ."

She trailed off as she tried to find the right words.

"He drinks," she finished lamely. "You know, too much, sometimes."

"Not around me."

They had argued about this before, ever since Jack had fallen down and cut his head on the edge of the table and Danny had come running for her, the old man's blood on his hands and shirt. His mother had thought that he had injured himself, and her relief when she discovered the truth quickly transformed into anger at the old man for putting her through such a shock, however briefly. Joe had come along and administered a little first aid, then spent a long time talking to Jack out on the old man's porch, and since then Jack had been a lot more careful. If he drank now, he drank in the evenings. He was also turning out paintings with a vengeance, though Marianne didn't think much of his art.

"He just paints the same view, over and over," she said to her son shortly after she and Danny had visited the old man for the first time, paying a neighborly call with cookies.

"It's not the same view," the boy protested. "It's different every time."

But she had merely glanced at the small watercolor that the old man had presented to the boy on their departure, the rocks on either side of the inlet a bluish gray, the sea a dark, threatening green. It was an ugly picture, she thought. All of the old man's pictures were ugly. It was as if he were unable to perceive anything but the most mundane, dreary aspects of the landscape before him. There were no people. Hell, he couldn't even paint birds or clouds, or if he could, he sure never bothered to place them in his pictures. Grays and greens and washed-out blues, that seemed to be the sum total of shades on his palette.

But the boy had placed the painting above his bed and was prouder of it than any of the dozens of other posters and cards and notes that obscured the walls, even prouder of it than he was of his own work, which his mother thought was far better than anything the old drunk was ever likely to produce. Marianne was never going to say that to Jack's face, though. The old painter might have his flaws, but an absence of generosity was not one of them. The house in which they now lived was rented from him and even by island standards he had asked little for it. She had that much for which to be grateful to him.

"Please, Mom," said Danny.

If she did not relent, there would be a tantrum and she would be distracted from the task at hand, and she could not afford to be distracted from it. She gave up and dismissed him with a wave.

"Go, go. But if you think that there's even the slightest thing wrong with Jack, you come straight back home, you hear me?"

He nodded solemnly, then broke for the door. His mother stood and walked to the window, her bedroom looking down on the path that wound between their property and Jack's house. In the beginning, she had led him along the way herself, either holding his hand or watching anxiously as he bounded ahead. After a while, she had started to let him make the short walk between the two houses alone. It wasn't far, and she could follow his progress every step of the way. She felt that it was important to allow him a little independence, a little room in which to grow. She wanted him to be tougher, while simultaneously fearing the consequences of releasing him from her protection. It was the dilemma of every parent, she knew, but a mother without a man to share the raising of a male child felt it more acutely. Sometimes she sensed that she was being forced to make choices that were against her nature in order to compensate for someone who wasn't there.

The boy trailed his way down, the soda can still clutched in his hand, like a small, bright fragment of canvas set adrift from the whole, his red windbreaker startlingly bright against the trees. Her eyes remained upon him until he reached the old man's door. She saw him knock and wait patiently, and then the door opened and he was gone.

Vincent "Jack" Giacomelli had come to Dutch Island in the spring of '67, after he had lost his job teaching at some fancy college on the East Coast. He was a walking history of art, even if his knowledge and appreciation had never enabled him to paint with even one iota of the talent and imagination of those of whom he spoke to others. Things had started to turn black in the summer of '65, when his wife left him for a professor of physics who drove the kind of fancy sports car that physicists (who were, in Jack's experience, so boring they made even mathematicians seem kind of entertaining) were not supposed to know existed. After she went away, Jack's life began to fall apart, or maybe it had been falling apart anyway and that was why she left. Jack was never too sure, and most of that period of his life remained a blur. Truth be told, the blur extended up to a couple of months back, when he had fallen and bumped his head, and Joe Dupree had sat him down on the chair and spoken to him in that way of his, that quiet way that told you that if you didn't shape up and take his advice, then you might as well pack your bags, lock your doors, and head for the mainland, because Joe Dupree wasn't going to have any nonsense on his island.

What Jack couldn't figure out was why he didn't feel any resentment toward the policeman. After all, people had been telling him to shape up for the best part of forty years and he hadn't given a red cent for their advice. But Joe Dupree was different. There was no other way to put it. When Joe Dupree looked at you in that strange, sad way of his, it was like being an onion beneath a knife held by a skilled hand, as layer after layer was exposed and discarded until only the very core remained.

Or until nothing at all remained, depending on how far he went, or the sort of onion you were. Jack had been kind of worried that if Joe Dupree kept peeling, he would find out some terrible truth about Jack that the old man himself had never even suspected existed or that he had somehow refused to face. It was the fear that he had nothing left to offer, nothing but bad art and broken promises, and that Joe Dupree was capable of revealing that truth. Once exposed, it could never again be hidden.

After that talk, Jack went on the wagon for a while. It didn't last, of course. It never had before, and even Joe Dupree wasn't likely to have that much of an impact on a hardened booze hound like Jack, but the old man was more careful now, drinking only in the evenings and never, ever, taking a bottle to bed with him as he used to do in the good old days. Instead, he began to paint at a faster pace than ever before.

He'd been dabbling with painting for a long time, of course. Jack made some money selling bad oil paintings and worse watercolors to tourists, sometimes from a little stand that he set up down by the waterfront in Portland on sunny weekends, laying on the old-salt act as thickly as he could, inventing the kind of family history that a lot of folks around here could claim for real but that in Jack's case was as false as the bottom of a magician's hat. But he earned enough to keep himself in reasonable comfort in a house long since paid for, which was now his to pass on to whomever he chose—a couple of cousins, a handful of nieces and nephews, or his sister, Kate, who, if Jack's will was anything to go by, was likely to be one disappointed lady once he was cold in the ground.

The doorbell rang. He wandered down the hallway, his old

sneakers making a slapping sound on the bare boards. Through the frosted glass of the door he could make out the shape of the boy, disintegrating into black and red shards like watercolors dropped on oil. He opened the door and stepped back in mock surprise.

"Hey, it's the Danmonster."

The boy stomped past him, not even waiting to be invited in. He walked quickly to the door of Jack's studio and then looked back at the old man for the first time.

"Is it okay?"

"Sure, sure. You go right ahead. I'll follow you in soon as I get my coffee."

Outside, daylight was already beginning to fade, igniting lights in the windows of distant houses. Jack retrieved his coffee cup from the kitchen, adding a little hot water to it to heat it up, then followed the boy into his studio. It was a small space, formerly a spare room, but Jack had transformed it by replacing one wall with sliding glass doors, so that the floor became grass that rolled slowly down until it eventually reached the trees that bordered the low cliff edge, the water beyond a dark, threatening blue. The boy was standing before the easel, looking at Jack's latest work in progress. It was another oil, and another attempt to capture the view over the water. Another *unsuccessful* attempt, Jack thought. It was the uncertainty principle in action: the damn thing kept on changing, developing, and the instant he attempted to capture it, he became complicit in a lie. Still, there was something calming about the exercise, even as it drew closer and closer to failure with every movement of his hand, every stroke of his brush.

"This isn't like the others," said the boy.

"Hmm?" said Jack, momentarily distracted by his own failings. "What did you say?"

"I said this isn't like the others. It's different."

"Different how?"

Jack joined the boy, then frowned and leaned closer to the canvas. There were marks upon it, like black streaks on the waves. He looked up at the ceiling and tried to determine if dirty water had somehow leaked down through a previously undiscovered crack, but there was nothing. The ceiling was white and unblemished.

Carefully, he reached out with a finger and touched the canvas, then drew his hand back slowly. The marks looked like paint, yet he couldn't feel the texture of the brush strokes beneath his touch. He looked closer and saw that the black marks were under some of his own strokes, the horizontals that he sometimes used in an effort to capture the movement of the sea. Somehow, it seemed that he had managed to paint over the blemishes without noticing.

But that was impossible. There was no way that he could have failed to notice the flaws in the canvas.

He took a couple of steps back and tried to understand what the marks represented, tilting his head as he went, then pausing as he reached the threshold of the hallway. Before him, the shapes became distinguishable as forms, and he knew what they represented. He knew also that there was no way that Jack Giacomelli had been responsible for the marks on the canvas, for Jack Giacomelli never added anything to the natural landscape that was his sole inspiration.

"They're people," said the boy. "You've put people in your painting."

The boy was right.

There were two bodies floating in the oiled waters of his painting.

The bodies of men.

* * *

The island had been quiet for so very long.

Its past slumbered gently beneath the surface, its exhalations causing the trees to sway, the waters to ripple, the dead leaves to chase one another across the grass like small brown birds in flight. It slept the way one who has endured great pain might sleep, its rest both escape and recuperation. The memory of those who had suffered and died upon it in years gone by drifted through its consciousness, so bound up with the land and the trees and the sea that it was impossible to tell if they had ever truly existed as separate entities.

But there were places on the island that were a testament to those who had once lived in its gift, and the manner of their passing had ingrained itself upon the very stones themselves. At the heart of the island, barely a mile distant from the Cove, was a small huddle of stones surrounding patches of sunken earth. Seen from the ground, their pattern was indistinct, the placement of the stones seemingly, but not quite, random. Viewed from above, the true nature of the clearing became apparent. Here were corners and fireplaces and chimneys; here were yards and outhouses and pens.

Here, once, were people.

Their end, when it came, scarred the island, and the foundations of the dwellings ran far deeper than those who had built them had ever intended or imagined, stone fusing with stone until the divisions were no longer apparent, the constructions of man and nature becoming one. Only the patterns visible from above, and the half-buried monuments surrounding a single raised cross, marked this place for what it was.

This was the Site.

For a time—fifty years in the memory of men, but barely a second in the life of the island—there had been no more killing here and the island had remained uninhabited once again, but then more men had come, men who were fleeing the consequences of their actions, for places with a history of pain and violence will sometimes draw further pain and violence to themselves. And the island tolerated their presence for a time, until at last it could take it no longer, the soil being incapable of soaking up any more blood, the stones resisting the blackening of fires set in anger.

The men who came to the island brought with them a woman, taken from Scarborough against her will. Soldiers were searching for them on the mainland, so they took to the sea, hoping to find a place in which they would be safe for a time.

They came at last to the island.

There were four men. They were armed and battle hardened. They had fought the Indians, the British, the French. They feared no one.

It was fishermen, blown off course by a storm and seeking shelter in the coves of the island, who eventually found the woman. She had built herself a little shelter in the ruins of the old village, feeding on wild fruit and birds and fish to keep herself alive, and had lit a fire in the hope of drawing help.

She had been there for two weeks, and was almost insane when they found her.

Of the men, there was no sign.

They brought her back to the mainland and she was questioned about all that had occurred. She could tell them little. On the first day, they had taken turns with her. On the second day, the men's boat had disappeared, although they had drawn it up on the shore and lashed it to a fallen tree.

On the third day, the whispering had started.

It sounded at first like the wind in the trees, yet there was no wind blowing. The voices seemed to come from all around, and the men grew uneasy. Indistinct shapes flitted through the margins of the forest. Knowing that she could not flee, they left her tied to a tree and headed into the woods on the morning of the fourth day. After a little time had gone by, she heard gunshots.

The men did not return.

Soldiers scoured the island, for these were vicious, dangerous individuals, but only one of them was ever found. The officer who discovered him thought at first that he was looking at the carcass of a small animal, until he touched it with his rifle and felt the skull beneath the hair. They began to dig, uncovering first his scalp, then his face, until finally his arms were revealed, outstretched in a crucifixion pose, and they were able, with difficulty, to pull him from the earth.

His name was Gabriel Moser, and he had been buried alive.

Except perhaps "buried" was not the right word, for there had been no signs of disturbance at his resting place and already there was grass growing around the crown of his head.

Gabe Moser had not been buried, it seemed. Gabe Moser had been pulled down beneath the earth and had suffocated in the darkness.

The man named Joe Dupree knew all these things. He knew the history of the island, just as his father and grandfather before him had known it, and they had bequeathed that knowledge to him.

"The first one who came was named Thomas Lunt, and he brought with him his wife, Katie, and their children, Erik and Johann. That was in the spring of 1691. With them came the Leggits, Robert and Marie. Marie was pregnant at the time and would later give birth to a boy, William. Others joined them in the weeks that followed. These are their names. You must remember them. It's important that you remember . . ."

At the time, Joe Dupree had not understood, for he was very young. Later, as he grew older, he learned more and more about the island, about what had taken place there. He understood the importance of maintaining peace on the island and of allowing nothing to disturb its calm. Inevitably, people sometimes did foolish things, for where there are people there will be faults, but there had been no wrongful deaths on the island for many years.

Dupree drove to Liberty Avenue and killed the Explorer's engine. Liberty ran southwest to northeast across the island in what was almost a perfect diagonal, except where it took a dip to avoid the Site. It had been renamed Liberty Avenue (instead of the rather more mundane Central Avenue) in the aftermath of Pearl Harbor, when Casco Bay had become the northern base of the Atlantic fleet. A big fueling depot was established on Long Island, and every kind of ship imaginable, from little cruisers to aircraft carriers, threaded a way through the channels of the bay to take on fuel. A cable capable of detecting the passage of metal objects was stretched across the ocean floor from Bailey Island to Two Lights, and two ships stood vigil over the submarine nets at Hussey Sound, waiting to open the nets in order to allow passage to military shipping.

The two largest coastal defense batteries were situated on Peaks Island, guarding the main approach to Portland, and Dutch Island, the largest of the outlying islands. Both were similarly equipped. The Dutch Island battery had two sixteen-inch guns, as big as any along the Atlantic coast, cast and fabricated at the Watervliet Arsenal in Albany. Each was sixty feet long, weighed fifty tons, and had to be transported to the island on a specially constructed barge. They were fired only once, during target practice, and promptly shattered every window on the island. They were never fired again, and when the war came to an end, they were removed and destroyed.

But the emplacements built to house them remained, great man-made mountains along the island's southeastern shore, and gradually they were reclaimed by grass and bushes and shrubs. A network of tunnels ran beneath them, their great iron doors now hanging from broken hinges, but even the bravest of the youths stayed away from the tunnels. Doors that stood open one day would be inexplicably locked by the next. There were echoes where there should not have been echoes, and lights where there should have been only darkness. The island's teenagers were content to use the remains of the emplacements for biking or, if they were of a more adventurous cast, for driving cars diagonally down at the maximum possible speed, their occupants wrenching the wheel to the right or left at the last possible moment and coming to rest facing the road, sweat streaming down their faces, still shrieking in exhilaration.

That was how Sylvie Lauter and Wayne Cady had come to be out here. They had boosted an old Dodge from the garage of one of the summer houses, since even if the car was damaged during their activities, it would be many months before the damage was discovered, assuming, of course, that they did not harm it so extensively that it had to be abandoned at the emplacement, as had happened on more than one occasion.

The couple had been drinking, for there were cans found strewn across the backseat of the car. Judging by the number of fresh tracks along the emplacement, they had managed two or three runs before Cady lost control of the car, sending it careening at top speed into the oak tree. There were still heavy tire treads marking the car's final path, and fragments of glass and metal lay strewn around the tree, its bark now heavily pitted and speckled with the sap that had bled from within it. Flowers had been placed around its base, along with a couple of beer cans and a pack of Marlboros with two unsmoked cigarettes left inside.

Joe Dupree ran his fingers along the great gouge in the tree, then rubbed them together, crushing grains of bark beneath his fingers. Wayne Cady had hit the steering column with so much force that it entered his chest, killing him within seconds. His girlfriend struck the windshield hard, but her death was caused by the crushing of her lower body. Old Buck Tennier, whose house lay about a quarter of a mile from the emplacement, had heard the sound of the crash and called the cops. By the time Dupree and Lockwood reached the scene, Buck was kneeling by the car, talking to Sylvie. It was then that she had spoken her last. The two cops cut Sylvie and Wayne from the car using the jaws of life after Doc Bruder, who was still registered as an assistant ME, declared them dead at the scene. The bodies were driven to the station house, in the back of the island's sole ambulance, prior to being transported to the mainland. Dupree had taken on the task of telling Sylvie's father and mother, and Wayne Cady's layabout dad. They had all cried in front of him, even Ben Cady, although Ben had been pretty liquored up when Dupree got to his door.

The huge policeman shivered. He kicked at the glass with the toe of his boot and stared into the darkness of the forest as Richie Claeson's words returned to him.

The others, in the woods.

The island had been quiet for so very long.

Now, something was awake.

CHAPTER TWO

Harry Rylance spread the map over the hood of the rental Mazda and watched as a bead of sweat engulfed Galveston. He had a vague recollection that Galveston had once been pretty much washed away and subsequently rebuilt. Harry had been to Galveston, and why they had bothered to rebuild the place was beyond him. Maybe he was just bitter. He'd once been ripped off by a Galveston hooker who stole his wallet while he was taking a postcoital leak, and ever since then he had been unable even to hear the word "Galveston" spoken without tensing inside. Thankfully, the opportunities to hear anyone talking about Galveston were comparatively few, which suited Harry just fine.

Now here he was looking at a dark patch of sweat slowly seeping into the map around that selfsame thieving-hooker hole in the ground. It could be a sign, he thought. Maybe if he hung his head over the map and let another bead of sweat drop, it might just hit the page and tell him where he was, because unless it did, Harry Rylance was likely to remain absofucking-lutely lost. That would have been okay with Harry if he had been alone on this godforsaken stretch of dirt road. Well, not okay, exactly, but at least he would have been able to figure out where he was in relative silence. Instead—

"Do you know where we're at yet?" said Veronica, and there was that bored, whining tone to her voice that just seemed to burrow into Harry's skull from somewhere right above the bridge of his nose and then keep going until it hit the center of his brain and began picking idly at whatever it found there.

Well, there it was. Harry wasn't alone. He had Veronica Berg with him, and while Veronica was pretty much all that a man could wish for in the sack, and a whole lot more (Harry was not an unimaginative man, but the things that Veronica was prepared to do once her back hit the sheets came close to frightening him at times), she could be a righteous pain in the ass outside the bedroom. She sat in the passenger seat, her shades on, an elbow propped up on the open window, a cigarette dangling from her fingers sending hopeless smoke signals up into the winter sky.

And that was another thing: it was unseasonably warm. Hell, it was January, and January had no business being hot. Harry Rylance was from Burlington, Vermont, and in Burlington, Vermont, January meant skiing and freezing your ass off and shoveling out the driveway. If you were sweating in January in Vermont, then you were indoors and the heat was up too high. The south was no place for a man to be in January, or any other time, if you asked Harry. Harry didn't do Dixie. He gave up looking at the blue-veined map of the United States in his Rand McNally road atlas, resigned to the fact that his attempt to exchange the trees for the forest had left him no wiser than before, and returned his attention to the local map. Harry wasn't a great reader of maps, a fact that he tended to keep to himself. A man who admitted publicly that he couldn't read a map might as well start riding side-saddle and listening to show tunes. Harry wondered if it was some kind of condition he had, like dyslexia. He just couldn't connect the map, with its tracery of blues and reds and its smears of green, to the landscape that he saw around him. It was like showing him the interior of a body, all veins and arteries and bloody meat, and asking him if he could tell who it was yet.

"I said—" Veronica began again.

Harry felt the pressure building in the center of his forehead. Her voice was drilling away nicely now. If she kept this up, his head would cave in.

"I heard you. If I knew where we were, we'd be someplace else."

"The hell is that supposed to mean?"

"It means that if you'd give me a damn minute's peace, then maybe I could figure out where we are and get us where we're meant to be instead."

"You should have stayed on the highway."

"I came off the highway because you said you were bored. You wanted to see some scenery."

"There is no scenery."

"Well, welcome to the south. The Civil War was the best thing that ever happened to this place. At least it brought in some visitors."

"You shouldn't have listened to me."

"You didn't give me much choice."

"Don't take that tone with me."

"Hey, I already got a wife back home. I don't need another one."

"Fuck you, Harry."

And he could hear the hurt in her voice and knew that he'd have to worm his way back into her affections if he had any hope of expanding his sexual horizons in the company of Veronica Berg. The annual convention of the Insurance Providers of America wasn't likely to be so riveting that Harry would want to spend the entire weekend sitting in the middle of a bunch of seersuckers, nursing a hard-on. He reached in through the car window and touched her moist skin lightly with the palm of his hand. She pulled her face away from him, sending him a clear signal: if she wasn't going to let him touch her face with his hand, then there was a pretty good chance that the rest of her skin would remain a covered mystery to him as well unless he started making up some lost ground.

"Baby, I'm sorry. I didn't mean that."

She dabbed at a make-believe tear with the tip of a finger. "Yeah, well, you ought to be more careful about what you say. You can be very hurtful sometimes, Harry Rylance."

"Sorry, " he repeated. He leaned over and kissed her on the mouth, trying to ignore the taste of nicotine on her breath. That was another thing: her damn smoking. If there was one thing—

"Harry, there's someone coming!"

He looked up, and sure enough, there was a cloud of dust and fumes heading their way. He skipped away from Veronica, took the map in his hand, and waved it at the oncoming vehicle. As it drew closer and the dust cleared some, Harry could see that it was a blue Ford truck, twenty years old at least. Behind the wheel was a young man with blond hair parted on the right and hanging down over one eye. He stopped and brushed the hair back onto his head with his fingers as he looked at the older man.

Behind him, he heard Veronica purr in approval. The kid

was good looking, Harry noticed, maybe a little on the pretty side because of that blond hair, but still a fine-looking young man. Harry wondered if he was turning queer, then decided that the mere fact that he was worried about turning queer probably meant that he wasn't. Still, thought Harry, that kid better not do anything that might offend the law, because if he went to jail, his cell mate would never have to buy cigarettes again.

"You lost?" asked the kid. His voice was a little high, almost eerily so. Harry walked over to him and realized that the young man was older than he had first appeared: early twenties at most, but he had the voice of a thirteen-year-old boy waiting for something to happen below his navel.

Backwoods freak, thought Harry.

"Took a wrong turn somewhere back down the road," said Harry, which wasn't actually an admission that he was lost but wasn't saying that he knew where he was either. It was a man thing.

"Where you bound?"

What the fuck? Where you bound? Who talked like that?

"We're headed for Augusta."

"You're a long ways from Augusta. That's a whole 'nother state away."

"I know that. We were planning on taking our time."

"You on vacation?"

"Business."

"What d'you do?"

"I sell insurance."

"Why?"

"Why what?"

"Why do you sell insurance?"

Harry's brow furrowed. This was all he needed. The kid

was obviously some kind of redneck retard driving a clapped-out old Ford up and down back roads, looking for folks to bother. They hadn't been off the plane more than two hours and already the weekend was turning to shit.

"People need insurance."

"Why?"

"Well, suppose something happens to them. Suppose you crashed your truck, what would you do?"

"It ain't my truck."

Jesus.

"Okay, well suppose you crashed it anyway, and the guy whose truck it is wanted something done about it."

"I'd fix it."

"Suppose it was so badly damaged that it couldn't be fixed?"

"There ain't nothing I can't fix."

Harry wiped his hand across his face in frustration.

"You get hurricanes down here, right?"

"Sure."

"What if your house blew away?"

The young man considered this, then nodded.

"If I had a house," he said, then started the truck up again. "Follow me," he told Harry. "I'll take you where you need to go."

Harry smiled in relief and trotted back to the car.

"We're going to follow him," he told Veronica.

"Okay with me," she said.

"And put your tongue back in your mouth," said Harry. "You're getting drool on your chin."

They followed the truck for five miles before Harry started to worry.

"The hell is he taking us?" he said.

"He probably knows a shortcut."

"A shortcut to where? Louisiana?"

"Harry, it's his country. He knows it better than we do. Calm down."

"I think the kid's retarded. He was asking me about insurance."

"You sell insurance. People ask you about it all the time."

"Yeah, but not like that. The kid acted like he didn't know what insurance was."

"Maybe he had a bad experience once."

"Like what?"

"Like trying to make a claim on your firm."

"Very funny. And it's *our* firm."

"I just answer the phones. I don't sell bum policies."

"They're not bum policies. Jesus, you talk like that to other people about what we do?"

"If they're not bum policies, how come they don't pay out like they should?"

"It's complicated."

"Explain it to me."

"You wouldn't understand."

"Fuck you, Harry."

"Now where is he going?"

Ahead of them, the Ford had made a right and was pulling up in front of an old farmhouse. The kid got out of the car and walked up the steps to the door, then opened it and disappeared inside.

"I don't believe this," said Harry.

He followed the driveway until he reached the old Ford. The place looked as if it had seen better days and could now hardly remember them. Trees bordered the yard, but it wasn't clear why they were needed because Harry couldn't see another house anywhere nearby. Once this might have been a working farm. There was a barn off to the right, and Harry saw a rusting John Deere standing in the open door, but its tires were flat and its exhaust was severed. He glimpsed overgrown fields through the trees, but nothing had been harvested from them in a very long time. The only thing being farmed here was dirt and weeds. It was quiet too: no dogs, no people, hell, not even a couple of scrawny chickens trying to survive on dust and stray seeds. A porch ran along the front of the house, great teardrops of white paint flaking from it. Paint was falling too from the facade, and from the window frames and the door. The whole house seemed to be weeping.

Harry opened the car door and called after their guide.

"Hey, kid! What's the deal?"

There was no reply, and suddenly Harry, who considered himself a calm man, all things considered, lost it.

"Fuck!" he shouted. "Fuck! Fuck! FUCK!"

He climbed out of the car and stomped up to the house. Behind him, he heard Veronica telling him to wait up. He ignored her. All he wanted to do now was get back on the highway, find a hotel, and hit the bar. Hell, maybe they might just drive into the night until they got to Augusta, and screw the idea of taking their time and kicking back along the way. Veronica could just kiss his ass.

He reached the door and peered into the house. The entrance led straight into a living room. All the drapes were drawn and the room was shrouded in darkness. He could see the shapes of chairs, and a TV in the corner. Facing him was a kitchen and, beside that, a bedroom that had been converted to storage. To his left, a flight of stairs led up to the second story.

Despite the heat, all of the windows were closed. There was no sign of the pretty boy.

Harry stepped inside, and his nose wrinkled. Something smelled bad in here, he thought. He heard flies buzzing.

"What's happening?" said Veronica, and there was that whining tone to her voice again, except this time Harry barely noticed it.

"Stay there," he called back. "And lock the car doors."

"What—"

"For Christ's sake, just do it!"

She was quiet then, but he heard a snapping sound as the doors locked. Beyond him, the darkness remained untroubled by sound or movement, but for the noise of the insects, still invisible to him.

Harry stepped into the house.

Many miles to the north, two police officers sat at a table in the Sebago Brewing Company in Portland's Old Port. It was shortly after four o'clock and already growing dark. There were few tourists around at this time of year, and the streets, like the bar, were quiet. There was talk of a storm brewing, and the coming of snow.

"I like it better without the tourists," said the first cop. She was small and dark, with short hair that barely troubled the nape of her neck. Her limbs were slim, and she appeared almost delicate out of uniform, but Sharon Macy was strong and fast. Cute too, thought Eric Barron. In fact, very cute. She'd joined up only six months before, and in that time it was all that Barron could do to stop himself hitting on her. Barron was smart, and he'd watched as the other cops had made moves on her in bars and clubs, hiding wedding bands in some cases, as if Macy would be dumb enough to fall for that. But Barron had held back, and now he believed that he was one of the few cops who could safely suggest to Macy that they head out for a beer or two after a tour, y'know, to unwind. He could feel her starting to trust him, to relax in his presence, and she didn't seem to mind any when he patted her arm or let his leg rest against hers. Baby steps. Barron was a great believer in baby steps. It might actually have made him a decent cop, if he had cared to be: not flashy, or glory seeking, but conscientious and careful. Unfortunately, Barron wasn't a decent cop. He had a lot of people fooled, maybe, but even the ones who considered him adequate at worst wouldn't have used the word "decent" of Barron. He gave off a bad vibe. Nobody was ever going to ask Barron to baby-sit a kid, or pick up a daughter after cheerleading practice. It wasn't anything that could be put into words, exactly, but if you were a parent, then Barron was the kind of guy who put you on your guard. Local kids, even the real troublemakers, knew better than to mess with him. Barron liked to pretend that it was because they respected him, but secretly he knew better. He could see it in their faces, those of the boys in particular.

Barron didn't usually go for women like Macy—hell, he didn't usually care much for grown women, period—but Macy was thin, with kind of a boyish ass, and Barron was all for experimentation. Plus, he'd been out of the loop for a time, keeping his head down. He'd let his appetites get the better of him a little while back, and had almost brought a ton of trouble down on his head. He needed an outlet for his frustrations.

"It'll be cold out there on the island," he said. He rubbed his hands over hers, as if trying to increase the circulation to frozen limbs. She smiled at him, then drew her hands away and hid them beneath the table.

Damn, thought Barron. Not a good sign.

"I don't mind," she said. "I'm kind of looking forward to it. I've never been out there before."

Barron took a long pull on his beer. "There's nothing 'out there,'" he said. "Just a bunch of yokels living some damn island fantasy. Inbreds, mostly. Banjo players."

She shook her head. "You know that's not true."

"You haven't seen it. Believe me, just twenty-four hours of island life and this place will seem like New York and Vegas combined."

Barron had that tone when he spoke, the know-it-all one that really grated on Macy. Then again, Macy was just a probationary patrol officer, while Barron was her field training officer. She'd put in her eighteen weeks of basic training, and now was at the end of her six weeks under an FTO. She had almost another two years of probation to go, with transfers to new duties every six months, but she didn't mind that so much. She would just be happy to get away from Barron. He creeped her out, and his attitude toward her wasn't simply that of a senior patrolman to one fifteen years his junior. Barron was just plain bad news. The force was already under federal review, and morale was suffering. A lot of good cops were simply working toward their twenty-five so they could retire and open a bar somewhere. Cops like Barron only made things worse.

Still, he'd offered to buy her a beer to celebrate the end of their time together and she hadn't been able to refuse. There were one or two other cops in the Sebago, although it wasn't a regular haunt. Barron didn't go to the cop bars. Macy figured that she wasn't the only one who felt uneasy around him.

Macy sipped her beer and watched the cars pass on Middle Street. She was still getting used to Portland, but it reminded her a little of Providence, where her parents lived. There were a lot of young people, although Portland's university wasn't quite as grand as the one back home, and it still had kind of a small-town feel. She liked the fact that there were good bars and decent places to eat in the center of the city. She didn't miss Providence too much, and was happy to leave the bulk of her bad memories there. If things had worked out better, then Macy would have been married to Max, might even have been talking about having a child. Things hadn't worked out, of course, which was why she was sitting in a bar 150 miles away with tired legs and an aching back.

It was strange, but one of the things that she had liked about Max was the feeling he gave her that, even half a century down the line, she would still be discovering new things about him. In the end, it had taken barely eighteen months for her to discover a new thing about Max that blew any hopes of marriage out of the water. Max couldn't remain faithful. Max would screw a keyhole if there wasn't already a key in it. When he couldn't pick up a desperate student on Thayer Street, or a bored secretary during the five-to-eight happy hour (which was how Macy, a bored secretary in a law office, had met him, come to think of it), he'd screw hookers. He even seemed to prefer hookers, she discovered, when he was released on bail and they'd met for that last time, after she had packed her bags and returned in humiliation to her parents. He confessed everything, spewing poison and bile out onto the table of the diner, so that it seemed that the Formica would corrode beneath it. He would tell the hookers that he was single and would get a kick when they asked how a good-looking guy like him could be single. Even as he spoke about it, his career in tatters around him (associating with hookers was the least of his professional problems, for he had been under surveillance for some time, a consequence of the investigation into the mayor's operation in Providence, and was now facing charges of graft and corruption), she sensed that he still found it flattering. Max was sick, but the sickness was moral as much as psychological. She was just grateful that she had found out the truth before the wedding and not after it.

That was two years ago, and Macy had begun toying with the idea of becoming a cop shortly after. She had been helping out at a center for women who were victims of domestic abuse, and had heard horror stories from some of them about their dealings with the police. There were good stories too, hopeful stories, but it was the bad ones that stayed with Macy. She wanted to make a difference. It was as simple as that. She had visited Portland in the aftermath of the breakup, while she was still trying to come to terms with what had happened, and had decided that it suited her. It was close enough to her parents to enable her to drive home when she chose, yet far enough away that she would be in no danger of meeting any of Max's old associates (or, God forbid, Max himself). The cost of living was reasonable, and the force was recruiting. Her modicum of legal knowledge and her experience in the battered women's shelter had made her a shoo-in as a recruit. She had no regrets, although working with Barron had been her most trying ordeal yet.

She noticed that Barron had gone quiet. She saw him looking across the bar, and the expression on his face was so hostile that she immediately wanted to leave him there, to get as far away from him as possible, even though his eyes were not on her. Instead, he was watching a man of slightly more than medium height talking to the bartender. He was kind of cute, thought Macy, in a brooding way. He flashed some form of ID, asked a couple of questions, then prepared to move on. He barely paused when he spotted Barron, but it was enough. He held the cop's eyes until Barron looked away, then left the bar.

Macy watched him climb into an old Mustang and drive toward the Franklin Arterial.

"Who was that?" she asked.

"Nobody. A fuckup."

He excused himself to go to the john and told the bartender to rack up two more beers. Macy was barely halfway through her first and she wasn't planning on having another. She looked around the bar and saw Odell from Property. He stepped up beside her and touched his glass to hers.

"End of your six," he said. "Congratulations."

She shrugged and smiled. "Hey, you know who that guy was, the one who was talking to the bartender a couple of minutes ago? Drives a Mustang."

Odell nodded. "Charlie Parker."

"The PI?" As an investigator, she knew Parker had managed to track down some bad guys. He had quite a reputation, even if it was a mixed one. She had heard talk that Parker was nosing about in the department. She was curious to know why.

"The very same."

"I got the impression that Barron doesn't like him."

"There aren't a whole lot of people Eric Barron does like, and Parker isn't the kind of guy to top that list. They had a run-in a couple of years back. Parker was looking into the death of a woman, Rita Ferris. She'd been hooking a little to make ends meet. After the case was closed, Barron saw Parker at Old Port Billiards and made some comments about the woman."

"And?"

"Barron went to the men's room. Couple of minutes later Parker followed him in. Only Parker came out. Barron never spoke about what happened in there, but he's got a scar at the right side of his mouth"—Odell pointed with his finger to his own mouth—"that maybe I wouldn't mention to him, you see what I mean?"

"People who mess with cops don't usually walk away from it so easily."

"You see anyone rushing to defend Barron's honor?"

"I guess not. I hear Parker's been asking about cops."

"Cops, rent-a-cops, private security. He's pissing off all the wrong people."

"You know why?"

"Case a couple of months back. Someone tried to pull a boy from the street, over in Gorham. Kid was huffing lighter fuel and was pretty much off his head to begin with, so he couldn't recall much, but he claimed the guy was wearing a uniform under his jacket, and he thought he could see a gun. His parents have money and they've hired Parker to ask some questions. They're afraid the guy might make a play again, either on their kid or someone else's."

Barron returned from the men's room, and nodded a curt greeting to Odell.

"See you 'round, I guess," Odell said to Macy. He nodded at Barron—"Eric"—then went back to his buddies.

"What did he want?" asked Barron.

"Nothing, just wanted to congratulate me on finishing my six." She could sense Barron simmering beside her. He had a short fuse, and it seemed a good idea to try to stamp it out before the powder keg ignited.

"Tell me more about the island," she said.

Barron told her that Dutch Island, or Sanctuary as it was sometimes known, was within the jurisdiction of the Portland Police Department, despite its status as the most remote of the inhabited islands on Casco Bay. Dutch wasn't the only island that required a police presence of this kind, but it was the least hospitable. Most Portland cops never had to spend time there. It had one resident policeman, and a couple of others who traveled out on a rotation system. On the other island policed by the Portland PD, Peaks Island, two officers headed out on a boat every day. But when the boat left for Dutch, there was often only one cop on board.

"Why has it got two names?"

"To make it sound interesting," said Barron. "But believe me, it isn't. What more do you want to know?"

"What's he like?" asked Macy.

"Who?"

"You know, Dupree."

Barron clicked his tongue in disgust. "Melancholy Joe? He's a freak."

"They say he's a giant. I mean, a real giant. Like in the circus, or like that wrestler guy, the one who died."

"Andre the Giant. No, Joe ain't as big as Andre. Still a big son of a bitch, though. Strong, too. Nobody fucks with Melancholy Joe."

"Why do they call him that?"

"Because he's a miserable bastard, that's why. Doesn't say much, keeps to himself. You better take some books out to Dutch Island, because you sure ain't going to be kept up nights talking to Joe."

"You spend time out there?"

"Just once, when flu took out half of the regular guys. Didn't care much for it. Didn't care much for Joe Dupree, either."

I bet it was mutual, thought Macy.

"I suppose nothing much happens out there."

"Not a whole lot. Bored kids stealing cars, breaking into summer houses. The occasional DUI. It's community policing, mainly."

"But not always?"

"What do you know?" asked Barron.

"Someone said—"

"Who?"

"Just someone. He said Joe Dupree once killed a man out on the island."

Barron made that clicking sound again. "Yeah, he killed one of the Lubey brothers. Ronnie Lubey. If he'd been a little faster, then maybe his partner might not have taken a load of buckshot in the leg. Lubey was drunk, Dupree and Snowman arrived—"

"Snowman?"

"Yeah, dumb fucking name for a dumb guy. If he'd taken the buckshot in the head, it probably would have done him less damage. Anyway, Dupree and him arrive, Snowman gets shot, and Dupree kills Ronnie Lubey. He was taken off duty for a while, but the investigation cleared him. That's it. Nobody shed too many tears for old Ronnie. He was a bad one. His brother still lives out on Dutch. He hates Joe Dupree like wood hates fire."

Barron paused. He felt dumb saying what he was about to say, as if Macy was going to laugh at him or call him a liar, but when he'd joined the force, his first partner, Tom Huyler, had sat him down over a beer and told him pretty much what he was about to tell Macy, and old Huyler wasn't the type to joke around. He was Dutch Protestant, and when those people cracked a smile, it was like watching Arctic ice break, but Huyler knew his history. After all, they were some of his people that went out there in the beginning.

His people who were slaughtered.

Because, sure, Dutch Island was quiet, most of the time. There was the odd domestic dispute, the occasional drunk that tried to drive up a tree. But he recalled Huyler telling him the story of the first settlers on the island, how they'd retreated out there after skirmishes with the local Indians in the late 1600s.

Then, according to the history books, there was some internal dispute among the islanders, and somebody had been banished. He'd come back, though, and he brought others with him. The entire population—ten, twelve families, all with children—had been slaughtered. It was only in the last hundred, hundred and fifty years that people had started returning to Dutch in numbers, and now the community was large enough to need full-time cops out there.

And sometimes, people went missing. They were the bad ones, mostly. That was the odd thing about it. They were the ones that were no use to anybody, not even to their own families. They were the fighters, the abusers, the wife beaters. True, not all of them went that way, and Dutch still had its share of bad sorts, but they tended to be pretty careful about where they walked and what they did. They didn't stray too far from their homes and they stayed away from the woods at the center of the island, and far away from what was known as the Site, the burial place of the original settlers.

Huyler was dead now, died of a heart attack two years before, but Barron could still see him sitting there, a glass of beer in his hand, talking in those soft tones of his, the occasional strange intonation creeping into his speech, a relic of his family's heritage. Barron had never doubted a word that he had said, not even when he'd told him about his final tour on Dutch Island, and the death of George Sherrin. Because George Sherrin was the reason Dutch's less salubrious residents didn't go walking in the woods at night anymore. Nobody wanted to go the way old George had, no sir.

There had always been talk about the Sherrins. Their kids were rebellious and educationally subnormal, real difficult types. Old Frank Dupree, Melancholy Joe's father, had been forced on more than one occasion to haul one or the other of the Sherrin kids back to his old man and tell him how the kid had been caught breaking windows or tormenting some poor dumb animal, and the kid would be quiet as he was led back to the house, and Frank would always feel a tug at his belly as the kid was led inside by George and the door closed silently behind them. Frank suspected that there was something going on there, something vile and rotten, but he could never convince Sherrin's mousy wife, Enid, to talk, and any social workers who ever went near the Sherrins risked getting a gun waved at them or had to run to escape the dogs barking at their heels.

And then, one day, George Sherrin went missing. He didn't come home from a trip out into the woods, his truck loaded up with a saw and chains so he could do a little illegal cutting and collect some cheap fuel for the winter. It was two days before his wife bothered to report it, and Frank Dupree figured that if she hadn't killed him herself, then maybe she was just relieved to have two days without his presence in the house, because if George Sherrin was doing bad things to his children, Frank didn't doubt that his wife knew about it, and that maybe she tried to get him to do bad things to her instead on occasion, just to give the kids a break.

So Frank Dupree and Tom Huyler had made their way into the woods, and after a few hours they'd found George Sherrin's truck, and beside it George's saw. There was a gash in a big pine tree nearby, where George had just started cutting, but then something seemed to have interrupted him, because he never got to finish his task. They had a good look around for

George, but there was no trace of him. Later they came back with twenty islanders and they formed a line through the forest and scoured the bushes and the trees, but George was gone. After a few days, they stopped looking. After a few weeks, they stopped caring. George's kids started getting on better in school and a social worker began calling at the house, and then a couple of times a month, Enid Sherrin and the kids took the little ferry over to the mainland and got to talk things through with a doctor who had Crayolas in her drawer and a box of Kleenex on her desk.

One year later, a bad storm hit the coast, and Dutch, being right out there, took the brunt of it. There was thunder, and two trees were felled by lightning bolts, and under one of those trees they found George Sherrin. The pine had been torn partway out of the ground but its fall was arrested by the surrounding trees so that its broad root structure gaped like a toothed mouth. In the hollow that it left in the ground, George Sherrin's remains were discovered, and a murder investigation was initiated. There was no visible damage to his bones—no breaks, no fractures, no entry wounds—but somebody must have put George Sherrin under that tree because he sure hadn't dug himself a hole beneath it and then covered himself up. They took Enid Sherrin in and quizzed her some, but she had her kids to back her up and they all told the same story. Their momma had been with them the whole time after their daddy disappeared. Who else was going to look after them?

There were more puzzles for the investigators to mull over. When the tree and the bones were analyzed, the results made no sense. The way the experts figured it, George Sherrin would have to have been buried under there for thirty years for the roots to grow through his bones the way they had, for they had curled around and through him as if holding him in place. But George Sherrin had been missing for only one year, and there was just no way to account for that degree of growth. No, there had to be some other explanation for the nature of the root spread.

Except nobody had ever come up with one.

"That's the story," said Barron.

Macy looked at him closely to see if he was joking. He wasn't.

"You say other people have disappeared?"

"*I* don't say. The only one I've heard about is George Sherrin. I think the others are just attempts to add to the legend. You know, people leave the island for their own reasons and don't come back, and suddenly there's another name in the pot. But what I just told you about George Sherrin, well, that's real. You can put that in the bank and watch it draw interest."

He knocked back his beer and raised his hand for another round. Instead, Macy pushed her untouched second beer in front of him.

"Take mine, I'm all done."

"You're going? Hey, don't go. Stay a little longer."

His hand reached for hers, but she went for her jacket instead, narrowly avoiding contact. She put it on and saw Barron's eyes following the zipper as she pulled it up over her breasts.

"No, I got to go. I have things to do."

"What things?" he said, and she could hear something in his tone, something that made her real glad that there were other people around them in the bar, that they weren't sitting alone in a car somewhere or, worse, back at Barron's place. He'd asked her back there that afternoon, suggesting they watch a movie on cable, maybe get some Thai food. She'd declined and they'd ended up here instead. Suddenly it seemed to her like the wisest decision she'd made in a very long time.

"Just things," she said. "Thanks for the beer and, y'know, looking out for me during training."

But Barron had left her and was now standing at the bar. He lifted her untouched beer, leaned over the counter, and poured it into the sink. She shook her head, picked up her knapsack, and walked out.

Macy thought about all that she had been told as she drove home, about Dupree and the island and George Sherrin. She thought too about Barron, and shuddered instinctively at the memory of his touch. The weeks of training under Barron had been difficult. At first it hadn't been so bad. Barron had kept his distance and played everything by the book. But gradually she became increasingly uneasy around him, conscious always of how close he would stand to her; of the relish with which he told self-glorifying stories of inflicting violence on "smart-mouths" and "punks"; and of the looks some of the street kids would shoot him when he approached them, like dogs that had been kicked once too often. It was only in the final weeks that Barron had started to put some tentative moves on her. He was careful, aware of the potential for harassment complaints, or of action by his superiors if they found out that he was even attempting to form a relationship with a probation cop in his charge, but the desire was there. Macy had felt it like a bad rash.

Macy knew that she was pretty, and that she possessed, superficially at least, a kind of vulnerability that drew a certain type of man to her. Scratch that: it drew a whole lot of different types to her, and she had learned to sidestep their attentions with a grace that would have befitted a ballerina. Barron was subtler than most, but it was perhaps that subtlety that was most off-putting. While most men made a frontal assault, Barron was the kind who crept up, like a sneak thief. They were the worst types and had to be watched most closely.

She thought too of an incident that had occurred the night before, one that still troubled her. Macy and Barron had been heading down Congress, doing their standard loop, when they saw him. The lights picked out a figure in a black Alpha Industries aviator's jacket, the hood of his gray jogging top hanging over the back of the jacket, a watch cap on his head. He took one look at the cruiser and started to walk briskly in the opposite direction.

"Will you look at this joker?" said Barron. He depressed the accelerator slightly, causing the patrol car to increase its speed to match the guy. Watch Cap looked over his shoulder, then ran.

"I mean, seriously," Barron continued. He could have been talking about the return of flared pants or the revival of progressive rock for all the concern in his voice. "Here's conclusive evidence that a whole lot of criminals are just plain dumb. If this guy could just have kept his head for ten seconds"—he swung the wheel to the right as the suspect made a turn onto Pine—"then he would have been free and clear. Instead, he decides to outrun Miss Crown Vic here, and I'm telling you now, I don't think this is a healthy man. Look at the vapor trail he's leaving. It's like chasing a crop duster. Okay, screw this. Let's light him."

Barron hit the gumballs and the siren, and put his foot down hard to the floor. Already, the guy was visibly wilting. When they swung into the parking lot behind him, he seemed almost grateful to be forced to stop. Barron stepped out from behind the wheel seconds later, and the two cops came at him in a narrowing V. The runner had his hands raised and was breathing as if he were about to bust a gut. Barron seemed to do a double take when he got close enough to identify the man. It was hardly noticeable, but it was there.

"Hey," said Barron. "Terry Scarfe. Look, Macy, it's Terry Scarfe. How you doin', Terry? They let you out? The fuck were they thinking?"

"Maybe they took a vote," said Macy. Scarfe's name had been on a circulated list of new parolees. According to the other cops, he was a well-known local lowlife. He was just over five feet tall and desperately thin. His face was heavily lined, despite his comparative youth, as though it still bore the imprint of the last foot that had stepped on it.

"Yeah, like a straw poll. You, Terry, are the weakest link. Now get the fuck out of our nice prison. You carrying, Terry?"

Scarfe shook his head.

"You sure now? Because I better not frisk you and find something that draws blood. I gotta say that if you think the airlines are kind of strict, then wait until you get a load of me. I find even a sharp fingernail clipping and I'm going to have you charged with carrying an offensive weapon. And that's in addition to you just being offensive, period. So let me ask you again, Terry. Anything in there we should know about? Sharps? Needles?"

Scarfe found his voice.

"I told you, I got nothing."

"On the ground," said Barron.

"Aw, come on, it's cold. I'm telling you—"

Barron came at him hard and shoved him to the ground. Scarfe landed on his knees and seemed about to protest, until Barron pushed him down fully and his chin hit the ground.

"You didn't have to do that," Scarfe whined while Barron patted him down.

"Get up," Barron said when he was done.

Scarfe got to his feet and rubbed the dirt from his hands.

"Why did you run away from us?" asked Barron.

"I wasn't running away from you. I was running *to* someplace."

"Someplace where?"

"Someplace else."

"You want us to take you in? How long you been out on parole?"

"Since Monday."

"Monday?" said Barron loudly. "You mean you been out just a couple of days and already we've got you for fleeing and for failing to cooperate with your local friendly police department?"

"I told you, I wasn't fleeing. I'm a busy man. I got shit to do."

"Is it the kind of shit you can do in jail?"

Scarfe looked at him in puzzlement. "No."

"Well, you seem in kind of a hurry to get back there. I just figured that maybe it was kind of nonspecific shit. You know, independent of geography."

Scarfe kept his mouth shut.

"You're an asshole, Terry," said Barron, and his tone was more serious now. "You're an asshole and you're going to get in some serious trouble again if you don't watch your step. Now get out of here."

Macy looked at Barron incredulously. "You're letting him walk?"

"What are we going to arrest him on? Dressing too young for his age?"

"He ran."

"Yeah, but— Hey, are you still here?"

Scarfe had stopped, seemingly uncertain of what to do now

that the two cops were arguing about him. "I told you to go so go, before I change my mind."

Scarfe took one final look at Macy, shrugged, then walked briskly from the parking lot and faded into the night. The two cops faced each other.

"Come on, Macy," said Barron. "Don't do that shit."

"What shit?"

"Criticizing me in front of a cockroach like Terry Scarfe."

"He wasn't running for nothing. He's got something going on."

"So, what were we supposed to do? Haul his ass in, then watch him sit on his hands for twelve hours until we get him to court? Maybe we get the right judge and his parole is revoked, and then what? So he serves another six months. Big fucking deal. Terry's more use to us out on the street now. He hears things, and maybe we can lean on him in the future. He owes us now. We got him over a barrel."

Macy said nothing. They got in the car and made their way back onto Congress.

"Come on, Macy," Barron repeated. "Let it go."

But Macy remained uneasy for the rest of the shift, and she spoke little to Barron until they were on the steps of the headquarters building. There, Barron had reached out a hand and grasped her arm.

"Are we okay?" he asked, and Macy looked into his eyes and knew better than to disagree.

"Sure. I just don't have a good feeling about Scarfe. We should have brought him in."

"He's dumb. If he is up to something, we'll spot it soon enough. At least if he goes down again, it will be for something more than time remaining."

He gave Macy his best shit-eating grin, then headed

toward the lockers. Macy watched him go, and wondered if she'd seen what she thought she'd seen: Barron frisking Scarfe, then palming the small bags of white powder that he'd found in the man's pocket. She said nothing about it to anybody. She didn't figure Barron for a user, and maybe he was holding on to the bags for future use, possibly as payment to snitch junkies, but that didn't sound right either. It simply wasn't worth the risk for Barron to carry drugs, no matter what the excuse.

Which left the possibility that Barron wanted to protect Scarfe. Once again, as she headed for home, Macy was glad that her time with Barron was now over, and despite his stories, she was curious about her upcoming island detail. Macy was not a credulous person, and while police work tended to encourage a certain amount of superstition—lucky shoes, lucky routes, lucky bullets—she was still a little surprised by what Barron had said, and more particularly by the sincerity with which he had said it. Barron really believed everything he had told her about George Sherrin and Dutch Island, or at least had fewer doubts about it than he might otherwise have been expected to entertain. Still, he had pricked her curiosity, although that would be as close as Barron ever came to pricking anything of Sharon Macy's.

She was curious too about the policeman, the one Barron and the others called Melancholy Joe. His story was pretty well known in Portland: his father and grandfather had both served as police officers, doing the bulk of their time out on Dutch Island. It was a peculiar arrangement, but it suited the department. They knew the island and its ways, and when police officers from outside the community had been tried on the island in the absence of a member of the Dupree family, the experiment had foundered. Crime—mundane crime, but crime nonetheless—had increased, and the nerves of the cops on temporary duty had become steadily more frayed. In the end, given that nobody particularly wanted to spend time out on Dutch anyway, the Dupree family had become the de facto first family of police work as far as Dutch Island was concerned.

But old Frank Dupree's marriage had produced only one son, and that son was big enough to have even other cops label him a freak. She heard that the cost of altering a police vehicle to suit his size had been met by the department. He carried the standard-issue Portland PD sidearm, the .45 Smith & Wesson, but he had adjusted the trigger guard in his own workshop so that one of his huge fingers could pass through it more easily. Occasionally, one of the local papers would do a story on "The Giant of Dutch Island," and during the summer, tourists would sometimes travel out there to catch a glimpse of him or to have their photographs taken alongside him. Joe didn't seem to mind; or if he did, it made no difference to his permanent expression of worried bafflement.

Melancholy Joe. Macy smiled and said the name aloud. "Melancholy Joe."

Her headlights caught the sign for the interstate, the wipers striking out at the first drops of rain, and she took the north ramp.

"Sanctuary," she said, testing out the name. She decided she liked that name better than Dutch. "Well, it's better than being on traffic duty."

Moloch lay in silence on his bunk. From a nearby television came the sound of a news bulletin, but Moloch tuned out the background noise. He had more pressing matters to consider.

His lawyer hadn't been able to tell him much about the grand-jury hearing when they'd met ten days before, across a bare steel table in the prison's visiting area. "All I know is that they have a guy named Verso."

Moloch's mouth twitched, but otherwise he gave no sign of his irritation. "Is Verso the target of this grand jury?"

"I don't know."

Moloch leaned in closer to the little man. "Mr. Braden, why am I paying you if you know nothing?"

Braden didn't back off. He knew Moloch was merely venting steam. "You finished?" he asked.

Moloch leaned back, then nodded.

"I'm guessing that Verso has spoken to them and offered them something in return for immunity from prosecution. Verso's a nasty piece of work, and you're already locked up for the foreseeable future, so it could be that the county prosecutor might like to see what you can offer them to put Verso away."

"What do I get in return if I testify? A cell with a view?"

"You'll be due for parole in eight to ten. Testifying will help your case."

"I don't plan to spend another decade in jail, Mr. Braden."

Braden shrugged and leaned back. "Your call. I'll be in the hallway during the proceedings. You can ask for time out as soon as you discover where their questions are leading. If in doubt, take the Fifth."

Moloch looked down at the table before he spoke again. "They have something," he said. "They don't want Verso, they want me. I'm the target."

"You don't know that for sure," said Braden.

"Yes," said Moloch. "I do." He placed his hands together, palm against palm. "I pay you well, Mr. Braden. You were engaged because you were smart, but don't believe for one moment that you're smarter than I am. I know where you live. I know your family's movements. I know the name of the boy your daughter—"

"You better stop—"

"—your daughter *fucks* in your basement while you're watching *The West Wing*. I know these things, Mr. Braden, and you, in turn, know me. I suspect that the commonwealth of Virginia has no intention of ever seeing me released. In fact, I believe that the commonwealth of Virginia has high hopes of executing me and freeing up my cell for someone else. They want capital charges. This grand-jury hearing is a trap, nothing more."

"I have no evidence—"

"I don't care about evidence. Tell me your instincts, your gut instincts. Tell me I'm wrong."

But Braden said nothing.

"So there's been talk."

"Rumors, suspicions," Braden said. "Nothing more."

"That Verso is not the target."

"That Verso is not the target," Braden echoed.

"Have you spoken to the prosecutor?"

"He wouldn't agree to a meeting."

"If Verso was the target, he would have met with you. You could have negotiated immunity from prosecution for me. You better believe that any true bill that comes out of this will have my name on it."

Braden spread his hands. "I'm doing what I can."

Moloch wondered if Braden might be secretly happy were he to be found guilty of capital crimes. He shouldn't have threatened the lawyer. The man was frightened enough of him already.

Moloch leaned in closer to his counsel. “Listen to me, Mr. Braden. I want you to remember a telephone number. Don’t write it down, just remember it.”

Carefully and clearly, Moloch whispered the seven digits to the younger man.

“When the details of the hearing are confirmed, I want you to call that number and pass them on. Do not call from your office. Do not call from your home. Do not use your cell phone. If you’re wise, you’ll take a day trip, maybe into Maryland, and you will make the call from there. Am I clear?”

“Yes.”

“You do this right and you’ll be free of me.”

Braden rose and knocked on the door of the meeting room.

“Guard,” he called, “we’re all done here.”

He left without looking back at his client.

Now the preparations were in place. Moloch had received a message, passed in code during an apparently innocuous telephone conversation. They were moving. Progress was being made. All would be ready when the time came.

He closed his eyes and thought of vengeance.

The gray-haired man sat in the Rue de la Course on North Peter, sipping coffee and reading the local throwaway. Groups of young men passed by the windows of the coffeehouse, heading for the depths of the French Quarter. He could hear a thumping bass beat coming from the Coyote Ugly bar close by, battling the light jazz being played on the sound system behind his head. He liked the Rue de la Course, preferring it to the Café du Monde, where, earlier, he had eaten beignets and listened to the street musicians trying to hustle a buck. At the

Café du Monde, coffee came either black or au lait, and the gray-haired man didn't care much for it either way. He liked it black, but with a little cold milk on the side. The Asian waitress at the Café du Monde wasn't prepared to accommodate him, so he had been forced to take his business elsewhere. The Rue de la Course had been a fortuitous discovery. In a way, it had been recommended to him by somebody else.

The Rue de la Course had ceiling fans and walls of what looked like beaten tin, and the tables were lit by green-shaded bankers' lamps. He was surprised that it was still a coffeehouse, what with the money that could be made by turning it into a bar. Maybe it had been a bar once, as white lettering on the door still indicated that it sold beer and wine, although the blackboard behind the counter only listed about forty different types of coffee and tea, all iced this and mocha that. The gray-haired man, whose name was Shepherd, preferred his coffee the old way, with the minimum of milk and fuss. It didn't bother him that he couldn't get a drink here. Shepherd wasn't much of a drinker. He hated the way that it made fools out of people. In fact, Shepherd had few, if any, vices. He didn't smoke, didn't use drugs, and his sex drive was virtually nil. He wasn't interested in women or men, although he'd tried both just to be sure that he wasn't missing something. Like his aversion to alcohol, it helped to keep his mind clear.

And so he sat sipping coffee from a mug decorated with the image of a man in a raincoat reading a newspaper at a table, which was very apt, for Shepherd too was wearing a raincoat and sitting at a table reading a newspaper. Circles within circles. Two tables away from him, a young woman wearing green hospital scrubs sat taking notes from a textbook. She seemed to feel his eyes on her, for she looked up. He smiled casually at her, then went back to the newspaper.

Shepherd didn't like New Orleans. It was a third-world city in a first-world country, so in thrall to graft that it had come to regard corruption as the norm rather than as an aberration. When he walked its streets, all he saw was ugliness, the baseness of the human condition unashamedly revealed. Earlier, he had watched a hard-faced man stand at the doorway of a glorified titty bar, a huge woman with an even harder face standing behind him, rolls of fat dripping over dirty white lingerie. Why would anyone go into such a place? Shepherd wondered: to be ripped off, maybe to be threatened, to smell the cheap scent on a woman one step above whoredom? Such corruption of the spirit and of the soul repelled him, but at least it was obvious, unhidden. There were other forms of corruption that were far more insidious.

The woman in the green scrubs stood, placed her textbook and notebook in a satchel, and left the coffeehouse. After a minute or two had passed, Shepherd also left. He stayed some way behind her, shadowing her from across the street as she headed up Decatur. He did not panic when he lost sight of her among the crowds, for he knew where she was going. To his left, starlings moved in great shrieking circles, hovering above an old chimney stack on Chartes. Above them, the January sky was gray and cheerless. Tourists watched the birds in momentary curiosity, then moved on, somehow unnerved by the sight. Slowly, the birds' numbers were depleted as they found their roosts inside the chimney, black shapes descending into a deeper darkness.

By the time he reached the top of Decatur, the woman was nowhere to be seen. He waited ten minutes, then walked to the security gates of a renovated condo and pressed the number nine, followed by the pound key. There was a click, and then a female voice said, "Who is it?"

"My name is Jeff. I called earlier to make an appointment."

He'd found her ad offering a "sensual massage" the day before, and had called to arrange a visit.

"Come on up," she said. The gate buzzed and he entered the yard, following the interior lights to a stairway. He climbed three flights and stopped before the door to number nine. He was about to knock when the door opened.

She had changed out of her scrubs and now wore a satin robe. The ends of her hair were still wet from the shower. She looked a little puzzled as she struggled to remember his face.

"You were in—" she began, then found Shepherd's gloved hand pressed firmly over her mouth as she was forced into the apartment. Shepherd closed the door silently behind him. He pushed her against the wall and removed his right hand from the pocket of his raincoat so that she could see the knife.

"If you scream, I will hurt you," he said. "I don't want to hurt you. If you answer my questions, I promise you that you will not be hurt. Do you understand me?"

She nodded and he released his grip.

"Sit down."

He followed her into her living room. The drapes were drawn and a single lamp, overhung with a red scarf, was the sole illumination in the room. A door to his right stood open. Inside he could see a massage table covered with a clean white towel.

"I'm sorry to have misled you," said Shepherd. He stood slightly to one side of her, his left leg slightly forward to protect his groin. He had encountered trouble with women before.

She seemed on the verge of tears. He could hear them in her voice as she asked: "What do you want?"

Shepherd nodded in satisfaction. "Good. I don't want to take up any more of your time than I have to. I'd like to know where your boyfriend is."

She didn't reply.

"Your boyfriend," he repeated. "Verso. Or have you forgotten him already?"

"I haven't heard from him."

Shepherd sighed. His hand moved in a blur of flesh and metal, drawing a red line from her left shoulder to the top of her right breast. She started to yelp and he again covered her mouth with his hand.

"I told you," he said. "I don't want to hurt you, but I will if you make me. I will ask you again: where is he?"

"The police have him."

"The police *where?"*

"In Virginia."

"Where in Virginia?"

"I don't know."

Shepherd raised the blade again and she said, louder this time: *"I don't know.* They keep moving him. He's not my boyfriend anymore. I haven't seen him since he turned himself in. All I know is that he's going to be in Norfolk soon. There's a grand-jury hearing. He's going to testify."

"When was the last time he called?"

She was silent for a time.

"There's a limit to my patience," he warned her.

"This morning," she said at last.

"Before or after I called?"

"After. I was just on my way out the door when the phone rang."

The phone lay on a table to Shepherd's left. There was an answering machine hooked up to it, but it was turned off.

"Why is your machine off?"

"I was going to go out tonight, catch a movie. You were my only appointment."

"Stand up," said Shepherd.

She did as she was told. He walked her to the phone table, then told her to kneel, facing away from him.

"Please!" she said.

"Just kneel. I want to star sixty-nine your phone, and I don't want you doing anything stupid while I dial."

Reluctantly, she knelt. Shepherd pressed the buttons, then listened.

"Chesapeake Inn and Suites," said a male voice. Shepherd hung up.

Asshole, he thought.

He stepped back from the kneeling woman. She didn't turn around.

"Please," she said. "Don't hurt me anymore."

"I won't," said Shepherd.

He was a man of his word. She didn't feel a thing.

Harry Rylance had never thought of himself as the nervous type. Nobody ever made a good living out of the insurance business by being nervous. Nervousness was for the suckers who bought the policies. The whole business was predicated on fear. Without it, the insurance industry would sink like a stone and Harry would sink along with it, but Harry had to admit that he was feeling pretty damn nervous now. The creepy retard kid had disappeared and Harry's instinct was to get the hell out of the house and hope that he and Veronica could find their own route back to the highway.

Except the house smelled of dead meat, and there were flies buzzing.

And curiosity was a terrible thing.

Harry padded softly across the floor of the living room,

wincing every time a board creaked. In the kitchen, he found a pile of take-out chicken buckets littered with the stripped bones of those midget chickens the fast-food companies raised on some irradiated Pacific atoll; no other way, thought Harry, that you got legs and wings that small. A frying pan stood on the range, pieces of burnt fat adhering to its base, and bugs floated on the surface of the foul-smelling stew that sat in a pot beside it. There was an ancient refrigerator beside the stove, humming and rattling like a crazy old man in a tin cage. Harry reached out to open it, then paused. He could see himself reflected in the metal, his features distorted. Something white was behind him.

Harry spun around and lashed out at the drapes that in the still air hung unmoving over the window. A plate fell from the drain board and shattered on the floor, sending ants scurrying in confusion. Somewhere, a cockroach clicked.

"Shit," said Harry, and opened the fridge door.

Apart from a carton of week-old milk, it was empty.

In the freezer compartment, Harry found meat packed in bags. There was a lot of it.

He closed the fridge doors, then went back into the living room. No sounds came from upstairs.

"Hello?" called Harry. "Kid, you okay up there?"

He began to climb and, for the first time, he heard it: two words of a song, repeated over and over, the needle caught in the groove of the record.

—don't care

—don't care

—don't care

Elvis, thought Harry. The King don't care.

He reached the top of the steps. There was a bedroom before him, but it was empty, the sheets on the bed thrown back where its occupant had departed, leaving it unmade. Beside it was a bathroom, judging by the tiles on the floor, but it stank so bad that Harry's eyes began to water. The door was almost closed. Harry nudged it with his foot, and it opened slowly.

There was a man sitting on the toilet. His pants were around his ankles, and a newspaper dangled from his hand. Instinctively, Harry started to apologize.

"Shit, sorr—"

Harry stepped back and covered his mouth with his hand, but it was too late. He felt the fluid on his fingers, then bent down to finish puking.

The guy on the john had been shot where he sat, a bloody cloud behind what remained of his head. There wasn't much of his face left either, but Harry figured from his stringy legs, his gray hair, and sagging flesh, that the guy was well into his seventies. His white T-shirt was sweat-stained yellow in places, and blood had soaked into the shoulders, leaving marks like epaulettes. His skin was split by gas blisters.

Harry wanted to run, but there was still the sound of Elvis coming from what was probably a bedroom at the end of the hall. He walked slowly to the door and looked inside.

The couple in the bedroom were younger than the old man in the can, much younger. Harry figured them for their late twenties, at most. The man had been shot on the floor and lay naked by an open drawer, its contents littering the floor. A box of ammunition had fallen and scattered around him, but there was no gun. There was a bullet hole in his back, barely recognizable amid the damage that had been done to his body. Harry retched, but he had nothing left inside and so he just belched acidic gas.

The woman had dark hair and sat slumped sideways against

the pillows and the headboard. She too was naked. The sheets had been pulled away from her body and she'd been cut up pretty bad as well. Despite himself, Harry stepped closer, and something registered in his head. This wasn't a frenzy, thought Harry. No, there was purpose to these wounds. There was—

"Jesus," whispered Harry.

She had chunks of flesh missing from her thighs and buttocks, where someone had hacked them out. There was flesh missing from the man as well: less flesh, admittedly, but then he was scrawny and muscular, a little like the old man in the john.

A mental image flashed in Harry's mind: the refrigerator, empty but for a carton of sour milk.

And meat. Fresh meat.

Harry ran.

He hit the stairs at speed, taking the steps two at a time. The front door was still open and he could see Veronica sitting behind the wheel, her fingers tapping an impatient cadence on the dashboard. Her eyes widened as she saw him emerge.

"Open the door," shouted Harry. "Quickly!"

She reached for the driver's door, still staring at him while her fingers fumbled for the handle. Then she was no longer looking at him but beyond and behind him. Harry heard her scream his name before the world spun around in a circle, and Harry found himself looking first at the car from a sideways angle, then at the ground, then the sky and the house and the grass, all tumbling in a crazy mixture of images that seemed to go on forever but in fact lasted barely seconds.

And Harry couldn't understand why, even as he died and his severed head bounced to a halt by the porch steps.

* * *

And out on Dutch Island, the man known to some as Melancholy Joe Dupree lay on his bed and watched the rain fall, harder and harder, until at last his view through the window was entirely obscured. His bones, his teeth, his joints, they all ached, as if the effort of supporting his great bulk were slowly becoming too much for them. Joe moaned and buried his face in his pillow, tears forcing themselves from the corners of his eyes.

Make it stop, he begged. Please make it stop.

A face appeared in the darkness beyond his window, a boy's face, the skin blue-gray, the eyes dark. The boy reached out as if to touch the glass, but made no contact. Instead, he watched the man in uniform curl in upon himself on the huge bed, until at last the pain began to ease and Joe Dupree fell into a troubled sleep, tormented by the sound of whispering, of gray figures and tunnels beneath the earth, and a boy with tainted skin who gazed upon him as he slept.

THE SECOND DAY

Not a shred in the papers,
Becoming all too clear
Not a one cares that she got away.

Now the fear of being found
A little less profound
On a face that's never been
Fit to laugh.

—Pinetop Seven, "The Fear of Being Found"

CHAPTER THREE

Know me, wife.

The dream ended, and now Moloch's features fell before him like rain. It was as though a great many photographs had been taken and shredded, the figures caught in the different frames intermingled, smiling familiarly while glancing against strangers from other pictures; yet in this downpour of images, this torrent of memories, he was ever the same. There he sat, beside parents unknown, amid siblings now lost and gone. He ran as a boy across sand and through sea; he held a fish on the end of a hook; he cried beside an open fire. This was his history, his past, yet it seemed to encompass not one life but many lives. Some images were sharper than others, some recollections more acute, but they were all linked to him, all part of the great chain of his existence. He was color, and he was sepia. He was black, and he was white. He was of this time, and he was of no time.

He was Moloch, and he was No One.

Moloch awoke, aware that he was being watched. His ear

felt raw where it had been touching the cheap material, the pillow once again drenched with his sweat. He thought that he could smell the woman against his face, could touch her skin, could feel the blade tearing through her flesh. He stirred on his bunk but did not rise. Instead, he tried to identify the man watching him through his smell, his breathing, the soft jangle of the equipment on his belt. Images from the dream still ran through his mind, and he was suddenly aware of how aroused he had become, but he forced himself to concentrate on the figure at the other side of the bars. It was good practice. His incarceration had taken the edge off his abilities in so many ways that he welcomed any opportunity to hone them once more. That was the worst of his imprisonment: the monotony, the terrible similarity of each day to the next, so that every man became a seer, a fortune-teller, capable of predicting the wheres and whens of each hour to come, his precise location at any given time, the irrevocable nature of it all threatened only by the occasional outbreaks of sickness and violence.

Every day the wake-up call came at six A.M., heralded by horns and coughing and the flushing of toilets. Two hours later, the doors opened and each man stepped outside onto the cold concrete to await the first count of the day. No words were permitted to be exchanged during any of the day's six counts. The shower followed (for Moloch took every opportunity offered to clean himself, viewing any lapse in hygiene as the precursor to a greater collapse), and then breakfast, always taken seated at the same plastic chair, the food seemingly designed solely to provide energy without nutrition. Then Moloch would head to the laundry for his day's work, socializing little with the other men. The noon count came next, then lunch, then more work, followed by an hour in the yard, then dinner, another count, and a retreat to his cell to read, to think. Eight count, then lights out at ten. In the first weeks, Moloch would wake for the late counts, at midnight and four, but no longer. He had received no visitors, apart from his lawyer, for over three years. He made few phone calls and fewer friends. A waiting game was under way and he was prepared to play his part.

Now the game was coming to an end.

Moloch shifted on his mattress, his body once again under his control. Eyes closed, he concentrated on smell and hearing.

Aftershave. Hints of sandalwood.

A small rattle in the throat as the man breathed out. Congestion.

Digestive noises. Coffee on an empty stomach.

Reid.

"Wake up, now," Reid's voice said. "It's your big day."

Moloch lifted his head and saw the thin man standing at the bars, the brim of his hat perfectly level against his forehead, the creases on his uniform like blades set beneath the cloth. Reid looked away and called for 713 to be opened. Moloch remained where he was for a moment or two more, breathing deeply, then rose from his bunk and ran his hands through his hair.

Moloch knew the date. Some inmates lost track of the days while in jail. Many did so deliberately, for there was nothing guaranteed to faster break the spirit of a man facing twenty years than an urge to count the days until his release. Days in prison passed slowly: they were beads on a long thread, an endless rosary of unanswered prayers.

Moloch was different. He counted the days, kept track of hours, minutes, even seconds when the urge took him. Every moment spent inside was an injury inflicted upon him, and when the time came to return those insults to his person, he wanted to be sure that he did not miss a single one. His count had reached 1,245 days, 7 hours, and—he glanced at his watch—3 minutes spent in the Dismal Creek State Penitentiary, Virginia. His only regret was that the one on whom he desired to revenge himself would not live long enough to enable him to vent his rage to its ultimate degree.

"Stand straight, arms out."

He did as he was told. Two guards entered, chains dangling from the arms of one. They secured his arms and his feet, the restraints attached in turn to a chain around his chest. The arrangement was known in the system as a "three-piece suit."

"Don't I even get to brush my teeth?" he asked.

The guard's face was expressionless.

"Why? You ain't going on no date."

"You don't know that. I might get lucky."

Reid seemed almost amused.

"I don't think so. You ain't got lucky by now, you ain't never gonna get lucky."

"Man's luck can always change."

"I never took you for no optimist."

"You don't know me."

"I know enough about you to say that you're gonna die wearing them prison weeds."

"Are you my judge and jury?"

"No, but come the time, I'll be your executioner."

He stood aside as the guards brought Moloch out.

"Be seeing you, Mr. Reid."

The older man nodded.

"That's right. Fact is, I aim to be the last thing you see."

There was a black Toyota Land Cruiser waiting for him in the prison yard. Standing beside it were two armed investigators from the district attorney's office. Moloch nodded a good morning to them, but they didn't respond. Instead, they watched as he was chained to the D ring on the floor of the SUV, then tested the chains and the restraints until they were satisfied that he was fully secured. A wire-mesh screen separated the backseat passenger from those in the front. There were no handles on the inside of the rear doors, and a second wire screen ran from the roof of the Cruiser to the floor of the trunk behind Moloch.

The door slammed shut noisily.

"You take good care of him now," said one of the guards. "Wouldn't want him getting bruised or nothing."

"We'll look after him," said one of the investigators, a tall black man named Misters. His partner, Torres, closed the door on Moloch, then climbed into the driver's seat.

"Settle back," he said to Moloch. "You got a long ride ahead of you."

But Moloch was silent now, content, it seemed, to enjoy a brief taste of life outside the prison walls.

Dupree was sipping coffee in the station house. It was technically his day off, but he was passing and . . .

Well, that was just an excuse. He couldn't stay away from the place. Most of the other cops knew that, and they didn't mind.

"Doug Newton," he said. He was sipping coffee from the market and eating one of the doughnuts that he had bought for the two cops on duty.

Across from him, Ron Berman was tapping a pencil on the desk, alternating each tap between the tip and the eraser end. Dupree found it mildly annoying but decided to say nothing. He liked Berman, and given that some of the other cops had far more irritating habits than tapping a pencil on the desk (for example, Dupree wondered if Phil Tuttle, Berman's partner on this tour, had ever washed his hands after taking a leak), he was happy enough to let Berman and his pencil be, for the present.

"Doug Newton," echoed Berman. "I took the call and put it in the log, but frankly, we both had other things to do, and it's not like it's the first time he's made that kind of claim."

Dupree reached over and took the log from Berman. There it was, in Berman's neat hand. At 7:30 A.M., almost as soon as Berman and Tuttle had settled in, and while it was still dark on the streets, Doug Newton had called in a report of a little girl in a gray dress tormenting his dying mother.

Again.

"You went out there last time, right?" asked Berman.

"Yeah, I went out. We organized a search. I even checked with Portland and with the state police to see if they'd had any reports of missing girls matching the description Newton gave me. There was nothing."

The first time, Tuttle had answered the call from the Newton place and, having kind of a short fuse, had warned Doug about wasting police time. Now, just this morning, Doug Newton had called in a third report, except this one was different.

This time, he'd claimed the little girl had tried to climb through the window of his mother's bedroom. Doug had heard the old woman's screams, and had come running just in time to see the little girl disappearing into the trees.

Or so he'd said.

"You think he's going crazy?" asked Berman.

"He lives with his mother and has never married," replied Dupree.

"Maybe he just needs to get laid."

"I never took you for a therapist."

"I'm multiskilled."

"You think you could multiskill that pencil back into your drawer? It's like listening to a drummer with the shakes."

"Sorry," said Berman. He put the pencil into the drawer, then closed it just in case the temptation to retrieve it proved too great.

"I guess Doug's maybe a little odd, but I've never taken him for crazy," said Dupree. "He doesn't have the imagination to make up stuff. He's only ever been to two states in his life, and I reckon he's not sure the other forty-eight exist, seeing as how he's never visited them himself. So either he's going crazy or a little girl in a gray dress really did try to get into his mother's bedroom last night."

Berman thought about this.

"So he's crazy, then?"

Dupree tossed the log back at him.

"Apparently he's mad as a coot. I'll go have a talk with him today. Last thing we need is Doug taking potshots at Girl Scouts selling cookies. Anything else on your mind?"

Berman looked troubled.

"I think Nancy Tooker, down at the diner, may have a thing for me. She gave me extra bacon yesterday. For free."

"There's a shortage of eligible men on the island. She's a desperate woman."

"She's a *big* woman."

"I'm sure she'd be gentle with you. At the start."

"Don't say that. That woman could break me in two."

"She's also kind of old for you."

"She's *seriously* old. You think it would make a difference if I told her I was married?"

"You're not married."

"I know, but I could get married. It would be worth it to keep her away."

"My advice is, don't take anything else from her for free. Tell her it's against department policy. Otherwise, you're going to end up paying for that bacon in kind."

Berman looked as if he was about to upchuck his breakfast. "Stop, don't even say things like that."

It struck him that Dupree was in surprisingly good humor this morning. Berman guessed that it might not be unconnected to Dupree's slow courtship of the Elliot woman but he decided not to comment upon it, partly out of sensitivity for the big cop's feelings and partly out of concern for his own personal safety.

"I think you'd make a nice couple," said Dupree. "I can just see the two of you together. Well, I could see Nancy, anyway. You'd be kind of lost somewhere underneath . . ."

Berman unclipped his holster.

"Don't make me shoot you," he said.

"Save the last bullet for yourself," said Dupree as he headed out. "It may be your only hope of escape."

Far to the south, close to the town of Great Bridge, Virginia, a man named Braun walked back to his car carrying two cups of coffee on a cardboard tray, packets of sugar poking out of his breast pocket. He crossed the street, slipped into the passenger seat, and handed one of the coffee cups to his companion, whose name was Dexter. Dexter was black, and kind of ugly. Braun was redheaded, but handsome despite it. He had heard all the redhead jokes. In fact, he'd heard most of them from Dexter.

"Careful," he said, "it's hot."

Dexter looked at the plain white cup in distaste.

"You couldn't find a Starbucks?"

"They don't have a Starbucks here."

"You're kidding me. There's a Starbucks everywhere."

"Not here."

"Shit."

Dexter sipped the coffee.

"It's not bad, but it's no Starbucks."

"It's better than Starbucks, you ask me. Least it tastes like coffee."

"Yeah, but that's the thing about Starbucks. It's coffee, but it doesn't taste like coffee. It's not *supposed* to taste like coffee. It's supposed to taste like Starbucks."

"But not coffee?"

"No, not coffee. Coffee you can get anywhere. Starbucks you can get only in Starbucks."

Braun's cell phone buzzed. He picked it up and hit the green button.

"Yeah," he said. He listened for a time, said, "Okay," then hung up.

"We're all set," he told Dexter, but Dexter wasn't paying attention to him.

"Look at that," said Dexter, indicating with his chin.

Braun followed the direction of the other man's gaze. On a corner, a small black kid who might have been in his early teens but looked younger had just exchanged a dime spot with an older kid.

"He looks young," said Braun.

"You get up close to him, see his eyes, he won't seem so young. Street's already worn him down. It's eating him up from the inside."

Braun nodded, but said nothing.

"That could have been me," said Dexter. "Maybe."

"You sell that shit?"

"Something like it."

"How'd you get out?"

Dexter shook his head, his eyes losing their glare just momentarily. He saw himself in his brand-new Levi's—Levi's then, not those saggy-ass, no-rep jeans that the younger kids wore now, all straps and white stitching—walking across the basketball court, glass crunching beneath the soles of his sneakers. Ex was sitting on a bench, alone, his feet on the seat, his back against the wire of the court, a newspaper in his hands.

"Hey, little man."

Ex, short for Exorcist, because he loved that movie. Twenty-one, and so secure in himself that he could sit alone on a fall day, reading a newspaper as if he didn't have a care in the world.

"What you want?"

He was smiling, pretending that he was Dexter's best buddy, that he hadn't crippled a twelve-year-old the week before for coming up short, the kid wailing and crying as Ex knelt on his chest and put the gun barrel against the kid's ankle, that same smile on his face as he pulled the trigger.

The kid's street name was Blade, on account of his father being called Gillette. It was a good name. Dexter liked it, liked Blade too. They used to look out for each other. Now there was nobody to look out for Dexter, but he would continue to look out for Blade, as best he could.

Ex's smile was still in place, but any residual warmth it might once have contained had begun to die from the eyes down.

"I said, 'Hey, little man.' You got nothing to say back to me?"

Dexter, thirteen years old, looked up at Ex and removed his gloved hands from the pockets of his Lakers jacket. He was unused to the weight of the gun, and he needed both hands to raise it.

Ex stared down the stubby barrel of the Bryco. He opened his mouth to say something, but it was lost in the roar of the gun. Ex toppled backward, his head striking the wire fence of the court as he fell and landed in a heap on the ground, his legs splayed against the back of the bench. Dexter looked down at him. The bullet had hit Ex in the chest, and he was bleeding from the mouth.

"Hey," he whispered. He looked hurt, as if the young boy had just called him a bad name. "Hey, little man."

Dexter fired the final shot, then walked away.

"Dexter? You okay?"

Braun nudged Dexter's arm with an elbow.

"Yeah, I'm here. I'm here, man."

"We got to go."

"Yeah, we got to go."

He took one last look at the kid on the corner—*Hey, little man*—then started the car and pulled away.

By coincidence, some twenty miles to the north, two men with a similar racial profile were also drinking coffee, except they had found a Starbucks and were drinking grande Americanos from big Starbucks mugs. One of them was Shepherd, the gray-haired man of few vices. His companion was named Tell. He was small and wiry, and he wore his hair in cornrows, like the basketball player Allen Iverson used to wear his, and probably for the same reason: because it made white folks uneasy. Tell was reading a newspaper. Tell was very conscientious about reading the newspaper every day. Unfortunately, that day's newspaper happened to be a supermarket tabloid, and in Shepherd's opinion, Tell could have been reading the back of a cornflakes box and been better informed. The gossip sheets weren't big on analysis, and Shepherd liked to think of himself as an analytical kind of guy.

Two seats down from them, in the otherwise deserted coffee shop, an Arab was talking loudly on his cell phone, tapping his finger on the table before him to emphasize his points. In fact, he was talking so loudly that Shepherd wasn't even certain that his phone was turned on. The guy behaved like he was trying to *shout* his message all the way to the Middle East, and was holding the cell phone only out of habit. He'd been talking like this for the better part of ten minutes, and Shepherd could see that Tell was getting pissed. He'd watched him start the same story about some has-been pop star's face-lift three times already, which was once more than Tell usually needed to take in what he was reading. Truth be told, Shepherd was kind of unhappy about it himself. He didn't like cell phones. People were rude enough as it was without having another excuse to be bad-mannered.

Tell looked up. "Hey, man," he said to the Arab. "Can you keep it down?"

The Arab ignored him. This led Shepherd to suspect that the Arab was either very arrogant or very dumb, because Tell didn't look even remotely like the kind of person you ignored. Tell looked like the kind of person who would remove your spine if you ignored him.

Tell's face wore a puzzled expression as he leaned in closer to the Arab.

"I said, can you talk a little quieter, please? I'm trying to read my newspaper."

Shepherd thought Tell was being very polite. It made him nervous.

"Go fuck yourself," said the Arab.

Tell blinked, then folded his newspaper. Shepherd reached an arm across, holding his friend back.

"Don't," he said. Over at the counter, a barista was watching them with interest.

"You hear what that raghead motherfucker said?"

"I heard. Forget it."

The Arab continued talking, even after he'd finished his coffee with a slurp. Tell stood, and Shepherd followed, blocking his partner's access to the Arab. Tell bobbed on the balls of his feet for a second or two, then turned and walked out.

"Show's over," said Shepherd to the barista.

"I guess." He sounded a little disappointed.

Tell was already waiting in the van across the street, his fingers tapping a rhythm on the steering wheel. Shepherd got in beside him.

"We going? You know, we got a schedule to keep."

"No, we ain't going yet."

"Fine."

They waited. Ten minutes later, the Arab emerged. He was still talking on his phone. He climbed into a black SUV, did a U-turn, and headed north.

"I hate SUVs," said Tell. "They're a top-heavy cab on a pickup's chassis, they drive like shit, they're dangerous, and they're ecologically unsound."

Shepherd just sighed.

Tell started the van and began following the SUV. They stayed with the Arab until he turned into an alleyway at the side of a trendy Middle Eastern restaurant. Tell parked, then opened the driver's door and headed toward the alleyway. Shepherd followed.

"Hey, you prick."

The Arab turned to see Tell bearing down on him. He tried

to hit the alarm button on his car keys, but Tell wrenched them from his hands before he got the chance. He hurled the keys to the ground, tore the Arab's cell phone from his left hand, and threw it after the keys. Finally, he dragged the Arab around the back of the building, so that they were hidden from the pedestrians on the sidewalk.

"You remember me?" he said. He pushed the Arab against the wall. "I'm Mr. Go-Fuck-Myself. The fuck do you get off talking to me like that? I was polite to you, you fuck. I asked you nice, and what do you do? You disrespect me, you SUV-driving motherfucker."

He slapped the Arab hard across the face. The Arab's face contorted with fear. He was fat, with chubby fingers over-loaded with gold rings. He was no match for Tell.

"I'm sorry."

"No, you ain't sorry," said Tell. "You're scared, and that ain't the same thing. I didn't come down here after you, you wouldn't have given me a second thought, and next time you was in Starbucks you'd have shouted your damn head off all over again, disturbing people and giving them a pain in the ass."

He punched the Arab in the nose and felt it break beneath his fist. The Arab curled up, cupping his damaged nose in his hands.

"So don't tell me you're sorry. Look at you. My people came over here in chains. I bet you flew your ass over here business class."

He hit the Arab hard across the head with the palm of his hand.

"Don't ever let me see you talking on that phone again, motherfucker. You get one warning, and this is it."

He began to walk away. Behind him, the Arab leaned

against the wall, examined the blood on his fingers, then bent down to retrieve his possessions: his car keys first, then his cell phone. The cell phone made a scraping noise against the concrete as he gathered it up.

Tell stopped. He looked back at the Arab.

"You dumb fuck," he said.

He walked back, drawing his gun from beneath his jacket. The Arab's eyes widened. Tell kicked him hard in the belly and he fell to the ground. While Shepherd watched, he placed the gun against the Arab's head and pulled the trigger. The Arab spasmed, and then his fingers slowly released their grip on the phone.

"I warned you," said Tell. "I did warn you."

He put the gun back in his belt and rejoined Shepherd. Shepherd cast a last glance back at the dead Arab, then fell into step beside Tell. He looked at his partner in puzzlement.

"I thought your people were from Albany," he said.

Leonie and Powell sat in silence outside the courthouse, watching as Moloch was led in by the two investigators from the DA's office. Leonie wore her hair in an Afro and looked, to Powell, a little like one of those kick-ass niggers from the seventies, Cleopatra Jones and Foxy Brown. Not that Powell would ever have called Leonie a nigger to her face, or even a dyke, although as far as Powell was concerned, she was both. He didn't doubt for one moment that Leonie would kill him if he uttered either of those words in her presence; and if, by some miracle, he did manage to avoid being killed (and the only way that he could see that happening was if he managed to kill her first), then Dexter would come after him and finish the job. Dexter and Leonie were like brother and sister. Braun seemed to get on okay with her too. Powell wasn't going to screw around with

Dexter and Braun, didn't matter how many funny stories Braun told, or how much high-fiving and smiling Dexter fit into a day.

Powell leaned back in his seat and ran his fingers through his long hair, losing them in the curls at the back. Powell was the type of guy who would say "nice mullet" and mean it. His hairstyle was trailer trash crossed with eighties glam metal, and he loved it. His face was unnaturally tan, and his teeth were bleached so white that they glowed at night. Powell had B-movie-star looks, the artificial kind that oozed insincerity. He had even gotten some professional shots taken five or six years back. A couple of newspapers had used them during coverage of his trial. Powell had been secretly pleased, although no offers of acting work had followed his eventual release.

"It's hot," said Powell.

Leonie said nothing.

He looked over at her, but her eyes were fixed on the courthouse. He knew Leonie hated his guts, but that was kind of why he was with her. He was with Leonie and Tell was with Shepherd because he and Tell were the new guys and they had to be watched closely. It was good practice, nothing more, and Powell didn't resent it. Powell would rather have been with Shepherd, but Tell was such a prickly motherfucker that there was no way of knowing what he might have said to Leonie if he was stuck with her for a day. Shit, they'd be cleaning what was left of him off the inside of the van for the next month. Compared to Tell, Powell was a regular diplomat.

So Powell kept his mouth closed and waited, amusing himself by imagining Leonie in a variety of poses with white girls, Chinese, Latinos, and Powell himself slap bang in the middle. Man, he thought, if she only knew what I was thinking . . .

* * *

Sharon Macy spent the morning doing laundry, collecting her dry cleaning, and generally catching up on all of the stuff she had let pile up while she was working. She then drove out to Gold's Gym over at the Maine Mall and did her regular cardiovascular workout, spending so long on the StairMaster that her legs felt like marshmallow when she stepped off, and the machine itself was drenched with her sweat. Afterward, she headed over to the Big Sky Bread Company and was tempted to undo all her good work with a Danish, but instead settled for the soup-and-sandwich deal.

She ate in one of the booths while looking over the southern edition of the *Forecaster*, the free newspaper that dealt with local news in South Portland, Scarborough, and Cape Elizabeth. A cop in the Cape Elizabeth PD was seeking donations of mannequin heads to display his collection of hats from police departments around the world; the South Portland Red Riots golf team had donated a new bus to the school system; and a pair of men's gloves had been found down by Pine Point Beach. Macy was still amazed by the fact that someone would take the time to place an ad in the *Forecaster* in order to return a pair of lost gloves. They were strange people up here: they kept to themselves, preferring to mind their own business and let other folks mind theirs in return, but they were capable of acts of touching generosity when the circumstances called for it. She recalled last year's first snowstorm, a blizzard that had swept up the coast from just above Boston and blanketed the state as far north as Calais. She had heard sounds in the early morning coming from the parking lot of her apartment, and had looked out to see two complete strangers digging out her car. Not just her car, either, but every car in the lot. They had then shouldered their spades and, identities still unrevealed, had moved on to the car in the next driveway. There was something hugely admirable about such anonymous kindness to strangers.

She skipped to the "Police Beat" page, scanning the names in the list of arrests and summonses: the usual DUIs, thefts by unauthorized taking or transfer, a couple of marijuana collars. She recognized one or two of the names, but there was nothing worth noting. If there had been, she figured that they would have heard about it on the grapevine by now.

Her meal finished, she drove downtown and parked in the public market's parking garage. She bought some fresh produce from one of the stalls in order to get her parking validated for two hours, then headed up Congress to the Center for Maine History. She walked down the little pathway by the side of the Wadsworth-Longfellow House and entered the reading room, ignoring the sign that invited her to register her name and the reason for her visit in the library's logbook. The librarian behind the desk was in his late seventies, she figured, but judging from the gleam in his eye as he smiled at her, he was a long way from dead.

"Hi, I'd like to see whatever you have on Dutch Island," she said.

"Sure," said the librarian. "May I ask what your interest is in Dutch?"

"I'm a police officer. I'm heading out there soon. I'm just curious to find out a little about it."

"You'll be working with Joe Dupree, then."

"Yes, so I understand."

"He's a good man. I knew his father, and he was a good man too."

He disappeared among the stacks behind the counter, and returned with a manila file. It looked disappointingly thin. The librarian registered her expression.

"I know, but there hasn't been too much written on Dutch. Fact is, we need a good history of the islands of Casco Bay, period. All we got here are cuttings, and this." He removed a thin sheaf of typescript pages from the folder, stapled crudely along the spine.

"This was written maybe ten years ago by Larry Amerling. He's the postmaster out on the island. It's about the most detailed thing we have, although like as not you'll find something too in Caldwell's *Islands of Maine* and Miller's *Kayaking the Maine Coast.*"

He retrieved the books in question for her, then settled back in his chair as Macy found a space at one of the study tables. There were one or two other people doing research in the library, although Macy was the youngest person in the room by almost half a century. She opened the folder, took out Amerling's *A Short History of Dutch Island*, and began to read.

Torres and Misters led Moloch back to the Land Cruiser, deliberately keeping up a fast pace, the restraints on Moloch's legs causing the prisoner to stumble slightly on the final steps.

"You asshole, Moloch," said Torres.

Moloch tried to maintain his concentration. The grand-jury hearing had been a bore for him. So they had found the body of a woman, and Verso—small, foolish Verso—was prepared to testify that he had helped Willard and Moloch dispose of her in the woods after Moloch had killed her.

SFW: So Fucking What?

As soon as the direction of the prosecutor's questions had become apparent, Moloch had begun to speak like a handicapped man, talking through his nose, the words barely intelligible.

"Is there something wrong with him?" the judge had asked, but it had been Moloch who provided the answer.

"Sorry, Your Honor," he'd said, modifying his speech sufficiently for his words to be understood. "But I was kissing your wife good night, and the bitch closed her legs."

That had been the end of the proceedings.

"You hear me?" repeated Torres. "You're an asshole."

"Why am I an asshole?" said Moloch. He didn't look at the men at either side of him. Neither did he look at the chains on his hands or his feet, so used was he to the shuffling gait their presence necessitated. He would not fall. The investigators would not allow him to fall, not with people watching, but still they kept him moving quickly, depriving him of even the small dignity of walking like a man.

"You know why."

"Maybe I just felt the urge to jerk that old judge's chain some."

"You sure jerked it," said Torres. "You surely did. And don't you think it won't come back on you, because it will. You mark my words. They'll take your books away, leave you nothing to do but shit, sleep, and jerk off."

"Then I'll be thinking of you, except maybe not when I sleep."

"You fucking asshole, you're a dead man. You'll get the juice for this, doesn't matter how much you mouth off to the judge."

"Sticks and stones, Mr. Torres, sticks and stones."

They reached the car, Moloch smiling at last for the cameras, then he was put in back and his chains locked once again to the D ring.

"It's been fun spending time with you both," Moloch said. "I appreciated the company."

"Well," said Torres, "I can't say I'm looking forward to the pleasure again."

"And you, Mr. Misters?" said Moloch, but Misters didn't respond. "Mr. Misters," repeated Moloch, savoring the words on his tongue, extending the "s" sounds into long washes of sibilance like water evaporating from the surface of a hot stove. "Wasn't that kind of the name of some suck-ass, white-bread band in the eighties? 'Broken Wings,' that was them, right?"

Misters remained silent.

"Your partner doesn't say very much, does he?" said Moloch to Torres.

"He's kind of fussy about who he talks to."

"Well, maybe he'll find it in him to say a few words before the journey's end."

"You think so?"

"I'm certain. I can be a very interesting conversationalist."

"I doubt that."

"We'll see," said Moloch. "We'll see."

And for the next five miles he hummed the chorus of "Broken Wings," over and over and over, until Torres broke down and threatened to gag him. Only then, when the young investigator was sufficiently rattled, did Moloch stop.

The surroundings of the library had faded around Macy. She was no longer conscious of the old librarian, the other researchers, or the occasional rattle as the main door opened, the cold air accompanying it. Instead, she was lost in the history of Dutch Island, the history of Sanctuary.

The Native Americans had fought hard to maintain their hold on the islands of Casco Bay. Like modern-day tourists, they summered on the islands, fishing and hunting porpoises and seals, even the occasional whale. Chebeague was their main base, but they used others too, and were resentful of the gradual encroachments of white settlers. The islands were the centers of population in the new colonies: they were easy to defend, safer than the mainland, and offered an abundant source of food from the ocean. Macy noticed that a lot of them, like Dutch Island, had multiple names: Great Chebeague was once Merry Island, then Recompense; Peaks Island was formerly Munjoy's, Milton's, and Michael's, the name changing as the owners changed.

Despite their relative safety, the islands were still frequently attacked in the late seventeenth century. Settlers who were fleeing the atrocities on Harpswell Neck and other islands nearer the coast built a fort on Jewell, on the Outer Ring. In September 1676, a bloody year with attacks on whites at Casco Neck and Back Cove, the families on Jewell were attacked by eight canoes of warriors and were so disturbed by the experience that they retreated to Richmond Island. For the remainder of the year, the natives rampaged along the coast, annihilating every settlement between the Piscataqua and Kennebec Rivers. The settlers dug in, although some gave up and found safer places to live inland. In 1689, the natives raided Peaks Island, the most accessible island from the mainland, and slaughtered many of its inhabitants. One year later, they returned and forced the remaining settlers from the island.

Dutch Island, named for a Dutch sailor named Chris Herschdorfer, who was briefly shipwrecked there toward the end of the seventeenth century, was a different matter. It was farther from the mainland, and the distance made the crossing difficult for the Indians, who had only birch-bark canoes in which to travel. Furthermore, they regarded the island with suspicion, and seemed content to leave it unexplored.

Shortly after the Indian raid on Peaks, Major Benjamin Church, whose soldiers had been present on Peaks during the course of the main attack, led an expedition to the island and found it to be heavily forested, with only a handful of suitable landings for boats. Yet it was to Dutch that a man named Thomas Lunt led a group of settlers in 1691, weary of the running battles he was forced to fight with the natives. In total, twenty settlers joined him in the first two weeks on the island that he renamed Sanctuary, among them survivors of the attacks on Jewell and Peaks, and their numbers continued to increase over the following months. They opted to settle away from the shore, hoping that the higher ground might make them less vulnerable to a surprise attack.

At this point, Amerling's history of the island became less detailed and more speculative, but it seemed that the behavior of one of the settlers, a man named Buer, grew increasingly unpredictable. He became estranged from his family, spending more and more time alone in the thick forest at the center of the island. He was accused of attempted rape by the wife of one of his fellow settlers, and when her husband and three other men attempted to hunt him down as he tried to flee, he killed one of them with a musket shot and then sought shelter with his wife, begging her to hide him, claiming that he had done nothing wrong. But she, fearful for her own life (for she was as disturbed as anyone by the change in her husband), betrayed him to his accusers. He was chained to a post in a barn, but somehow he escaped from the island, stealing a boat and disappearing to the mainland.

He returned some months later, in the winter of 1693, at the head of a party of armed men and renegade Indians, and led the slaughter of the settlers on Sanctuary, including his own wife. One of the settlers, a woman, survived her wounds long enough to tell of what had occurred. Even now, three hundred years later, Macy found herself wincing at the details. There was rape and torture. Many of the women were assaulted, then bound and thrown alive into a patch of bog, where they drowned. No distinction was made between adults and children.

The search for the killers was led by three hunters from the island who had traveled to the mainland to trade on behalf of the settlement and were therefore absent when the massacre occurred. It was said that they tracked down a number of those involved in the attack and dispensed swift justice upon them. Years later, the son of one of those hunters would be among those who resettled Sanctuary. His name was Jerome Dupree.

Crow had stolen away from the group almost as soon as the canoes touched land, grateful only that he had survived the voyage. He had positioned himself behind the White Leader in the second canoe, his hand upon his knife throughout the journey, hidden beneath a rough, woven cloak. If they tried to take him, he would place his knife upon the throat of the White Leader and hold him hostage until they reached the mainland. He suspected that the White Leader knew what he was planning, for he could see the knowledge in his eyes, and his lieutenant, the man named Barone, remained seated in the bow of the boat with his back to the coast, a musket on his lap as he watched Crow.

From the safety of the woods, Crow saw the White Leader kill the Mi'kmaqs in their sleep. In truth, Crow had been planning to kill them himself. There had long been tension between his people and their own, and it was only the hand of the White Leader, and the protection offered by his guns, that had kept him from slitting their throats before now. Crow would like to have killed the White Leader, and considered remaining close to the camp in the hope of disposing of him, but English soldiers had come, alerted to the presence of the men whom they sought, and a skirmish had commenced. Crow escaped from the woods in the confusion, and when he returned, three of the White Leader's killers were dead and one was a captive.

The Indian's plan was to make for the area around the Chandiere River. It was inhospitable territory, but there he believed he would be safe for a time from his own people, and from the English who had placed a price upon his head. Crow longed to regain his place among his tribe, which now dwelt by St.-Castin's settlement on the Bagaduce River. There, the Frenchman, who had reestablished French control over southwestern Acadia after its occupation by the English, had built a habitation that broke with the traditional model typically adopted by the Europeans. There were no defensive walls around the main dwelling and the storehouse. Instead, protection came from the thirty-two wigwams surrounding the settlement, housing 160 Wabanaki, whom the French termed Etchemin. St.-Castin had even married into the tribe, taking for his bride Pidiwamiska, the daughter of the sachem Madockawando, and sister to Crow. It was his objection to the union, and subsequent revolt against his father's rule, that had led to Crow's banishment.

Crow despised the Europeans. He knew that more would come, and St.-Castin's marriage to his sister represented the beginning of the dilution of the old ways. Already, there was less game to hunt, and great numbers of his people were dying in strange, unfamiliar ways, taken by invisible ailments that had never existed before the coming of the whites. Gluskap, the great creator of the Maine natives, had fled when he sensed the coming of the Europeans, abandoning them to their fate. Crow believed that Gluskap would never return as long as Wabanaki dwelt with the Europeans, giving to them their women and protecting them from their enemies. Through the White Leader, Crow was able to strike back at the hated French and English, but by the time of the raid on Sanctuary, he knew that the uneasy alliance was drawing to an end, and that the hour would come when the White Leader's musket would be used upon his guide.

So Crow turned his back to the sea, and headed for the wilderness to the west, not knowing that three new names had been added to the list of those who hunted him.

The three hunters, the last living remnants of the settlement on Sanctuary, searched for their prey without rest, and, once found, disposed of them without mercy.

It took them four years.

The names and descriptions of the men whom they sought had been obtained from the English in Portland, who had tortured their captive, a man named Mundy, until he informed on his companions. They were aided in their aims by the reluctance of the perpetrators to leave for long the northeastern territories familiar to them, and in which they had families and allies who might give them succor.

The first they killed in Wells, as he tried to make his way south to establish contact with his brother, who lived near Fort William & Mary. Two died at Winter Harbor, fleeing the Indian raid on the settlement and falling instead to the knives of the hunters. As Queen Anne's War raged around them, they hanged one at Norridgewock, taken as he and two fellow cutthroats shadowed the Hilton expedition in the hope of stealing supplies. They tracked another north through Acadia, eventually confronting him by the shores of the Northumberland Strait, and as he pleaded for mercy they drowned him in the icy waters.

Of Barone and the man the natives termed the White Leader, they found no trace. At the end of their long hunt, they were weary of bloodshed and revenge, and had made the decision to travel back to the islands when they encountered a small French patrol escorting parties of natives to the Saint Lawrence River, where they hoped to find shelter from the English under French protection. Aiding the French was a guide, his tribal tattoos defaced with hot irons, a man who always stayed apart from the families he was guiding.

It was the Wabanaki killer known as Crow.

The hunters tracked the party beyond the Dead River, where the natives were handed over to the care of more soldiers. After resting for three days, the French soldiers, ten of them in total, prepared to make the journey east once more in order to winter in Acadia, with Crow as their guide.

By now, the hunters were more accomplished killers than the soldiers, and they had no love for the French. One day into their journey, when the soldiers stopped to make camp for the night, they were attacked as they sat around their campfire. Tired, and unprepared for fighting, the first five died in the glow of the flames. Three more were taken in the woods, and two escaped to tell of what had occurred.

The hunters trapped Crow by the banks of the river. He held a knife in one hand, and an ax in the other. His musket, its shot wasted in the confusion of the initial attack, lay at his feet. He watched silently as the three men emerged from the trees, their faces hooded, their bodies draped in furs. They stopped when they were some twenty feet from him, and their leader raised his hands and dropped the hood that hid his features.

"Do you know who I am?" he said.

Crow merely shook his head.

"My name is Dupree. You killed my wife."

"When?" said Crow.

"Four years ago, on an island called Sanctuary."

For a moment, Crow did not move. It seemed almost as though the tension in his body dissipated as he realized that the hunt was now over, and that the time to join his ancestors had come at last. Then his hands tightened on his weapons, and he opened his mouth wide as he ran toward his pursuers, his last great scream echoing through the night as the first snows of winter fell upon him.

The muskets roared, and Crow fell backward into the water.

The river carried him away, and his name was never spoken again.

According to Amerling's history, Buer, the one Crow knew as the "White Leader," and his lieutenant, Barone, evaded capture. There were those who said that Buer was not his real name, and that a man fitting his description but with the name of Seera was wanted in Massachusetts in connection with the deaths of two women there. In any event, he disappeared after the events on Sanctuary, and was never seen again. Barone also vanished.

Amerling went on to cover the abduction of a woman in 1762, the disappearance of the men who had taken her to Dutch, and the subsequent discovery of one of them buried in the forest. The Dupree name cropped up again and again, and it was one of Joe Dupree's ancestors who had made the stone cross that still stood amid the sunken remains of the old settlement and the graves of those who had died there. There was no mention of George Sherrin, who was found entangled in tree roots.

It was Amerling's final paragraph that most intrigued Macy. It read:

> To those looking in upon the island from outside, its history may appear bloody and strange. Yet those of us who have lived here for many years, and whose fathers and grandfathers and great-grandfathers lie buried in the island's cemetery, have grown used to the strangeness of Dutch Island. Here, paths through the forest disappear in the space of a single week, and new paths take their place, so that a man may one day walk a trail familiar to him, yet find himself directed toward new surroundings by the end of it. We are used to the silences and we are used to the sounds that are native only to this small patch of land. We live in the shadow of its history, and walk by the gift of those who have gone before us.

Macy closed the slim volume and returned to the desk, the names encountered in Amerling's history still rattling around in her head. Church. Lunt. Buer. Barone.

Barone. Barron.

It was probably just a coincidence, she thought, although it would explain why Barron was such a creep if his unpleasantness was part of a proud family tradition.

"You find what you were looking for?" asked the librarian.

"No," said Macy. "I was hoping for answers."

"Maybe you'll have better luck on the island."

"Maybe," she said.

Out on Sanctuary, Joe Dupree was also finding himself short on answers. He had taken a ride out to Doug Newton's house, as he had promised Berman. Newton and his mother lived near Seal Cove, close to the southernmost tip of the island.

Their house was one of the oldest on Sanctuary, and one of the most carefully maintained. Doug had given it a fresh coat of paint the previous spring, so that it seemed to shine amid the trees that surrounded it.

The old woman wasn't long for this earth. Dupree could see it in her face, could smell it in her room. When she died, the doctors would find some complicated way to explain her demise, but for Joe and Doug, and perhaps for the old woman herself, there was nothing complicated about it. She was just old. She was in her late eighties and her body was losing its final struggle to keep her alive. Her breathing was shallow and rasping, and the skin on her face and hands was almost translucent in its pallor. She was in no pain and there was nothing that a hospital could do for her now, so her son had taken her home to die. Debra Legere, who had some nursing experience, dropped by for four or five hours each day, sometimes a little longer if Doug had some work to do, although he was pretty much retired by now. Dupree figured that there was an arrangement between Debra, who was a widow, and Doug, who had never married, but he wasn't about to pry into it. In any case, they were both strict Baptists, so there appeared to be a limit to the amount of arranging that they could do.

Dupree stood at the window of the old woman's room and looked down to the yard below. It was a sheer drop. This side of the house was flat. There was a kitchen below, but since Doug had never found the need to extend it farther, it remained flush with the main wall. The way Dupree saw it, there was just no way that a little girl could reach the topmost window in the house.

"Did she have a stepladder, Doug?" he asked softly.

Doug's mother had awakened briefly when they entered

the room but had now slipped back into her troubled sleep.

Doug seemed to think about bristling, then decided that it wasn't worth the trouble.

"I know what you're thinking," he said. "It's nothing that I haven't asked myself: how did she get up here? The answer is that I don't know. I'm just telling you what I saw."

"The window was locked?" Dupree tested the sash with his hand. It seemed solid enough.

"As far as I remember. It could be that I didn't close it properly and the wind might have blown it open, except that there was no wind that night and, anyway, who ever heard of a wind that could blow a heavy sash window upward?"

Dupree stared into the forest. The window faced northeast. He could see the island's central watchtower from where he stood, and part of the border of sunken trees that marked the boundary of the Site.

"You think I'm crazy?" asked Doug.

Dupree shook his head. He didn't know what to think, except that it still seemed unlikely that a little girl could magic her way twenty feet off the ground in order to attack an old woman in her bedroom. "You always seemed pretty levelheaded to me," he said at last. "What can I say? Keep the windows locked, the doors too. You got a gun?"

Doug nodded. "More than one."

"Well, for crying out loud, don't use any of them. The last thing I want to do is to have to haul you in for shooting someone."

Doug said that he would bear it in mind. It wasn't exactly a promise that he wouldn't shoot anybody, but it was better than nothing.

Dupree was about to leave the room when a piece of paper, seemingly caught by a draft, rose from a corner by the drapes and then settled again. The policeman leaned down to examine it more closely, and found himself looking at a moth. It was ugly and gray, with yellow markings along its body. Its wings fluttered feebly.

"Doug, can you get me an empty mayo jar, or something with a lid on it?"

The older man found a jelly jar. Dupree scooped the moth from the floor, then refitted the lid carefully. He used his pocketknife to bore a hole in the top, in order to allow the insect some air, although he guessed that it didn't have long to live.

Holding the jar up to the light from the window, he examined the moth, turning the bottle slowly to look at its wings and its markings. Doug Newton squinted at it, then shook his head.

"I've never seen a moth like that before," he said.

Beside him, Dupree felt an uncomfortable ache spreading across his belly. Suddenly, Doug Newton's tale of a levitating girl didn't seem so far-fetched. He swallowed hard.

"I have," he said.

They were four miles from the prison, following the banks of the river, when they saw the body. The Dismal Creek State Penitentiary lay at the end of an isolated road, with little traffic apart from prison vehicles. Anyone who found himself in trouble on that road was likely to be waiting a long time for help.

"Hell is that?" asked Misters.

"Looks like a woman," said Torres. "Pull over."

The woman lay by the side of the road, her legs splayed, her shoulders and head hidden in the long grass that grew by the hard shoulder. Her legs and buttocks were exposed where her skirt had ridden up over them. They pulled up a few feet from her and Torres got out, Misters about to follow until Torres told him to stay back.

"Keep an eye on him," said Torres.

"He's going nowhere," said Misters, but he still remained close to the car and aware of Moloch, who was watching the proceedings with interest.

The woman was not moving, and Torres could see blood on her back. He leaned down and spread the grass that obscured her head.

"Oh sweet—"

He saw the red exposed flesh where her head should have been, then turned his face away in time to catch the slug on the bridge of his nose. He crumpled to the ground as Misters went for his own weapon, but a shadow fell across him and he looked up to see one of his own, a brother, holding a shotgun on him. From the grass at the other side of the road another man emerged, this one younger, with blond hair and a pretty, almost feminine, face. Behind him was a muscular man with short red hair, wearing tight faded jeans and a T-shirt decorated with the Stars and Stripes. The red-headed man took Misters's gun, then used plastic restraints to tie the investigator's hands behind his back. Meanwhile, the blond kid knelt by Torres and removed the keys from his belt and the gun from his holster. Then he walked over to the Land Cruiser, opened the door, and released Moloch from his chains.

Moloch stretched as he emerged from the car, then took Torres's gun from the kid and walked over to where Misters squatted. He raised the gun and pointed at the investigator's head.

"Now, *Mr.* Misters, do you have anything to say to me?"

Misters didn't open his mouth. He looked up at Moloch with mingled fear and disgust.

"I could shoot you," said Moloch, "shoot you like the boorish dog that you are."

He aimed the gun.

"Bang," he said. He tipped the muzzle to his mouth and blew a stream of imaginary smoke from the barrel.

"But I'm not going to shoot you," he said.

"We taking him with us?" asked Dexter.

"No."

"If we leave him, he'll identify us."

"Really?" asked Moloch.

He stared hard at Misters.

"Oh that my eyes might see and my tongue might speak," he said. "Of what wonders might I tell."

He turned to the young white boy.

"Blind him, then cut his tongue out. He never had much use for it anyway."

They worked quickly, pushing the SUV into the river, the body of Torres and the woman inside it. Misters they left, bleeding and in shock, by the riverbank. The whole operation had taken less than three minutes.

Braun made a call on his cell phone, and seconds later, they were joined by Powell and Leonie, who had been driving the lookout vans positioned two hundred yards at either side of the ambush area, their sides decorated with the removable logo of a nonexistent forestry company so that, if any other car had taken that road before their work was done, they could be held back with a story about a fallen tree. In the event, no other vehicle had troubled them. Then the little convoy, five men and one woman in two vans, headed at speed toward the highway, and the north.

Dexter, Leonie, and Moloch drove in silence for a time, Dexter glancing occasionally in his side mirror. Three cars behind were Braun, Powell, and the boy, and that suited Dexter just fine. The boy Willard gave him the creeps, the beauty and seeming innocence of him all the more unsettling for what lay beneath. Still, Moloch liked him, and he had proved useful in the end. He had found the woman, trawling the side roads, the bars, and cheap motels for almost a week before he'd come across "a suitable candidate," as he'd described her. Then he had killed her and brought her remains to the meeting place on time.

Dexter was a clever guy, maybe not as clever as he thought he was, but still pretty smart, all things considered. He'd done some reading, and liked books on psychology. Dexter figured that if you were going to be dealing with people, then you should try to find out as much as possible about the general principles behind them. He particularly liked the abnormal stuff because, in his line of work, abnormal was what he dealt with on a day-to-day basis. He knew all about sociopaths and psychopaths and assorted other deviants, and had begun to categorize the freaks he had met according to his diagnosis of their particular abnormality.

But Willard . . .

Dexter hadn't found a book that dealt with anything quite like Willard before. Willard was off the scale. In fact, Dexter wasn't even sure that Willard was entirely human, although that wasn't the kind of thing that he was about to say out loud in the company of Moloch or anybody else. But sometimes he found Willard staring at him, and when he looked into the kid's eyes it was like falling into a void. Dexter figured that dying in space might feel something like seeing oneself reflected in Willard's eyes: there was only nothingness masquerading as blackness. It wasn't even hostile. It was just blank.

"What are you thinking about?" asked Moloch.

"Stuff."

"Don't you go giving too much away now."

"Like I said, just stuff."

Beside him, Leonie just stared silently at the passing cars.

"Willard stuff?" said Moloch.

"How'd you know that?"

"I was watching you. I saw you look in the mirror. Your face changed. I can read you like a book, Dex."

"I don't like him. I've never been anything but straight with you, and I'm telling you the truth of it now. He's out there."

"He's been useful."

"Yeah."

"And loyal."

"To you."

"That's all that matters."

"With respect, man, you been in jail these past three years. Difficult to work with someone who don't answer to anyone but a man in a prison suit."

"But you managed it."

"I got a lot of patience, and the Verso thing was a piece of luck."

"Yes," said Moloch. "I take it something is being done about him."

"As we speak."

"You should have gotten Willard to do it. He never liked Verso."

"I never liked him either, but I didn't dislike the man enough to sic Willard on him. You see what he did to the woman? He cut on her pretty bad."

"Before or after?"

"I didn't ask."

"Then I'm not planning on asking either."

"Me, I figure before."

"Is this conversation leading somewhere, Dexter?"

"Take a look at the newspaper. It's somewhere back there."

Moloch, seated in the semidarkness at the back of the van, checked among the boxes and drapes until he found the newspaper. Its front-page story detailed the discovery of four bodies in a house south of Broughton.

Four bodies—three male, one female—and two heads—one male, one female—in the refrigerator. One female body, minus a head, remained unaccounted for.

"It's all over the TV too. Way I figure it, Willard was probably holed up there for a time. You can bet your last nickel that somebody saw him around there and pretty soon his face is going to be plastered right up there beside yours. He's getting worse."

In the darkness of the van, Dexter heard Moloch sigh regretfully.

"You're saying he's a liability."

"Damn straight."

"Then I must be a liability too."

Dexter glanced back at him.

"You're the reason we're here. Willard ain't."

It was some minutes before Moloch spoke again from behind Dexter.

"Keep a close eye on him, but do nothing for now."

Man, thought Dexter, I been keeping a close eye on him since the first time I met him.

Powell was dozing, and there was no conversation between Braun and Willard in the van behind. That suited Braun just fine. Unlike Dexter, the redheaded man didn't have too much against Willard. He just figured him for another one of Moloch's crazies, but that didn't mean he wanted to talk to him more than was absolutely necessary. Of the five people who now accompanied Moloch north, Braun was probably the closest to being a regular guy. Although a killer, he, like Shepherd, did not favor unnecessary violence, and had willingly acceded to their request to watch the road while they disposed of the investigators. Braun was in it for the money: he was a good wheel man, a reliable operator. He stayed calm, even in the worst situations. Every group needed its Braun.

Braun just wanted his share of the cash. He figured that some people were going to get hurt in the process, but that was nothing to do with him. That was down to Moloch. Braun would quite happily have walked away without hurting anyone as long as the money was in his hand, but Leonie and Dexter and Willard and the others needed more than that. They liked a little action. He looked over at Willard, but the boy's attention was elsewhere, his gaze fixed on the road. Braun didn't mind the silence, just as he didn't mind Willard.

Still, he patted the hilt of the knife that lay along the edge of his thigh, and felt a small surge of reassurance.

Braun didn't *mind* Willard, but he sure as hell didn't trust him either.

Braun was smarter than any of them.

Willard stared at the blacktop passing beneath them, and thought of the woman. It had taken her a long time to stop screaming after the man had died. She had tried to start the car, and had almost succeeded before Willard got to the window and broke it with the blade of the machete. When he took the car keys in his fingers and yanked them from the ignition, something faded in the woman's eyes. It was the death of hope, and though she started pleading then, she knew it was all over.

Willard had shushed her.

"I ain't going to hurt you," he had told her. "I promise. Just you calm down now. I ain't going to hurt you at all."

The woman was crying, snot and tears dribbling down her chin. She was begging him, the words almost indistinguishable. Willard had shown her the machete then, had allowed her to see him tossing it away.

"Come on now," he said. "See, you got nothing to be scared about."

And she had wanted to believe him. She had wanted to believe him so badly that she allowed herself to do so, and she had permitted him to take her hand and help her from the car. He had turned her away from the remains of the man—"You don't have to see that"—as he led her toward the house, but something about that gaping doorway, and the blackness within, had set her off again. She tried to run and Willard had to tackle her and take her down by holding on to her legs. He let her scream as he hauled her toward the house by the legs, her nails breaking as she tried to get a grip on the dirt. There was nobody to hear her. Willard cast a longing glance over at the machete lying in the grass. It was his favorite. He could always go back and get it later, he thought.

And he had lots of other toys inside.

Shepherd saw the pizza-delivery car first. The Saturn had a big plastic slice strapped to the roof, like a shark fin. Shepherd hoped the guy was making a lot in tips, because the job didn't come with a whole heap of dignity. He started the van and pulled in alongside the kid as he retrieved the pizza boxes from the insulated bag on the backseat. He heard the back of the van open and pulled his ski mask down over his head. Seconds later, Tell, his face also concealed by a mask, forced the kid into the van at gunpoint. There were no other people in the parking lot of the motel.

"Look, man," said the kid, "I don't carry more than ten bucks in change."

"Take off your jacket," said Tell.

The kid did as he was told, handing it over to Tell. Shepherd leaned across the bench seats at the front of the van and tapped the kid on the shoulder with his gun.

"You stay there and you keep quiet. My friend is going to deliver your pizza for you. After that, we're gonna drive away from here. We'll drop you off along the way. It's up to you if you walk out, or we dump what's left of you. Understand?"

The kid nodded.

"You go to college?" asked Shepherd.

The kid nodded again.

"Figures. You're smart."

The van door closed, leaving them alone together. Tell, now wearing the kid's red Pizza Heaven jacket, climbed the stairs to the second floor of the motel and knocked on the door. He pulled the ski mask from his face and waited.

"Who is it?" said a voice.

"Pizza," said Tell.

He saw a face at the window as the curtain moved, then the door opened. There was a guy in a white shirt and red tie standing before him. Behind him was a tall white man with receding hair and a beer gut.

"What do we owe you?" said the DA's investigator as Tell reached a hand into the insulated bag.

"For Mr. Verso," said Tell, "it's on the house."

The bottom of the bag exploded and the investigator staggered backward. Tell's second shot sent him sprawling across the bed. Verso tried to run for the bathroom, but Tell shot him in the back before he got to the door, then stood over him and fired two shots into the back of his head. He fired one more into the man on the bed, then walked swiftly back down to the van. Shepherd started it as soon as Tell reached the door.

"Your mask," he said.

"Shit." Tell pulled it back down before he climbed in. Behind him, the pizza-delivery guy sat with his knees drawn up to his chin.

"You okay?" asked Tell.

"Yeah," said the kid.

"You did good," said Tell. "You got nothing to worry about. Put this on your head."

He handed the insulated bag to the kid, who did as he was told. They drove back onto the highway, then pulled over at a deserted rest stop. Tell opened the back door and helped the kid over to one of the wooden picnic benches.

"There's a phone to your right. I was you, I wouldn't use it for about another twenty minutes, okay?"

"Okay."

"You breathing okay under that thing?"

"I'm fine."

"Good."

"Mister?" said the kid.

"Yeah."

"Please don't kill me."

As Shepherd had noted, the kid was smart. Tell raised the silenced pistol and pointed it at the insulated bag.

"I won't," he said as he pulled the trigger.

* * *

They bought hamburgers at a fast-food joint off exit 122, and ate them seated in the back of the van while they waited for Shepherd and Tell to join them. They were avoiding toll booths and were sticking to the speed limits. In the back of the van, Moloch had clipped his hair, shaved his beard, and now wore a pair of black-rimmed glasses. His driver's license claimed that he was John R. Oster of Lancaster, Ohio.

"How much longer?" Moloch asked.

"Hour, maybe," said Dexter. "We can rest up then."

Moloch shook his head. "We move on. They're already looking for me, and pretty soon my picture will be on every TV station from here to Canada. We need to find her, and find her fast."

Despite what he said, he wasn't too concerned yet. He had sometimes spoken of Mexico as his preferred final destination in the event of an escape from custody, because Mexico, following a decision by the Mexican Supreme Court that life sentences breached a constitutional article that stated all men were capable of being rehabilitated, would not extradite Americans facing life sentences. Moloch didn't believe that for one moment, but he figured that there would be those in the prison population who would recall his comments and who would pass them on. It would not be enough to prevent checks to the north and west as well as to the south, but he hoped that it might force the police to concentrate their efforts on monitoring the southern routes.

He sat back in the van and closed his eyes. He was strong, and he had a purpose. He allowed himself to drift into sleep, and dreamed of a woman.

A woman dying.

CHAPTER FOUR

Danny was pleading.

"Mom, just ten more minutes. *Five* more minutes. Please!"

Marianne peered at him from over the rim of her glasses. Danny was in his pajamas, which was something, but it had taken her an hour to convince him to do even that. He seemed to have grown up so much in the last year, and she was beginning to find him more and more difficult to handle. He was always questioning, always doubting, testing the limits of her authority in every little thing. But that incident with the bird had thrown him, exposing his vulnerability and drawing him back to her for a time, his head pressed against her breasts as he cried over—

Over what? Over the fact that Joe Dupree had been forced to kill the dying bird with his bare hands to put it out of its misery, or because Danny hadn't been allowed to touch it, to play with it first? Danny sometimes hurt creatures: she had watched him do it, had caught him burning ants with a piece of broken bottle or tormenting cats by flinging stones at them. She supposed that a lot of boys behaved that way, not fully understanding the pain that they were causing. In that, maybe Danny was just being a typical six-year-old. She hoped so. She didn't like to think that it might be something deeper, something that he had picked up from his father, some faulty gene transmitted from generation to generation that would manifest itself in increasingly vicious ways as he grew older. She did not like to think of her Danny—because he was *her* Danny, make no mistake about that—becoming such a man.

And he was asking questions now, questions about *him,* and it bothered her that the lies she was forced to tell Danny caused him pain. Danny seemed to have vague memories of his father, and he cried when she told him that he was dead. Not the first time, curiously, but rather on the second occasion, as if it had taken him the intervening days to absorb the information and to come to terms with what it meant to him and for him.

How did he die?

A car accident.

Where?

In Florida.

Why was he in Florida?

He was working there.

What did he work at?

He sold things.

What things?

Misery. Pain. Fear.

He sold cars.

Is he buried, like the people in the graveyard?

Yes, he's buried.

Can we visit him?

Someday.

Someday. Just as someday she would be forced to tell him the truth, but not now. There would be time enough for anger and hurt and blame in the years to come. For now, he was her Danny and she would protect him from the past and from the mistakes that his mother had made. She reached out to him and ruffled his hair, but he seemed to take her gesture for one of acquiescence and bounced back to his perch on the couch.

"No, Danny, no more. You go to bed."

"Mom."

"No! You go to bed now, Danny Elliot. Don't make me get up from this seat."

Danny gave her his most poisonous look, then stomped away. She could hear him all the way up the stairs, and then his bedroom door slammed and his bed protested as he threw the full weight of his tantrum upon it.

She let out a deep breath and removed her glasses. Her hands were trembling. Perhaps it was surprising that Danny was as well adjusted as he was, given the lifestyle that he had been forced to lead. For the first two and a half years they had stayed on the road, never remaining long in any place, criss-crossing the country in an effort to stay ahead of any pursuers. Those years had been hellish. They seemed to coalesce into a constant blur of small towns and unfamiliar cities, like a movie screened slightly out of focus. The early months were the hardest. She would wake to every floorboard squeak, every rustle of trash on the street, every tapping of branches upon the window. Even the sound of the AC clicking on in cheap motel rooms would cause her to wake in a panic.

But the worst times came when car headlights swept across the room in the dead of night and she heard the sound of male voices. Sometimes they would laugh and she would relax a little. It was the quiet ones she feared because she knew that when they came for her, they would do so silently, giving her no time to react, no time to flee.

Finally she and Danny had arrived here, settling in the last place that *they* would look, for she had spoken so often about the West Coast, about a place with year-round sunshine and beaches for Danny. She had meant it too. It had long been her dream that they would settle at last out there, but it was not to be. She feared the ones who were looking for her (for they were surely looking, even after all this time) so much that the entire West Coast was not big enough to hide her. Instead, she had retreated to cold and to winter darkness, and to a community that would act as an early-warning system for her if they came.

She looked to the refrigerator, where she still had a bottle of unopened wine in case one of her new friends called and offered to curl up in front of the TV for an evening of comedies and talk shows. She so wanted to open it now, to take a single glass, but she needed to keep her head clear. On the kitchen table before her were spread the household accounts, abandoned since the previous night in the hope that a little sleep might make them less forbidding. She wasn't earning enough from her job at the Casco Bay Market to cover her expenses, and Sam Tucker had already asked her to stay home for the rest of the week, promising to make up the hours within the month. That meant that she would either have to look for another job, possibly in Portland—and that was assuming that she could find a job and someone to baby-sit Danny after school or in the evenings—or she could dip back into the "special fund." That would necessitate a trip to the mainland, and the mainland always made her nervous. Even the larger banks were a risk: she had already dispersed the funds into accounts in five different banks over three counties—no more than $7,000 in each account—but she was always worried about the IRS or some strange bank inspector of whom nobody had ever heard spotting the connections. Then she would be in real trouble.

And there was the fact that she didn't like using the money. It was tainted. Wherever possible, she tried to get by on what she earned. Increasingly, that was becoming harder and harder to do. True, there was the knapsack itself, hidden among boxes and spare suitcases in the attic, but she had vowed not to touch that. There was always the chance of succumbing to temptation, of taking out too much and giving Danny and herself some treats, thereby drawing attention to herself. This was a small community, and even though Mainers didn't go interfering in one another's business, that didn't mean that they weren't curious about that business to begin with. It was the downside of living in such a comparatively isolated community, but a sacrifice worth making.

There was also the fact that the money was their escape fund, should she and Danny ever need to move on again quickly. If she began dipping into it for little things, there was the danger that she would come to take its contents for granted, and the little dips would become big dips, and pretty soon the fund would be gone.

And yet there was so much money in it, so much: nearly $800,000. How bad could it hurt to take a little, to buy a decent television, some new clothes, maybe even the game console that Danny wanted? Such small things from so much . . .

She forced the temptation away. No, a bank trip was the only option. She folded her glasses and put them back in their case, then began to gather the papers together.

She was almost done when the knock came on the door.

* * *

It had been decided that Leonie would knock. Anyone looking out would see an attractive black woman, smiling brightly. She could pose no threat.

Leonie heard footsteps coming toward the door, and a curtain moved aside in the semidarkness. She smiled in an embarrassed way, and raised the map that she held in her hands. Hey, I'm lost, and it's a cold night. Help me out here. Tell me where I went wrong, huh? She didn't even glance to her left, where Dexter stood holding a gun by his thigh, Braun behind him, or to her right, where the boy-man Willard waited, unblinking, his left hand shielding the blade of the knife in case a porch light caught it and drew attention to them. Moloch had remained apart, for the time being, with Shepherd, Powell, and Tell.

Seconds passed, followed by the sound of a chain being undone, and a lock being turned.

The door opened.

Joe Dupree stood on Marianne's doorstep, out of uniform. She had to look up slightly to see his face, his eyes shining brightly amid the shadows that congregated around them.

"Joe? Is there some problem?"

But Dupree merely shook his head. "I was just passing. I brought this for Danny."

From behind his back he produced a small wooden gull and handed it to her. She took it carefully in her hands and held it up to the light. It seemed almost crudely carved in places, but it was clear that it was not from lack of craft or care. Rather, the primitivism of the carving was designed to capture something of the bird, a reflection of its nature. He had taken great pains, with the head in particular, depicting the beak as slightly open. She could even see a tiny carved tongue in its mouth. The paint was newly dry.

"It's beautiful," she said, and she marveled at how the big man's hands had created something so small and wondrous, for she had difficulty imagining him even holding the knife in his fist. It must have taken him hours to do it, she thought. He killed the bird, then spent hours re-creating it in wood.

"Would you like to come in?"

"I don't want to disturb you."

"I've finished what I was doing. I was about to open a bottle of wine," she lied.

He hesitated, and she pressed home her advantage.

"You're not on duty, right?"

He didn't need much persuasion, just a little. She recalled again all those months that he had spent circling her, like a small male spider working toward a female, unsure of the safety of approaching, in fear of his life. In this case the physical proportions were reversed, but she still had the power. She had wondered why it was taking him so long to approach her, for she had seen the way he'd looked at her when she'd begun working in the market, the bashfulness with which he spoke in response to her polite remarks. She had the answer almost as soon as she asked herself the question. She knew it was because of how he looked, his consciousness of his own difference, and so it was she who had broken the ice between them, taking the opportunities, when they arose, to talk with him, walking with him along Island Avenue when their paths crossed, attracting nudges and smiles from the locals. She wasn't sure, even then, that she was interested in the man himself. Instead, it was his timidity that drew her, the fragility of his self-esteem strangely enticing in such a huge figure.

She stepped aside to let him enter and caught the scent of him as he brushed by her: he smelled of wood and sap and saltwater. She breathed it in as discreetly as she could and felt something tug inside her. He was not a conventionally handsome man. His teeth were gapped in places, seemingly too small to create a single wall of enamel in his great mouth. His face was long, but widened at the cheeks and chin. She could see wrinkles around his eyes and mouth, and knew at once that they were the consequence of some pain, perhaps physical, perhaps psychological, and that this man was frequently in distress. She was a little surprised when she began to find him attractive and guessed that it was, at least in part, a combination of his power and size along with the capacity for gentleness and subtlety that had enabled him to carve the bird out of a piece of driftwood; to deal sensitively with Jack the painter and his problems; in fact, to interact with most of the islanders in such a way that they both liked and respected him, even when he was forced to come down on them for some minor infraction. Marianne Elliot had spent so long among the kind of men who used their power to hurt and intimidate that Joe Dupree's graciousness and humanity naturally appealed to her. She wondered what it might be like to make love to him, and was surprised and embarrassed by the surge of warmth that the fantasy brought. She had not considered her own desires for so long, subsuming them all in order to concentrate on Danny and his wants, and on their combined need for constant vigilance.

Now, as she watched the big policeman gingerly sit down at the kitchen table, the chair too low for him so that his own legs remained at an acute angle, she was conscious of the muscularity of his shoulders, the shape of his chest beneath his shirt, the width of his arms. His hands, twice as large as hers, hovered in the air before him. He cupped them and placed them on the table, then unclasped them and moved them to his thighs. Finally, he folded his arms, jolting the table as he did so and causing a china bowl to tremble gently. He seemed even larger in the confines of the little kitchen, making it appear cluttered even though it was not. She had not seen the inside of his house but was certain that it contained the minimum of furniture, with the barest sprinkling of personal possessions. Anything fragile or valuable would be stored safely away. She felt a great tenderness for the big man, and almost reached out to touch him before she stopped herself and turned instead to the business of the wine. There was a bottle of Two Roads Chardonnay in the fridge, a treat for herself bought in Boston. She had been saving it for a special occasion, until she realized that she had no special occasions worth celebrating.

Marianne was about to open the bottle, by now instinctively used to doing everything for herself, when he asked her if she would like him to take care of it. She handed over the bottle and the corkscrew. The wine looked like a beer bottle in his hand.

He read the label. "Flagstone. I don't know it."

"It's South African."

"Robert Frost," he said.

"Sorry?"

"The wine. It's named after a Robert Frost poem. You know, the one about the two roads diverging in a forest."

She hadn't noticed, and felt vaguely embarrassed by her failure to make the connection.

"It's hard to forget a poem like that on an island covered by trees," he said, inserting the corkscrew.

"At least you can't get too lost if you take the wrong road," she replied. "You just keep going until your feet get wet."

The plastic cork popped from the bottle. She hadn't even seen him tense as he drew it out. She placed two glasses on the table and watched him pour.

"People still get lost here," he said. "Have you been out to the Site?"

"Jack took Danny and me out there, shortly after we arrived. I didn't like it. It felt . . . sad."

"The memory of what happened still lingers there, I think. A couple of times each summer, we get tourists in to the station house complaining that the trails out to it should be more clearly marked because they went astray and had trouble finding the road again. They're usually the worst ones, the loudmouths in expensive shirts."

"Maybe they deserve to get lost, then. So why don't you signpost it better?"

"It was decided, a long time ago, that the people who needed to find it knew how to get to it. It's not a place for those who don't respect the dead. It's not a place for anyone who *doesn't* find it sad."

He handed her a glass and touched it gently with his own.

"Happiness," he said.

"Happiness," she said, and he saw hope and sadness in her eyes.

If Marianne was curious about the giant, then he was no less interested in her. He knew little about the woman, except for her name and the fact that she had brought with her enough money to rent her small but comfortable house, yet he had recognized an attraction toward her and thought, however unlikely it might at first appear, that she might feel something for him too. It had taken all of his courage to propose a dinner date, after months of gentle probing, and it had taken a moment or two after she replied for him to realize that she had accepted.

Yet something about her troubled him. No, that wasn't true. It was not about *her,* precisely, but to do with some undisclosed element of her life. Joe Dupree had learned to read people well. His father had taught him the importance of doing so, and life on the island, with its exposure to the same faces, the same problems day after day, had enabled him to hone his skills, weighing his first perceptions against the reality of individuals as their characters were inevitably revealed to him. He glanced at the woman's fingers as she put the cork back in the bottle and replaced it in the fridge. She sat down opposite him, and smiled a little nervously. Her right hand toyed with her ring finger, yet there was no ring upon it.

It was something that he had seen her do a lot, usually when a stranger came into the store or a loud noise startled her. Instinctively, she would touch her ring finger.

It's the husband, thought Joe.

The husband is the element.

Bill Gaddis was not a happy man. There were a lot of reasons why Bill was unhappy even at the best of times, but now he had a specific reason. He was leaving a fine woman in the sack to answer an insistent knocking at his door, and that made him very unhappy indeed. He might even have been tempted to ignore the knocking, under other circumstances, but around here people had a habit of being good neighbors and the good neighbor at the door might take it into his or her head that, what with the lights being on and no reply coming from the Gaddis house, maybe somebody had had an accident, taken a tumble down some steps or slipped on some water in the kitchen, and nobody wanted to be the one who had to say,

"Hell, I was out there just last night, knocking and knocking. If only I'd checked through the windows, or tried the back door, they'd still be alive today." And Bill didn't want old Art Bassett or Rene Watterson coming in the back way, hollering and nosing about, expecting to see someone lying on the floor with blood pooling, only to find Bill with his ass in the air and his mind on other things.

He wondered now why they had even decided to settle here. It was Pennsylvania, goddamnit. *Pennsylvania.* As far as Bill was concerned, the only people who settled here willingly were religious zealots who regarded buttons as sinful, and folks who regarded buttons as sinful were likely to cast a harsh eye on Bill Gaddis's activities. Compared to those people, Billy Gaddis was virtually the Antichrist. Camp Hill, Pennsylvania, didn't even figure on most maps, but Bill knew that was why they were here, precisely because you had to look hard to find it.

It had its good points, though. His wife had picked up a job at the Holiday Inn in New Cumberland, just off the turnpike, working the desk a couple of evenings each week. On weekends, she worked a few hours at the Zany Brainy over at the Camp Hill Mall, as though spending some time in a big children's store could make up for the fact that she was never going to have any of her own. Two Sundays a month, she worked in the Waldenbooks at the Capital City Mall. The manager there, a guy named Jim Munchel, gave her books to take home and read, and she seemed to get along with the other folks who worked in the store. She told Bill that they were good people. Bill got the feeling that they knew just enough about him to not like him, so he stayed out of their way. A little independence of spirit on his wife's part was a small price to pay for keeping her out of his hair.

Bill got himself a job driving trucks for a paper company,

and they saw just enough of each other to remind themselves why they preferred to see only that much. In the first weeks, Bill would drive over to the Holiday Inn and take a seat in the Elephant & Castle, the English pub attached to the hotel. When she finished her shift, he and his wife would eat there, largely in silence, then return home and sleep at the two farthest extremes of their bed. Eventually, she got herself her own little car, but Bill kept going back to the Elephant & Castle. He'd met a woman there named Jenna, a little older than he was but still good looking, and pretty soon Bill had even more reason to be grateful for the time his wife spent working, and the regularity of her hours. Now someone was knocking on the door, depriving him of some much-needed R&R.

Bill shrugged on a robe, rearranging it to conceal his dying hard-on, and shuffled to the door, swearing as he went. He left the lights out in the hallway and pulled back the curtain at the side window. He didn't recognize the woman on the step, but she looked fine, maybe even finer than the woman he'd just left, and that was saying something. She had a map in her hands.

Bill swore louder. How hard could it be to get lost with a mall slap bang in front of you? Christ, if Bill stood on his lawn, he could see the mall, clear at the top of Yale Avenue. He took his time looking the woman over, lingering at her breasts. Bill swore once again, this time under his breath and more in admiration than in anger, then opened the door.

He barely had time to register the gun in the woman's hand before she jammed it into the soft flesh under his chin and forced him against the wall. Behind her came a redheaded man, and after him two others, a real pretty boy and a Richard-Roundtree-after-a-beating motherfucker with a big 'stache, who brushed past Bill and headed straight into the house.

"The f—"

"Shut up," said the woman. She ran her left hand over Bill's body, stopping briefly at his groin.

"We disturb something?"

From the bedroom Bill heard a scream, followed by the sound of Jenna being dragged from the bed.

"Just the two of you?" asked the black woman.

Bill nodded hard, then stopped suddenly as he considered the possibility that the action might get his head blown off. The pretty boy stayed by the half-open door while Bill was forced back into the living room. Jenna was already there, a sheet wrapped around her. She was sobbing. Bill made as if to go to her, but the woman stopped him and gestured toward the wall. Bill could only shoot Jenna a look of utter helplessness.

And then he heard the front door closing, and footsteps coming along the hallway. Two people, thought Bill. The pretty boy and—

Moloch entered the living room. "Billy boy!" said Moloch. His eyes flicked toward the woman, then back again. "I see you haven't changed a bit."

"Aw, Jesus, no," said Bill. "Not you."

Moloch moved closer to him, reached up to Bill's face, and grasped his hollow cheeks in the fingers of his right hand.

"Now, Billy boy," said Moloch. "Is that any way to greet your brother-in-law?"

Dupree nodded approvingly.

"The house looks good," said Joe. "You've done a lot with it in the last year."

He was holding the glass as delicately as he could while she showed him around her home. To Marianne, the glass still looked lost in his grip, with barely enough capacity to offer the policeman a single mouthful. They had paused briefly at her bedroom door and she had felt the tension. It wasn't a bad feeling. After looking in on Danny, who was fast asleep, they went back downstairs.

"I wanted to put our own stamp on it, and Jack didn't object. He helped us out some, when he could."

"He's a good man. There's been no more trouble, has there? Like before?"

"You mean drinking? No, none that I've seen. Danny likes him a lot."

"And you?"

"He's okay, I guess. Lousy painter, though."

Joe laughed. "He has a distinctive style, I'll give him that."

"But he was friendly, right from the start, and I'm grateful to him. It was kind of hard when we got here. People seem a little . . . *suspicious* of strangers, I guess."

"It's an island community. People here tend to stick pretty close together. You can't force your way in. You have to wait for them to loosen up, get to know you. Plus, the island's changed some recently. It's not quite a suburb of Portland, but it's getting there, with people commuting to the mainland for work. Then you have rich folks coming in, buying waterfront properties, forcing up prices so that families that have lived here for generations can't afford to help their kids set up homes. The assessments for waterfront properties out here are based on one sale made last year, and the assessor in that case only went back three months to make his valuation. Lot prices increased one hundred percent because of it, almost overnight. It was all legal, but that didn't make it right. Island communities are dying. You know, a hundred years ago there were three hundred island communities in Maine. Now there are sixteen, including this one. Islanders feel under siege and that makes them draw closer together in order to survive, so outsiders find it harder to gain a foothold. Each group is wary of the other, and never the twain shall meet."

He drew a breath. "Sorry, I'm ranting now. The island matters to me. The people here matter to me. All of them," he added.

She felt the tension again, and luxuriated in it for a moment.

"But working in the store, that's a good way to start," he continued. "Folks get to know you, to trust you. After that, it's just plain sailing."

Marianne wasn't sure about that. Some of those who came into the store still limited their conversations with her to "Please" and "Thank you," and sometimes not even that. The older ones were the worst. They seemed to regard her very presence in their store as a kind of trespass. The younger ones were better. They were happy to see some new blood arriving on the island, and already she'd been hit on a couple of times. She hadn't responded, though. She didn't want to be seen as a threat by any of the younger women. She had thought that she could do without the company of a man for a time. To be honest, she'd had her fill of men, and then some, but Joe Dupree was different.

Joe wasn't like her husband, not by a long shot.

Moloch sat in one of the overstuffed armchairs and sipped a beer.

"Fooling around, Billy boy?" he said. "Out with the old, in with the new?"

Bill had stopped weeping. He'd had to. Moloch had threatened to shoot him if he didn't.

Bill didn't reply.

"Where is she?" asked Moloch.

Bill still said nothing.

Moloch swallowed, then winced, as if he had just swallowed a tack.

"Queer beer," he said. "I haven't had a beer in more than three years, and this stuff still tastes like shit. I'll ask you one more time, Bill. Where is your wife?"

"I don't know," said Bill.

Moloch looked at Dexter and nodded.

Dexter grinned, then grabbed Jenna's arm. She was a big woman, verging on plump, with naturally red hair that she had dyed a couple of shades darker. The mascara on her face had run, drawing black smears down her cheeks. As she struggled in Dexter's grasp her sheet fell away, and she tried to pick it up again even as Dexter pulled her back toward the bedroom. She hung back, using her fingers to try to release his grip on her.

"No-o-o," she said. "Please don't."

She looked to Bill for help, but the only help Bill could offer was to sell out his own wife.

"She works late tonight." The words came out in a rush. "Down at the motel." He finished speaking and appeared about ready to retch at what he had just done.

Moloch nodded. "What time does she finish?"

Bill looked at the clock on the mantel.

"About another hour."

Moloch looked at Dexter, who had paused by the doorway of the bedroom.

"Well?" Moloch said. "What are you waiting for? You have an hour."

Dexter's grin widened. He drew Jenna into the bedroom and closed the door softly behind him. Bill tried to move away from the wall, but the black woman's gun was instantly buried in his cheek.

"I told you," said Bill. "I told you where she was."

"And I appreciate that, Billy boy," said Moloch. "Now you just sit tight."

"Please," said Bill. "Don't let him do anything to her."

Moloch looked puzzled.

"Why?" he asked. "It's not as if she's your wife."

Joe helped her put the glasses away.

"I have to ask you something," he said.

She dried her hands.

"Sure."

"It's just—" He stopped, seemingly struggling to find the right words. "I have to know about the folks who come to the island. Like I said, it's a small, close-knit community. Anything happens, then I need to know why it's happening. You understand?"

"Not really. Do you mean you want to know something about me?"

"Yes."

"Such as?"

"Danny's father."

"Danny's father is dead. We split up when Danny was little, then his daddy died down in Florida someplace."

"What was his name?"

She had prepared for this very moment. "His name was Server, Lee Server."

"You were married?"

"No."

"When did he die?"

"Fall of ninety-nine. There was a car accident outside Tampa."

That was true. A man named Lee Server had been killed when his pickup was hit by a delivery truck on the interstate. The newspaper reports had said that he had no surviving relatives. Server had been drinking, and the reports indicated that he had a string of previous DUIs. There weren't too many people fighting for space by Lee Server's graveside when they laid him down.

"I had to ask," said Joe.

"Did you?"

He didn't reply, but the lines around his eyes and mouth appeared to deepen.

"Look, if you want to back out of tomorrow night, I'll understand."

She reached out and touched his arm.

"Just tell me: were you asking with your cop's hat on, or your prospective date's hat on?"

He blushed. "A little of both, I guess."

"Well, now you know. I still want to see you tomorrow. I've even taken my best dress out of mothballs."

He smiled, and she watched him walk to his car before she closed the door behind him. She let out a sigh and leaned back against the door.

Dead.

Her husband was dead.

Maybe if she said it often enough, it might come true.

Bill had curled himself into a ball against the wall, his hands over his ears to block out the noises coming from the bedroom. His eyes were squeezed tightly closed. Only the feel of the gun muzzle against his forehead forced him to open them again. Slowly, he took his hands away from his ears. There was now silence.

It was a small mercy.

"You're a pitiful man," said Moloch. "You let another man take your woman, and you don't even put up a fight. How can you live with yourself?"

Bill spoke. His voice was cracked, and he had to cough before he could complete a coherent sentence.

"You'd have killed me."

"I'd have respected you. I might even have let you live." He dangled the prospect of life before Bill, like a bad dog being taunted with the treat destined to be denied it.

"How did you find me?"

"If you're going to run away, Bill, then you keep your head down and try not to fall into your old ways. But once a bad gambler, always a bad gambler. You took some hits, Bill, and then you found that you couldn't pay back what you owed. That kind of mistake gets around."

Bill's eyes closed again, briefly.

"What are you going to do with me?" he asked.

"Us," corrected Moloch. "You know, Bill, I'm starting to think that you don't really care about your wife, or that woman in the bedroom. What is her name, by the way?"

"Jenna," said Bill.

Moloch seemed puzzled. "She doesn't look like a Jenna. She's kind of dirty for a Jenna. Still, if you say so, Bill. I'm not about to doubt your word on it. Now that we've rephrased the question to include your lady friend and your wife, we can proceed. I think you know what I want. You give it to me, and maybe we can work something out, you and I."

"I don't know where your wife is."

"Where *they* are," said Moloch. "Jesus, Bill, you only think in the singular. It's a very irritating habit that you may not live long enough to break. She has my son, and my money."

"She hasn't been in touch."

"Willard," said Moloch.

Willard's bleak, lazy eyes floated toward the older man.

"Break one of his fingers."

And Willard did.

Joe Dupree checked in briefly with the station house. All was quiet, according to Tuttle. As soon as Berman returned, he'd turn in for an hour or two, he said, try to get some sleep.

Dupree drove down unmarked roads, for most of the streets on the island were still without names. It took the cops who came over from the mainland a few years to really get to know the island, which was why those who took on island duty tended to stick with it for some time. You had to learn to always get a phone number when anyone called, because people still referred to houses by reference to their neighbors—even if those neighbors no longer lived there, or had died. You figured out landmarks, turnings, forks in the road, and used them as guides.

Dupree returned again to thoughts of Marianne and her past. He had seen something in her eyes as she spoke of Danny's father. She wasn't telling him the truth, at least not the full truth. She had told him that she had not been married to Danny's father, but he had watched as her hand seemed to drift unconsciously toward her ring finger. She had caught herself in time and tugged at one of her earrings instead, and Dupree had given no indication that he had noticed the gesture. So she didn't want to talk about her husband with a policeman, even one with whom she had a date the following evening. Big deal. After all, she hardly knew him, and he had sensed her fear: fear both of her husband and of the implications of any disclosure that she might make about him. He was tempted to run a check on this Server guy, but decided against it. He wanted their date tomorrow to be untainted by his professional instincts. Perhaps, if they made this thing between them work, she would tell him everything in her own time.

Dexter came out of the room just as Bill stopped screaming.

"I'm glad you did that now, and not earlier," he told Moloch. "You might have put me off my game."

Bill was crying again. His face was pale with shock.

"You okay, Bill?" asked Moloch. He sounded genuinely concerned. "Nod if you're okay, because when you've recovered, Willard can move on to the next finger. Unless, of course, you think you might have something more to tell us?"

Bill was trembling. He looked up and saw the clock on the mantel over Moloch's left shoulder.

"Aw, shit," he said. His eyes flicked toward the half-open bedroom door. He could see Jenna's shadow moving against the wall as she tried to dress herself. Moloch watched him with amusement.

"You worried about her coming back, maybe finding out about your little piece on the side? Answer me, Bill. I want to hear your voice. It's impolite to nod. You nod at me again, or make me wait longer than two seconds for an answer, and I'll have Willard here break something you have only one of."

"Yes," croaked Bill. "I'm worried about her finding out."

"A more self-aware man might have realized by now that he had bigger problems to face than his wife discovering his affair.

You are a remarkable man, Bill, in your capacity to blind yourself to the obvious. Now, where is my family?"

"I told you, she hasn't been in touch, not with me."

"Ah, now we're making progress. If she hasn't been talking to you—and I've got to be honest here, Bill, I'd prefer not to be talking to you either, so I can understand her point of view—then she has been talking to her sister, right?"

"Yes."

"But you're such a piece of shit, Bill, that even your own wife won't tell you where her sister is."

"She doesn't tell me anything."

"But you must know how they communicate?"

"Phone, I guess."

"Where are your phone records?"

"In the cabinet by the TV. There's a file. But she never uses the house phone. I've looked."

"Does she receive mail?"

"Yes."

"Where does she keep it?"

"In a locked box in the bottom drawer of her nightstand."

Moloch nodded at Willard, and the boy went into the bedroom to search for the box.

As he left the room, car headlights brightened the hallway, briefly illuminating their faces and casting fleeting shadows across the room. Leonie pressed the gun against Bill's teeth, forcing him to open his mouth, then shoved the barrel inside.

"Suck it," she whispered. "I see your lips move from it and I'll pull the trigger."

From the bedroom came the sound of sudden movement: Jenna was trying to make for the window to raise the alarm, Moloch guessed. Willard was too quick for her, and the movement ceased. Moloch heard the car door closing; footsteps on the path; the placing of the key in the lock; the door opening, then shutting again; the approach of the woman.

She stepped into the living room. She was older than he remembered her as being, but then it had been more than four years since they had last met. In the interim, Moloch had been betrayed and they had run, scattering themselves to the four winds, inventing new lives for themselves. Even with Moloch behind bars, they remained fearful of reprisals.

Patricia had long, lush hair like her younger sister's, but there was more gray in it. She wasn't as pretty, either, and had always looked kind of worn down, but that was probably a consequence of being married to an asshole like Bill. Moloch, who didn't care much either way, still wondered why she had stayed with him. Maybe, after all the fear, she needed someone even semireliable to stand beside her.

Patricia took in her husband, huddled on the floor, the woman's gun in his mouth; Dexter, his shirt still untucked; Braun, an open magazine on his lap.

And Moloch, smiling at her from an armchair.

"Hi, honey," he said. "I'm home."

All was quiet. Even Bill had stopped sobbing and now simply cradled his damaged hand as he watched his wife. She stood before Moloch, her head cast down. Her left cheek was red from the first slap, and her upper lip was split.

"Look at me," he said.

She did not move and he struck her again. It was a light slap, but the humiliation of it was greater than if he had propelled her across the room with the force of the blow. She felt the tears roll down her cheeks and hated herself for showing weakness before him.

"I'll let you live," said Moloch. "If you help me, I'll let you and Bill live. Someone will stay here with you, just to make sure you don't do anything stupid, but you will be allowed to live. I won't kill her. I just want my money. I don't even want the boy. Do you understand?"

Her mouth turned down at the edges as she tried to keep herself from sobbing aloud. She found herself looking at her husband. She wanted him to stand by her, to be strong for her, stronger than he had ever been. She wanted him to defy Moloch, to defy the woman with the gun, to follow her even unto death. Yet he had never shown that strength before. He had always failed her, and she believed that even now, when she needed him most, he would fail her again.

Moloch knew that too. He was watching what passed between them, taking it in. There might be something there he could use, if only—

Willard came out of the bedroom. There was blood on his hands and shirt. A spray of red had drawn a line across his features, bisecting his face. Life was gradually seeping back into his eyes. He was like a man waking from a dream, a dream in which he had torn apart a woman whose name he had barely registered, and whose face he could no longer remember.

Bill screamed the name of the dead woman in the bedroom, and his wife knew at last that all she had suspected and feared was true.

"No, Bill," was all that she said.

And something happened then. They looked at each other and there was a moment of deep understanding between them, this betrayed woman and her pathetic husband, whose weaknesses had led these men to their door.

"I'm sorry," he said. "I'm sorry for it all. Tell him nothing."

Bill smiled, and although there was a touch of madness to

it, it was, in its way, an extraordinary thing, like a bloom in a wasteland, and in the midst of her hurt and fear, she found it in her to smile back at him with more love and warmth than she thought she would ever again feel for him. Everything was about to be taken from them, or what little they had left, but for these final moments they would stand together at last.

She turned and stared Moloch in the eye.

"How could I live if I sold out my sister and my nephew to you?" she whispered.

Moloch's shoulders sagged. "Dexter," he said, "make her tell us what she knows."

Dexter's face brightened. He started to walk across the room, and for an instant, Leonie glanced at him. It was Bill's opportunity, and he took it. He struck out with his uninjured hand and caught Leonie on the right cheekbone, close to the eye. She stumbled back and he reached for the gun, striking her again with his elbow. The gun came free.

Across the room, Braun was already reaching for his weapon. Willard still looked dazed, but was trying to remove his own gun from his belt. The gun in Bill's hand panned across the room, making for Moloch. Moloch grabbed Patricia and pulled her in front of him, using her as a shield.

From the corner of his eye, Bill registered the guns in the hands of the two men, Willard frozen in place, Leonie rising to her knees, still swaying from the impact of the blows, the voices shouting at him.

He looked to his wife, and there came that smile again, and Bill loved her.

He fired the gun, and a red wound opened at his wife's breast. For an instant, all was noise.

Then silence.

* * *

They said nothing. Bill lay dead against the wall. Shepherd and Tell were at the door, drawn by the commotion. Patricia Gaddis was still alive. Moloch leaned over her where she lay.

"Tell me," he said. "Tell me."

He touched his finger to the wound in her breast, and she jerked like a fish on a line.

"Tell me and I'll make it stop."

She spit blood at him and started to tremble. He gripped her shoulders as she began to die.

"I'll find her," he promised. "I'll find them both."

But she was already gone.

Moloch stood, walked over to Willard, and punched him hard in the face. Willard stumbled back and Moloch hit him a second time, driving him to his knees.

"Don't you ever do that again," said Moloch. "Don't you ever lay a hand on anyone unless I give you permission to do so first. I will tell you what I want from you, and you will do it. From now on, you breathe because I allow you to breathe."

Willard mumbled something.

"What did you say?"

Willard took his hands away from his ruined nose.

"I found it," said Willard. "I found the box."

The letters were postmarked Portland, Maine. Patricia should not have held on to them—her sister had warned her against it—but it was all that she had of her, and she treasured every word. Sometimes she would sit alone in the bedroom and try to catch a hint of her little sister, some trace of her perfume. Even when the scent of her had faded entirely, Patricia believed that she could still detect some faint remnant, for the memory of her sister would never leave her.

"It's not a big city, but she still won't be easy to find," said Dexter. They were already leaving the scene, departing Camp Hill. Initially, Moloch wasn't sure if the gunshots had been registered by the neighbors, for nobody was on a step or in a yard when they left the house, but minutes later they heard sirens. They had ditched the van that had been parked at the back of the house as a precaution, but the risk had been worth it.

"And she won't be using her own name," Dexter continued.

Moloch raised a hand to silence him.

She won't be using her own name.

If she was using an alias, she would need identification, and she could not have assembled that material for herself. She must have approached someone, someone who she believed would not betray her. Moloch went through the names in his head, exploring all of the possibilities, until at last he came to the one he sought.

Meyer.

Karen Meyer.

She would have asked a woman.

They headed for Philly, where they took rooms at a pair of motels off the interstate. Dexter and Braun ate at a Denny's, then brought back food for the others. Both Willard and Leonie had injuries that might have attracted attention, and Moloch could not risk having his face seen. Shepherd and Tell watched TV in their room. A reporter was talking about the rebuilding of Afghanistan.

"Man, we bombed those bastards back to the Stone Age," said Tell.

From what Shepherd could see of their houses, these people weren't far from the Stone Age to begin with. All things considered, it was a short but eventful trip for most of them. Still, Shepherd figured that they'd asked for it.

"Eye for an eye," said Tell.

"It's the way of the world," Shepherd agreed.

As usual, Dexter and Braun shared a room. Braun read a book while Dexter watched a DVD on his portable player.

"What are you watching?" asked Braun.

"The Wild Bunch."

"Uh-huh. What else you got?"

"*Butch Cassidy and the Sundance Kid. The Thing. The Shootist.*"

Braun put his book down for a moment.

"You always watch movies where the leading men are doomed to die at the end?"

Dexter looked over at Braun.

"They seemed . . . *appropriate.*"

Braun held his gaze.

"Yeah," he said. "Whatever."

He returned to his book. He was reading Thucydides's history of the Peloponnesian War. Braun believed in knowing about the past, particularly the past as it pertained to the military, having been an army man himself at one point. The Athenians were about to send out their great fleet, loaded with archers, slingers, and cavalry, to take Sicily, against the advice of the more prudent voices among them. Braun didn't know the intricacies of what was to occur, which was why he had taken up the book to begin with, but he remembered enough of his military history to know that the Athenian empire was sailing toward its ruin.

* * *

Moloch lay on the bed in his room and channel-surfed until he came to a news bulletin and saw the Land Cruiser being pulled from the river and the shrouded bodies being carried to the waiting ambulance. A picture of Misters appeared on the screen. He still had his eyes and his tongue when the photograph was taken. The cops were looking for eyewitnesses to the incident. They were also making casts of the tire tracks from the vans. It would not take them long to make the connection between the killings in Philadelphia and the escape. Moloch calculated that they had twenty-four, maybe forty-eight hours to do what needed to be done before the net began to spread farther north.

It would be enough.

CHAPTER FIVE

Strange now, or so it seemed, but Marianne had once liked his name. He called himself Edward; not Ted or Ed or Eddie. Edward. It had a kind of patrician ring to it. It was formal, no nonsense.

But she had never liked his second name and had not understood its provenance until it was too late. It was only when she learned more about his ways and began to pick away at his facade that she came to realize the nature of the man with whom she was involved. She had once read a newspaper article about a sculptress who worked with stone and who claimed that the piece she was creating was already present within the medium, so that her task was simply to remove the excess material that was obscuring what lay beneath. Later, Marianne would liken herself to that sculptress, gradually coming to see that what lay concealed under her husband's exterior was something infinitely more complex and more frightening than she had ever imagined; and so it was that she began to fear his name when at last she commenced her search for clues about the man she had married and the secret things that he did.

It had so many forms, so many derivations: Moloch, Malik, Melech, Molech. It could be found in Ammonite traditions, in Canaanite and Semite. Moloch: the ancient sun god; the bringer of plagues; the god of wealth to the Canaanites. Moloch: the prince of the Land of Tears; Milton's Molech, besmeared with the blood of human sacrifice. The Israelites surrendered their firstborn to him, burning them in fire. Solomon was reputed to have built a temple to him near the entrance to Gehenna, the gates of hell.

Moloch. What kind of man was called by such a name?

And yet, in the beginning, he had been sweet to her. When you lived in Biloxi, Mississippi, where the permanently moored casinos drew the worst kinds, the ones who couldn't afford to go to Florida or Vegas, or who didn't care what their surroundings looked like as long as there was a table, a card shoe, and maybe a cocktail waitress who might be persuaded to offer comfort for a fifty-dollar chip, then any man who didn't try to grab your ass was practically an ambassador for his sex.

And Moloch *was* different. She was working on the *Biloxi Black Beauty*, an imitation showboat painted—despite its name—so many shades of pink that it made one's teeth hurt just to look at it. The cocktail waitresses were forced to wear white corsets, like nineteenth-century hookers cleaning up after a john, and bunched skirts that, one hundred years before, would have revealed no more than a flash of shin but were now so high that the lower curves of their buttocks were on permanent display, the ruffles of the skirts like stage curtains that had been raised to reveal the main act. In theory, the men weren't supposed to touch them anywhere other than on the back or the arm. In reality, the tips were better if you didn't stick too closely to the letter of the law and allowed them to indulge themselves just a little. If they got too frisky, it was enough to nod at the security guards who dotted the casino in their green blazers, as omnipresent as the artificial potted palms, although the palms were probably more likely to develop as individuals than the *Beauty*'s Deputy Dawgs. They would lean over, one at either side of the drunk (because they were always drunks, the ones who behaved in that way), scooping up his chips and his drink even as he was quickly hustled away from the table, talking to him all the while, calm and quiet, but keeping him moving for, being a drunk, he would find it hard to argue, walk, and keep an eye on his remaining chips all at the same time.

Then he would be gone, his departure ignored by the dealer, and eventually someone else would move to take his place at the table. It didn't pay to complain too often, though. There were a lot of girls ready and willing to take your place if you got a reputation as a troublemaker or as a woman who couldn't handle a little attention from the men happily throwing away their savings for a couple of complimentary, watered-down bourbons.

Marianne had been born into a family in the town of Tunica, in the cotton country of northwestern Mississippi, close to the Arkansas border. She was raised almost within sight of Sugar Ditch, where slave descendants had lived beside open sewers a couple of blocks from Main Street. Her father ran a little diner on Magnolia Street, but Tunica was so poor it could barely support this meager enterprise. The bank took over the diner and covered its windows with wooden boards. Her father fell apart, and his family fell apart along with him. He grew depressed, then violent. On the day after he struck Marianne so hard across the head that she was deaf in one ear for a week, her mother packed up their things and moved her two daughters to Biloxi, where her own sister lived. They existed close to penury, but Marianne's mother could squeeze a nickel until the buffalo shat, and her daughters received schooling and, eventually, found places of their own. Later, she and her husband were reconciled, and he came to live with his wife and her sister for the last three years of his life, a pathetic man destroyed by bad luck, poor judgment, and an inability to stop drinking before the bottle ran dry. He was buried back in Tunica, and two years later his wife was buried alongside him, but by then Tunica had changed. Casinos had brought wealth to what had once been merely a staging post on the way to better things. There was now a carillon clock that played hymns on the hour in a little park downtown, free garbage pickup, even street signs (for in Marianne's youth Tunica could not afford to extend to visitors the luxury of a formal indicator of their whereabouts, a situation of which the late Harry Rylance would undoubtedly have disapproved). Marianne had been considering moving back there to escape Biloxi, for there would be work in Tunica's casinos and the quality of life was considerably better there than on Marianne's stretch of the Gulf Coast, until she met Edward Moloch.

The nature of her father's disintegration, and the sights that greeted her each evening in the casinos, had made her wary and intolerant of those who drank even moderately, but Moloch didn't drink liquor. She asked him for an order as soon as he sat down and placed his chips carefully upon the table, but he refused the offer of a cocktail and instead tipped her a ten for every soda she brought him. He played seven-card high-low stud quietly, declaring high and low more frequently than any other player, and at least tying each way three times out of five. His clean white shirt was open at the neck beneath a black linen jacket without a single crease. He was a big man for his height, with broad shoulders tapering to a slim waist, and strong thighs. His hair was dark, with no trace of gray, and his face was very thin, with vertical creases running down from each cheekbone and ending on the same level as his mouth, like old wounds that had healed. His eyes were blue-green, with long, dark lashes. Marianne wouldn't have called him handsome, exactly, but he had a charisma about him. He smelled good too. He wore the kind of aftershave that made women pause as they passed him, so that it slipped in under their defenses. And he came out ahead, not so far as to draw attention to himself, but sufficiently above the average for the house to breathe a light sigh of relief when he surrendered his chair. Due in no small part to his generosity, Marianne finished her shift that night with $200 in bills tucked into her purse. It almost made up for the drunks and the maulers.

When her shift finished, she decided to walk home in order to stretch her legs and allow for a little time to herself. Marianne was an attractive woman, and had learned to play it up on the casino floor but to tone it down for the streets, so she drew few glances as she headed toward Lameuse Boulevard and Old Biloxi.

The guy came at her from an alleyway beside a boarded-up diner. Even in the brief time that she had to see his face before his left hand closed around her mouth and his right around her throat, she knew him. He'd been thrown out earlier for slipping his hand between her legs, working at her painfully with his fingers, and she hadn't been able to get away from him, so firm was his grip. Even the dumb-ass security guys had seen how shaken she was, with her mouth pressed so tightly closed that her lips were almost white. She was asked by the pit boss if she wanted to press charges, but she shook her head. That would be the end of her time at the *Biloxi Black Beauty,* and she would have trouble getting work anywhere else too once it came out that she'd asked for the cops to be called and the casino's name appeared in the police blotter, maybe in the local rags too. No, there would be no charges. When she returned to the tables, the man in the black linen jacket with the soda in front of him said nothing to her, but she was certain that he had witnessed all that had occurred.

Now here was the mauler again, some bruising to his cheek where maybe his mouth had gotten him into a little more trouble than he'd anticipated with casino security, his blond hair matted with sweat, his tan suit wrinkled and torn at the left shoulder. He shifted his grip, pulling her backward into the darkness, whispering in her ear as he did.

"Huh, bitch? Huh, remember me, you fucking bitch?" Over and over. Bitch. Bitch. Bitch.

The alley was L-shaped, an alcove to the right hidden entirely from the street ahead. He spun her around almost gracefully when they reached it and sent her sprawling over a pile of black garbage sacks. Something sharp bit into her thigh. She opened her mouth to scream and he showed her the knife.

"Scream, bitch, and I'll cut you bad. I'll cut you so fucking bad. Take them jeans down, now, y'hear?"

He was fumbling at his own trousers as he spoke, trying to release himself from his pants. He moved forward and made a pass at her with the knife, the blade whistling by the tip of her nose.

"You hear me, bitch?" He leaned toward her and she could see the spittle on his chin. "You take them off!"

Now she was crying and she hated herself for crying, even as she worked at the button on her jeans, hating the way it parted from the hole so easily, hating that this thing was going to happen to her at the hands of this man.

Hating, hating, hating.

There was a click, and the guy stopped moving. His eyes

moved slowly to his right, his head remaining still, as though he hoped that his eyeballs would continue their passage, rotating through his hair so that he could see the man behind him, the man with the gun now pressed into the back of his head.

The man in the white shirt and the creaseless linen jacket.

"Drop the knife," he said.

The knife fell to the ground, bouncing once on the tip of its blade before coming to rest in the trash.

"Walk to the wall."

Her attacker did as he was told. She caught the sharp whiff of ammonia as he passed close to her, and knew that he had wet himself with fear.

And she was pleased.

"Kneel," said the man with the gun.

The guy didn't move, so the gunman stepped back and raked the barrel of the gun across the back of his head. Her attacker stumbled forward, then fell to his knees.

"Keep your hands pressed against the wall."

The man with the gun turned to her.

"You okay?" he asked.

She nodded. She could feel something sour bubbling at the back of her throat. She swallowed it down. He helped her to rise to her feet.

"Go to the end of the alley. Wait for me there."

She went without question. The would-be rapist remained facing the wall, but she could hear him sobbing. At the end of the alleyway, she bent over against the wall, put her palms on her knees, and leaned down. She sucked great breaths of stale air into her lungs, tasting polluted water and grease. Her whole body was shaking and her legs felt weak. Without the wall to support her, she felt certain that she would have collapsed. Passersby glanced at her but no one expressed any concern.

This was a fun town, and people didn't want their fun spoiled by a sick woman.

Her rescuer—for that was how she already thought of him—followed her a minute or two later. In the interim she heard sounds, like a wet towel slapping against a hard surface. As he walked toward her, he was adjusting the leg of his pants.

"Come on."

"What did you do to him?"

"Hit him some."

"We should call the police."

"Why?" He seemed genuinely curious.

"He may try to do it again."

"He won't do it again. You call the cops, you do it only because you need to, because it makes you feel happier. Believe me, he won't try anything like that again. Now, you want to call them?"

He paused beside her. She thought of the interview she would have to endure, the questions asked at the casino, the face of her boss as he told her that she wouldn't have to come in Monday, wouldn't have to come back ever, sorry, you know how it is.

"No," she said. "Let's go."

He walked with her for a block or two, then hailed a cab. He dropped her off at the door of her apartment, but declined her invitation to come up.

"Maybe I'll see you again?" he said.

She wrote her number on the back of a store receipt and handed it to him.

"Sure, I'd like that. I didn't get your name?"

"My name is Edward."

"Thank you, Edward."

Once she was safely inside, the cab pulled away from the

curb. She closed the door, leaned against it, and at last allowed herself to cry.

The guy's name was Otis Barger. Moloch read it out loud from his driver's license. Otis was from Anniston, Alabama.

"You're a long way from home, Otis."

Barger didn't answer. He couldn't answer. His hands and feet were bound with wire taken from the trunk of Moloch's car, and there was tape over his mouth. One eye was swollen shut, and there was blood on his cheek. His right foot was curled inward at an unnatural angle, broken by the heel of Moloch's boot to ensure that he didn't try to crawl away while Moloch took the woman back to her apartment. He was lying on the garbage bags where, only twenty minutes earlier, Marianne had lain as he prepared to rape her.

Moloch drew a photograph from Barger's wallet. It showed a dark-haired woman—not pretty, not ugly—and a smiling, dark-haired boy.

"Your wife and child?"

Barger nodded.

"You still together?"

Again, Barger nodded.

"She deserves better. I've never met her, but that woman would have to be hell's own whore to deserve you. You think she'll miss you when you're gone?"

This time Barger didn't nod, but his eyes grew wide.

Moloch kicked at the wounded ankle and Barger screamed behind his gag.

"I asked you a question. You think she'll miss you?"

Barger nodded for the third time. Moloch raised the leg of his pants and drew the pistol from the ankle holster. He looked around, kicking at the garbage until he found a discarded chair cushion. He walked to where Barger lay, then squatted down beside him.

"I don't believe you," he said. "What was it you called that lady you tried to rape? Bitch? That was what you called her, wasn't it?"

He slapped Barger hard across the head.

"Wasn't it?"

Barger nodded for the fourth, and final, time.

"Well," said Moloch. "She's my bitch now."

Then he placed the cushion against Barger's head, pushed the muzzle of the gun into the fabric, and pulled the trigger.

Marianne knew nothing of this, although, as the years went by, she thought often of that night and wondered what had become of the man in the alley. Moloch would say only that he had beaten him and told him to get out of town. Since he was never seen in Biloxi again, she assumed that was the truth.

Except—

Except that during their years together, most of them spent in a little house in Danville, Virginia, she had grown increasingly fearful of this man: of his mood swings, of his intelligence, of his capacity for cruelty to her. He knew where to hit her so that it hurt most and bruised least. He knew places on her body where the mere pressure of his fingers was enough to make her scream. There was money, for he always had money, but he gave her only enough to feed their little family of three, for a son had been born to them during that terrible second year. She was required to produce receipts for everything, and every penny had to be accounted for, just as every moment of her day had to be described and justified.

It had begun almost as soon as they were married. It seemed to her that the marriage license was all that he wanted. He had wooed her, made promises to her, provided them with a house to live in. She had given up the job in Biloxi two weeks before the wedding, and he had told her not to take on anything else for a time, that they would travel, try to see a little of this great country. They had a short honeymoon in Mexico, blighted by bad weather and Moloch's moods, but the proposed road trip never materialized. She quickly learned not to mention it, for at best he would mutter and tell her that he was too busy, while at other times he would hold her face, beginning with a caress but gradually increasing his grip until his thumb and forefinger forced her mouth open, and just when the pain began to bring tears to her eyes he would kiss her and release her.

"Another time," he would say. "Another time." And she did not know if he was referring to the trip, or to some promised treat for himself.

The first time he hurt her badly was when he came home from a "business meeting" in Tennessee, less than a year into their marriage. She told him that she had found a job for herself in a bookstore. It was only two afternoons each week, and all day Saturday, but it would get her out of the house. You see—

"I don't want you working," he said.

"But I need to work," she replied. "I'm kind of bored."

"With me?"

The lines in his face deepened, so that she almost expected to glimpse his teeth working through the holes in his cheeks.

"No, not with you. That's not what I meant."

"So what did you mean? You say you're bored, a man's going to take that to mean something. I don't do it for you anymore? You want somebody else? Maybe you've found somebody else already, is why you want a job, so you'll have an excuse to leave the house."

"No, it's not that. It's not that at all."

He was talking as if he was jealous, but there was no real hurt in his words. He was playing a role, and even in her fear she could see that, but it made it harder for her to argue with him when she didn't understand why he was so annoyed. She reached for him and said, "Come on, honey, it's not like that. You're being—"

She didn't even see him move. One moment they were talking and she was extending her hand toward him, the next her face was pressed against the wall and her arm was being wrenched behind her back. She felt his breath close to her ear.

"I'm being *what*? Tell me. You think you know me? You don't. Maybe I should teach you a little about me."

His left hand and the weight of his body held her in place while his right hand slipped beneath her sweater and found her skin. His fingers began moving on her, exploring.

And then the pain began: in her stomach, in her kidneys, in her groin. Her mouth opened in a silent cry, the agony increasing, turning from yellow to red to black, and the last words she heard were: "Are you learning now?"

She regained consciousness with him moving on top of her as she lay on the kitchen floor. One month later, she found out she was pregnant. Even now, years later, it still hurt her to think that Danny, her wonderful, beautiful Danny, could have resulted from that night. Perhaps it was the price she had to pay to be given him. If so, then she had continued to pay the price for a long time after, and sometimes, when their infant son cried just a little too much, she would see the light appear in Moloch's eyes and she would run to the boy and quiet him, nearly suffocating him against her.

The child had been a mistake. Moloch wanted no children, and had talked of an abortion, but in the end he had relented. She felt that he did so because he believed it would tie her more closely to him, even as he told her that they were now a family, and would always be a family.

He did not hate her. He loved her. He would tell her that, even as he was hurting her.

I love you.

But if you ever try to leave me, I'll kill you.

His mistake was to underestimate her. Men had always underestimated her: her father, her uncle (drunk at Thanksgiving, stealing kisses from his niece in the quiet of the kitchen, his mouth open, his hands reaching and touching while she maneuvered herself away, trying to placate him without offending him so that she would not put her family's tenuous status in his house at risk), the men for whom she worked or with whom she slept. It suited her. Where she grew up, men feared and hated women whom they suspected were smarter or stronger than they were. It was better to keep your head down, to smile dumbly. It gave you more room to move, when you needed it.

And so she began listening to snatches of telephone conversations, and using her little car, with its small allowance of gas, to track her husband. She picked up receipts for nonexistent purchases, just a few here and there, for Moloch had become distracted and no longer checked every item in the kitchen and bathroom. She looked for three-for-two offers, for buy-one, get-one-frees, then squirreled away the freebies for use later. It took her the better part of a year but, slowly, she began to accumulate a little money.

There were places that were out of bounds to her—the shed, the attic—but now she began to take chances even in those places. In a fit of daring that left her sleepless for days, she called in a locksmith, explaining to him that she'd lost the keys to the garden shed and the attic and that her husband would be furious when he found out.

Then she began to explore.

First, she marked the location of everything in the shed on a piece of paper and made sure always to return each item to its spot on the plan. The attic was more difficult, seemingly littered with trash and old clothes, but still she made a drawing there too.

In the shed she found nothing at first but a gun wrapped in oilcloth and hidden in a box of nails and screws. It took her two more searches—including one during the course of which Moloch had returned home and she had been forced to keep her hands thrust firmly in her pockets for fear that he would see the dirt and rust upon them—to find the hole in one of the boards on the floor. It looked like a flaw in the wood, an absent knot, but when she lifted it she discovered the bag.

She did not have time to count all of the money that it contained, but she reckoned it was close to $900,000, all in twenties and fifties. She put the board back, then returned to the shed twice more to check that she had left no sign of her presence.

In the attic there were items of jewelry, some old, others quite new. She found a small stack of bearer bonds, worth maybe $50,000 in total. She discovered bank account details in the names of unknown men and women, and credit card records carefully noted, even down to the three-digit security number to be found on the backs of the cards.

And she came across a woman's driver's license in the name

of Carol-Anne Brenner, a name that caused a buried memory to resonate softly. The next day, while shopping, she stopped at the Internet café at the mall and entered the name Carol-Anne Brenner on a search engine. She came up with a doctor, an athlete, a candidate for beatification.

And a murder victim.

Carol-Anne Brenner, a widow, fifty-three. Killed in her home in Pensacola, Florida, three months earlier. The motive, according to the police, was robbery. They were searching for a man in connection with the crime. There was a photofit picture with the report. It showed a young man with blond hair; very pretty rather than handsome, she thought. Police believed that Carol-Anne Brenner might have been having an affair with the young man and that he had wheedled his way into her affections in order to rob her. They had no name for him. Brenner's accounts had been emptied in the days prior to the discovery of her body, and all of her jewelry was missing.

The next day, during her attic search, she found more items of jewelry, and purses, empty, and photographs of women, sometimes alone, sometimes with their families. She also found four drivers' licenses and two passports, each with her husband's photograph upon it but each in a different name. The drivers' licenses were tied together with an elastic band, while the passports were in a separate brown envelope. There was a telephone number written on the outside flap.

Marianne remembered the envelope being delivered. A woman had brought it, a woman with short, dark hair and a vaguely mannish stride. She had looked at Marianne with pity and, perhaps, a little interest. The envelope had been sealed then, and Moloch had been furious at the fact that Marianne had been entrusted with it, until he confirmed that the seal was intact.

Marianne had memorized the number.

Two days later, she called it.

The woman's name was Karen Meyer, and she met Marianne at the mall, Danny sleeping beside them in his stroller. Marianne didn't know why she was trusting her, but she had felt something that day when the woman called with the envelope. And for what she needed, Marianne had nowhere else to turn.

"Why did you call me?" asked Meyer.

"I need your help."

"I can't help you."

"Please."

Meyer looked around, checking faces. "I mean it. I can't. Your husband will hurt me. He'll hurt all of us. You, of all people, must know what he's like."

"I know. I mean, I don't know. I don't know what he is anymore."

Karen shrugged.

"Well, I know what he is. That's why I can't help you."

Marianne felt the tears begin to roll down her cheeks. She was desperate.

"I have money."

"Not enough."

Karen got up to leave.

"No, please."

Marianne stretched out her hand to restrain her. It locked on her wrist. Karen stopped and looked down at the younger woman's hand.

Marianne swallowed, but kept her eyes on Karen's face. She released her grip, then slipped her hand into the other woman's palm. Tentatively, she touched her gently with her fingers. For a moment, she thought that she felt Karen's hand tremble, until it was suddenly pulled away.

"Don't call me again," said Karen. "You do and I swear I'll tell him."

Marianne didn't watch her leave. Instead, fearful and humiliated, she hid her face in her hands until Karen was gone.

Karen came to the house three days later. Marianne answered the door to find her there, ten minutes after Moloch had left for the day.

"You said you had money."

"Yes, I can pay you."

"What do you need?"

"New identities for Danny and me, and maybe for my sister and her husband as well."

"It'll cost you fifty thousand dollars, and I'm nailing you to the wall at that price."

Marianne smiled despite herself, and after a second's pause, Karen smiled back.

"Yeah, well," she said. "I'm being up front about it. You're being charged above the going rate, but I need to cover myself. If he finds out, I'm going to have to run. You understand that?"

Marianne nodded.

"I'll want half now, half later."

Marianne shook her head. "I can't do that."

"What do you mean? You said you had money."

"I do, but I can't touch it until just before I leave."

Karen stared at her.

"It's his money, isn't it?"

Marianne nodded.

"Shit."

"There's more than enough to cover what you ask. I promise you, you'll have it as soon as I'm ready to leave."

"I need something now."

"I don't have half, or anything close to it."

"What can you give me?"

"Two hundred."

"Two hundred?"

Karen slumped against the wall and said nothing for at least a minute.

"Give it to me," she said at last.

Marianne went upstairs and retrieved the roll of bills from the only safe place she could find in which to keep it: the very center of a carton of tampons. It was a peculiarity of Moloch's. He would not even sleep beside her when she had her period. She handed the roll of ones and fives to Karen.

"Do you want to count it?"

Karen weighed the roll of bills in her hand.

"I figure this is everything that you've hidden away, right?"

Marianne nodded, then said: "Well, I kept fifty back. That's all."

"Then that'll be enough, for now."

She moved to go.

"How long will it take?"

"They'll be ready in two weeks. You can pick them up when you're leaving, and I'll take the rest of my money then."

"Okay."

Marianne opened the door. As she did so, the older woman reached out and brushed her cheek. Marianne didn't flinch.

"You'd have done it too, wouldn't you?" said Karen softly.

"Yes."

Karen smiled.

"You need to work on your seduction technique," she said.

"I've never had to use it before, under those circumstances."

"I guess your heart just wasn't in it."

"I guess not."

Karen shook her head sadly, walked to her car, and drove away.

Marianne never understood why Moloch had kept the licenses, the purses, the little personal items from the women. She suspected that they were souvenirs, or a means of recalling the women from whom they had come, a kind of aide-mémoire. Or perhaps it was simply vanity.

Moloch had never told her what he did for a living, exactly. He was, when she asked in those first days, a "businessman," an "independent consultant," a "salesman," a "facilitator." Marianne believed that the women, and what had happened to them, were only part of what he was. Now, when she read of raids on stores or banks, and saw her husband's cash reserve increase; when she heard of a businessman being killed in his car for his briefcase, the contents later revealed to be $150,000 in under-the-counter earnings, and an amount just under that was briefly added to the bag in the shed; when a young woman disappeared in Altoona, the daughter of a moderately wealthy businessman, and her body was found in a ditch after the ransom was paid, she thought of Moloch. She thought of Moloch as she fingered the money; she thought of Moloch as she smelled the burnt powder in the gun among the nails; and she thought of Moloch as she spied the hardened dirt in the treads of his boots, carefully picking it away and placing it in a Ziploc bag that she bound tightly and squeezed into a tampon inserter.

In those last days, she became aware of an increase in the pitch of his activities. There were more calls to the home phone, the phone that she was not allowed to answer. There were more frequent, and longer, absences. The mileage on his car climbed steadily in increments of two hundred miles. He grew yet more distracted, now barely glancing at the receipts from the market and failing even to check the total spent against her allowance for the week.

There were three things that Marianne had learned about Moloch's final operation, through careful listening and the maps and notes that he had locked away in the attic. The first was that it would take place in Cumberland, far to the north of the state and close to the borders of both Maryland and Pennsylvania. The second was that it would involve a bank.

The third was that it would take place on the last Thursday of the month.

She made her plans carefully. She called Karen from a pay phone and told her the exact time at which she would arrive to pick up the material. She contacted her sister, who lived only a few miles away, yet from whom she had become virtually estranged because of Moloch's paranoia, and told her of her plan, and of the possibility that she and her sorry-ass husband might have to leave the state at some point in the future, but with money in their pockets. Surprisingly, Patricia seemed unconcerned by the prospect of uprooting herself. Bill had recently been let go from a plant job and she saw it as a chance for them both to start over again.

Marianne prepared three changes of clothing for Danny and herself, using what little cash she had left to buy them each a new set of clothes cheaply at Marshalls: no-name jeans, plain T-shirts, cotton sweaters from beneath the yellow, black, and red REDUCED sign. These she placed at the bottom of their respective piles of clothing, although she need not have worried, Moloch becoming ever more withdrawn as the day of the operation approached. This was to be his big score, she sensed.

What she could not have known was that Moloch's recent actions were merely one of a number of scams and crimes that he had put into operation over the years, and that there were other men involved, committing insurance frauds, drug rip-offs, minor bank raids in small dusty towns.

Murders.

And these were only the enterprises that produced a profit, for Moloch had his hobbies too. He had more in common with the would-be rapist Otis Barger than might once have seemed possible, except he picked his targets more carefully, from the ranks of whores and addicts and lost souls, and there was never a risk of them talking, because when he was finished with them, he disposed of their remains in forests and mountain bogs. Moloch's peculiarity—one, if the truth be known, of many—was his disinclination to have vaginal sex with his victims.

After all, he did not wish to be unfaithful to his wife.

Yet even if she had known all of this at the time, had recognized the unsuspected depths of her husband's degeneracy, Marianne would still have acted as she did, independently and without making a formal approach to the authorities. She would still have contacted Karen. She would still have set in motion her escape.

She would still have told the police of the details of the bank job.

She called them shortly after she had retrieved the cash from the hollow beneath the shed floor and placed it in the trunk of her car, alongside the two small bags that represented all of the possessions she was prepared to take with her. She planned to drive to the rendezvous point, meet Karen, then head on to the bus station and abandon her car there. From there, she would pay cash for two tickets to three different destinations, each bought at a separate window. She would travel on to only one of them, New York, and there she would buy three more tickets to three different cities, and again head to only one of them. It seemed like a good plan.

She strapped her son into the baby seat, then drove to the mall and parked by the pay phone. She lifted the boy out and carried him, still sleeping, to the phone. From there she dialed the dispatcher at the Cumberland PD and asked to be put through to Detective Cesar Aponte. She had read his name in a newspaper one week earlier, when he was quoted during an investigation into a domestic assault case that had left a woman fighting for her life. If he was not on duty, she had three other names, all taken from the newspapers.

There was a pause, then a man's voice came on the line. "Detective Aponte speaking."

She took a breath, and began:

"There will be a bank robbery today at four P.M. at a First United in Cumberland. The man leading the robbery is named Edward Moloch. He lives at . . ."

Using RACAL, the call was traced back to the pay phone at the mall. By the time the local cruiser arrived, Marianne was gone, and nobody could recall what the woman who had made the call looked like. The only thing that the old woman behind the counter at the Beanie Baby Boutique could remember was that she had an infant boy asleep on her shoulder. Stuck behind the pay phone was an envelope, just as Marianne had told them there would be. It contained Moloch's various false

IDs and some, but not all, of the material from the attic relating to what she believed were his past crimes. Most of it remained in the house.

By then, Marianne had arrived at the meeting place, a disused gas station half a mile outside town. She was five minutes late. There was no sign of Karen's car, and for a moment she panicked, fearing that she had been abandoned. Then Karen appeared from the back of the lot, waving her around. She drove and parked beside a beat-up Oldsmobile.

She got out of the car and saw that Karen had a manila envelope in her hand.

"You've got it? You've got it all?"

"You've got my money?"

Marianne popped the trunk. The black knapsack she had taken was zippered closed. When she opened it, dead presidents blinked in the bright sunlight. Ten of the sealed bundles had been opened, then rebound. Marianne handed them to Karen.

"Fifty thousand. I counted it this morning."

"I trust you."

She handed over the envelope. Marianne slit it with her thumbnail.

"Don't *you* trust *me*?"

"If I didn't trust you, do you think I'd be opening the trunk in front of you?"

"I guess not."

She examined the passport, the driver's license, the card bearing her social security number. She was now Marianne Elliot instead of Marian Moloch. Her son's name, according to his new birth certificate, was Daniel. Where his father's name should have been, the word "Unknown" had been written.

"You've left me with my own first name, almost."

"You've never done this before. The first thing that will

give you away is your failure to answer to your new name. It will arouse suspicion and attract attention to you. Marianne is close enough to your given name for you to avoid that problem."

"And Danny's father?" She had asked Karen to give her son the name Daniel. It was the name that she had always wanted for him, but Moloch had given him his own name, Edward. Now he was Daniel. In her mind, he had always been Daniel.

"You get asked, his name was Lee Server, and he's dead. In there is an obituary for Server. It will tell you all you need to know about him."

Marianne nodded. She found a set of documents and IDs for both Patricia and Bill, the photos a little old because they were the only ones she had at hand when Karen had agreed to help her. Once again, they had been left with their own first names.

"I should ask you for more money," said Karen. "I had to pay off some people. The paper trail goes right back, even down to death certificates for your father and mother. There's a typewritten sheet of paper in that envelope. Memorize the details on it, then burn it. It's your new family, except you'll never get to know them now. You're an only child. Your parents are dead. It's all very sad."

Marianne stuffed the material back into the envelope.

"Thank you."

"How the hell did you ever get involved with this guy?" asked Karen suddenly.

"A man tried to rape me," she replied. "He saved me."

There was a pause.

"Did he?" Karen asked sadly.

"I trusted him. He was . . . strong." She started back toward her car.

"I gave him those names, the ones on the papers that you found in the attic," said Karen.

Marianne stopped.

"What do you mean?"

"I created them, all but one. He came to me and I did it."

"Who is he? Who is he really?"

"I don't know. The only name that I didn't give him is the one he used with you. Moloch was how I knew him, right from the beginning. I guess he likes that name a lot."

She tossed a set of car keys to Marianne.

"This is your car now. Registration is in the glove compartment. It's clean."

"I'll give you more money."

"Didn't cost me much. I'd kept it hidden away in case I ever had to run. I guess your need's greater than mine right now."

Karen helped her move the bags into the trunk of the new car, then shifted the baby seat to the Oldsmobile while Marianne carried Danny. He was awake now, and had begun to cry.

"You'd better get going," said Karen.

Marianne strapped the still-howling child in, then stood at the driver's door.

"I—"

"I know."

Then, without even knowing why, Marianne walked quickly up to the older woman and kissed her tenderly on the mouth, then hugged her. After a moment, Karen responded, hugging her tightly in return.

"Good luck," she whispered.

"And to you."

Then Marianne got in the car and drove away.

* * *

There were three First Uniteds in Cumberland, and each was monitored after Marianne's warning. It was not her fault that the information she had given was wrong. Cumberland was merely the base: the bank itself was in Fort Ashby, ten miles south. It was taken just as the doors were being locked for the day. Nobody was killed, although the security guard was pistol-whipped and would never fully recover from his injuries. The silent alarm was not set off until the robbers—five of them—had left the bank. By the time the police could react, the thieves were gone.

Moloch got back to his house shortly before daybreak. The street was quiet. He made one full circuit of the block, then parked at the end of the driveway and entered the house. He walked straight to the back door, passed through the garden in darkness, and unlocked the shed door.

He saw the space where the board should have been, and the empty hollow where his money once lay, and then there were flashlight beams, and shouted orders, and dogs barking.

And as he emerged blinking into the phalanx of armed men, he thought:

Bitch. I'll kill you for this.

THE THIRD DAY

Widow'd wife and wedded maid,
Betrothed, betrayer, and betray'd!

—Sir Walter Scott, "The Betrothed"

CHAPTER SIX

It was close to dawn when they neared their destination. Already there was a faint glow visible in the east, as of a fire distantly glimpsed. They had agreed on a rotation for sleeping and driving, as Moloch was reluctant to pause for any reason. He had the scent of her now, of that he was certain. It had proved easier than expected, for elements outside his control had fallen into place for him: foolish Verso, who had hoped to trade Moloch's life for his own; his idiot brother-in-law, risking his anonymity in order to gamble on meaningless outcomes; and Dexter's casual remark that his wife would not be using her own name, causing tumblers to fall in Moloch's mind.

For most of the journey, he remained silent and awake, watching the red lights of the cars on the road streaming toward the void, fading into the distance until they were swallowed up by the blackness. Moloch had been incarcerated for so long that he found himself fascinated by the small details of the lives being lived around him, although there was a remoteness, perhaps even a coldness, to his interest: it was the curiosity of a small boy marveling at the industry of termites or ants in the moment before he annihilates their mound or torches their nest. He watched the cars go by, their occupants only occasionally visible in the brief flare of a match or the comforting illumination of the dashboard lights, and wondered how so many could be on the roads and highways at this time, for what mission could be so urgent, what destination so compelling, that it caused them to give themselves up to a journey through the night, forsaking sleep? Moloch suspected that, for some, there was no destination. There was no home waiting, no husband drowsing, no wife sleeping or children dreaming. There was only the illusion of progress and momentum offered by the cocoon of the automobile in the surrounding night. These people were not traveling; they were fleeing, taunted by a false belief that if they ran fast and hard enough they might somehow escape their past or their present, that they might even somehow escape themselves. Moloch recalled those who had crossed his path and faded from the view of the world as a consequence. For some, he thought, it might almost have been a relief. He closed his eyes and waited for the coming of the dream.

Braun, weary now of Willard's unsmiling company, had joined Dexter and Moloch in the lead van, while Leonie had taken the wheel of the second. Farther back along the road, Tell and Powell were engaged in a lengthy discussion of their various sexual conquests, both real and imagined, while Shepherd sat in silent judgment upon them. As the trip had worn on, Shepherd had begun to draw away a little not only from the younger men in the car but from the group as a whole. There had been no opportunity for him to talk with Dexter and Braun since Moloch's escape, and the need to do so was now pressing. They knew one another well, these three men, for they had worked together before under Moloch's aegis. Leonie too shared a history with Dexter, although she largely kept her own counsel, choosing to reveal her thoughts only with Dexter and trusting him to relay them, if necessary, to the rest of the group.

Shepherd was concerned about recent developments, including the killing of the investigator down at Dismal Creek and the mutilation of his companion, and the deaths of Moloch's sister-in-law and her husband. He also had real worries about the sanity of at least one of their group.

Of Powell he knew little and, in truth, cared to know even less. He had come highly recommended, and had state time behind him in Maryland and Tennessee. Shepherd found him boorish and ignorant, and the snatches of conversation that were coming from Shepherd's right did nothing to alter that perception. Tell, he liked, but while he understood the possible justification for taking the life of the young pizza-delivery man (he was smart, argued Tell after the fact, and might have noticed more than he pretended), he was not convinced that it was necessary, and Tell's inability to make that distinction troubled him. The incident with the cell phone also indicated that Tell's temper was somewhere between short and nonexistent. Shepherd, as previously noted, wasn't a big fan of cell phones. He believed they were contributing to the creation of a ruder, less caring society. There was a time, and it wasn't so very long ago, when people kept their voices down in public, not only because they wished to enjoy a little privacy in their conversations but also because talking too loudly disturbed the people around them. Now, all that was going out the window, along with leaving your car unlocked or your front door open. The fact that people now locked their doors and secured their houses to protect them from criminals like Shepherd was beside the point. Still, Shepherd had never really considered solving the cell phone problem by killing anyone who used one in a discourteous manner. It was a pity that nobody would ever know that excessive conversational volume was the reason behind the Arab's murder. Otherwise, he might have made a nice example to others, convincing them to change their ways. Shepherd figured that Tell would be okay if he could just calm down some, maybe take a deep breath once in a while instead of pulling a trigger. Shepherd would work on him.

But the principal source of Shepherd's unease was Willard, and he knew that Dexter shared that disquiet. Shepherd was a man who believed himself to be in control of his own appetites. He also knew, from past experience, that discipline and restraint in any operation increased the odds of its success, and that once those qualities began to dissipate, a breakdown of some kind inevitably followed. Willard, quite clearly, was incapable of exercising self-control, making Tell look like a Buddhist by comparison. He was an immature man defined by his appetites. Shepherd did not know what ties bound Willard to Moloch, or what made the older man show such indulgence toward the younger. Sometimes, Moloch seemed to demonstrate toward Willard the tenderness of a lover. At other times, he appeared almost paternal, protecting the younger man while reluctantly disciplining him. Whatever Moloch's feelings about him, Willard was becoming more and more unpredictable. As a consequence, they were leaving a trail for others to follow, and there would be a reckoning because of it. Shepherd had no intention of sitting on death row, waiting to see if the chair or natural causes would take him first. His share of the money would buy him a comfortable life, if he was careful, and he had every intention of living long enough to spend it. He needed to talk with Dexter and Braun, for something had to be done about Willard.

If Leonie felt unease at the prospect of spending time in Willard's company, she did not show it when Braun asked her to switch vehicles. Braun, for one, suspected that Leonie felt little of anything at all, and that under the skin she and Willard might well be blood relatives. Dexter had used her for jobs a couple of times, with Moloch's agreement, but Braun still knew nothing about her other than a story Dexter had once told him. Leonie was heading out of some dyke bar in South Carolina—Braun was less surprised to hear that Leonie ate at home than that she'd managed to find a pickup joint in South Carolina—when a pair of guys jumped her in the parking lot. Braun knew their kind, had grown up alongside them: they hated women, particularly independent women, and there was nothing more independent than a woman who didn't need a man for sex. They bundled her into the trunk of their car and drove her to a shack out in the woods. Braun didn't need to know anything more about what had happened to Leonie after that, and Dexter didn't tell him much anyway, but he could guess. Afterward, when they saw that she hadn't buckled, they beat on her some, then dumped her at the back of the dyke bar, her clothes torn and bloody. She didn't go back inside, though. Instead, she walked to her car, where her gun lay taped beneath the dashboard—she hadn't bothered to carry it into the bar, a mistake that she would never again repeat—and returned to her apartment, where she washed and douched and treated her cuts, then took a couple of sleeping pills and went to bed.

The next morning, she called Dexter. She told him all that had occurred, and he drove down to be with her. It was Dexter who pulled the two guys from the street and brought them back to the shack, where Leonie was waiting. Then he sat outside in his truck, smoking and listening to R. L. Burnside while he watched the road. He heard that hunters found the two men a couple of days later. One of them was still alive, although he died as soon as the medics tried to move him. Dexter figured that Leonie would be kind of unhappy to hear that only one of them had survived for so long. Usually, she was precise about these things, but then she'd been pretty upset by what had been done to her, so it might have clouded her judgment some.

It wasn't that part of the story that had stuck with Braun, though. The guys had gotten what they deserved, make no mistake about that, and Braun wasn't about to shed any tears for them. No, what gave Braun an insight into Leonie was what those guys saw before they died. One had been married, while the other was dating a woman who worked nights providing technical support for her local ISP. Leonie had visited them both while she was waiting for Dexter to pick up the two men, and just as they'd had fun with her, well, she'd had fun with their women. She'd even taken some pictures before she left.

Dexter said they'd come out pretty good, considering the amount of red in them.

No, Willard wouldn't be screwing with Leonie, not if he had any sense in that pretty-boy head of his.

Tell and Shepherd, meanwhile, appeared to have

bonded. Shepherd had told Braun that he was reasonably impressed with how Tell had handled the Verso thing. Like Shepherd, Braun wasn't so sure that Tell had really needed to kill the pizza guy, but there was no way of knowing how much he had taken in, so Tell had probably erred on the side of caution.

Whatever occurred, at least there was Dexter. Braun had known Dexter longer than almost any other human being. They were like brothers bound by blood. They shared cars, rooms, even women, although if Braun ever met a woman that he liked as much as Dexter, then he planned to marry her and not share her with anyone, not even Dexter.

This did not strike Braun as at all odd.

"You ever wonder about names?" asked Dexter, from out of nowhere.

"Wonder how?" said Braun.

"About how only some colors become names, and not others."

"Like?"

"Like black. You know, Mr. Black. Or Mr. White. You got Mr. Green too, and your Mr. Brown, but that's about it. You ever meet anybody called Blue, or Yellow, or Red? Doesn't happen, except in movies. You think that's strange?"

"You know, it never struck me before."

"You think it's interesting?"

"No. You got too much time on your hands, is what I think. You need to be doing something useful to keep your mind off shit like that. Just drive."

"There was a time," said Dexter, "when you thought I had a lot of interesting shit to say."

"I thought you were deep. Then I got to know you."

"You saying I'm not deep?"

"If you were a pool, little kids could paddle in you."

"If you were a pool, little kids would piss in you."

"Just drive, will you? The sooner we get to where we're going, the sooner I can get away from your shallow black ass."

But both men were smiling as Dexter tapped the gas, Moloch momentarily forgotten in the darkness behind them.

Shoot the women first: it was an axiom of antiterrorist units, quite literally a maxim to live by. The women were more fanatical. They had more to prove, and when they made a decision, they were less likely than their male peers to experience doubts or second thoughts about it. Women attempted suicide less frequently than men, but they were far more likely to follow the attempt through to its fatal conclusion. Similarly, when a woman picked up a gun and put her finger on the trigger, there was a good chance that someone's body was about to be endowed with an extra hole.

If Willard was the most unpredictable of the little band of killers slowly making its way north, and Tell the most volatile, then Leonie was the most lethal. Braun was right to suspect as much, and Moloch, had he been asked, would have confirmed that his faith in her resolve was based entirely on the evidence of his own eyes. Leonie enjoyed power. Specifically, she enjoyed wielding the power of life and death, and had always done so. As a child, spiders and insects had briefly provoked her interest. They were simple to catch, and had enough easily detachable limbs to keep her amused in the clean little bedroom of the clean little unit that she shared with her mother in one of Philadelphia's more desirable low-income housing projects. The young Leonie quickly tired of bugs, though, for there was no challenge to them. Similarly, unlike some of the boys who shared her environment, she did not enjoy tormenting cats and dogs. Instead, Leonie retreated into her own world, growing slowly quieter, a stillness creeping over her as she sat at her window and waited for the time when fantasy and reality might coalesce.

It was from that window that she watched as the slim black boy walked across the basketball court toward the one who called himself Ex. Ex had touched her once, while she was coming back from the store with an armful of groceries. She had been unable to move, fearful that she might drop the bag in her arms. It was the middle of the month, when money was always short for her momma, and so she had endured Ex's touch, and the sour taste of his breath when he placed his mouth upon her own. Ex had grown bored when she did not respond, and called her some names that she did not understand. Secretly, her stillness had disturbed the young dealer, who found it unnerving the way her eyes had never left his, not even blinking while he fondled her. Since then, he had not approached her again, even as she matured into the fine-looking woman she would eventually become.

Now the boy was facing Ex, and Ex was saying something to him. Leonie felt her mouth grow dry. She pressed her fingers and face against the glass, a smear of breath pulsing, then fading, upon it.

She knew what the boy was about to do. She felt it from him, could see it in his stance.

Kill him, she thought. Kill him now.

And he did.

By the time Ex's body hit the ground, the girl was running to the door of her apartment. She intercepted the boy on a patch of waste ground that led to the river. Already, she could hear sirens. The boy could hear them too. He looked scared.

"Give me the gun," said Leonie.

The boy didn't move. Instead, he just stared at the pretty girl with the thick black hair who stood before him. She was a year or two younger than he was, he guessed, but everything about her spoke of a maturity beyond his own.

"Give it to me," she repeated. "They won't search me."

To their right, a patrol car made an arc into the project, spraying dirt and water from the rutted concrete. A second car came in from the left, effectively cutting off his exit. He couldn't understand how they'd gotten there so fast.

Suddenly, the girl moved toward him, her hands slipping beneath his jacket as she hugged herself to him. She buried her face in his chest, then pulled back and kissed him on the cheek.

"Gotta run," she said. "I'll see you later, baby."

And as the cops approached she skipped away across the dirt, the gun tucked into the waistband of her skirt, her shirt hiding the butt. He watched one of the cops glance at her, and saw her reward him with a little smile.

Then she was gone, and Dexter never saw the gun again.

But he saw the girl, and although that kiss was the only one she would ever give him, Dexter loved her, and he knew that she loved him too, in her way.

Still, he had never crossed her, and he never would. If it came down to it, he believed that she would kill him. She loved him more than she loved anyone else in the world, yet she would take his life if he failed her.

Dexter figured that, where Leonie was concerned, the rest of humanity didn't stand a chance.

It was the absence of lights that alerted Karen Meyer. She heard the van pulling up outside her house, but no headlights matched its progress. Her first thought was that it was the cops coming, and she ran through a mental checklist as she climbed out of bed and pulled on a pair of jeans over her panties. The dummy passports and driving licenses were hidden in a panel behind her gas stove, accessible only by taking apart the oven from the inside, and she deliberately kept it thick with grease and food waste to discourage any possible search, even if it meant that the oven was rendered practically unusable as a result. Her inks, pens, and dyes were all in her studio, and were indistinguishable from the materials she used in her regular design work. Her cameras were an expensive Nikon, a cheaper Minolta, and a Canon digital. Again, she could argue that these were an essential part of her job, since she often had to take photos as part of her initial preparations. The last batch of material had gone out a few days before, and there was nothing on the slate. She figured that she was clean.

She had moved up to Norwich, Connecticut, to be close to her mother. Her mother had suffered a bad stroke that left her with impaired mobility, and Karen, as the only daughter in the family, had felt responsible for her. Karen's brothers lived over on the West Coast, one in San Diego, the other in Tacoma, but they each sent money to boost the coverage offered by their mom's insurance and to help Karen out, although, unofficially, Karen didn't need their help because her sidelines were quite lucrative. Still, she wasn't one to turn down free money, and the cash had helped her to rent the pretty house on Perry Avenue in which she now lived. Much as she loved her mom, she couldn't live with the old woman, and her mom wanted to retain some degree of independence anyway. She had a panic button and a day nurse, and Karen was three minutes away from her. It was the perfect arrangement for all of them.

She looked out of the window and saw the van. It was black and comparatively clean—not so beat up that it might attract attention, and not so clean as to stand out.

There was no other vehicle in sight.

Not cops, she thought.

Her doorbell rang.

Not cops.

She went to her dresser and removed the gun from the drawer. It was a Smith & Wesson LadySmith auto, its grip designed for a smaller, woman's hand. She had never fired it anywhere except on the range, but its presence in the house reassured her. Although Meyer made a point of no longer dealing with violent criminals, there was no telling what some people might do if they were desperate enough.

Barefoot, she padded down the stairs, the gun held close to her thigh. She did not turn on any of the house lights. The street lamps cast the shadow of a woman against her door.

"Who is it?" she said.

She glanced to her right, where the display panel for the alarm system was mounted, and began checking the sensors in each zone. Front door: OK.

"Karen?" said a woman's voice. "Karen Meyer?"

"I said, 'Who is it?'"

Living room: OK.

"My name is Leonie. I'm in trouble. I was told you could help me."

"Who told you?"

Dining room: OK.

"His name is Edward."

Garage: OK.

"Edward what?"

Kitchen: DISARMED.

Her stomach lurched. She felt metal at the nape of her neck. A hand closed over her gun.

"You should know my name," said a voice. "After all, it's the only one that you didn't give me."

Dupree awoke to pain.

His joints and muscles, even his gums, still ached, although he'd taken some painkillers the night before. He felt too weak to lift his own weight from his bed, so he lay still, watching shadows on the ceiling rise and fade like smoke. He wondered sometimes if the symptoms he felt were phantoms too, shadows cast by the knowledge of his impending mortality. The pain had been coming more frequently in recent months. He had been warned by old Doc Bruder that his size and build left him open to a variety of ailments, and the pain he was experiencing could be the onset of any one of those.

"You're not frail by any means," the retired physician had said while Joe sat on a couch in the old man's den, Gary Cooper striding down a dusty street on the TV screen, forsaken by his darling, "but you're not as strong as you look, or as people seem to think you are. Your job puts stresses on you. You're complaining to me of pains in your chest, aches in your joints. I'm telling you that you need to get yourself checked out."

But Dupree had not taken Bruder's advice, just as Bruder had known that he would not. Dupree was afraid. If he was told that he could no longer do his job, then that job would be taken away from him. His work on the island was more important to him than anything else. Without it, he would be lost. He would die.

Dupree was thirty-eight now, and would be thirty-nine in

May. He recalled a picture he had once seen of Robert Pershing Wadlow, the so-called Alton Giant, the largest man on record, Wadlow towering over the two men at either side of him, their heads barely reaching his elbows. At eight feet, eleven inches tall, he was taller than the enormous bookcase behind him. His hands were buried in the pockets of his dark suit, and he appeared to be teetering to his left, as if on the verge of toppling over, his thin frame buffeted by an unseen wind. Dupree guessed that Wadlow was twenty when the photograph was taken. Two years later he was dead, felled by the great curse that was his condition.

Lying on his bed in the house in which he had grown up, Dupree remembered his father's stories, his tales of old giants, told to reassure a boy who felt himself alienated from his peers by his size. His father had lied to him. They were lies of omission, but lies nonetheless, for his father had tailored his stories to the boy's problems, cutting, distorting, softening.

For his stories were not truly about giants.

They were about the death of giants.

Outside it was still dark. Ordinarily he would have been on his way to the station house by now, but he had juggled the rotation so that he could spend the evening with Marianne. He lay back on his bed and tried to rest.

Sharon Macy sat in the tiny kitchen of her apartment, sipping a mug of hot milk. She had a lot on her mind. Her father was due to enter the hospital the following week for a series of tests after he had complained of pains in his back and chest. He was laughing off the concerns of his wife and daughter, but there was a history of cancer in the family and Macy knew that the fear of it was with each of them. Under other circumstances she might have returned home immediately, but the department was already buckling under the combined weight of illness and leave—which was why Macy, although still on probation, had found herself on the island rotation—and she suspected that only a real emergency would enable her to absent herself from duty. Anyway, her father had told her in no uncertain terms that he did not want her hanging around the house fussing over him. Her tour on Sanctuary would leave her with five days off at the end of it. She would drive down to Providence as soon as she was back on the mainland, and would examine her options in the light of what, if anything, her father's tests revealed.

Macy thought too of Barron and the drugs that she had seen him take from Terry Scarfe. Maybe she was mistaken in what she believed had occurred, but she didn't think so. She wished that she had someone with whom she could talk about these things, and for the first time since the breakup of their relationship, she felt herself missing Max, or at least missing what he had once represented for her.

To hell with him, she thought. To hell with all of them.

She placed the empty mug in the sink, returned to bed, and at last fell asleep to the sound of a ship in the bay, its horn rising like the cry of a sea creature lost in the darkness, seeking only to return to the safety of its kind.

The call woke Terry Scarfe from a deep, alcohol-induced sleep, and so it took him a couple of seconds to recognize the voice and the distinctive Eastern European accent.

"We have a job for you. Someone has purchased your expertise."

Even in his dazed state, Terry knew that whatever expertise

he might have was worth next to nothing, unless you were dealing in pesetas and were happy just to count the zeros.

"Sure," he said. Terry wasn't going to argue. He needed some cash. Even if he hadn't needed it, these people weren't the kind you refused. They owned Terry Scarfe, and he knew it.

"You'll get a call, usual place, fifteen minutes," the man said, then hung up.

Terry rose, swayed a little, and pulled a pair of sweatpants and an old T-shirt over his scrawny body. He found his heaviest overcoat, then walked two blocks to the pay phone, along the way picking up a coffee at the Dunkin' Donuts to warm his body and his hands.

Life had not been particularly kind to Terry Scarfe. Most of the time it seemed to treat him like he had screwed its sister. Other times, it went after him like he had screwed its mother as well. He had one failed marriage behind him, a failure that was due, Terry felt, to a combination of factors, including excessive alcohol intake on the night that he had proposed, his arrest and incarceration shortly after the wedding itself, and the unforgiving (and, in fact, downright unpleasant) nature of the woman to whom he had attached himself. His wife had divorced him while he was in jail on burglary charges, then married someone else while Terry was locked up for possession of a controlled substance. Her significant life events, Terry concluded, seemed to coincide with his government vacations. Maybe if he stayed out of jail for a while, her life wouldn't be quite so good, while the quality of his own existence would improve considerably.

A smarter man than Terry might have concluded that his criminal ambitions for himself far exceeded the talents available to him to achieve them, but like most criminals, Terry wasn't particularly smart. Unfortunately, his career options were now even more limited than they had been to begin with, and few of them were likely to meet with the approval of the forces of law and order, which was why he was standing beside a telephone in the darkness waiting to talk to someone he had never met and who was unlikely to offer Terry a job tasting beer or testing feather beds for softness. Just as Terry was starting to notice that he could no longer feel his feet, the call came through.

"Terry Scarfe? My name is Dexter."

Terry thought the guy sounded black. It didn't bother him, except that black people tended to stand out some in Portland, and if the guy was planning on coming up, it could present problems.

"What can I do for you?"

"There's an island, somewhere off the coast there. It's called Dutch Island."

"Yeah, Dutch. Sanctuary."

"What?"

"Some folks still call it Sanctuary, that's all, but Dutch, yeah, Dutch is good."

He heard the black guy sigh.

"You done?"

"Yeah. Sorry."

"We need you to find out as much as you can about it."

"Like?"

"Cop stuff. Ferries. Points of access."

"I'll need to bring in someone else. I know a guy lives out there. He's got no love for the big cop on the island."

"Big cop?"

"Yeah, fuckin' giant."

"You're shitting me."

"Nope, for real."

"Well, find out all you can. And get your friend to track

down a woman. She's using the name Marianne Elliot. She'll have a little boy with her, about six years old. I want to know where she lives, who she's friendly with, boyfriends, shit like that."

"When do you need this by?"

"Tonight."

"I'll do my best."

Terry thought that he heard, in the background, a soft pop. Terry knew that sound. Somebody had just taken a bullet.

"No," said Dexter, "you'll do better than that."

Dexter stared down at the body of Karen Meyer. She had never been a pretty woman, but Leonie and Willard had removed what little superficial attractiveness she might have had. They worked well together. It was kind of worrying. Dexter would have to talk to her. He didn't want her getting too close to Willard. He and Shepherd had talked, and the way things were going, Willard wasn't going to be around much longer.

Meyer had been easy to find. She'd transferred her business north, but had left word with the kind of people who might need her services in the future. It had taken Dexter just one phone call to find out where she was.

He'd always thought Meyer was smart, and relatively unsentimental. It was all money with her, and he guessed that the woman had given her a big share of Moloch's stash in return for her help. It must have been a lot to make her risk crossing Moloch. He hoped that she'd had a good time with it because, in those final minutes in her basement, she had paid in spades for what she'd done.

"Did you find someone?" asked Moloch.

"Yeah. He'll cost us five Gs to our friends in Boston, plus a straight ten percent of whatever is on the island and some favors in the future."

"He'd better be worth it."

"They threw in a bonus, as a sign of goodwill."

Moloch waited, and Dexter smiled.

"They gave us a cop."

The changeover went smoothly. Lockwood and Barker came out on the first ferry and started the weekly test of the medical and fire equipment at the station house. At eleven A.M., Dupree checked in with them, then drove down Main Street to the post office, parking the Explorer in the lot on the right-hand side of the white clapboard building. He had called Larry Amerling that morning to tell him that there was something he wanted to talk to him about. It struck him that Amerling might have been expecting the call.

Amerling knew more about the island than anyone else, maybe even more than Dupree himself. His home was filled with books and papers on the history of Casco Bay, including copies of his own pamphlet, printed privately and sold at the market and at the bookstores over in Portland. Amerling was a widower, and had been for ten years. His children lived on the mainland, but they visited regularly, little trains of grandchildren in tow. Dupree usually spent Thanksgiving with Amerling, as it was his family's tradition to return to the island and celebrate the feast together. They were good people, even if it was Larry Amerling who had first christened the policeman Melancholy Joe. Only a handful of people used that name, and few of them said it to his face, although among the cops assigned to the island the name had stuck.

Dupree thought that Amerling would be alone when he called, as the old man usually took a half-hour's time-out at eleven A.M. to get some paperwork done and drink his green tea, but the postmaster had company that morning. The painter, Giacomelli, was standing against the wall, drinking take-out coffee from the market. He looked troubled. So did Amerling. Dupree nodded a greeting to them both.

"I interrupt something?" he asked.

"No," said Amerling. "We've been waiting for you. You want some tea?"

Dupree poured some of the green tea into one of Amerling's delicate little Chinese cups. He held the cup gently in the palm of his hand. The three men exchanged pleasantries and island gossip for a time before lapsing into an uneasy silence. Dupree had spent the morning trying to put his concerns into words, to explain them in a way that did not make him sound like a superstitious fool. In the end, Amerling saved his blushes.

"Jack's here for the same reason you're here, I think," Amerling began.

"Which would be?"

"There's something wrong on the island."

Dupree didn't respond. It was Jack who spoke next.

"I thought it was just me, but it isn't. The woods feel different, and . . ."

"Go on," said Amerling.

Jack looked at the policeman.

"I haven't been drinking, if that's what you're thinking, least of all not enough for this."

"I didn't think that at all," said Dupree. There was no way to tell if he was lying or not.

"Well, you may reconsider when you hear this. My paintings are changing."

Dupree waited a heartbeat.

"You mean they're getting better?"

There was a burst of laughter that eased the tension a little and seemed to relax the painter slightly.

"No, smart-ass. They're as good as they're gonna get. There are marks appearing on the canvases. They look like men, but I didn't put them there. They're in the sea paintings and now they're in some of the landscapes as well."

"You think someone is sneaking into your house and painting in figures on your work?"

He tried to keep the disbelief from his voice. He almost succeeded, but Jack spotted it.

"I know it sounds weird. The thing of it is, these figures aren't painted on."

He reached down to the floor and lifted up a board wrapped in an old cloth. He removed the cloth, revealing one of his seascapes. Dupree stepped closer and saw what looked like two men in the shallows. They were little more than stick figures, but they were there. He reached out a finger.

"Can I touch it?"

"Sure."

Dupree ran his finger over the board, feeling the traces of the brush strokes against his skin. When he came to the figures, he paused, then raised the tips of his fingers to his nose and sniffed.

"That's right," said Jack. "They've been burned into the board."

He picked up a second painting and handed it to Dupree.

"You know what this is?"

Dupree felt uncomfortable even looking at the painting. It was certainly one of Jack's better efforts. He sucked at sea and hills, but he did good trees. They were mostly bare and in the background of the picture, almost hidden by mist, Dupree could make out a stone cross. It was definitely a departure for the painter.

"It's the approach to the Site," he said. "I have to tell you, Jack, you're never going to sell this painting. Just looking at it gives me the creeps."

"It's not for sale. I do some of these for, well, I guess out of my own curiosity. Tell me what you see."

Dupree held the painting at arm's length and tried to concentrate on it.

"I see trees, grass, marsh. I see the cross. I see—"

He stopped and peered more closely at the detail on the canvas.

"What is that?"

Something gray hung in the dark place between two trees, close by the cross. He almost touched it with his finger, then thought better of it.

"I don't know," said Jack. "I didn't paint it. There are others, if you look hard enough."

And there were. The closer he looked, the more apparent they became. Some were barely blurs, the kind of smears that appeared on photographs when someone moved and the shutter speed was kind of slow. Others were clearer. Dupree thought he could distinguish faces among them: dark sockets, black mouths.

"Are these painted on?"

Jack shrugged his shoulders. "They look painted to you?"

"No, they look like photographs."

"You still afraid I might be drinking too much?"

Dupree shook his head. "I'd say you're not drinking enough."

Amerling spoke.

"You going to tell me you came here because you're worried about raccoons, or have you felt something too?"

Dupree sighed. "Nothing specific, just an unease. I can't describe it, except to say that it's a sensation in the air, like the prelude to an electrical storm."

"That's about as good a description as I've heard. Other people have felt it too, the older folk, mostly. This isn't the first time something like this has occurred. It happened before, in your daddy's time."

"When?"

"Just before George Sherrin disappeared, but it wasn't quite like this. That buildup came quickly, maybe over a day or two, then was gone again just as quickly. This one is different. It's been going on for longer."

"How long?"

"Months, I'd say, but it's been so gradual most people haven't even noticed it until now, if they've noticed it at all."

"But you did?"

"I've been feeling it for a while. It was the accident that confirmed it; the accident, and what the Lauter girl said before she died."

"She was in pain. She didn't know what she was saying."

"I don't believe that. I don't think you do either."

"She was talking about the dead."

"I know."

Dupree walked to the window of the little office and looked out on Island Avenue. It was quiet, but it wasn't peaceful. Instead, it was like a community awaiting the outbreak of some long-anticipated conflict, or perhaps that was just a tormented policeman, a drunk, and an old romantic trying to impose their own interpretation on an innocent world.

"People have died on the island before now, some of them pretty violently," Dupree said. "We've had car crashes, fires, even a homicide or two. You think they all saw ghosts before they died?"

"Maybe."

Amerling paused.

"But I'd guess not."

"So why the Lauter girl, and why now?"

"Your father, he told you about the island?"

Once again, Dupree glanced at Jack. He remembered taking the old man out on his porch, after Danny Elliot had found him with blood pumping from a deep scalp wound. He had been furious with the painter, maybe because he saw in him some of his own flaws, but mostly because he had scared the boy. Now he was about to reveal a part of himself that he had kept hidden from everyone. Jack, however long he might have been on the island, was still an outsider.

Amerling guessed his thoughts.

"If you're worried about Jack, then I'd lay those worries to rest. He's more sensitive to this place than some who have grandparents buried in the cemetery. I think you can speak safely in front of him."

Dupree raised his hands helplessly before the painter.

"I understand," said Jack. "No hard feelings."

"He told me," began Dupree. "He went through the histories of the families, right from day one. He made me memorize them all. He told me about the slaughter and the new settlement that followed later. He told me about George Sherrin and why he thought Sherrin had been taken. He told me all of it. I never fully understood. I don't think I even believed some of it."

"But he tried to explain it to you?"

"Yes. He told me what he himself believed. He believed that this place was always different. The natives didn't come out here, and they used most of these islands before the whites arrived, but for some reason they wouldn't come out to this one."

Amerling interrupted. "They had pretty good reasons for not coming here. This island is kind of an anomaly. It's big, but it's way out on the outer ring. They only had bark canoes to get them out here. I think it was just too far away for them to worry about it."

"Well, anyhow, then the settlers came," continued Dupree, "and they were killed. My father thought like his father: what happened to them tainted the island, and some remnant, some memory of those events, clung to this place. The violence of the past never went away. Something of it stayed here, like a mark in stone. Now there's a balance on the island, and anything that endangers that balance has to be dealt with. If it isn't . . ."

He swallowed the last of the tea.

"If it isn't dealt with, then something else on the island will deal with it in its own way. My father thought that it had found a way to purge itself of anything that might threaten it, the way a person's system will flush out toxins. That's what happened to Sherrin. He was toxic, and the island dealt with him. That's what my father believed."

He finished and stared at the leaves in the bottom of his cup. It sounded absurd, but he remembered the look on his father's face as he told him the history of the island. His father was not a superstitious man. In fact, he was the most realistic, no-bullshit man that Dupree had ever met. Frank Dupree was the kind of man who would carry his own ladder around with him just so he could walk under it to show up more credulous folks.

Amerling poured himself some more tea, then offered the pot to Dupree. The policeman declined.

"Why do you drink this stuff, anyway?"

"It keeps me calm," said Amerling.

After a pause, Dupree reconsidered and extended his cup. "Any port in a storm," he said.

"Your father knew that this place was different," said Amerling. "We talked about it some, and we both came to more or less the same conclusion. Sometimes, bad things happen in a place and it never truly recovers. The memory of it lingers. Some people are sensitive to it, some aren't. I read once that Tommy Lee Jones, you know, that actor fella, he lived in the cottage where Marilyn Monroe committed suicide, or was murdered, or whatever you believe took her from this earth. Didn't bother Tommy Lee Jones none. He's not that kind of fella, from what I've read. But me, I don't think I could have lived in a place like that, knowing what happened there. I believe, and I may be a fool, that something of its past must remain there, like damp trapped in its walls.

"What happened on Sanctuary was so much worse than a single murder. Like you say, it tainted this island, marked it forever. Then a bunch of rapists took a woman here a long time after, and they disappeared. Flash forward to George Sherrin, and he winds up under the roots of a tree. I was there when they dug him up, and I saw what the roots had done to him."

Amerling leaned forward, grasping the teacup in both hands.

"He was an evil son of a bitch. There were stories about him, after he died. He tormented and abused his own children and they say he might have hurt children on the mainland."

"I heard that too," said Dupree. "My father believed it was so."

"Well, if your daddy believed it, then it was true. I got no doubt in my mind now. The island, or whatever dwells here, wouldn't tolerate him, and it got rid of him. There's no better way of putting it than that."

"But where does that leave the Lauter girl, and Wayne Cady? You're saying they deserved what happened to them?"

"No, I don't think the island played any part in that. They died because they'd been drinking and decided to boost a car. But I think something was drawn to that place as they died, because there's an awareness now. This tension that we've all felt, it's there for a purpose. I think when the crash happened, the nature of the tragedy—sudden, frightening—drew something. It came to see what was happening."

"Something? Something like what?"

"I don't know. Have you been out to the Site lately?"

"Not for a while."

"It's almost impossible to get to. The path's become overgrown. There are fallen trees, briers. Even the marshes seem to be getting bigger."

"You said 'almost impossible.' Does that mean you've been out there?"

Amerling paused. "Yesterday. Jack went with me. We didn't stay too long."

"Why?"

"It's stronger out there. It's like getting too close to the bars of the lion's cage. You can feel the threat."

"And there are no birds," said Jack.

"Not out there, not anywhere," said Amerling. "Haven't you noticed?"

To tell the truth, Dupree hadn't, but now that he thought about it, there was a silence to the island that he had never experienced before. The only bird that he had seen was the dying gull on Marianne's lawn.

"That's where your daddy and I differed about the island.

He believed it was something unconscious, like a force of nature. A tree doesn't think about repairing breaches in its bark, it just does it. He thought the island operated on that level."

"But you don't?"

"No, and the Lauter girl's last words just confirm what I believe. Whatever is out there is conscious. It thinks, and reasons. It's *curious*. And it's getting stronger."

Jesus, thought Dupree, I can't believe I'm having this conversation. If anyone from the department heard me, they'd have me jacketed and locked up in a padded room. But the brass don't come out here, so they don't know what it's like. They don't understand it. Most of them don't understand much about any of the islands, but this one in particular is beyond them. All I can do is hope that nothing happens that would force me to try to explain it to them.

Well, Chief, I guess you could say that the island is haunted, and I think some dead people came to take a look at Sylvie Lauter. Oh, they had lights, did I mention that? They must go through a hell of a lot of batteries, so that's our main lead. We're scouring the island for batteries . . .

"So, why now? Why should it be so strong now?"

"A convergence of circumstances, maybe. A new factor on the island that we don't recognize, or haven't noticed."

"You're thinking it's dangerous?"

"Maybe."

"Do you think it's—" Dupree paused, uncertain that he wanted to use the word that came to mind, then relented.

"Do you think it's evil?"

"Evil, that's a moral concept, a human concept," said Amerling. "It could be that whatever is on this island has got no concept of morality and no need for it. It just wants what it wants."

"Which is?"

"I don't know that. If I knew it, we wouldn't be having this conversation."

"I'm not sure I even want to be having this conversation as it is."

The postmaster grinned.

"Anyone else apart from us three was here, they'd say we were two foolish old men and a giant driven simple by what was ailing him." Larry Amerling was never one to sugarcoat his words, but Dupree felt as if the older man had been reading his thoughts.

Jack interrupted.

"I heard from her father that there was some question about the Lauter girl's death," he said.

"Yeah, I heard that too," said Amerling, "although I heard it from you." He cocked an eyebrow at the painter.

"I just thought you might like to know," said Jack. "Hell, you know just about everything else. I figure a gap in your knowledge would bug you more than most folks."

Dupree didn't answer immediately. He wasn't sure that he should, but then both men already seemed to know as much as he did, or more.

"They found insect matter in her mouth, and beneath her fingernails," he said. "It came from a moth, a tomato hornworm. They're big and ugly and they're all dead by September, and I'm not sure that I've ever even seen one on this island until recently."

"I saw one on a tree in the cemetery, when they were laying Sylvie Lauter down," said Jack. "I took it home, looked it up in a book, then pinned it to a board. Thought I might paint it sometime."

"Paint it badly," said Amerling. "You'd have to stick a note on it so folks would know what it was."

"I'm not that bad," said Jack.

"Yes, you are."

"You came to my exhibition at the Lions Club."

"There was free food."

"I hope it poisoned you."

"Nope, it was pretty good, unlike what was on the walls."

Dupree interrupted them.

"Gentlemen! You're like two old dogs fighting. It's embarrassing."

He picked up his cap and flicked at some dust.

"I was out at Doug Newton's place. There was a moth there too, same type. I saw it on the curtains in his mother's bedroom."

But he wasn't talking to the two older men as much as to himself. He ran his hands through his hair, then placed his cap carefully on his head. Moths. Why moths? Moths were attracted to flames, to light. Was that what it was, some form of attraction toward Sylvie Lauter and the old Newton woman? What did they have in common?

The answer came to him immediately.

Dying, that was what they had in common.

"How long have we got?" asked Dupree.

"Not long," said Amerling. "I go outside, it's like I can hear the island humming. The birds were the last sign. It's bad news when even the birds fear to fly."

"So what do we do?" asked Dupree.

"We wait, I guess. We lock our doors. We don't go wandering near the Site at night. It's coming soon, whatever it is. Then we'll know. For good or bad, then we'll know for sure."

CHAPTER SEVEN

Moloch allowed them to rest for the remainder of the day, choosing to travel north under cover of darkness. Later that morning, Powell and Shepherd headed down to Marie's Home Cooking and bought enough takeout for the day. On the way back to Perry Avenue, they stopped off at Big Gary's Liquor Store and picked up two bottles of Wild Turkey to keep out the cold. Dexter and Braun took an opportunity to rest, once they had finished conversing softly with Shepherd in Karen Meyer's kitchen.

Moloch had learned enough about Meyer from their past dealings to know that she was the kind of woman who would have few visitors. Her house was the last on the street, sheltered by trees and not overlooked by any of her neighbors. He didn't know if she had a lover, but there were no photographs on the refrigerator, no little tokens of love on the shelf by the cookbooks. He went through her studio, heedless of the fingerprints that he left behind. If they found him, they already had more than enough evidence to justify the taking of his life. It mattered little to him if they added Karen Meyer's name to the final tally.

The studio was neat and her computer was password protected. Moloch guessed that anyone trying to gain access to it without the password would probably have just two or three chances before the computer automatically commenced erasing its memory. He searched her bedroom and found a shoe box on the top shelf of her closet. It contained a collection of letters from a woman named Jessica, most of them expressions of love except for the most recent, dated October 1997, which detailed her reasons for ending the relationship. Jessica had met someone else, apparently. Moloch found it curious that Karen Meyer had retained the breakup letter. It seemed to suggest to him an element of emotional masochism in the forger's personality. Perhaps some part of her might even have enjoyed what Willard and Leonie had done to her in the basement, although he somehow doubted it.

Her body still lay on the basement floor. She had resisted for longer than he expected, which surprised him. He had always thought of Meyer as a pragmatist. She must have known that she would have to tell him what she knew eventually, but something had made her hold out for so long that he feared she would die before she revealed the location of his wife and son. She had feelings for them. Moloch wondered if Meyer and his wife had been lovers. The possibility angered, and aroused, him.

Marianne Elliot. She had kept her first name almost intact, simply expanding it from the original Marian. It was a smart move, typical of Meyer. Moloch knew that those who assumed new identities sometimes gave themselves away in the first few months by failing to hear their new name when they were addressed by it, or by signing checks, rental agreements, or bank documents with their old name. The easiest way to avoid it was to give them a new name that began with the same letter, preferably even the same two letters, as their old name. So James became Jason, Linda became Lindsay.

Marian became Marianne.

His son was now named Danny, not Edward as they had agreed. Well, perhaps "agreed" wasn't the right word. His wife had wanted something simple and boyish, but Moloch liked formal names. Trust the bitch to give his son a name like Danny as soon as she was out of his sight.

Moloch didn't much care what happened to the boy. He might take him with him when he left the island, or he might leave him. He might kill him, or he might corrupt him. He hadn't decided yet. All he knew was that he felt no paternal instincts whatsoever toward him, but his wife would understand before she died that it was within his power to do whatever he chose with his son.

He overturned the shoe box and watched as a jumble of photographs fell on Karen Meyer's unmade bed. He went through them with his fingertips, turning over those that had landed facedown, until he found the one that he had suspected—even hoped—might be among them. She was a little different now: her hair was darker and she seemed to be downplaying her natural good looks. When he had met her first in Biloxi, she had used makeup with a delicacy that had impressed him, his experience of casino waitresses having led him to expect all of them to resemble the brides of Mary Kay. Now her face was completely unadorned, her hair lank. Her face was very pale and the photograph, taken in a photo booth, suggested that she had not slept well in a very long time. A perceptive man might look twice at her and begin to see something of the beauty that she was trying to disguise, and a very unusual man might suspect something of the history of pain and abuse that had led her to take such steps. The boy was on her lap, his finger raised to the camera, a birthday crown upon his head.

He had underestimated her, and that was what troubled him more than anything else, even more than the betrayal itself. He had thought that he knew her, knew her as intimately as only one who had explored both pleasure and pain through her could know her. He believed that he had broken her, for what was she but a thing to be used, part of a front to fool those who might come after him, the loving family man with the neat house, the pretty wife, the little boy who must surely have represented the first step on the road to a home filled with children and grandchildren?

Moloch's was not the routine abuse of drunks and petty sadists, the kind that might at last force the object of their hatred to turn on them with a gun or a knife out of an instinctive desire for survival. No, Moloch's capacity to hurt—emotionally, physically, psychologically—was more refined than that. The pain, the stress could never be allowed to become unbearable, and needed to be interspersed at times with moments of kindness, even tenderness; reminders of love, need, dependence. Yet somehow, despite it all, she had managed to keep something hidden from him, some vital part of herself that he was unable to touch, and it was that which had enabled her to escape him. He was impressed by what she had achieved. Perhaps they were closer in spirit than he had ever imagined.

He placed the photograph in his jacket pocket, then went back downstairs and turned on the television. Already, the TV news bulletins were describing how the search for the escaped man was expanding, extending the net to take in not only those states along the border but also the southern states as far north as Maryland. Worse, they had trawled for possible accomplices and now, in addition to Willard, he had to worry about Dexter and Shepherd. Their pictures had appeared on every news show, along with all known aliases. Their continued involvement was a risk, but a calculated one. Once they got to Maine, they could complete their work in a matter of hours, then head for Canada. Most of the routes across the border were unpatrolled, and those who chose to make the journey could easily slip across. Dexter would make sure of it.

Dexter was clever. That was why he had been entrusted with so much of the organization once it became apparent that Moloch would be forced to face the grand jury. Where Dexter went, Braun and Leonie would follow. As for Shepherd, he was a curious beast. He seemed to drift through his existence, never allowing himself to experience the extremes of pleasure or hatred. He appeared to take little from life, apart, occasionally, from the lives of others. There was no sentimentality to him, and while he was loyal, it was the loyalty of one who has signed a contract and proposes to remain strictly within its bounds. Any breach of its clauses by another would render the contract null and void and Shepherd would do whatever was necessary to extricate himself from its requirements.

As for the redneck, Powell, and the belligerent Tell, with his cornrows knitted tightly against his skull, tight as his pent-up rage at the world, Moloch knew little of them, except that Dexter vouched for them. They were men who would work for the promise of money, and that was enough. Moloch was not sure how much of his cash the bitch had spent, but there would be enough, he felt certain, to divide the best part of $500,000 between them, maybe even $600,000. The hardest parts—the escape, the associated killings, and the pinpointing of her location—were already behind them. With luck, their work would be done quickly and they would be scattered within two days. If there was less money than they had expected, then Powell and Tell were expendable. The others could take whatever was left. Moloch needed only enough to get him out of the country. After that, he would find ways to make some more. Perhaps he would ask Dexter to join him, once the time was right.

Except there was now a fatalism to Dexter that Moloch had not noticed before, although Moloch had often seen it develop in men like him. After years of violence, the odds in favor of meeting a violent end increased with every passing week. They had stayed too long in the life to imagine that they could enjoy an easy escape at this late stage. Dexter had not become reckless, as some of his kind did, and neither did he appear to have become overly cautious. Instead, that fatalism, that resignation, was written across his face. He looked like a man who wanted to sleep, to sleep and forget.

Moloch had seen him talking with Braun and Shepherd. He had not intervened. He knew the subject of their conversation: Willard, who now lay sleeping in the room across the hall. Moloch loved Willard, and knew that the love was reciprocated. There was a purity to Willard that was almost as beautiful as the boy himself, and unlike Shepherd, he would be loyal unto death. Moloch could only guess at what went on inside Willard's head, and sometimes wondered what it would be like to probe the younger man's mind. He feared that it would be similar to briefly inhabiting the consciousness of a vaguely self-aware spider: there would be blackness, patience, and a ceaseless, driving appetite that could never be sated, but there would also be inquisitiveness and rage and sensuality. Moloch had no idea where Willard had come from. He had not sought Willard out; rather, Willard had found him, and attached himself to him. He had approached Moloch for the first time in a bar on the outskirts of Saranac Lake, but the older man had been aware of him for some time, for Willard had been hovering at the periphery of his vision for a number of days. Moloch had made no move against him, although he took to sleeping with his gun close at hand and the locks in his hotel rooms carefully secured. The boy interested him, without Moloch really knowing why.

Then, exactly three days after Moloch had first sighted him, the boy had entered the bar and taken a seat in the booth across from him. Moloch had seen him coming, and in the time it had taken the boy to walk from the door to the booth, Moloch had unholstered his pistol, secured it with a silencer beneath the table, and wrapped the gun in a pair of napkins. It now lay between his legs, Moloch's right index finger resting lightly upon the trigger.

The boy sat down carefully and placed his hands flat upon the table.

"My name is Willard," he said.

"Hello, Willard."

"I've been watching you."

"I know. I was beginning to wonder why that might be."

"I have something for you."

"I'm straight," said Moloch. "I don't want what you have to sell."

The boy showed no offense at the deliberate insult. Instead, his brow simply furrowed slightly, as though he didn't fully understand the import of Moloch's remark.

"I think you'll like it," he continued. "It's not far from here."

"I'm eating."

"I'll wait until you're done."

"You want something?"

"I've eaten."

Moloch finished his plate of chicken and rice, eating with his left hand, his right remaining beneath the table. When he was finished, he laid down a ten and two ones to cover the food and his beer, then told Willard to lead the way. He picked up his coat, wrapped it around the gun, then stayed behind the boy until they left the bar and found themselves in the parking lot. It was a midweek night and only a handful of cars remained. Willard began walking toward a black Pontiac, but Moloch called him back.

"We'll take mine," he said.

He tossed Willard the keys.

"And you can drive."

As the boy caught the keys, Moloch struck him hard with the butt of his gun and forced him against the Pontiac. He pushed the gun into the boy's head, then frisked him. He found nothing, not even coins. When he stepped back, there was blood on Willard's face from the wound in his scalp. His face was completely calm.

"You can trust me," said Willard.

"We get to where we're going, I'll help you clean up that cut."

"I been cut before," said Willard. "It heals."

They got in the car and Willard drove, unspeaking, for about ten miles, until they were close to High Falls Gorge. He turned left off 86, up a secluded driveway, then pulled up outside a two-story summer house.

"It's in here," he said.

He opened the door and moved toward the front of the house. Moloch stayed about five feet back from him.

"Anything happens, anything at all, and I'll kill you," said Moloch.

"I told you, you can trust me."

Willard knelt down and took a key from the flowerpot by the door, then entered the house. He hit the hall lights so Moloch could see that they were alone. Despite his assurances, Moloch searched the house, using the boy as a shield as they entered each room. The house was empty.

"Who owns this place?"

Willard shrugged. "I don't know their names."

"Where are they?"

"They left on Sunday. They come up here for weekends, sometimes. You want to see what I have for you? It's in the basement."

They reached the basement door. Willard opened it and turned on the light. There was a flight of stairs leading down. Willard led, Moloch following.

Near the back wall was a chair, and in the chair was a girl. She was seventeen or eighteen. Her mouth was gagged and her arms and legs had been secured. Her hair was very dark and her face was very pale. She wore a black T-shirt and a short black skirt. Her fishnet stockings were torn. Even in the poor basement light, Moloch could see track marks on her arms.

"No one will miss her," said Willard. "No one."

The girl began to cry. Willard looked at her one last time, then said: "I'll leave you two alone. I'll be upstairs if you need anything."

And seconds later, Moloch heard the basement door close.

Now, years later, Moloch thought back to that first night, and to the bound girl. Willard knew him, understood his appetites, his desires, for they existed in a similar, though deeper, form within himself. The girl was a courtship gift to him and he had accepted it gladly.

Moloch loved Willard, but Willard was no longer in control of his hunger, if he had ever truly been able to rein it in. The death of the woman Jenna and the damage inflicted on the bait for the escape indicated that Willard was spiraling down into some dark place from which he would not be able to return. Moloch loved Willard, and Willard loved Moloch, and love brought with it its own duties.

But then, as Moloch knew only too well, and as his wife was about to find out, each man kills the thing he loves.

Danny was kicking up a fuss, as he always did when his mother tried to leave him for an evening. It came from not having a father around, she believed. It had made him dependent, maybe even a little soft, and that worried her. She wanted him to be strong, because at some point he was going to have to learn about the world they had left behind, and the man who had contributed to his creation. But she also wanted him to be strong for her own selfish reasons. She was tired; tired of the constant fear, tired of looking over her shoulder, tired of having nobody on whom she could depend. She wanted Danny to grow up to be big and tough, to protect her as she had protected him. But that day, it seemed, was a long way off.

"Where are you going?" he asked again, in that whining voice he adopted when he felt that the world was being unfair to him.

"I told you already. I'm going out to dinner."

"With Joe?"

"Yes."

"I don't like Joe."

"Don't say that, Danny. You know it's not true."

"It is true. I hate him. He killed a bird."

"We went through this before, Danny. He had to kill it. It was hurt. It was in so much pain that the kindest thing Joe could have done was to put it out of that pain."

She had given him the gull carved for him by Dupree. He had looked at it for a moment, then had cast it aside. Later, when she went to retrieve it from the floor, it was gone, but she had glimpsed it on the shelf in Danny's room before they left the house. Her son was a complex little boy.

The car jogged as it hit a dip in the road, the headlights skewing crazily across the trees for a moment. She wondered if she should bring up what had been troubling her since earlier in the evening, or if she should just let it rest until the morning.

She had gone outside to put some water in the car and her attention had been drawn to the little grave that Joe had created for the dead gull. The stone that marked the spot had been moved aside, and the earth was scattered around what was now a shallow hole. The bird was gone, but she had found blood and some feathers nearby. It could have been an animal that had dug up the bird, she supposed, except that Danny had dirt beneath his nails when he'd eaten earlier that evening, and when she'd questioned him about it, he'd simply clammed up. It was only later, when she examined the grave, that she had begun to suspect what had happened.

She decided to leave matters as they were. She hoped to enjoy the night and didn't want to leave her son after an argument.

"Will Richie be at Bonnie's?"

"I'm sure he will," said Marianne. Richie's mental age wasn't much more than Danny's, but he seemed to care a lot about Danny, and Danny liked the fact that Richie deferred to him. That didn't happen a lot for Danny, who had found it hard to make friends and to settle on the island.

She hung a left into Bonnie's driveway and killed the engine. Danny undid his seat belt and waited for her to come around and open the door. Light shone upon them as Bonnie appeared on the steps, her hair loose around her shoulders, a cigarette dangling from the fingers that cupped her elbow. Bonnie Claeson had endured a hard life: a husband who beat her, then ran off with a line-dance teacher; a son who would always be dependent on her; and a succession of men who were at best unsuitable and at worst unstable. Sometimes, Marianne thought, Bonnie Claeson appeared to live her life as if she were being paid by the tear. Then there was the accident, the one in which her nephew Wayne Cady had been killed. Marianne had attended the funeral, along with much of the island's population, watching as the coffin was lowered into the ground at the small cemetery beside the island's Baptist church, Bonnie's sister so distraught with grief that when the time came to drop dirt on the coffin, she had fallen to her knees and buried her face in the damp earth, as if by doing so she might somehow burrow beneath the ground and join the dead boy.

Bonnie had been strong for her sister that day, but then she was strong in so many ways. It wasn't easy for her raising a disabled son alone, and the state's overburdened mental health system had been of little help to her during her son's life. Much of the funding had traditionally gone to placing mentally ill children in psychiatric hospitals or residential programs, but Bonnie had resisted that from the start. For a time the state had provided at-home help to her after her husband left, but cuts in funding and the prohibitive cost of sending someone out to the island on a regular basis meant that the service was withdrawn after less than a year. Marianne was suddenly terribly grateful that Danny would never be so reliant on her, and that at some time in the future she might be able to lean on him for support.

Bonnie had been good to her from the beginning and she had returned that goodwill as much as she could, taking Richie for a night to give Bonnie a break, or bringing him on movie trips with Danny on weekends. She had never discussed her past with Bonnie, but Marianne knew that the older woman suspected more than she ever said. Bonnie had been a victim of enough bad men to recognize a fellow sufferer when she met her.

"Thanks for doing this," Marianne said as she approached the step, her hand on Danny's shoulder.

"It's no problem, hon. How you doing, Danny?"

"Okay," mumbled Danny.

"Just okay? Well, we'll see if we can change that. There's popcorn and soda inside, and Richie has got some new computer game that I'm sure he's just dying to show you. How does that sound?"

"Okay," repeated Danny in that same monotone.

Marianne raised her eyes to heaven, and Bonnie gave her an "I know" shrug in return. "If I'm not late, I'll drop by to pick him up. Otherwise, I'll be by first thing in the morning."

"Don't sweat it, hon. You just have a good time."

Marianne kissed Danny on the cheek, hugged him, and told him to be good, then went back to her car. She waved good-bye as she drove, but Danny was already heading inside and his thoughts of her, and his anger with her, would soon be forgotten with the promise of new games to play. She picked up speed once she was back on the main road, which became Island Avenue. She parked across the street from Good Eats, the sound of bluegrass music coming to her from inside, and checked her makeup in the mirror. She touched up her lipstick, tugged at her hair, then sighed.

She was thirty-two years old and she was going on her first date in years.

With a giant.

Joe Dupree was waiting for her, a beer in front of him. He was seated at a table in the back of the restaurant, turned slightly sideways so that his legs didn't hit the underside. Once again, she was struck by how out of place he must often feel.

Nothing ever sits right for him. Things are always too small, too tight, too narrow. He lives his life in a constant state of displacement. Even the island itself doesn't seem big enough to hold him. He should be out in open spaces, somewhere like Montana, where he would be dwarfed by the scale of the natural world.

He rose as he saw her approach, and the table shuddered as he struck it with his thigh. He reached down to save a water glass from falling, liquid splashing the table and the single red rose in the vase at its center shedding a leaf as his hand made the clumsy catch. The restaurant was half full, mainly with local people, although she saw a young couple stealing curious glances at the big man. Visitors. Funny how, even after only a year here, she resented the presence of outsiders.

"Hi," he said. "I was starting to worry."

"Danny was kicking up some. He still doesn't like it when I head out without him. If he had his way, he'd be sitting here now demanding french fries and soda."

"Nothing wrong with that."

She raised a quizzical eyebrow. "You want me to go back and get him?"

He lifted his hands in surrender. "No, you're just fine."

He reddened, thought briefly about trying to explain what

he meant, then decided that it would only get him into further trouble.

In truth, it had been a long time since Joe Dupree had found himself in a social situation with a woman, and he figured that his skills in that area, limited as they were to begin with, were probably pretty rusty by now. Women occasionally came on to him, or they used to when Joe Dupree would take time out from the island to frequent the bars of the Old Port, the island's little diesel ferry taking him over on its last scheduled run. He would drink in the city's bars until one or two in the morning, then call Thorson and have him come pick him up. The old ferry captain didn't usually mind. He didn't sleep much anyway. On those rare occasions when Thorson couldn't make it, Dupree would either hire a water taxi or take a small single room at a cheap hotel, where he would remove the mattress from the bed and place it on the floor, using cushions to support his legs where they overhung the end.

And in those bars, particularly the ones off the tourist trail, he would sometimes attract the attentions of women. He would hear them, two or three of them, laughing in that way that women with alcohol on their breath and sex on their minds will sometimes laugh, a hoarse, unlovely thing from deep inside them, their eyelids heavy, their eyes narrowing, their lips slightly pursed. Their comments would crawl across the dusty floor

I wonder if he's big all over.

The hands and the feet. You always look at the hands and the feet.

or seep like smoke between the tables

I could make room for him.

Hon, they'd have to take something out of you to make room for what he's got.

until at last they reached him and he would acknowledge them with a thin smile, and they would giggle some more and look away, or perhaps hold his gaze for a time with a look that spoke of tainted promises.

Sometimes he had taken them up on the offer made, and had usually regretted it. The last time it happened, he had accompanied the woman back to her little house in Saco, so neat and feminine that he instantly felt even more out of place than usual, afraid to move for fear that he might dislodge a china doll from the congregation of pale faces that seemed to gaze at him from every shelf, every ledge. She undressed in her bathroom and entered the bedroom wearing only a too-tight bra and black panties, a little fat spilling out over the straps at her back and the elastic at her waist. She was holding a cigarette, and she placed it in her mouth as she pulled back the sheets on the bed, undid the clasp of the bra, and slid it down her arms before hooking her thumbs into the waistband of her underwear and stepping out of them without once glancing at him. She climbed into the bed, drew the sheets up to her waist, then smoked her cigarette as he removed his own clothing, his face burning with shame and self-loathing.

He saw in her eyes not lust or need, not even curiosity, but merely the prospect of the temporary alleviation of her boredom with herself and her own desires. She took a last drag on the cigarette before she stubbed it out in the ashtray on the nightstand and pulled back the sheet, inviting him to join her. As he climbed into bed beside her, he heard the springs creaking beneath his weight, smelled the stale odor of smoke upon the pillows, felt her nails already raking five white trails along his thigh as her hand moved toward his sex.

He left her snoring, the china dolls watching him impassively as he slipped through the house, his shoes in his hands.

He tugged them on as he sat on her porch steps, then called a cab from a pay phone and returned to the Old Port. On a bench by the Casco Bay Ferry Terminal he waited until light dawned, then walked down to Becky's diner on Commercial and ate breakfast with the fishermen, working his way methodically through a plate of eggs and bacon, keeping his head down so that he would not catch the eye of any other diner. And when Thorson's ferry drew toward the dock, carrying those who had jobs in the city, Joe Dupree was waiting for it, barely nodding at those who disembarked, until at last the boat was empty. He took a seat at the back of the ferry and when no further passengers appeared, Thorson started the engine and carried Joe Dupree away from Portland, the wind wiping the smell of perfume and booze and cigarettes from his clothes and hair, cleansing him of the proof of his sins.

Since then, he had not returned to the bars of the Old Port, and now drank little. He could see the surprise in the faces of the wait staff and in the smile of Dale Zimmer when he rose to greet the woman who now sat across from him. He didn't care. It had taken him the best part of a year to work up the courage to ask her out. He liked her son. He liked her. Now she was saying something, but he was so lost in himself that he had to ask her to repeat it.

"I said, it's hard to do anything in secret here. Seems like everyone knows your business before you do."

He smiled. "I remember Dave Mahoney—he was heading on for seventy years of age, the old goat—got himself all worked up over a widow woman named Annie Jabar, who lived about half a mile down the road from him. Nothing had happened between them, nothing more than glances over the bingo table at the American Legion, I guess, or hands almost touching across the shelves at the market, but she was coming on to him, without a doubt. So one day Dave takes it into his head to do something about it. He puts on his best jacket and pants under his slicker, and heads out in the rain to walk down to Annie Jabar's house. When he got there, she was waiting for him."

He shook his head in amusement.

"Who?" asked Marianne. "The widow woman?"

"Nope. Dave's wife. Don't know how she did it, but she got there before he did. I figure she must have sprinted through the woods so that she'd be waiting for him, and she wasn't much younger than Dave. She had a gun too, Dave's varmint rifle. Dave took one look at her, turned around on his heel, and headed straight back home. Never again looked at the widow woman, or any other woman except his wife. She died a couple of years ago, and I heard tell that Annie Jabar might have hoped that she and Dave could get together now that his wife was gone, but far as I know he's never gone next to near her since that day his wife confronted him and made him look down the barrel of his own rifle."

"He loved her, then."

"Loved her and was scared half to death of her. Maybe he figures she might still find a way to get back at him from the next world if he steps out of line, or maybe he just misses her more than he ever thought he would. I talk to him sometimes and I think he's just waiting to join her. I think he realized how much she loved him when he saw that she was prepared to shoot him rather than let another woman take him, even at seventy years of age. Sometimes maybe you have to love someone an awful lot to be prepared to kill them."

His attention was distracted momentarily by movement close to the door, so Dupree did not see the look that passed across Marianne's face. Had he done so, their evening together might have come to an abrupt end, for he would have felt compelled to question her about it. Instead, he was watching a bulky man in a red-checked shirt, accompanied by his equally bulky wife, approaching the exit. As they left, the man gave Dupree a nod that was part acknowledgment, part dismissal. Marianne glanced over her shoulder, grateful for the distraction, and the man smiled at her before his wife gave him a sharp nudge in the ribs with her elbow that nearly propelled him through the door.

"Tom Jaffe," said Dupree.

"His father runs the construction business, right?"

"That's right. He's near sixty-five himself now, but still won't hand over the running of the business to Tom. Doesn't trust him. Tom still believes he's the Great White Hope. He was valedictorian the year I graduated from high school. Liked to think of himself as an orator."

"How was his speech?"

"Terrible. It was basically an extended 'Screw you' to everybody he'd ever known. Somebody tried to run him over in the parking lot afterward."

"Maybe it was just a misunderstanding."

"Nope. I went around for a second try after I missed him. He could run, I'll give him that."

She laughed then, and for the first time, Dupree began to relax. The little restaurant filled up as the evening progressed, but there was never anybody left standing, waiting for a table. They talked about music and movies, and each spoke a little of the past, but not too much. In Joe's case, his reticence was a result of embarrassment, shyness, and a feeling that his life on the island would seem somehow parochial and isolated to this woman with a soft southern accent, a young son, and a firsthand knowledge of places far from this one.

But the woman? Well, her reason for silence was different.

She spoke little of her past, because all that she could give him in return was lies.

They were on dessert when the restaurant door opened and Sally Owen entered. She was one of the bartenders at the Rudder, and had been for as long as Dupree could remember. Rumor was that, when she was younger, she once dragged a guy across the bar for not saying "please" after he'd ordered his drink. She was older now, and a little calmer, and contented herself with shooting dark looks at the ruder customers. Now she walked quickly up to their table and spoke to Joe.

"Joe, I'm real sorry to be disturbing you, but Lockwood is dealing with a possible burglary over on Kemps Road, and Barker is out with one of the fire trucks tending to a car fire."

Dupree couldn't hide his displeasure. He'd asked the cops on duty to try to give him a little space tonight, even if they were snowed under, which seemed unlikely at the start of the day. Still, it wasn't their fault that cars were burning and houses were being burgled, although if they found the people responsible for either event, Joe Dupree was going to have some harsh words to say to the culprits.

"What is it, Sally?"

"Terry Scarfe is in the Rudder, and he's not alone. He's got Carl Lubey in there with him and they're thick as thieves. Just thought you should know."

Marianne watched Dupree's expression darken. There was sorrow there too, she thought, a reminder of events that he had tried to forget. She knew the story of Carl Lubey's brother. Everybody on the island knew it.

Ronnie Lubey had been a minor-league criminal, with convictions for possession with intent and aggravated burglary. On the night that he'd died, he had a cocktail of uppers and alcohol in his belly and was spoiling for a fight. He'd started shooting out the windows of his neighbor's house, yelling about tree trunks and boundaries, and by the time Joe and Daniel Snowman, who had since retired, arrived out at the house, Ronnie was slumped against a tree trunk, mumbling to himself, puke on his shirt and pants and shoes.

When the two policemen pulled up, Ronnie looked at them, raised the shotgun, and shot wildly from the hip. Snowman went down, his left leg peppered with shot, and after an unheeded warning, Dupree opened fire. He aimed low, hitting Ronnie in the thigh, but the shot busted Ronnie's femoral artery. Dupree had done his best for him, but his priority had been his partner. Snowman survived, Ronnie Lubey died, and his little brother, Carl, who also lived on the island, had never forgiven the big policeman.

Marianne didn't know who Terry Scarfe was, but if he was keeping company with Carl Lubey, then he wasn't anyone she wanted to know. During her first month on the island, Carl had tried to come on to her as she sat with Bonnie at the bar of the Rudder. When she'd turned down his offer of a drink, Carl called her every name he could think of, then tried to reach for her breast in the hope of copping a consolatory feel. She had pushed him away, and then Jeb Burris had climbed over the bar and hauled Carl outside. The young policeman Berman had been on duty that night. Marianne remembered that he had been kind to her and had warned Carl to stay away from her. Since then, she had endured only occasional contact with him when he came into the market. When she passed him on the street or saw him on the ferry, he contented himself with looking at her, his eyes fixed on her breasts or her crotch.

"I'd better go take a look," Dupree said as Sally nodded a good-bye and returned to the bar. "You excuse me for a couple of minutes? I'll be back as soon as I can."

He rose and laid his hand gently on her shoulder as he passed by her. She brushed his fingers with her hand, and felt his grip linger for a moment before he left her.

Dupree walked down Island Avenue and made a right. Straight downhill on the left was the island's ferry terminal and across from it was the Rudder Bar. It had an open deck at its rear, which filled up with tourists during the summer but was empty now that winter had come. Inside, he could see lights and a half dozen people drinking and playing pool.

He entered the bar and saw Scarfe and Lubey immediately. They were sitting at the bar, leaning into each other. Lubey raised his glass as Sally came out from the small kitchen behind the bar.

"Hey, Sal, you got any shots that taste like pussy?"

"I wouldn't know what pussy tastes like," said Sally, glancing at Dupree as he drew closer.

Lubey lifted a finger and extended it to her.

"Then lick here," he said, and the two men collapsed into laughter.

"How you doing, boys?" said Dupree.

Both men turned in unison to look at him.

"We're not your boys," said Lubey. His eyes were dull. He swayed slightly as he tried to keep Dupree in focus.

"It's the Jolly Green Giant," said Scarfe. "What's wrong, Mr. Giant? You don't look so jolly no more."

"We don't usually see you over here, Terry. Last I heard, you were doing three to five."

"I got paroled. Good behavior."

"I don't think your behavior is so good tonight."

"What's your problem, *Off-fis-sur*?" said Lubey. "I'm having a drink with my buddy. We ain't bothering nobody."

"I think you've had enough."

"What are you going to do?" asked Lubey. "Shoot me?"

Dupree looked at him. Lubey held the gaze for as long as he could, then glanced away, a dumb smile playing on his lips. Dupree returned his attention to Scarfe.

"I want you off the island, Terry. Thorson has a crossing in ten minutes. You be on that ferry."

Scarfe looked at Lubey, shrugged, then slid from his stool and picked up his jacket.

"The Green Giant wants me off the island, Carl, so I got to go. I'll be seeing you."

"Yeah, be seeing you, Terry. Fight the power."

Dupree stepped back and watched as Scarfe headed unsteadily for the door, then turned back to Lubey.

"You drive here?" he asked.

Lubey didn't reply.

"I asked you a question, Carl."

"Yeah, I drove," said Lubey at last.

"Give me your keys."

The other man dug into his pockets and found his car keys. As Dupree reached out for them, Lubey dropped them to the floor.

"Whoops," he said.

"Pick them up."

He climbed from the stool, bent down gingerly, then toppled over. Dupree helped him to his feet, picking up the keys as he did so. Once he was upright again, Lubey shrugged off the policeman's hand.

"Get your hands off me."

"You want me to put you in cuffs, I will. We can get a boat over here and you can spend the night in a cell."

Lubey reached for his coat.

"I'm going," he said.

"You can pick up your keys from the station house in the morning."

Lubey waved a hand in dismissal and headed for the door. Behind the bar, Jeb Burris took off his apron and said: "I'll give him a ride back."

Dupree nodded and gave him Lubey's car keys.

"Yeah, do that."

Back outside, he watched as Terry Scarfe and two other people, tourists who'd been eating at the restaurant, climbed onboard Thorson's ferry and headed back to Portland.

Scarfe kept looking back at the island, and Dupree, until the ferry faded from view.

Marianne had enjoyed a couple of glasses of wine at dinner, Dupree a single beer. He offered to drive her back to her house and said he would arrange to have her car dropped at her door before eight the next morning. She sat in the passenger seat of Dupree's own Jeep and stared in silence through the side window. Dupree wanted to believe that it was a comfortable silence, but he sensed her sadness as he drove.

"You okay?"

She nodded, but her mouth wrinkled and he could see that she was near tears.

"It's been a long time, you know?"

He didn't, and he felt foolish for not knowing.

"Since what?"

"Since I had a nice evening with a man. I'd kind of forgotten what it was like."

He coughed to hide his embarrassment and his secret pleasure.

"You always cry at the end of a nice evening?"

She smiled and wiped at the tears with the tips of her fingers.

"Hell, I must have snail trails running down my face."

"No, you look good."

"Liar."

He hung a right into the driveway of her small house and pulled up outside her door. She looked at him.

"Would you like to come in? I can make you coffee."

"Sure. Coffee would be good."

He followed her inside, and sat on the edge of the living-room couch as she went to the bathroom to fix her makeup. When she came out, she went straight to the kitchen and put the kettle on the stove, then swore.

"I'm sorry," she called out. "I've only got instant."

"It'll be just like home."

She peered around the corner of the doorway, unsure if he was being sarcastic.

He caught the look.

"No, honest, it will be just like home. All I ever make is instant."

"Well, if you say so. Put on some music, if you like."

He rose and walked to the pile of CDs that lay stacked against the wall. A JVC system stood on the third shelf of the Home Depot bookcase. He tried squatting and looking sideways at the CDs, then kneeling. Finally, he lay flat on the floor and ran his finger down the spines.

"I don't recognize any of this stuff," he said as she came into the room carrying two mugs of coffee on a tray.

"You're out of touch," she said.

"Radio reception sucks this far out, and I don't go over to the mainland as much as I used to. Hey, are the Doobie Brothers still together?"

"I hear Michael McDonald left," she said. "Things aren't looking so good for Simon and Garfunkel either."

He smelled her perfume as she knelt down beside him, and her arm brushed his hair gently as she reached across and carefully removed a disc from the pile. He placed his hand against the discs beneath, steadying them so that they would not fall. She put a bright blue CD into the player, then skipped through the tracks until she got to number six. Slow funk emerged from the speakers.

"Sounds like Prince," he said.

She cocked an eyebrow at him. "Maybe you're not so out of touch after all. You're close. It's Maxwell. This track's called 'Til the Cops Come Knockin'.' I thought you might appreciate the humor."

"It's good," he said. "The song, I mean. The humor I'm not so sure about."

She swiped at him playfully, then rose and sipped her coffee, her body swaying slightly to the music. Dupree watched her from the floor, then turned awkwardly and stood from the knees up. He lifted his coffee mug, instinctively grasping it in his hand instead of trying unsuccessfully to fit his finger through the handle. Little things, he thought. It's the little things you have to remember.

Marianne walked to the window and looked out on the dark woods beyond. Her body grew still. He waited for her to speak.

"The bird—" she began, and he felt his back stiffen in response. Had she also noticed their absence? Instantly, his conversation with Amerling and Jack returned to him, and the pleasure of the evening began to dissipate like smoke.

"The gull that you put out of its misery?"

He felt relieved for a moment, until he thought about Danny and the look on his face after he had killed the bird.

"Like I said, I'm sorry about that," he interrupted. "I should have made him walk away."

"No, it's not that. I think Danny dug it up, after you'd left. I think he dug it up and . . . did something to it."

"Like what?"

"I found blood and feathers." She left her fear unspoken, hoping the policeman would pick up on it.

Dupree put his cup down and stood beside her.

"He's a boy. They can be curious about things like that. If you want, I can talk to him."

"I guess I'm just worried."

"Has he ever hurt any living animals?"

"I've told him off for throwing stones at cats, and he's mischievous about bugs and stuff, but I don't think he's ever really hurt anything."

"Well, then. I'd maybe leave him be this time."

She nodded, but he sensed once again that she was far away from him, walking in the country of her past. He finished his coffee and placed the mug carefully on the tray.

"I'd better be going," he said.

She didn't reply, but as he moved to get his coat, her hand reached for him and laid itself softly upon his arm. He could feel the heat of her through the fabric of his shirt. She looked up at him, and the expression on her face was unreadable.

"I'm sorry," she said. "Like I said, it's been a long time. I've forgotten how this should go."

Then he inclined his head and body toward her, bending almost double to reach her. He kissed her, and her mouth opened beneath his, and her body moved against him. Later, she led him into her bedroom and they undressed in darkness, and he found her by the light of her eyes and the paleness of her skin and the fading scent of her perfume. For a time, all of their pain was forgotten, and the night gathered them to itself and wrapped them, briefly, in peace.

The painter Giacomelli sat in his studio, the lamp on the table casting its harsh light across brushes and paints and leaning canvases. Jack wanted a drink. He wanted a drink very badly, but he was too afraid to drink. After his conversation with Dupree and Larry Amerling, he had gone for a late-afternoon walk along the wooded trails that crisscrossed the center of the island, but he had not gone as far as the Site. Instead, he had stood at a forest of dead trees, the roots drowned by bog, and looked toward the dark interior in which the ruins lay. There was a stillness there, it seemed, the kind of quiescence that comes on late-summer days when the sky is overcast, the heat oppressive and unyielding, and the world waits for the weather to break and the skies to explode violently into rain. He stood on the trail, looking out over the patch of dead beech trees, their trunks gray and skewed as their decaying root structures failed to hold them upright. A mist seemed to hang about them—no, not a mist, exactly, but rather it appeared as if their slow decay had now become visible, the tiny fragments combining to cast a veil over the trees and the ground. He dragged his fingers across the front of his coat and raised his hand before him, expecting to see them coated in gray, but they were clean.

He walked no farther that day.

Now he sat and stared at one of the flawed paintings, which were, in their way, better than anything that he had ever done before, for the waves seemed to move over the bodies, causing them to bob slightly in the tide, and there was a silver light over the waters and the rocks that he had never previously managed to capture, for it had never been apparent to him until now. In fact, he admitted, he couldn't recall adding the sheen of light to the picture either, and no moon hung in the dusk sky of his work, or what used to be his work.

Moloch woke.

For a moment, he felt himself in the semidarkness of the prison, for in the cell block a dull light hung over all things, even at night. He could hear men snoring, and footsteps. He raised himself from the sweat of his pillow and ran his hands through his hair, then saw Willard, now also awake, watching him from his post beneath the window, the curtains drawn to discourage snoopers.

He had been dreaming again, but this time there was no girl and no killing. Instead, he was alone among the trees, walking through wooded trails, dead leaves crunching beneath his feet, moonlight gilding the branches. Yet when he looked up there was no moon visible, and the skies were black with clouds. Ahead of him lay a darkness, marked only by the thin shapes of dead beech trees, impaled upon the earth like the spears of giants.

Something waited for him in the shadows.

I could map this place, he thought, this landscape of my dreams. I know it well, for I have seen it every night for the last year, and each time it becomes more familiar to me. I know its paths, its rocks, the landings along its coastline. Only that darkness, and what lies within it, is hidden from me.

But in time, I will know that too.

He got to his feet. Willard remained seated, his eyes fixed on him.

"You okay?" asked Moloch.

"Dexter doesn't like me," said Willard. "Shepherd neither."

"They don't have to like you."

"I think they want to hurt me."

Moloch was grateful for the cover of darkness.

"They won't do that. They'll do what I say."

"What you say," echoed Willard. He spoke in a monotone.

"That's right. Now let's go downstairs, get something to eat."

He waited until Willard rose. For a moment, they stood together at the doorway, each seemingly unwilling to turn his back on the other. At last, Willard stepped through, and Moloch followed him, just as Moloch had followed him from the bar years before.

I trust you.

Followed him to a house.

They'll do what I say.

Followed him to a woman.

What you say.

And bound himself to Willard in damnation.

THE LAST DAY

And how can man die better
Than facing fearful odds . . .

—Macaulay, "Horatius"

CHAPTER EIGHT

The giant was gone. He left her before the clock read five, for he would soon have to relieve the patrolmen on duty and allow them to catch the ferry back to the mainland. A new cop was coming over on the return leg; a rookie, he said, one who had never been given island duty before. He stroked her hair as he spoke, his arm holding her to him as they lay close together in the false intimacy resulting from their lovemaking.

For it was false. Dupree wanted to be close to her, but how could he draw near when she would tell him so little and when he suspected the veracity of even those small details that she chose to reveal? In the restaurant, he had been startled by how beautiful she looked. During her time on the island, it had seemed to him that she did all that she could not to attract attention, to downplay and even to camouflage her looks. But when she'd entered Good Eats that night, heads had turned, and Dupree had tried hard not to look smug as she walked to his table. It made him determined that the night should be special for her, for them both. Without being asked, Dale Zimmer had taken personal responsibility for their meal, moving between the kitchen and the dining room, solicitous without being overbearing. From their window table overlooking the water they could see the lights of the neighboring islands shining brightly, like small night suns hoping to dazzle the stars. In the candlelight, he had found himself occasionally overawed by her and had concentrated so hard on trying not to break or spill anything that his head hurt by the end of the meal. The only taints upon the evening were the encounter with Lubey and Scarfe at the Rudder, and Dupree's niggling concern at the fact that his companion was still keeping things from him.

Marianne was aware of his unease. Her years spent moving and hiding had heightened her perceptions, making her acutely sensitive to how others were regarding her. Now, alone, she replayed the events of the previous night in her mind, recalling his reactions, his hesitations, the fleeting changes in expression as he listened to her speak. She had not intended the night to end as it had, or if she had, then she had not admitted it to herself. But as the evening went on, and the wine began to have its effect, she wondered what it would be like to make love to him, to take him inside her. She had been a little afraid; afraid of the weight of him, his bulk, and the awkwardness that came with it, for there was little that was graceful about him. He was a man constantly waiting for the sound of falling objects, a man always out of step with the world. But then he came to her bed, and he was gentle, and his touch was surprisingly tender.

She felt guilty for lying to him about her past, but she had no choice in the matter. To tell him the truth could lead to her losing Danny. Worse, it would expose her, and then *he* would find out.

And his people would come.

Lost amid regrets, the warmth of him still upon the pillow, Marianne began to cry.

Dupree drove first to his own house, where he showered and changed into his uniform. In his bathroom, as he listened to the water running in the shower, he smelled Marianne upon him and felt a twinge of regret that her scent would soon be washed from his body. Later, after he had changed, he picked up his shirt from the night before and brought it to his face. There was a small stain on the material where her face had pressed against him and he touched the traces of makeup with his fingertip. Then he carefully placed the shirt in the bathroom closet, above the laundry basket.

Barker was sitting in the office reading a novel when Dupree arrived. The sound of running water came from the open bathroom door, where Lockwood was brushing his teeth.

"Sleep well?" asked Barker. He was grinning.

"Pretty good," said Dupree, maintaining a poker face.

"Dinner good?"

"That was pretty good too."

"Breakfast?"

"I haven't eaten breakfast yet."

"You should eat breakfast. You need to keep up your strength. I like a woman to make me breakfast the morning after."

Dupree scowled at him. "Is this in the real world, or the fantasy one?"

Now it was Barker's turn to frown. "Hey, my wife makes breakfast every morning, now that I come to think of it. Sometimes we even have sex the night before. Not often, but sometimes."

"More than I need to know," said Dupree. "*So* much more than I need to know."

Lockwood came out of the bathroom. He walked like a dancer on the balls of his feet. He and the overweight Barker were an unlikely pairing, but Dupree liked them both in their own way.

"I borrow you for a few minutes?" Dupree said to Lockwood. He wanted someone to help him take Marianne's car back to her house, but he wasn't about to ask Barker to do it. Lockwood was less likely to use his suspicions about Dupree's nocturnal activities as a source of humor.

"Sure."

Lockwood grabbed his jacket and followed Dupree outside.

"I have to take a car back to its owner. I'd like you to follow me in the Explorer, you got nothing else to do, and give me a ride back here afterward."

"No problem."

"I appreciate it."

They drove out to Marianne Elliot's house. Dupree parked outside her front door, leaving the keys in the ignition. He looked up at the window of her bedroom, but the drapes were closed. He wondered what she was doing, until he saw the drapes move slightly and then Marianne was standing at the window, looking down on him. She smiled nervously and gave him a little wave. He waved back, then walked over and got into the Explorer next to Lockwood.

Lockwood looked at him.

"So, did she make you breakfast?"

Dupree reddened.

"I asked you to come along because I didn't think you were as big a horse's ass as Barker."

Lockwood shrugged.

"Not smaller, just quieter."

They drove along in silence for a time, until Lockwood asked Dupree if Sally Owen had found him last night.

"Yeah, I took care of it."

"Lubey give you any trouble?"

"Nope, just shot his mouth off some."

"You think he and Terry Scarfe were just catching up?"

"I don't know. Maybe they're thinking of forming a book club."

"A picture-book club. Those guys are dumb."

"Lubey is, but Scarfe is a little smarter. He's like a rat. He'd sell his mother's corpse for cash, if he could bother to dig her up."

"You think he was dealing on the island?"

Dupree winced. He'd been so distracted by Marianne that he hadn't bothered to search either Scarfe or Lubey, yet he didn't believe Scarfe would be stupid enough to bring drugs over with him. But he hadn't known that Scarfe and Lubey were friendly, and even though they were laughing together the night before, he still got the feeling that they weren't particularly close. Scarfe wanted something from Carl Lubey and that couldn't be good because Carl Lubey had nothing positive to offer anyone.

"I'll keep an eye on Lubey," he said at last. "You hear anything about Scarfe over in Portland, maybe you'd give me a call."

"Will do," said Lockwood. They turned onto Island Avenue. It was still dark, but the sky was brightening slightly.

"Anything else I should know?" asked Dupree.

"Well, we're still having trouble with the radios. Phones too."

The problems with the radios were a recent development. The radio system in the Explorer was a dual arrangement. When the Portland PD had updated the island's equipment, the old radio had been left in the Explorer and a second, portable system had been plugged into it. The new radio allowed the patrol cop to stay in touch with both the island base and dispatch over in Portland. The old system, meanwhile, enabled the island police to contact outside agencies such as the state police or the fire department. Over the last week, there had been gaps in transmission. Each of the island cops, Dupree included, had experienced some difficulty in raising either Portland or the station house, while on other occasions there had been the equivalent of a crossed line, faint voices audible in the background of regular transmissions. The radios had been checked and judged to be in perfect working order. "Ghosts in the machine," as Lockwood had put it. Now the problem seemed to have spread to the phone lines.

"What about the phones?" asked Dupree.

"Same as the radio. Line was dead at least four times last night, just for a couple of seconds. You know, I picked up, there was nothing, then the dial tone kicked in. Other times there was light static. Could be the storm. Weathermen are saying that it's going to hit the coast sometime tonight, although I've never heard of an approaching snowstorm affecting communications in that way before."

Dupree didn't reply. He was reminded of the previous day's conversation with Amerling and Jack—*It's like the buildup before an electrical storm*—and the task that he had been putting off until after his dinner with Marianne: the visit to the Site.

"You know anything about this rookie cop Macy?" asked Dupree.

"I know she's cute."

"That'll be a big help."

"With respect, Joe, it's not as if she's entering a war zone."

"No," said Dupree. "I guess not."

While the two men drove together, Sharon Macy stood in line for the small ferry. She'd heard tales about Thorson and his ferry, most of them, she hoped, gross exaggerations. One of the other field training officers, Christine McCalmon, had jokingly offered her the use of a life jacket for the trip. Macy had gone down to the dock the day before to take a look at the ferry as it left for its early-evening sailing. It looked a little rickety, but Macy figured it was better than rowing across Casco Bay in a teapot.

There were three other people beside her at the dock on Commercial Street, all with their eyes fixed on the little diesel boat, which was currently occupied by Thorson and his crewman. Thorson didn't appear to be in too much of a hurry to get going. Macy thought he looked kind of hung over and figured that she could probably arrest him for some form of seagoing violation if she chose, but she guessed that nobody would thank her for it. Maybe if she took out her gun and forced him at gunpoint to get his ass in gear, then she might get their support and admiration. It was cold on the dock and the wind nipped painfully at her nose and ears.

"Cap'n," said the man beside her, "what the hell are we waiting for?"

"Supplies," said Thorson. "I promised Huddie Harris that I'd carry over some machine parts. His sister said she'd bring them along before five."

"It's five-fifteen now."

"Ayuh."

That was it, thought Macy. Thorson's "ayuh" was the equivalent of a shoulder shrug, a complete abdication of responsibility. He had promised Huddie his parts, Huddie had probably promised him a couple of six-packs and some cash in return, and nobody was going to be allowed to get in the way of their arrangement. She kicked at a stone and pushed her hands deeper into her pockets as a woman wearing a quilted jacket shuffled along the dock pulling a beat-up metal box on wheels. Erin Harris; she lived in Portland but spent weekends out on Dutch with her brother. Macy recalled her face from an altercation outside the Eastland Hotel a month or two back, when the wife of one of Erin's sometime boyfriends had decided that enough was enough and that Erin should quit messing with her man. Macy found it kind of difficult to figure out what the man in question saw in either of the women because Erin Harris was ugly on the outside and uglier still on the inside, but she was a bargain compared to the woman with whom she had been slugging it out that night. Barron had tried to intervene but Erin Harris had taken a swing at him and Macy had been forced to spray her. Maced by Macy, as Barron had put it later. It had all been kind of ugly. Macy kept her head down and watched quietly as the box was passed down to Thorson. Erin shot a glance at Macy as she passed. There was no disguising the hostility in her face. Macy didn't look away.

"Okay," said Thorson. "All aboard. We're good to go."

The four passengers climbed aboard the ferry, three occupying the wooden benches on the lower deck while Macy took a seat on the exposed upper deck. Minutes later they were heading out to sea, the gulls crying above them and gray waves breaking at the bow. Macy was already in uniform. An L. L. Bean backpack lay at her feet. She had taken Barron's advice and brought a couple of books with her, as well as a Discman and a bunch of CDs. She slipped a CD into the player as Portland grew smaller behind her, the first bars of the Scud Mountain Boys' "Freight of Fire" filling her ears as the spray splashed her face, the lead singer Joe Pernice advising her to bring her guns and all her ammunition; and she felt the weight of the pistol beneath her jacket and smiled as she recalled Barron's tales of giants and the bones of men buried beneath pine trees.

Dupree was dealing with another reporter, one who was clearly trying to kill time during the early shift. This one was calling from Florida, so at least the interview didn't have to be conducted face-to-face, which was something. Like most beat cops, Dupree had a natural distrust of reporters. There had been an accident down in the Keys a couple of days earlier in which three teenagers had drowned after a stolen car went off a bridge. The reporter was trying to pull together a feature about the danger of wayward teens and the accident on Dutch was a good tie-in.

"Yeah, the boy was dead when we got there," said Dupree. "There was nothing we could do for him. The girl was badly injured. She died at the scene." He grimaced even as he said the words, then listened to the next inevitable question about what safety measures had been introduced in the aftermath.

"We're doing everything we can to ensure that a tragedy like this never happens again. We're looking at ring-fencing the entire area, maybe sowing the slopes with scrap metal to stop anyone taking a car up there."

It should have been done years before, thought Dupree. I should have forced them to do it, but they wanted to leave the emplacement as it was, and anyway, kids will be kids. There had never been an accident on the slope before the deaths of Wayne Cady and Sylvie Lauter. It was just one of those things.

The reporter thanked him, then hung up. The clock on the wall read 6:25 A.M. The ferry would be due in soon, bringing with it his partner for the next twenty-four hours. Barker was already down at the little jetty, smoking a cigarette and kicking his heels impatiently, Lockwood sitting quietly beside him.

Dupree wondered again about Sharon Macy. The arrival of a new face was always difficult. The older cops were used to Joe by now, but the younger ones could never hide their feelings toward him when they encountered him for the first time; usually it was just surprise, sometimes amusement, and very occasionally a kind of uneasiness. He knew that there were those who referred to him as a freak. In addition, rookies and trainees rarely got sent out to the islands, but the rotation had been hit by illness, family obligations, and amassed vacation time. The department was filling in the gaps with whatever it had.

He climbed into the Explorer and drove down to the dock, trying to pick out the ferry in the semidarkness. The ferry service was subsidized by a small tax levied on the island's residents each year. Nobody ever complained about the tax; they valued their independence, but the islanders still needed the safety net that Portland provided, with its stores and hospitals and movie theaters and restaurants. In the event of a medical emergency, like that time Sarah Froness had fallen off her roof and broken her back while stringing up Christmas lights, the cops on duty could radio for a helicopter pickup from the baseball diamond north of Liberty. It had taken the chopper crew just thirty minutes to get to Dutch on that occasion, and Sarah Froness could still be seen ambling into the market to buy her weekly supply of trash magazines and six-for-five beers, although she didn't go climbing ladders on December 1 anymore and she walked a little more gingerly than before. Sylvie Lauter hadn't been so lucky, and Dupree blamed himself for what had occurred. He replayed the events of that night over and over, wondering what might have happened if they had gotten to the crash site a little earlier, if old Buck Tennier had made the call as soon as he'd noticed the revving of the car's engine instead of waiting until he heard the crash. But it wasn't his fault. Dupree and the other cops should have patrolled the area more often, making it too risky for the wilder kids to use it. But Sanctuary was still a big island for a pair of cops to cover. They couldn't be everywhere, and now two young people were dead.

Sanctuary: he had found himself using that name more often in recent days, not only when he was talking to older islanders like Amerling or Giacomelli, but also to visitors and new residents. He had even caught himself using the name when he was speaking with the reporter earlier that morning. He always thought of it as Sanctuary in his own mind, but over the years he had managed to make a distinction between that name and its official name in his day-to-day work. Sanctuary was its past, Dutch was its present. The fact that he was increasingly slipping into the old usage indicated a leaching of the past into his perception of the island, an acknowledgment of its grip upon him, upon all of them.

He thought of Sylvie Lauter's final moments, of her pain and of the blood that had stained his clothing. He thought too of the autopsy and the peculiarities it had uncovered; there had been damage to the back of Sylvie Lauter's tongue and throat, as if something had been forced into her mouth. Maybe she and Wayne had been arguing or fooling around before the crash, and somehow she had managed to wound herself. As he had told Jack and Amerling, gray matter had been found in one of the cuts, and had subsequently been identified as wing material from a moth: *Manduca quinquemaculata,* the tomato hornworm moth, a member of the sphinx moth family. Dupree had never seen one, and didn't even know what the insect looked like until a specimen was sent to him from a sympathetic university researcher up in Orono. It had a four-inch wingspan and a large body that tapered almost to a point. Five or six pairs of yellow spots ran down its abdomen. There was a kind of beauty to its wings, which, even on this dead specimen, seemed to shimmer, but overall Dupree thought the insect ugly, the markings on its body and its strange pointed rear making it seem like some peculiar hybrid of moth and reptile.

He had no idea how fragments of that kind of insect, however small, could have found their way into Sylvie Lauter's mouth. Most moths were dead by July or August. This moth's season was June to September, but it was now January and no moth could survive the temperatures on the island. He had asked around, but nobody on the island bred moths. Killed plenty of them, sure, but didn't breed them. Yet somehow Sylvie Lauter had come into contact with a tomato hornworm, the same species of moth that Dupree had found in the Newton woman's bedroom and that now lay dead in its jelly jar beside the original specimen from Orono. It was peculiar, he told himself, but nothing more. For a second, he almost believed it.

Now the ferry could be clearly seen, a finger trail of diesel fumes rising behind it. Joe took his binoculars from the floor and trained them on the boat. It was still too far away to distinguish faces, but he counted six people onboard. He experienced a tingling in his fingers. His feet felt too big for his shoes, and despite the cold, the Explorer felt stuffy and warm. He rolled down the window, and as the icy breeze hit his face, he realized that he was sweating.

The ferry passed Fort Gorges, rust seeping in tear trails from the bars on its windows, then followed the mail-boat route between the Diamonds and Peaks, passing Pumpkin Knob on the right, then Long Island, before leaving Great Chebeague on its left and moving into Luckse Sound, skirting Chebeague once again as it headed into Broad Sound, slaloming between Bangs and Stave, Bates and Ministerial, the tiny islands that dotted Casco Bay, so many of them that they had been christened the Calendar Islands because it was once erroneously believed that there were 365 in all.

Slowly, a larger island began to emerge, rising slightly at its wooded center, the white finger of an observation tower visible at its highest point, a small, unmanned lighthouse at its northeastern extreme: Dutch Island, although Macy preferred the old nomenclature of Sanctuary. Macy had been curious about why Sanctuary should have remained in the jurisdiction of Portland. After all, Long Island, which was closer to the shore, was outside the jurisdiction of the Portland Police Department. Sanctuary, meanwhile, was farther out, beyond even Jewell Island.

Barron had shrugged when she'd asked. "It goes way back," he said. "It's tied up with the first settlers and with the ones who came after. It's to do with the Duprees as well. They used to be pretty wealthy, and they funded a lot of development in Portland, particularly after the fire of eighteen sixty-six. That money's gone now, but the ties remain. The folks out on

Dutch voted to remain under Portland's jurisdiction, they pay taxes, and with Melancholy Joe out there being a martyr and doing more than his fair share, it doesn't cost the city too much."

Macy could see a black-and-white Explorer parked above the passenger shelter. The slowly rising sun shone on the windshield.

The giant was waiting.

The ferry docked and Macy shouldered her bag. Erin Harris was the first to disembark. Her brother was waiting for his machine parts beside a red Dodge truck. She could see the family resemblance, since they were both ugly and both looked like men. He glanced once at Macy, recalling her from his efforts to bail his sister out, but there was no hostility in his look. After all, it was his sister she had maced, not him, and it didn't look as if he was too fond of her anyway. She spotted the two cops, Barker and Lockwood, and exchanged some words of greeting. They wished her luck, she thanked them, and then headed up to the Explorer.

The door of the vehicle opened and a man climbed out. Her first instinct was to wonder how he had managed to get into the Explorer to begin with. His great frame unfolded like that of some huge dark insect, until he towered almost two feet over her. His eyes were hidden behind a pair of shades and he wore no cap. He extended a hand the size of a shovel blade.

"Joe Dupree," he said.

She allowed her own hand to be briefly engulfed in his, like a little fish being swallowed up by an eel.

"Sharon Macy."

He released her hand. "Put your stuff in the back. You want the tour?"

"Sure. Do we get to stop and take pictures?"

He laughed briefly. It sounded, she thought, like tectonic plates might sound as they rubbed against one another beneath the earth.

"I think you can safely leave your camera in your bag."

They did a U-turn, then headed up the short road that led from the jetty to the main intersection. Dupree hung a left.

"You always meet the ferry?"

"Try to. It's more important in summer than winter. We get a lot of people through here in July and August. I was only kidding about the pictures. This place is beautiful in summer and there are some pretty expensive summer homes dotted around the island. Mantle, the guy who runs the Fable computer company? He has a house here. Big Time Warner executive named Sandra Morgan owns a cottage out by Beech Cove, and there are a couple of others too. They'd be real pissed if someone trashed their houses."

He pulled in at the redbrick municipal building.

"We do it all out here. There's a doctor comes out from the mainland two afternoons a week, and Doc Bruder is still here, although he's officially retired, but we're the first point of contact. We're also the fire department, game wardens, school patrol, crossing guards, and dogcatchers."

He left the Explorer. Macy followed. The sliding garage doors were open, revealing four vehicles parked inside. "Medcu Fourteen," said Dupree, pointing at the ambulance inside the door. "If an emergency arises, we go out in this, do what we can to get the patient comfortable, then get them to the ferry landing or, in a really urgent case, out to the baseball diamond for a chopper pickup."

He moved on to the red fire trucks, and patted the first.

"This is Engine Fourteen. We use it mostly to pump water. Over there is Ladder Fourteen, the primary attack vehicle.

That's what we take out to fires while we're waiting for the local volunteers to get organized. That smaller truck in the corner is Tank Fourteen. Basically, it's just a big bucket on wheels. We haul it out to those places on the island that don't have hydrants."

"Are there many of those?"

"A couple," he said, in a tone of voice suggesting that half the island was probably without hydrants. He carried on into the station house. There was an open area with a table and two chairs, some books and magazines on the table. To the left was the communications center: a radio, a computer, a bulletin board pasted with notices, reminders and scribbled notes. A large map of the island dominated one wall.

"We have a secretary?"

"Nope. All nine-one-one calls go through the dispatch center in Portland, but most people just call us direct. Paperwork, filing, well, we do that ourselves."

Across the main reception area was a second room, housing an emergency generator, various pieces of equipment, and a locker containing a single shotgun.

"This is it for weapons?" said Macy.

"We don't have too much call for SWAT teams out here," said Dupree. "Last time I used this was to kill a rabid raccoon. It had been so long since I'd fired it, I was just grateful that it didn't blow up in my face."

Macy took the Mossberg pump-action from his hands. It had been cleaned recently, she noticed.

"Doesn't look so bad," she said.

"I gave it a pretty good cleaning a day or two back," said Dupree.

She glanced at him, alerted by his tone.

"Why, something happen?"

"No," he said. "But you never know."

He wasn't smiling.

"Guess not," she said.

Upstairs was a sofa bed, a TV, some chairs, a small kitchen area, and a bathroom with a shower stall and toilet.

"No cells," she said.

"Nope. If we make an arrest, we call Portland. They send out a boat and take the prisoner back. Until then, there are two steel loops in the main reception area. I've had to use them a handful of times."

"We've only got one patrol vehicle?"

"We used to have a golf cart as well, but it broke down. I live about two hundred feet from here and I've got my own Jeep if we need another vehicle. Come on, I'll buy you a cup of coffee and introduce you to some people."

As Macy followed him from the building she rubbed her fingers together, feeling the oil on her skin. She couldn't be certain, but from the smell of the shotgun it had been fired recently.

Somebody had been practicing.

Dupree introduced her to the folks at the market, to the Tooker sisters at the diner (Nancy Tooker half-jokingly warned her to stay away from "her" Berman), to Dale Zimmer and Jeb Burris, and, finally, to Larry Amerling. By then it was time for lunch, and Dupree suggested to Macy that she take the Explorer and drive around the island in the company of the postmaster while he made some calls. Amerling, the old Lothario, was quite content to spend his lunch hour in the company of an attractive young woman, especially one who had read his book.

"If he tries anything," Dupree warned her, "shoot him."

"What if she tries anything with me?" Larry protested.

Dupree looked hard at Macy. "You get that desperate, shoot yourself."

There was no road leading directly to the Site, which was surrounded on three sides by patches of bog. Instead, Dupree parked at the top of Ocean Street, which ran north from Island Avenue almost to the center of the island, and walked along the trail toward the burial ground. The forest was mainly evergreens, but there were also scattered maples and beech and hemlock. Amerling was right; the trail was obscured by the fallen branches and the last dry leaves, but tan winter maleberry had also encroached, some of its round seed capsules cracking beneath his feet, along with gray-black winterberry bushes and tattered larches. Within ten minutes, Dupree was in trouble. The trail had virtually disappeared, and only his own knowledge of the island enabled him to continue in what he thought was the right direction. It came as a shock to him when he found himself approaching a stretch of road and realized that, somehow, he had walked southwest instead of southeast, and was now back on Ocean Street, except maybe half a mile below where he had started.

Frustrated, he retraced his steps and found that he had mistaken a secondary walking trail for the main path, for bushes and briers had obscured the principal artery so effectively that there was no way to distinguish it from the rest of the forest unless one knew where to look. He hacked a way through using his Maglite and continued along the path, almost losing his way twice more when it once again began to disappear. As he drew nearer to the Site, he noticed that more and more trees were dying, and that the patch of bog at the island's center appeared to be increasing in size. Still water lay like a black mirror, almost level with the narrow causeway formed by the trail as it crossed the marsh. If heavy rains came in the spring, the trail would be submerged. Here the greenery was at least understandable, leaf retention being reasonably common among bog plants. Bog rosemary, bog laurel, and labrador tea grew steadily beside green tubular pitcher plants, the remains of insects still trapped in their inner pools. The trees here appeared stunted, their trunks lost beneath the encroaching bog. Others had their shallow roots layered with a dark green sphagnum moss and lush, creeping vines. The life here was hidden, visible only to those who were patient and knowledgeable enough for it to reveal itself: back swimmers and beetles, dragonfly larvae and mayfly nymphs, and smaller mammals like voles and squirrels moved busily through this world. What seemed quiet and dead was secretly alive; wary, but alive.

And yet there were no birds. Increasingly, Dupree was aware of the silence created by their absence. It was so quiet that the snapping of the twigs beneath his feet rang like small-arms fire in the forest, and his breathing sounded loud enough to be heard offshore. He continued to walk, leaving the bog behind him and entering the deepest part of the forest. At last, he could see ahead of him the shapes of stones through the trees. Once again there appeared to be some recent growth of briers and shrubs along the trail, but these were not green. In fact, their branches broke dryly in his hand when he touched them. They seemed dead, and long dead, yet somehow they were still growing.

He was almost at the entrance to the Site when he saw movement. A patch of gray drifted between the trees, perhaps fifty feet ahead of him, at the farthest edge of the Site. It seemed to hang in the air for a moment, then was absorbed into a tree trunk. An image of Jack's painting flashed in his mind, with its gray shapes that were almost figures. It was an illusion, that was all. Still, he removed his gun from its holster, but kept it pointed toward the ground as he forced his way through the final curtain of briers and branches and found himself standing before the remains of the settlement. Even from this angle he could see what once were the corners of houses, the remains of chimneys, the frames of doors. In winter the patterns were more noticeable, for during the summer the rich greenery of the island obscured the man-made forms. Some unexplained growth had also occurred here, although not to the same extent as on the trail. At the very center of the Site stood the stone cross that his ancestor had raised, almost as tall as Dupree himself. The names of those who had died here were etched upon it, for most of the graves were unmarked and there were those whose remains had never been found, among them the settlers who had been cast into the marsh. Dupree thought that he had never seen this place so silent, so still.

He advanced, walking carefully around the tilted gravestones, until he reached the cross. He rested his hand upon it to draw a breath, then pulled it away as though it were a column of heated metal. He took three steps back and looked up at the cross, then slowly extended his hand again and allowed it to come to rest on the stone.

He had not been mistaken. The cross was vibrating. He could almost hear it hum.

Dupree knelt, maintaining his contact with the stone all the way down. The intensity of the vibration seemed to increase as he neared the ground. Finally, he laid a palm flat upon the earth and felt the pulse resonate through his fingers, passing along his arm and into his body until his ears rang with it and his own heart seemed to beat in time with the reverberation. It was like standing above a mine and feeling the rhythmic throbbing of the machinery far below.

From the trees at the edge of the Site, the flash of gray came again. Dupree rose and moved toward it, the gun now extended before him.

Twenty feet.

Fifteen.

Ten.

Something touched his face. He fell back a step, nearly loosing off a shot in his surprise, his left hand swinging and striking a glancing blow at the thing in the air. He looked down and saw the moth lying stunned upon the ground, its narrow, pointed wings moving slightly. It was another hornworm. There were more of them on the tree trunk ahead of him, the yellow spots on their abdomens like mold on the bark. Slowly, the insect on the ground rose, then joined its fellows on the tree. As Dupree drew closer, he could distinguish moths upon the branches around him, moths upon the stones, moths hidden in the tangles of the dead briers. Dupree had never encountered anything like it before. They did not belong on this island at any time, for even in the summer there were no tobacco plants, no potato plants or tomato plants, upon which they might feed. In winter, their extinction was guaranteed. They should not be here, thought Dupree.

They should be dead.

Then he turned and saw that his surroundings—the remains of the houses, the grave markers, even the great cross—were now entirely obscured by the insects, their slow movements seeming to bring the stones to life. Dupree could hear the moths brushing against one another, the sound of them like a soft whispering carried on the breeze. With the back of his hand, he touched those on the nearest tree and felt their wings trembling against his skin, but not a single insect fled from his touch or took to the air.

Small fragments of their tissue adhered to his fingers, coating them lightly with a pale dust. He thought that he could taste them in his mouth, just as Sylvie Lauter must have tasted them in her final moments.

Dupree stood silently among them as the sun crossed the sky and the clouds lowered, until at last he left that place, the pitch of the whispering increasing in intensity as he went before abruptly ceasing entirely, as though some secret, half-heard conversation had concluded at last in unity and resolve.

CHAPTER NINE

Barron was having a very bad day.

In fact, Barron was having his second bad day in a row. The first had commenced with the phone call from Boston, advising him that his services would be required in the very near future. Barron had tried to explain to the man on the other end of the line that this wasn't a good time for him, that he was under pressure. The appearance of Parker in the bar had rattled him badly. He had no idea how much the private detective knew, or even suspected, but Barron feared his persistence. He wanted to keep his head down and behave like a model cop for a while. Still, he told the caller nothing about Parker. He was afraid that they might scent trouble and feed him to the department. They had photographs. Christ, they had a video. Barron would have to eat his gun, because there was no way he was doing jail time. No way.

Then there was Terry Scarfe. Part of Barron's deal with the Russians was that he would look out for Scarfe. Scarfe had contacts. He was a fixer. Scarfe also owed them, and he couldn't pay them back if he was stuck in jail. Barron knew that they had their hooks in Scarfe until his dying day, and that he would never be permitted to pay in full the debt that he owed. Barron understood this because he feared that he was in the same terrible position. What worried Barron was that Scarfe knew about him, and Scarfe was a screwup. The dipshit had run from him that night he was on patrol with Macy. If he had kept his head down, they might well have passed by him. Instead, Barron had been forced to chase him, to search him, and then to empty him out because the moron was carrying. If another patrol had picked him up ten minutes later and found his stash, Barron might have been compelled to explain how he had missed it during his search, assuming Scarfe didn't hand him over on a plate to save his own skin. True, he could have argued that Scarfe had been clean during the first search, and nobody would have been able to contradict him, but there was still the danger of arousing suspicion.

Then there was Macy to contend with. Barron didn't know how much Macy had seen during his search of Scarfe, but trainee cops had buckled under pressure in the past and Barron didn't know if Macy would be a stand-up girl if push came to shove. Even if she kept her mouth shut, Barron didn't like the idea of Macy having anything on him.

The Russian didn't listen to Barron's objections. He was bought and paid for. He was to wait for a call. When that call came the following morning, it marked the start of Barron's second bad day.

Because the call came from Scarfe.

Dupree made it back to town in time for the arrival of the twelve-thirty P.M. ferry, still shaken by his experience at the

Site. Amerling was right. Things were happening, and there was nothing that they could do except hold on tight during the ride and pray that it was over quickly.

He smelled perfume close by. He looked to his left and saw that Marianne Elliot was beside him, smiling shyly. There was a knapsack on her back, and she was sipping coffee from a steel travel mug.

"Hi," she said.

"Hi. You going over to the mainland?"

"I've got some things to do," she said. "I'll get the ferry back this evening."

"And Danny?"

"He's still with Bonnie Claeson. I dropped by to say hi. I think he's forgiven me for last night. Anyway, I promised to bring him back something from Portland and he seemed happy with that."

She touched his sleeve.

"I had a good time with you last night," she said quietly.

"Thank you."

"You're supposed to say that you had a good time too," she teased.

"I had the best time," he said.

She leaned in the window, kissed him quickly on the lips, then headed toward the dock. Over by the diner, Nancy Tooker, who had witnessed the exchange, raised her hand and gave him a cheerful wave.

Dupree tried to sink deeper into his seat.

Barron met Scarfe in the parking lot behind the Levi's store in Freeport. It was relatively quiet there, and most of the cars had out-of-state tags. They sat in Barron's Plymouth, watching the lot.

"They're coming in today," said Scarfe. "They want to meet you."

"No way," said Barron.

"I don't think you're in a position to argue."

Barron's right hand lashed out, catching Scarfe on the side of the face. Scarfe's head struck the passenger window.

"Don't you ever talk to me like that again! The fuck you think you are, talking to me that way?"

He stared straight ahead, gripping the wheel tightly, working at the plastic. Scarfe said nothing. Barron wanted to scream, to rage at the injustice of it all. He was a cop. These people had no right to put him through this. He could smell Scarfe beside him. He stank of sweat and unwashed clothes and desperation. Barron needed to get away from him.

"Give me the keys."

Scarfe handed over the keys to an Isuzu Trooper parked out at the Maine Mall. The Trooper, sourced by Scarfe, was scanner equipped. Barron was to use the Trooper for his part of the job, then just leave the keys in it and walk away. Scarfe would take care of its disposal.

"Now get out of the car," said Barron.

Scarfe climbed out silently. There was a red mark on his left cheek, and his left eye was tearing.

"You didn't have to hit me," he said.

"I know," said Barron. "I did it because I wanted to."

Then he drove away.

CHAPTER TEN

They ditched the vans at a wrecking yard just outside Brockton and prepared to pick up some replacements. Powell and Tell took care of the details, although Powell, who had grown fond of driving the Econoline, expressed his regret at seeing it go.

"Well, maybe we could hold on to it, just for you," suggested Tell. "We could get something written along the side, like 'We Are the Guys You're Looking For!'"

They watched as the Econoline's roof collapsed inward under the pressure of the crane's jaws. Glass shattered, and the van shuddered as if in pain. It reminded Powell of the way a man's face will crumple when he's shot.

"Yeah, you're right. Still, we had some good times in that van."

Tell tried to figure out if Powell was joking, but couldn't. "You need to make some more friends, man," he said.

They headed for the battered trailer that functioned as the lot's office. It smelled bad. An ancient gray filing cabinet spewed yellowed paper from an open drawer, and the carpet was dotted with cigarette burns. Nicotine-smeared blinds obscured the windows.

"Looks like business is booming," said Powell. "You guys must be planning to float on the stock exchange pretty soon."

There were three men waiting for them, and none of them smiled. Two pieces of ex-Soviet muscle stood at either side of a third man, who sat behind a cheap plastic desk. The seated man was wearing a plaid jacket over a vile sports shirt. The other men favored leather blouson jackets, the sort that bad disc jockeys wore to public events. Even Powell, who still missed the days when a guy could wear the sleeves of his pastel jacket rolled up to his elbows, thought the men were kind of badly dressed.

Tell, meanwhile, was trying to figure out where the guys were from. Dexter had told him that the main man was Russian, so he figured the others were probably Russian too. They were dressed like shit, which was kind of a giveaway. Tell didn't know what it was about the new breed of immigrant criminals, but they had the dress sense of fucking lizards. Everything had to shine. If these guys were making money, they were spending it all on acrylics.

The seated man had skin like a battlefield. He'd tried to mask the damage with a beard but it was scraggly and untidy. His hair was thinning unevenly. A patch of pink showed over his left ear. Tell wondered if the guy had some kind of disease, and was relieved that he hadn't been forced to shake his hand. He had introduced himself as Phil. Yeah, right, thought Tell: Phil, short for Vladimir.

"Dexter didn't come himself, no?" asked Phil.

"Dexter's kind of busy right now," said Tell.

"I'm offended that he would not take the time to visit an old friend."

"You get his Christmas card? 'Cause I know he sent it."

"No card," said Phil.

"Well, that's a shame," said Tell.

"Yes," said Phil. "It is."

He looked genuinely hurt.

Tell was getting antsy. Dexter had warned him to stay cool, Shepherd too, but Phil was beginning to get on his nerves and he'd been in his company for only a couple of minutes.

"We're in kind of a hurry here," said Tell.

"Yes, always hurry," said Phil. "Too much rush."

"It's the way of the world," said Powell. "People don't take the time to stop and smell the roses."

Tell looked at him, but Powell appeared to be genuine. The only thing Tell was smelling in here was rotting carpets and cheap aftershave.

"Your friend know," said Phil. "He understand."

Tell was going to have words with Powell once they got outside. He didn't want Powell to start thinking of himself as some kind of mystic.

Phil picked up a brown envelope from the desk and tossed it to Tell. "Two vans," he said.

"We wanted three."

"No three. Two only. No time."

"Too much rush," said Tell.

Phil smiled for the first time. "Yes, yes, too much rush. You tell Dexter to come see me."

Tell raised the envelope in farewell, and tried to smile back. "Yeah, you bet."

He and Powell turned to leave. They were at the door when Phil said: "And, hey!"

Tell looked back. Phil was now standing, and all three men had guns in their hands.

"You tell him to bring my money when he comes," Phil said. "And you tell him to hurry."

Macy was enjoying Larry Amerling's company. She could tell that he was used to charming the pants off the women who came by the post office (literally, in some cases, she felt certain), but he was funny and knowledgeable and Macy was already beginning to get some sense of the geography of the island.

Amerling told her to hang a right and they followed the road uphill until they came to the main lookout tower. It had five stories, four of them with horizontal slit windows on three sides, a concrete lip overshadowing each window. There was a single chimney at the top. Five glass-strewn steps led up to the reinforced-steel doorway. The door was open.

"Kids," said Amerling. "Joe tries to keep the towers locked up, but they just break right back in again."

"Mind if I take a look?" asked Macy.

"Hold your nose," said Amerling. "I'll stay here and smoke a cigarette."

They both got out of the Explorer. Amerling walked down to the road to light up, stealing a glance back at Macy as she climbed the steps. Fine-looking woman, thought Amerling. If I was only . . .

He tried to make the calculation, then gave it up as too depressing.

Macy pushed the door open and stepped inside. To her left, the words "Toilet Here" had been spray-painted on the wall over what had once served as a fireplace. She decided not to look down. There were no windows on this level, and the floor was bare concrete. To her left, a flight of concrete steps led up to the next level. She took them and came to the second floor. The slit windows were masked with layers of Plexiglas, and dead insects were trapped inside. Macy continued to climb until the concrete steps were replaced with wooden stairs to the top floor. A ladder hung down from a square access door leading to the roof. She climbed up and slipped the bolt.

The wind hit her as she stepped onto the roof, causing her jacket to flap outward like the wings of a startled bird. She zipped it up and walked to the edge. The tower stood high above even the tallest trees, and from her vantage point she could see the Cove, the smaller towers along the coastline, the neighboring islands, ships heading out to sea, even the mainland itself in the distance. The air smelled clean and fresh, with a faint hint of smoke, but the skies were heavy and gray and there was a bitingly cold edge to the wind. She turned to her right and saw Amerling smoking his cigarette. He looked up and waved, and she raised a hand in return until she was distracted by the sight of a blue truck rolling up the road. It was in bad shape, because gray-blue exhaust fumes not only curled from the pipe but seemed to envelop the vehicle entirely. That can't be right, Macy thought. He's moving fast, and the wind is blowing against him anyway. How can the fumes surround him in that way?

Then, as she watched, the truck slowed and the smoke appeared to peel away, forming two columns that faded into the forest to the left and right and then dispersed. Macy waited for a moment or two longer, still unsure as to quite what she had seen, then climbed back down the ladder and headed to the door.

She didn't notice the crude drawings of dying men and

burning houses carved into the concrete with a piece of discarded stone, or the length of white hair caught in the bottom rung of the ladder.

Or the child's cloth doll that watched her impassively from the corner of the room, its body shimmering as the moths moved upon it.

The truck had pulled up alongside Larry Amerling. The man leaning out of its window wore a dirty green windbreaker and a Sea Dogs baseball cap. His face was permanently tanned from years of working outdoors, but his nose was red and swollen and veins had broken badly across his cheeks. He made a sucking sound with his teeth as Macy approached and allowed his eyes to linger on her thighs and crotch. She was relieved to note that Amerling looked embarrassed on the man's behalf.

"This here's Carl Lubey," said Amerling. "He lives up the road. Carl, this is Officer Macy."

"Pleased to meet you," said Lubey. He made it sound like an invitation to his bed.

Macy contented herself with a nod and gave no indication that the man's name meant anything to her. So this was the brother of the man Dupree had killed. She hated herself for agreeing with Barron's assessment, but if his brother had been anything like Carl, then Dupree might have done society a favor. Carl Lubey was making her skin crawl.

"You got something wrong with your truck?" she asked him.

"Truck's running fine," he replied.

"Seemed to me like you were producing a lot of fumes. You ought to get it looked at."

"Don't need looking at. I told you, truck's fine."

"If you say so. It happens again and you could be picking up a citation."

Lubey made that sucking noise through his teeth again.

"You want to come over, maybe help me clean out my pipes, you let me know," he said. He winked broadly at her, then put the truck in gear and went on his way. This time, there was only a hint of exhaust smoke.

"Does he live alone out there?" asked Macy.

"Does Carl look like the kind of guy who has women beating down his door? Yeah, he's alone. I don't think he ever got over—"

He stopped.

"I know about it," said Macy.

"Yeah, well, then you understand. He always did have a lot of bitterness inside him. What happened to his brother just added a little extra piss to his vinegar, if you'll excuse the phrase. Pardon me saying it, but it didn't look like there was anything wrong with his truck."

Macy shook her head. "When he was coming up the road, it seemed like he was surrounded by gray smoke. Then it just sort of . . . faded away. It was real odd."

She turned to Amerling but he was looking away, staring at the road Carl Lubey had just taken, as if hoping to see some trace of the smoke for himself.

"I'd best be getting back," he said. He stomped his cigarette out on the ground, then picked up the butt and put it in the pocket of his jacket. "Mail won't sort itself."

They drove in silence for a time, until Macy said, "I couldn't see the Site from the top of the tower. That's what they call it, isn't it, the Site?"

Amerling took a moment to reply.

"Trees keep it hidden."

"Even in winter?"

"Even in winter. There's a lot of evergreens out here."

"It's over to the south, isn't it?"

"That's right, but you can't get there by car, and even on foot you need to know where you're going. At this time of year, with the light fading so early, I'm not even sure I could find it."

"Another time, then," said Macy.

"Sure," Amerling lied. "Another time."

Moloch saw Dexter staring back at him in the rearview. Leonie and Dexter sat up front, Braun behind them, and Moloch farther back. There was a hollow panel in the floor, big enough for a man to lie in, if necessary, although if he was there for longer than a couple of minutes, he'd probably suffocate. Moloch knew it was for weapons, maybe even drugs. It was a last resort for him in the event of a police search, and nothing more.

"You okay?" asked Dexter.

Moloch nodded. They had been traveling for about three hours, and his back ached. They had passed the toll booth at the New Hampshire state line shortly after nine and entered Maine. The traffic was light, most of it headed south toward Boston. They took the Kittery exit, and pulled up outside the Kittery Trading Post. Braun and Leonie went inside, leaving Moloch to rage alone silently.

As they had drawn closer and closer to Maine, Moloch had felt a pain building in his head. He found himself drifting into sleep, his eyes closing and his chin nodding to his chest, until a charge like a jolt of electricity forced him back into waking once again. But in those glancing moments of semirest, his body racked by exhaustion, he was tormented by visions, images of pasts both known and unknown, at once familiar and strange.

He saw himself as a small boy, hands pressed against the window of a black car as it pulled away from a suburban house, the boy's bicycle momentarily forgotten, his fingers brushing the glass as the car sped up, a man struggling in the backseat, his eyes wide with panic, two men holding him down. The man's hand reached out, as if somehow the boy could save him, but nobody could save him.

Dad?

No, not Dad, not really, but the closest he had come to finding one, a foster father and a foster mother on a street of identical houses, each with a small square of green lawn, its quiet disturbed only by the hiss of sprinklers and, now, the noise of the car as it pulled away from the curb.

Inside the house, the woman was crying. She lay slumped in a corner of the kitchen, blood running from her nose and mouth. She had been baking a cake, and now flour and broken eggs covered the floor around her. The boy went to her, and she took him in her arms and held him to her.

The next day, more men came, and they were forced to leave the house. The boy fled with his not-mother, moving from town to town, watching her as she grew more and more desperate, descending into some terrible dark place all her own, where men came and pounded on her body and left piles of ragged bills on the dresser when they were done. And the boy wondered, as he grew older: Who am I, and where have I come from, if I am not of this woman?

Then there were other women—mothers, sisters, daughters—flashing before him, and he heard half-familiar names spoken. He was in a house by a lake. He was on a streetcar, a man holding his hand.

He was on the island, and his voice was whispering: *Know me, wife.*

Moloch jerked into wakefulness again. Dexter was now reading a newspaper. Moloch closed his eyes again.

This is not my past. It is a past, but it is not mine. I am more than this.

The island returned to him and he smelled the sea and the pines, and he heard a sound as of a moth tapping on glass, struggling to escape the darkness.

Or to embrace to it.

The others returned about a half hour later. They had bought warm clothing, waterproofs, and a selection of minor weaponry: knives, mainly; a handheld ax; and a hunting bow for Dexter. As for guns, they already had what they needed.

Powell handed Dexter the bow case. Dexter opened it and removed the big bow contained within.

"I don't understand why you need that," Moloch said. He still felt groggy and ill. He wanted sleep, proper sleep. The tapping sound that he had heard in his dream had not gone away now that he was awake. Instead, it remained there, like water trapped in his inner ear.

"It's not about needing. I like the feel of a bow."

"You ever kill a man with a bow?" asked Powell.

"No. Killed one with an arrow, though." Dexter grinned.

"You really think we're going to need all this stuff up here?" Braun asked Moloch.

Moloch shook his head, as much in answer as in an effort to rid himself of the infernal noise in his head.

"We get there, find her, make her return my money, then we kill her. We don't want to make trouble for ourselves and bring them down upon us. If everything goes according to plan, we'll have her before they even know we've been there."

"So, like I asked, why do we need all of this?"

Moloch looked at him the way he might have looked at a slow child.

"Because nothing ever goes according to plan," he said simply.

The ferry to Portland contained just two passengers: an old man going to see his oncologist, and Marianne. She missed Danny and wished that he were with her, but she had to visit the banks and he would quickly have become bored with the waiting and the filling out of forms.

Bonnie had asked her little about her date, apart from inquiring whether it had gone well. She told her that Danny and Richie had enjoyed their evening together, and she didn't mind if he stayed with her for the best part of another day. Richie had cheered at the news. Richie was a wonderful kid—she could never think of him as anything but a kid—and the people on the island looked out for him. In some ways, Dutch was the best environment for a boy like him. No harm could come to him, and in the close-knit community, he knew affection and support. To Danny, he was almost like a big brother, even though Danny, who was a smart boy, recognized that his playmate was different and that, in some ways, Danny had to look out for Richie more than Richie had to watch out for Danny.

But she had warned Danny not to follow Richie when he went exploring on the island. She knew that Richie liked to ramble through the woods and that Bonnie had given up trying to discourage him from doing so because Richie would go anyway, sneaking out of the house and sending her wild with worry. Better that he told her where he was going than to have him simply disappear without a word. While Marianne liked Richie, she knew that he was incapable of looking after her son, and Danny had been told, on pain of eternal grounding and loss of his allowance for the rest of his life, not to go anywhere with Richie unless Bonnie went along too.

Ahead of her, she could see the boats bobbing at the docks on Commercial. Resigned now to a day without Danny, she was looking forward to getting a few things done. She planned to visit her hairdresser, eat a leisurely lunch, maybe even head out to the Maine Mall for a while. She would have the best part of four hours to herself.

But first, there was the money to take care of. Once that was done, she would breathe a little easier. She was wearing a money belt beneath her sweater, and while she would certainly have preferred not to have to carry so much cash around, Portland's streets didn't worry her. She would not be walking them at night.

Behind her, gray clouds gathered. There would be snow by morning, according to the Weather Channel. She had checked the forecast before leaving, and the worst of the weather would not hit until much later that night. Thorson had announced that the ferry would leave Portland at six-thirty that night, with a final sailing at ten. She would probably make the six-thirty, or else the last sailing with time to spare, and she and Danny would be locked up safely at home by the time the snows came.

In her kitchen, Bonnie Claeson was watching CNN while chopping vegetables for dinner. She thought that she might make something special, since Danny was with them: a pot roast, perhaps, and a pumpkin pie.

On the TV, she could see a vehicle being pulled from a river somewhere in the south. It looked hot down there, and the backs of the policemen's shirts were dark with sweat. She wondered if Mike, her current boyfriend, might be persuaded to chip in some cash so that they could take Richie away this summer. She'd ask him when she saw him next weekend. Mike drove trucks for a living and was sort of quiet, but he was patient with Richie and kind to her, and that was enough for Bonnie for the present.

Now the picture had changed, and a man's face filled the screen. He looked handsome, she thought, apart from his eyes. They were sort of narrow, an impression accentuated by the thin vertical lines that ran down each cheek, and the intelligence in them was marred by contempt. Maybe it was just the law he despised, she mused, but she didn't think so. She figured this guy hated just about everything.

Bonnie turned the TV up in time to hear his name.

Moloch. Wasn't that a biblical name? It sounded kind of biblical. Bonnie wasn't much of one for churchgoing or Bible thumping, but the name gave her the creeps. She went back to preparing her food. The soaps would begin soon, her "stories" as her mother used to call them.

Soon she forgot all about the man named Moloch.

But her son did not. He continued to stare at the television with rapt attention, watching the parade of faces. There was the man with the piercing eyes, and the black man, and the young man with the blond hair. Their pictures had been on TV a lot lately.

Richie sat very still and took them all in.

They arrived in Portland shortly before one. Moloch had by now moved into the front bench seat, sick of being incarcerated in the back of the van. The changes he had made to his appearance meant that only someone who took the time to examine him very closely would even begin to connect him with the face on the news reports, and if Moloch found someone examining him that closely, well, that person wouldn't live long enough to tell anyone what he or she had seen.

They pulled up on Commercial and looked out to sea. Close by was the dock for the Dutch Island ferry. There was nobody onboard. Braun had gone to check the schedule.

"Last sailing is at ten," he said when he returned. "Ferry comes back to the mainland first thing tomorrow morning."

Moloch considered this. "For now, we rest up, get some motel rooms away from the center of town. We can talk about it again after we meet Scarfe."

Dexter nodded. There was a Days Inn out by the mall. He'd seen the sign on the way into town. Dexter liked Days Inns. Once you got used to the fact that they all looked the same, they became a little like home.

Marianne had no problems at the banks. In total, she withdrew some $8,000 from three separate accounts, depositing each wad of notes carefully in the belt beneath her sweater. When she was done, she treated herself to a cab ride out to the Maine Mall, and allowed herself to be pampered in the hairdresser's for a couple of hours. Then, feeling better than she had in many months, she ate Chinese food at the mall's food court, then walked across the parking lot to T. J. Maxx, where she bought herself a DKNY leather jacket that, according to the tag, had been reduced by $300. She bought new sneakers for Danny and added them to the Harry Potter trading-card game in her bag.

She considered going to the movies. It had been so long since she'd sat in a movie theater to watch something that wasn't a cartoon or a kids' comedy. Maybe she could make the twilight showing over at the Maine Mall Cinema. She glanced at her watch, saw that it was just after six, and broke into a trot as she headed for the theater.

"What the fuck is wrong with her mouth?" said Dexter.

He and Braun were watching a pay-per-view movie in their motel room. Tom Cruise was some kind of deformed guy in love with a Spanish chick with dark hair. Tom had dumped Cameron Diaz for the dark-haired chick, which made no sense to Dexter at all, especially since the dark-haired chick seemed to have picked up the wrong mouth somewhere along the line.

"Well?" he said to Braun. "Look at it."

"Looks good to me," said Braun. Dexter had run out of movies to watch on his DVD player, and had turned on the TV. Braun couldn't concentrate on his book with the movie playing, so he had contented himself with watching the screen. There was nothing else for them to do anyway, not until Scarfe contacted them.

"Nah. I ain't saying she ain't pretty or nothing. Hell, I'd fuck her for free. But her mouth . . . I don't know, it's just too big for her face. Who is she, anyway?"

"Penelope Cruz."

"She married to him or something?"

"No, Cruz with a *z*. I hear he's dating her, though."

"Fucking Tom Cruise. You think it's true about him?"

"What? That he's—"

"Yeah."

"No. You think he could be going out with her if he was?"

"It might be a front."

"Hell of a front. Hell of an ass too."

"Yeah, but that mouth. It just looks *wrong*. . ."

Tell and Shepherd were sitting in the IHOP beside the Days Inn, eating pancakes with lots of sugar and butter and cinnamon on top. Shepherd was listening to Tell. Tell was full of shit sometimes, but it was kind of interesting shit.

Like, there they were in the IHOP, and this guy had rolled by in his wheelchair. He was wearing khakis and one of those black POW/MIA T-shirts. His legs were gone from the knees down, and his trousers were pinned up. His arms were huge. Shepherd figured the guy must be pushing himself up the side of mountains to get arms that big. Then Tell said: "You know my brother was a cripple?"

"No shit?"

"Lost a leg in Vietnam, couple of months before Tet."

"Which leg?"

"Right leg."

"No shit?"

"Came home on crutches with one trouser leg pinned up, just like that guy, except he still had one leg. He was real upset."

"Man had a right to be upset, he lost a leg."

"Sure. Terrible thing, losing a limb. He stayed in his room, drinking, sleeping in his own filth. Wasn't nobody could get through to him. Then he got this phone call. Ed Sullivan—you remember Ed Sullivan?"

"Yeah, he was a strange-looking guy. Head and body didn't look like they matched."

"He had short arms, was what it was. Anyway, Ed was a big

supporter of the war, and he wanted he should do his part, so he invited some vets on to the show and my brother was one of them. He loved Ed Sullivan."

"So he went to the show?"

"Hell, yeah, he went. He and his buddies were flown in, driven to the studio in big limousines, given front-row seats, the whole deal. They'd all lost limbs in Vietnam—arms and legs and shit. Ed insisted that all the guys should be cripples, otherwise they could be just anybody, you know? Anyhow, during the dress rehearsal for the show, Ed calls for the lights and cameras to be pointed at them, and he starts making a big fuss, and the audience starts whooping and hollering. So Ed looks at the boys, and smiles that big smile he had, and tells them to take a bow. I mean, it's Ed Sullivan, telling them to take a bow. So my brother and his buddies, they stand up to take their bow."

"Yeah? So they stand up . . . ?"

"And my brother fell over. He only had one leg. He stood up, kind of wavered for a second, then went sideways. Banged his head. Most of the other guys who'd lost legs managed to stay upright by supporting themselves on their seats, although they all looked kind of unsteady. Not my brother, though. He was gonna stand up straight and take a bow if Ed Sullivan told him to. He loved Ed Sullivan."

"A man's got to love another man to try to stand straight on one leg just because he told him to do it. Your brother must have been kind of pissed at Ed, though."

"No, he wasn't pissed at all. Fact was, he said he kind of appreciated someone treating him like he still had both legs. So after that my brother got himself a false leg. He wanted to be able to stand upright next time someone important told him to. He used to take it off to sleep, though. That's how he died.

There was a fire in his apartment block, and when the alarms went off there was smoke and shit, and he died trying to find his false leg. He didn't want to be no cripple hobbling out. He wanted to preserve his dignity. *The Ed Sullivan Show* taught him that. He loved Ed Sullivan."

"No shit."

"No shit."

Shepherd thought that was kind of interesting. That was what he meant about Tell.

"We did a bank job once, over in Pensacola," said Shepherd, not wanting to be outdone in the storytelling stakes. "Spent two weeks casing the bank. This was in the old days, before all them new security systems, and lasers and shit."

"It was a different time. Man needs a degree to take down a bank now."

"Yeah, they do make it hard for a man these days, and no mistake. Anyway, we get to the bank, morning of the job. Manager goes in, his staff after him, and we come in behind them before they got a chance to close the door."

"And?"

"And there's two guys with masks already in there, waiting to hold up the bank. They'd come in through the roof during the night, and they were standing waiting when the manager arrived."

"No shit?"

"Well, we were kind of perturbed, you know? We must have been casing the same bank during that same two weeks, and we never saw each other."

"Can happen."

"Surely can. So we got this moment, right, where we're looking at them wearing their masks, and they're looking at us wearing our masks, and the manager and his people are looking at all of us. So I say, 'The fuck are you doing? This is our bank.' And this other guy says: 'The fuck it is. We spent a month on this job.'"

"Bullshit."

"No, I don't think so. Coming in through the roof, that takes some planning."

Tell relented. "I guess."

"So there's a standoff, until I say, 'Well, why don't we split the take?' and the two guys look at each other and kind of shrug, and say, 'Okay.'"

"So you split the take?"

"Fifty-fifty, seeing as how they'd had to come in through the roof and all."

"That was damn Christian of y'all."

"Yep, mighty white. Like you said, it was a different time. That happened now, there'd be a bloodbath. But people had principles then. They had standards."

"So y'all went away happy?"

"Kind of. The two guys got to their car and we held them up, took their share of the cash."

"Survival of the fittest."

"Absolutely. We didn't kill them, though."

"Course not. You had standards."

"Damn straight. It was a different time."

"You said it. A different time. More pancakes?"

"Sure," said Shepherd. "Why not?"

Willard stood in the parking lot of the Days Inn, smoking a cigarette. There was the IHOP maybe one hundred feet away, where Shepherd and Tell were eating. Willard could see them at the window. They hadn't asked him to come along with them. They were probably talking about him at this very minute, plotting how to get him out of the way. Willard wasn't too worried about Tell, but Shepherd and Dexter were real threats, maybe Braun too.

Willard hated Shepherd, Dexter, and Braun.

He pulled the baseball cap lower on his head and looked at himself in the side mirror of the van. With his blond hair covered, and a thin growth of beard, he didn't look too much like the picture of him that they were showing on TV. Moloch had warned him against going out, but Willard wanted some air.

He started walking and had almost finished his cigarette by the time he reached the sidewalk. He took a last long drag on the butt and watched the woman approach. She stood at the entrance to the theater parking lot. Willard registered the disappointment on her face.

"It's closed," he said. Willard thought that it looked like it had been closed for some time, a couple of months at least.

She looked at him. She said nothing for a moment or two, then replied:

"I'd forgotten."

"I think there's another theater somewhere around here," said Willard. He had seen something about it in the guest-services book in his room.

"Yeah," said the woman. "I know. I'll just give it a miss."

Willard smiled his best smile—"You take care now"—and wondered what it would be like to cut her.

Marianne smiled back and turned away. She walked quickly, but not too quickly. She didn't want to give anything away, even as her insides churned and she thought: Willard. It's Willard.

They're here.

* * *

It was only coincidence that had exposed her to the man named Willard. It was during the last days, when she was becoming more and more fearful of Moloch and his ways. She thought that he might in turn be growing suspicious of her, that he was concerned by what she might know and of what might happen if the police forced her to reveal any knowledge of his activities, or if she chose to do so of her own volition. One day, one week before the date she had chosen for her escape, she had seen Willard sitting in a car outside their house, and knew that Moloch had told him to watch her. She recognized the pretty young man from his photograph in the newspaper, the one linking him to the death of the older woman, and from one previous occasion, when she had arrived early for a rare dinner with her husband and had seen him at the bar, talking intently to Willard, his mouth almost touching the younger man's ear, so that she had thought at first that they might be lovers. She had kept her distance, and had approached her husband only after the other man had gone.

It was Karen Meyer who told her the young man's name, after Marianne explained how she had seen Willard waiting near the house. That was why she hadn't been in touch. Karen had been angry. It was their next-to-last meeting, arranged in advance to clear up any remaining details or concerns. They were standing in a single stall in the ladies' room at the mall.

"You took a risk coming here, a risk to both of us."

"No, I didn't. He followed me for two days. He didn't know I'd spotted him, and I gave him no indication that I knew. I behaved like an angel, and I know that's what he told Edward."

Karen relaxed a little.

"Who is he?" asked Marianne.

"His name is Willard. I don't know anything more than that about him. He just looks pretty. There's something wrong with him, though, real deep down. Look in his eyes and you'll find yourself dying in a thousand different ways, with his hands on you right to the end. You see him coming for you again and you take off, you hear me? You take off and you never look back. We'll come up with another way to get the stuff to you, but you see Willard coming up your garden path and he's only going to be coming for one reason. He might drop by to check up on you again before then, so act naturally over the next few days. Don't give them any cause to suspect."

And that was what she had done, walking calmly, ignoring the presence of the man her husband might be planning to have kill her. On the last day, the day of Moloch's bank job, she knew she was safe. Willard would be with him, or close to him, but it was not until she was two hundred miles from the city, Danny asleep in his seat, that she began to relax even slightly. She continued to move from city to city, town to town, never staying long in any one location, before settling at last upon the island, the place to which she had decided to flee many months before after reading a feature about the Maine islands in a travel magazine, content that, for now, her trail was unlikely to be uncovered.

But she had never forgotten Willard, or the potential threat that her husband, even incarcerated, might pose to her. It could have been merely a coincidence, of course, that Willard was now up north, far from home, but she didn't think so. No, they were here, and they were coming for her, for if they were in Portland, then they knew she was on the island, and soon they would arrive on it. As she walked away from Willard—not too fast, not too slow—she tried to retrace their steps, figuring out how they had found her. Only two people could have told.

Karen.

And her sister.

Marianne walked to Maine Mall Road and tried to hail a cab, using the opportunity to pause and glance back to where Willard still stood. He was not looking at her. Then he turned, and his eyes seemed to alight on her face. Marianne waited for him to head into the IHOP, or back toward the motel. Instead, Willard began to walk quickly along the sidewalk.

He was heading straight for her.

Willard didn't talk much. He guessed that a lot of folks considered him dumb, seeing as how he had never been much for school, and maybe they thought he was afraid to open his mouth because people might laugh at what came out. But Willard wasn't afraid of anyone, and those who might have felt the urge to laugh at him would quickly have suppressed it as soon as they looked in Willard's eyes. Sure, Willard had trouble with reading, and he wasn't so good with figures, but he had the instincts and intelligence of a natural hunter, combined with a curiosity about the nature of pain and hurt when applied to others.

He had sensed something from the woman when she had looked at him. It was more than the natural fear that he frequently recognized in women: the care they took not to get themselves trapped alone with a stranger; the grip with which they held on to their purses; the casual look around the smarter ones took as they prepared to open their car door in the parking lot. No, this was different, keener. Separated, thought Willard, with a husband who isn't taking it too well; or maybe trying to avoid a boyfriend who doesn't want to split from her, because then he'll have to find someone else to beat on. Willard's nostrils were almost twitching as she stood before him. He liked the scent of her. It aroused the predator in him.

He wasn't so sure about her hair, though. She'd dyed it some dowdy color that didn't suit her, streaking it more than altering it entirely. He couldn't figure out why she'd do something like that, except he'd heard on TV that it was kind of the fashionable thing to do a few years ago. If so, this woman needed to get back on the fashion train, because it was surely leaving the station without her.

Willard watched her walk away. She had slim legs, and a nice ass beneath her coat. He could see the shape of it as she pulled the coat against herself. On another occasion, he might have followed her, learned more about her, just in case he decided to visit her at some point in the future, but Moloch had warned him after the incident with the woman in the bedroom. Willard hadn't liked the way Moloch spoke to him. Neither had he appreciated the look that had passed between Moloch and Dexter afterward, like a principal and a teacher agreeing on the unspoken decision to expel an errant student from school.

Willard saw the woman try to hail a cab. She looked anxious. Strange, he thought. She walks to the movie theater from the mall, and now she suddenly has to get a cab? He rubbed his foot across the still-smoldering cigarette butt, crushing it into the sidewalk. And then there was that hair: it was shitty, almost as if it was designed to make her look more common than she was. There was a good-looking woman under there, but she seemed to be deliberately trying to hide her presence. A mental picture flashed: a woman standing beside Moloch at the state fair, the woman smiling uneasily. Willard tried setting the image of the woman with the dyed hair beside Moloch's wife.

Shit.

Marianne saw the cab at almost the same instant that Willard began to speed up his progress. The lights were changing to amber over by Chili's restaurant, and the cabdriver seemed inclined to stop. She waved her hand frantically, causing cars to honk their horns as she ran across the road, and saw the driver glance to his right, where a competitor was exiting from the Hampden Inn with an empty cab. In that second, he made his decision and hit the accelerator, shooting through the lights as they turned to red in his rearview mirror. He pulled in alongside her and she clambered in, just as Willard started to run.

"Commercial," said Marianne. "Please, and quickly."

The cabdriver glanced in the rearview as he got ready to pull out, and spotted Willard.

"Hey," he said, "you know this guy?"

Marianne looked back. Willard was running between the traffic, dodging the oncoming hoods almost gracefully. He was maybe thirty feet from the cab.

"A guy I once dated," she said. "I really don't want to talk to him. There's ten bucks in it for you."

"For an extra ten, I'll date him myself," said the cabdriver. He swung out and shot away from the curb. Marianne heard a noise from behind, like fingers vainly dragging along the trunk of the cab, but she did not look back.

Willard stood on the curb, watching the cab head off toward Portland. Had the lights at the mall entrance gone red, then he might have caught up with them, but the cab had a free run to the main intersection. Willard took a deep breath and debated whether or not he should tell Moloch what had occurred. He might have been wrong about the woman, of course, but the look on her face as she had seen him approach through the back window of the cab told him that his suspicions were correct. It was her. She knew who he was, and if she knew that, then she must also know that they had come for her at last. The shock on her face told him one more thing: she didn't know that Moloch was free, otherwise she wouldn't have been trying to pass an idle evening with some shitty movie.

He had to tell Moloch. Already, the woman would be preparing to run again.

Willard was surprised by how calm Moloch appeared to be, at least initially. As it turned out, the calm didn't last long.

"You're certain it was her?" said Moloch.

"Pretty sure. Her hair is different, and she looked kind of dowdy, but I saw her face as that cab pulled away. She knew me."

"How? There's no way that she could have known who you are."

"Maybe she picked up on me when I was tailing her, back before she ran."

"If she did, then you're the shittiest tail I ever knew."

Willard bridled at the insult but said nothing.

"You should have caught her. Now she knows we're here."

"Where can she go? There's no way she could have made the ferry."

"You think that's the only boat down there? They have

water taxis. She could go to another island and get someone to bring the kid to her. You think we have time to scour every island for her? Get the others. Describe her to them, and set them to looking for her in town. If nobody has found her by seven, we bring everything forward." Willard left him. Moloch called Braun in his room. Braun listened, then hung up.

"We need to get going," he told Dexter.

"The hell are you talking about?" asked Dexter. "This shit is only starting to get good."

"Willard saw the wife. He thinks she made him."

Dexter swore, then turned off the TV. They packed up and joined Moloch and the others in his room. Shepherd and Tell had just arrived. Tell still had sugar on his sweater.

"An extra twenty-five thousand for the one who finds her," said Moloch. He looked at Willard. "And I want her intact, you hear?"

Willard didn't even nod, but he could see Dexter grinning at him. Once again, he recalled the look that had passed between Dexter and Moloch. Willard decided that he was going to have to deal with Dexter, and sooner rather than later.

The cab dropped Marianne on Commercial, footsteps from the ferry dock. The dock was empty and she could see the lights of the ferry disappearing into the evening darkness. She swore and felt the fear wash over her. It almost reduced her to tears. She tried to hold herself together.

They would be expecting her to head back to the island, if only to get Danny. Maybe if she could get someone to pick up Danny and get him off the island, then she could avoid going back to Dutch at all. Briefly, she considered calling the cops and telling them everything, but Marianne was afraid that they would take Danny away from her, perhaps even jail her. No, the cops were not yet an option.

Except . . .

She dialed 911 and told the dispatcher that she had seen a man out by the mall who looked like the guy on TV, you know, the blond guy. She gave an accurate description of Willard's dress, right down to the baseball cap, then hung up.

That would give them something to think about.

She didn't have much time. She dropped some coins in the slot and rang Bonnie Claeson's number. The phone rang three times and then was picked up.

"Hello?" she said.

There was static on the line, but it wasn't regular static. It ebbed and flowed. At first, it sounded a little like soft cotton being rubbed between someone's fingers. For an instant, an image came to her unbidden: an insect beating its wings, while around it a host of others did the same in preparation for some great flight.

Then the line died.

She tried again, and got only a busy signal. She tried three more numbers, including Jack's, with the same result.

Finally, Marianne gripped her bag and ran for a water taxi, just as the first flurries of snow began to fall.

Shepherd arrived first at the pier, only to see the water taxi disappearing from sight, a tiny puff of smoke seeming to mock him as it went. He removed a pair of binoculars from his pack and found the woman in the prow of the boat. She was, as far as he could make out, the only passenger. As he stared at her, she looked back toward the pier and he was certain that she was looking at him. He thought he could read fear in her eyes.

Tell appeared beside him, and Shepherd smiled.

"She's going home."

Willard's instincts were honed to perfection. He saw the patrol car before the cop inside could spot him, and slipped into the Starbucks in the Old Port, stripping himself of his coat and hat as he went. He didn't know who they were looking for, but he could guess. The woman had seen him, and she had called the cops to make life difficult for him.

Willard didn't care. Life had always been difficult for him.

He ordered a coffee, then slipped back out onto the streets and lost himself from view.

As soon as Willard told him of his encounter with Marianne, Moloch called Scarfe and headed for the meeting place he had suggested, the rocky outcrop by the twin lights in Cape Elizabeth. The rocks and the small beach were deserted. With the approaching storm, even the locals had retreated to their homes.

There were two men waiting on the beach, snow already whitening their shoulders and hair. One was Scarfe. The other was Barron.

"So this is the tame cop?"

Moloch looked at the policeman with a mixture of distaste and amusement. Barron was wearing jeans, sneakers, and a padded jacket. He looked nervous.

"I'm not your tame cop," he said.

"What would you prefer to be called? Pedophile cop? Child

molester cop? Please, let me know. I want you to be as comfortable as possible in your dealings with me."

Barron's face flushed, but he didn't reply.

"You should have been more careful, Officer. Your tastes have made you the bitch of anyone to whom your creditors choose to offer you."

"Just tell me what you want," said Barron softly.

Moloch turned to Scarfe. "I've heard a lot about you, none of it very impressive. I advise you not to let me down. Now, tell me about the island."

For the next ten minutes, Scarfe detailed all that he had discovered from Carl Lubey, including the presence and routines of the giant cop, Joe Dupree, and the reported arrival that morning of the rookie cop Macy. ("A rookie?" Moloch had interrupted. "Maybe our luck is holding.")

"And the woman, Marianne Elliot?"

"She's out there. Her house is over on the southeastern shore. There aren't too many other houses around there. The boy is with her."

"Does she have a boyfriend?" asked Moloch.

Scarfe swallowed.

"Lubey says she's been seen around with the cop Dupree. They had dinner together last night."

Moloch motioned him to continue, but he looked unhappy at the development.

"There's a boat waiting for you down at the Marine Company. You go in after dark on the northern shore, some ways from the woman's house. There are no good landings over where she is, except for a little inlet that belongs to an old painter guy who watches the bay like a hawk. You try coming in that way and if he spots you, he'll start making calls. The sea there is threaded with rocks anyway. Even experienced sailors steer clear of it. You need to stay as far as possible from the dock on Island Avenue on your way in, and from any houses along the shore. Like the painter, people on the island keep a close eye on what happens there, and who comes and goes. The northwestern shore is virtually unpopulated, though. Lubey will meet you at the landing. He has a truck. He'll take you to the woman's house, then bring you back to the boat when your business is done. He doesn't want money. He has one favor to ask."

"Go on."

"He wants you to kill Dupree if you get the chance."

"No cops," interrupted Barron. "Nobody gets hurt, that was the deal."

"I don't remember making a deal with you, Officer," said Moloch. "You will do as you're told, or your superiors will receive information that will end your career and make you the whore of every disease-ridden rapist that your state's prison system can put your way. Don't interrupt us again."

He turned back to Scarfe.

"I make no promises about the cop."

"It might be easier to get rid of him at the start." It was Leonie.

Moloch bit at his lip. If the cop was seeing his wife, then the cop deserved what was coming to him. There was nothing worse than the thought of another man inside his wife.

Scarfe unfolded papers from his pocket. "This is a map of the island. I've made some copies. It's kind of rough, but it shows the main roads, the town, and the location of the woman's house and those of her nearest neighbors."

Moloch took the map, examined it, then folded it and handed it, along with the copies, to Leonie.

"I couldn't help but notice that you said 'you' in your

detailing of the arrangements made. 'You,' not 'us.' That worries me."

"I've done what you asked me to do."

"You're coming with us."

"You don't need me."

"You know about boats, and you know this area. Some of my associates have experience of such matters, but these are unfamiliar waters and there is bad weather approaching. And if your friend Mr. Lubey lets us down, we will have someone to fall back on. Heavily."

Scarfe nodded.

"I understand."

Moloch turned to Barron.

"Your role in this affair is simple, Officer. You monitor the police bands. If there is even a hint of police activity that might concern us, I want you to nullify it. I understand that there is no cell phone coverage on the island?"

"There are pockets, but only close to town. The eastern shore is out of range."

"You will take up a position on the dock. If our return is jeopardized in any way, you will signal us with your headlights as we return to land. Is that clear?"

"That's all?"

"For now. Mr. Scarfe, you'll come with us. Our departure is imminent."

Moloch, Dexter, and Willard dropped Leonie and Braun on Commercial. The two older men sat in the van close by the Casco Bay Ferry Terminal while Willard stayed in the shadows and watched the approaches along Commercial. The plan was virtually unchanged: one group would make for the island with

Scarfe, while Leonie and Braun would follow by water taxi and land at the Cove, as the late ferry crossing had been canceled due to Thorson's innate caution and the early arrival of the snow. Barron would keep an eye on all new arrivals, just in case the woman managed to slip by them and make it back to Portland.

"I didn't want her to see us before we came," Moloch said to Dexter. "I didn't want her to know. I wanted to see the shock on the bitch's face myself."

"You'll still see it. I reckon she has a lot of shock left in her."

Moloch didn't look so happy, Dexter thought. He had been sleeping badly. Dexter had heard him crying out. That happened to men who had been jailed, Dexter knew. Even after their release, part of them always remained incarcerated, and that was the part that intruded on their dreams.

Dexter, meanwhile, had his own worries.

"I don't like this whole island deal," he said. "Too many things can go wrong. I don't like having just one escape route. I don't like having to leave the same way I came in. And we don't know shit about this Lubey guy."

"We have a boat. One of us will stay with it the whole time. Like I told you, we can take her and be gone before anyone even knows we've been there. We just need to stay out of trouble. As for Lubey, he's a driver, nothing more."

"Do you trust the cop?"

"No, but I think he's too frightened of the consequences to cross us. Plus, our friends in Boston have promised him a little gift for his cooperation. His fear and his lust should combine to keep him in line."

"And the policeman out on the island?"

"When they get there, Braun and Leonie will kill him, if only for having the temerity to fuck my wife."

"And Willard?"

Something like regret flashed across Moloch's features. "No pain," he said. "I want him to feel no pain."

In the shadows, Willard was looking at a small map of the bay held behind a protective Plexiglas screen. He had changed his clothes and was now wearing a tourist's fleece with a lobster on the front. He had darkened his hair in a men's room with a kit he had bought in a drugstore, and it was now a shimmering black. With the index finger of his right hand, he traced the route of the ferry, following each little dot as carefully as if he were tracing the route onto paper. His finger stopped on the island, then he jerked it back suddenly.

A spider was crawling across the map. Its body covered the island. Somehow, the spider had found its way inside the case and now it was trapped, vainly seeking a way out. Maybe it had been trying to shelter from the cold, but now the case would be its tomb. There would be no insects in there for it to feed on and eventually it would grow thin and die. Willard watched it crawl, its legs occasionally slipping on the surface of the map, causing the spider to drop an inch or two before its silk arrested its slide. At last it crawled back up to the top-right-hand corner of the case and huddled there, waiting for its end.

Willard's mouth was dry. He looked up from the map and stared out to sea, trying to find light in the distance, but he could not. His stomach felt bad. He was concerned about Dexter and Shepherd, but he was worried too about the island. Willard had a survivor's instincts, and now that little inner voice on which he had relied for so long was telling him to leave, to make his escape while he still could. But Willard wasn't going to run. Deep inside, he still trusted Moloch. He *wanted* to trust him. He needed him. He lived for the light of Moloch's approval. It was his weakness. Willard was crazy, crazier than even he himself knew, crazier even than Moloch suspected, but, deep down, he just wanted to be loved.

CHAPTER ELEVEN

Powell was having trouble with the boat guy. He was fat and old and dumb, with grease stains on his shirt. He didn't smell so good. Powell had to turn his face away anytime the guy spoke to him, his breath was so bad. Powell just hoped his boat didn't stink as bad as he did. Powell wasn't happy on the sea. He didn't need any encouragement to puke on boats, but he suspected that the stench from this guy's boat might be about to give him a little push in the right direction, just for good luck.

The boat was a fifteen-footer, with a small, enclosed wheelhouse barely big enough for two men. Powell knelt down close to it, took a sniff, and backed off. It reeked of rotting fish and the boat guy's breath, as if it were so toxic that it had stuck to the hull and cabin like gum. Powell had read somewhere that all smells are particulate, which meant that tiny little molecules of the boat guy's stench were now wending their way through his nasal passages. It made Powell even more irritated with the boat guy than he already was, and Powell had been pretty pissed at him before he even got within ten feet of his stinking boat. The guy wasn't even supposed to be here, but he had started to worry about his boat being taken out in bad weather and had come down to the dock to express his concerns. Now Powell was left to clear up the mess before Moloch and the others arrived, because if they got here first, then the boat guy was dead. The way Powell saw it, the last thing this operation needed was more dead people. They already had enough corpses to form a conga line from here to Virginia. Scarfe had assured Powell that the boat guy would keep his mouth shut, just as he had done in the past. Powell hoped that, for his sake, the boat guy started shutting up pretty soon, because Powell was beginning to feel seriously nauseous.

"You got paid, right?" said Powell. "I know, 'cause Scarfe says he did it."

"Yeah, I got paid. I got the money right here."

"So?"

"That boat is worth more than you paid me."

"We're renting it," said Powell, his patience wearing thin as paper. "We don't have to pay you what the boat is worth. That's why it's called 'renting' and not 'buying.'"

"But suppose something happens to it. Scarfe said—"

The fat guy looked over Powell's shoulder to where Scarfe stood in the shadows. Scarfe looked away. The boat guy was on his own. Powell reached out and grabbed his shoulder in order to keep him focused, then instantly regretted touching him.

"I could give a rat's ass what Scarfe said. With luck, you'll have your boat back tonight. Four, five hours, tops. We've been more than generous. You got insurance, right?"

"Yeah, I got insurance, but insurance never pays like it should."

"Why are you telling me? Go write your congressman. All I want is the boat."

"It's nothing illegal, is it?"

Powell looked hard at the guy. "Are you for fucking real? Where do you get off asking a question like that? You want me to tell you?"

The boat guy started to back off. "No, I don't want to know."

"Then take your money and get your fat, stinking ass out of my sight. This piece of shit is all fueled up, right?"

"Sure, it's ready to go."

"Okay, then. We have any problems with this, and we're not going to be looking for a refund, you understand? We're going to want a different level of compensation."

"I understand. You'll have no problems with her."

For a moment, Powell looked confused.

"How do you know—" he began, then stopped. The boat, he was talking about the boat. Shit. Powell let out a deep breath.

"No problems with her," he echoed. "Good. Now go buy yourself some Tic Tacs."

Moloch, Dexter, and Willard arrived shortly after the boat guy had gone on his way, and Tell and Shepherd emerged from out of the shadows. They had wrapped up warm in preparation for the crossing, and had put on the waterproofs purchased in Kittery. The wind had picked up in the last half hour. The snow blew hard against their faces. Powell noted with some amusement that the snowflakes were settling neatly along the lines of Tell's cornrows, contrasting nicely with his dark skin. Powell thought that it made the little man look kind of decorative, Dexter too come to think of it. He didn't consider sharing this observation with them. He suspected that they wouldn't find it funny.

"Storm coming in with a vengeance," said Scarfe.

"Good," said Moloch. "So are we."

Powell, Shepherd, and Dexter clambered down into the boat after Moloch, Scarfe following, then Willard. Scarfe started the motor. He glanced behind him, watching the four men shrug themselves into life jackets, then take their seats on the plastic benches, Powell alone and holding on grimly to the side. Tell untied the boat, tossed the rope down to the deck, then clambered aboard.

Moloch stood beside Scarfe in the wheelhouse. Scarfe was looking at the sky and the thickening snow. The docks around them were already nearly lost to sight and the sea beyond was a vision in static. They were alone on the water.

"How long will it take us to get across?" asked Moloch.

"There's a head wind, and visibility sucks. We'll have to take it slow. We don't hit anything and nothing hits us, then we'll make it in under two hours."

"She could have been there and gone by the time we get to her."

Scarfe shook his head. "Uh-uh. She's facing the same difficulties as we are, plus I reckon that there's going to be no more traffic into and out of the island until morning. The ferry is bedded down for the night. Thorson is no Captain Crunch. He won't take her out if there's even a smell of danger. Unless she gets someone to take her off the island in a private boat, and I don't think that's going to happen, then she's stuck there. Problem is, we may be stuck there too."

Moloch raised his hand, gripped Scarfe's chin, and turned the smaller man's face to his.

"That's not going to happen. You understand?"

Scarfe's reply was muffled because Moloch's grip was so tight, but it was clear that he knew where he stood. Moloch released his grip, and Scarfe pulled the boat away from the dock.

Already, Powell's face was gray. Across from him, Dexter took a package from his pocket and unwrapped it, revealing a meatball sub. As the boat moved away, Powell's cheeks bulged.

"Don't puke on my shoes," warned Dexter.

Powell didn't.

He puked on his own shoes.

Braun and Leonie had some trouble convincing the water taxi to take them over to Sanctuary. The guy didn't want to go, but Leonie, who had read up on the island during the hours at the Days Inn, gave him a sob story about being a cousin of Sylvie Lauter, and how she had come hundreds of miles to console Sylvie's mother. Leonie's tale would have broken a softer man, but the boatman looked like he was made of teak, with a mahogany heart. Braun stayed out of it, figuring that if they both began to work on the guy, they would intimidate themselves out of a ride.

Leonie gave him $150. The boatman relented. She watched him fold the bills and place them in a waterproof wallet that hung on a string around his neck, then tuck the wallet under his shirt. Satisfied, she turned away.

Leonie had none of the scruples of Powell and Braun. She did not like leaving loose ends.

She would get the money back from him when she killed him.

Marianne sat beneath the awning of her water taxi, her arms curled tightly around her, her chin buried beneath folds of coat and scarf. She was shaking uncontrollably. The boatman, thinking her cold, offered her coffee from his flask and she thanked him and wrapped her gloved fingers around the tin cup.

But still she shook.

She had tried calling her sister before the boat left, but the phone had rung out. She had called Karen Meyer, with the same result. She knew in her heart that both were dead, that she had cost them their lives. It was her fault, all her fault.

But if she died, then Danny would also die, and it would all have been in vain. There was still a chance for them, if she could get to Danny in time. Thorson had canceled his final sailing, and appealing to his better nature was not an option. She knew his reputation and doubted if he would make even one leg of the journey and risk being stranded in Portland. Even if he was willing to go to sea, Marianne feared that someone would be watching the ferry in case she tried to escape, certainly from the mainland and possibly from the island itself.

But there were others who might be prepared to take them off the island, if not as far as the mainland, then at least to one of the larger neighboring islands. Carl Lubey had a boat and sometimes made runs if someone was in enough trouble and was prepared to pay him handsomely for it. He was an option, although the idea of being at his mercy was unappealing. Her other option was Jack the painter. He also had a boat, and she knew that he cared for Danny. If he was sober, he was their best chance.

There were lights to her right and left: the houses on nearby islands, their windows hanging suspended in the darkness like fissures in the fabric of the night, or the promise of new worlds. She fantasized about taking Danny and disappearing through one of them, sewing it closed behind her so that nobody could ever find them again. The lights disappeared as the snow thickened and the wind picked up. The little boat tossed on the waves and she held tightly to the ropes, spray drenching her face and chilling her hands. She wore the boatman's spare oilskins, but water was still finding its way through. She thought of her son, and she thought too of Joe Dupree. She could turn to him, but the risks were too great. She would be forced to reveal the truth about herself and she couldn't do that.

But there was another reason that she was unwilling to ask him for help. She had seen Willard, and knew that Moloch must be close by. There would be others too, perhaps not as bad as her husband and the pretty, dangerous boy-man, but bad enough.

Joe Dupree was not strong enough to stand against them.

If she turned to him for help, they would kill him.

They would kill them all.

Dupree stood at the station house door and watched the snow fall. Already, Island Avenue was empty. The stores had closed early and the Rudder and Good Eats would not be opening for business. The ferry would return to port any minute now and Thorson would kill the lights on the dock and hang out a "Sailing Canceled" sign. The snow was already sticking to the sidewalks, the shadows of the flakes made huge by the glow of the streetlights as they descended. No cars were moving anywhere on the island. The risks of ending up in a ditch or, worse, taking a tumble into the cold sea were too great.

He heard footsteps behind him. Macy was wrapped up warm. She had added an extra sweater to her uniform, and her hands were double wrapped in a pair of woolen gloves and a leather pair from the station locker.

"No luck," she said. She had been trying to raise Portland on the radio for the last hour, but there was only static. The phone line, meanwhile, had exchanged a dial tone for a steady hum. Dupree had wandered over to check with Larry Amerling in his house behind the post office, but his phone was also without a proper tone. It looked as if the entire island was going into communication meltdown.

"Did you get out to the Site?" Amerling asked Dupree as the policeman prepared to leave.

"Yes, I went out there."

"And?"

"There were moths. A *lot* of moths."

"That's all?"

Dupree debated telling him about the vibrations in the ground, then decided against it. The postmaster looked edgy enough as things stood.

"That's all, and after this snow I don't think we'll be seeing too many more moths on the island until the summer. Stay warm, Larry. I'll check in with you at the post office tomorrow morning."

He left the postmaster, pulling the front door closed behind him. A moment or two later, he heard the sound of the dead bolts locking.

Now, beside him, he saw Macy trying to dial a cell phone number. The display showed a ringing phone symbol, indicating that it was attempting to make a connection, then returned to the Verizon home screen. The aerial strength indicator read virtually nil. Even the reception on the TV in the rec room was terrible.

"Guess we batten down the hatches," she said.

"Guess so."

He didn't even look at her.

Quiet time, she thought. I can do quiet time. I just wish you'd close the damn door.

Macy's day had been spent on largely mundane matters. There was the B&E that turned out to be nothing more than an embarrassed husband who had climbed in through the kitchen window while dead drunk the previous night, broken plates, and knocked over the portable TV in the kitchen, then fallen asleep in the spare room because he was afraid of waking his wife, unaware that she had popped enough sleeping pills to allow half of San Francisco to sleep through an earthquake. His wife had eventually come to, spotted the damage, and called the cops. The first her husband knew about it all was when Macy arrived at their door while he was throwing up in the john. The woman began hollering at her husband and calling him ten types of asshole while he just held his head in pain and shame.

Macy left them to it.

Apart from the happy couple, she had issued a warning to the owners of a scrawny mongrel dog that was trying to bite passing cars, and talked to a couple of kids who were smoking and probably drinking (they'd hidden the beer cans somewhere in the undergrowth, but Macy was damned if she was going to go beating the bushes with a stick for a couple of Miller High Lifes) out by the old gun emplacement. She'd taken their names, then told them to haul their asses back home. One girl, dressed in a black leather motorcycle jacket and combat pants, with a Korn T-shirt underneath and a spiked dog collar around her neck, hung back.

"Are you going to tell my mom and dad?" she asked Macy. The girl's name, according to her driver's license, was Mandy Papkee.

"I don't know. You got any reason why I shouldn't?"

"We weren't doing any harm. We just came out here to remember Wayne and Sylvie."

Macy knew about the accident on the island the week before. A lot of the people she had met that day insisted on talking about it, if only to assure her that things like that didn't happen very often on Dutch. Sometimes, the older ones said "on Sanctuary," reinforcing the seemingly dual nature of the island's existence.

"You knew them?"

"Everybody knows everyone else out here," said Mandy. "I mean, duh, it's an island."

"Duh?" repeated Macy, pointedly.

"Sorry," said Mandy. "Look, we're not going to be back out here, not for a long time. I can promise that."

"Why?"

"Because it gives us the creeps. This was, like, a stupid dare. We shouldn't have come here. It just feels wrong."

"Because of what happened to your friends?"

"Maybe."

Mandy clearly didn't want to say anything more, but she looked around at the trees, as if half expecting Sylvie and Wayne to emerge bloodied from the undergrowth, looking for a beer and a toke.

"Look, just give us a break, okay?"

Macy relented. "Okay," she said, and watched Mandy follow her friends back to the road. Something flitted across the grass toward Macy's feet. It was a moth, an ugly gray one. Macy flicked her foot at it and the moth flew away. She strolled over to the damaged tree against which the stolen car had finally come to rest and saw the little shrine that had been raised in memory of the dead teenagers. She touched nothing.

By the time she got back to the Explorer, Mandy and the other kids were gone.

That was about as interesting as things got. For the most part, she drove around the island, familiarizing herself with its roads and trails, talking to people as they went about their daily business. Occasionally she made contact with Dupree, but he seemed distracted. When the light began to fade, she returned to the station house and stayed there.

She went upstairs to the little galley kitchen beside the rec room, poured chicken soup from a can into a plastic bowl, then placed the bowl in the microwave. She took a book from her pack, lay back on the sofa, and started to read. There was still some time to kill before the ferry arrived.

Out on Sunset Road, Doug Newton checked on his mother. Her breathing was shallow and the dark patches around her eyes were like new bruises. He touched the old woman's skin with the backs of his fingers. She felt cold, even though the radiators were turned up as high as they would go. Doug went to the hall closet and took out another comforter. He laid it on her bed, tucking it in beneath her chin, then walked to the alcove window and looked out onto his yard. The exterior lights were on and he could see the snow falling and the shapes of the trees slowly emerging as the flakes came to rest upon them. Beyond, there was only darkness.

Doug tugged at the lock on the window. It was firmly closed, as were all the windows in the house. He recalled what he believed he had seen: a little girl at his mother's half-open window, her fingers prising at the gap to widen it. When Doug had entered the room, the girl had stared at him for no more than a second or two, then retreated. By the time Doug reached the window, she was gone from sight. The girl was five or six years of age, or so he had told Joe Dupree, but Doug had said that last part with a slight tremor of doubt in his voice, because the girl might have had the body of a child, but her eyes were much older, and her mouth was all wrong. It was very round, like it was about to give a kiss.

The funny thing about it was that Joe Dupree, old Melancholy Joe himself, hadn't laughed at him, or accused him of wasting police time the way that other cop Tuttle had. Instead, Joe had told him to do just what he was doing: keep his mother warm, and keep the doors and windows locked, just in case.

Just in case.

Doug went back downstairs, turned on the TV, and tried to watch a game show through a snowstorm worse than the one outside.

On Church Road, Nancy and Linda Tooker were arguing over the dogs. They'd taken the collie and the German shepherd indoors because of the snow, but now the dogs just wouldn't stop whining. Nancy had opened the kitchen door to see if they wanted to go back out, but the dogs had instead retreated farther into the house and were now lying in the darkness at the top of the stairs, still crying.

"It was you who wanted pedigree dogs," said Nancy. "Damn things are too highly strung. I told you."

"Can it!" said her sister. She was trying to connect to AOL, but with no success. Eventually, the screen just froze and she was forced to unplug the computer from the wall. When she tried to restart it, nothing happened.

"Nancy," she said. "I think I broke the computer."

But Nancy wasn't listening. Instead, she watched through the kitchen window as gray shapes danced across the snow. Her sister joined her, and together they stood in silence as the insects flew among the snowflakes, seemingly untroubled by the wind that shook the windows and caused closed doors to strike against their frames. Once or twice they banged against the glass and the Tookers got a clear look at the ugly moths.

Without consulting each other, the two sisters locked all the doors, secured the windows, and took their places with the dogs.

In his little bedroom, Carl Lubey wrapped himself up warm and pulled on a pair of steel-capped boots. The wind tugged at the windows of his house, causing them to rattle furiously. What little warmth there was seeped out through countless cracks and gaps in the woodwork. Ron was the one with the talent for houses, not Carl. Carl was the mechanic; Ron was the builder, the handyman. Now his brother was gone and Carl was left alone to deal with the wind and the rain and the snow as best he could.

He went to his bedside locker and removed the Browning. It had a shitty plastic grip plate that was supposed to look like wood but didn't, and the magazine catch jammed on occasion, but Carl wasn't fussy. He didn't think he'd have much call to use it, not if the visitors came through for him. If things went like they were supposed to, his brother would sleep easy in his grave tonight.

At the heart of the island, close by the Site, there was movement among the trees and beneath the earth. Despite a wind that blew hard from the west, shrubs bent toward the east, and flurries of snow rose in spirals and formed shapes that almost resembled the bodies of men, before they disintegrated and tumbled gently toward the ground. Seen from above, it might have appeared that gray light was seeping out from the ground, or a thin, dirty smoke that left no mark on the snow.

There were no more whispers. Now the wind sounded like voices, and the voices were joyful.

CHAPTER TWELVE

Macy spotted the ferry pulling into port from her vantage point on the second floor. Its arrival had been delayed by the weather, Thorson unwilling to push the ferry's speed into little more than double figures. The faint streamer of smoke was barely visible through the thickening snow, although Thorson had lit the boat itself like a Christmas tree. It almost hurt her eyes to look at it.

"Ferry's in," she called to Dupree.

He was catching up on paperwork in the little office. The doors leading outside were now firmly closed and the heating had kicked in enough to enable him to remove his jacket.

"You don't have to go," he said. "I'm pretty sure it's my turn."

"Nah, I'm dressed for it. Besides, it will give me something to do."

"Thanks," he said, and returned to his reports.

The wind had picked up force and the snow blew directly into her face, stinging her cheeks. She removed the windshield cover from the Explorer and tossed it on the passenger seat, then started the engine and drove carefully down to the dock, parking over by the passenger shelter until the ferry came in. The chains on the wheels made a ratcheting sound on the road, and the snowplow attachment that she and Dupree had fitted earlier that evening rattled against the grille.

A handful of passengers disembarked from the ferry, all of them apparently locals who raced for their own cars or caught rides from friends or family. Macy watched them leave, then saw another, smaller vessel heading into port. The water taxi docked and a harried-looking woman was helped out by the boatman. There seemed to be some argument, and Macy was about to head over and intervene when the boatman abruptly turned away, cast off, and headed out of port. He paused briefly to exchange some words with Thorson, who leaned over from his roost to talk, then continued on his way.

The woman did a double take when she saw the Explorer, then headed straight up the hill to where her car was parked. Macy followed, pulling in alongside her as she fumbled with her car keys.

"Everything okay, ma'am?"

The woman looked at her and tried to smile.

"Yes, thank you, everything's fine. I'm just late to pick up my son, that's all. He'll be worried."

Macy smiled, as if she really understood what it was like to have a child waiting for her to return, but the woman was no longer looking at her. Instead, she was staring over Macy's shoulder, looking back out to sea. Macy glanced in her rearview mirror, but the ferry was the only boat in sight. The water taxi was already lost amid the snow.

"Can I ask your name, ma'am?"

The woman jerked as if she'd just been hit with an electric shock.

"Marianne Elliot," she said. "My name is Marianne Elliot."

"Were you having trouble with the taxi?"

"Just a disagreement about the fare, that's all. In the end, I paid a little over the odds, but it's a bad night. It was good of him to take me over after I missed the ferry."

Macy examined the woman's face but saw no reason to doubt her story. She patted the car roof and moved back.

"Well, Miss Elliot, you take care on the road. I know you're in a hurry, but you want to get back to your son safe and sound, don't you?"

For the first time, the woman seemed to truly notice her.

"Yes," she said. "More than anything else in the world."

Thorson was sipping coffee in the cabin of the ferry when Macy came onboard.

The captain offered her his flask and a spare cup, but she declined.

"You're not making another crossing, right?" she asked. Dupree had told her to check, although he had been pretty certain that Thorson would not be taking the ferry out again.

Thorson stared out into the night. He even looks like a ferry captain, thought Macy: white beard, red cheeks, yellow oilskins. He was a good captain, according to Dupree; in all its long history, there had never been an accident involving Thorson's ferry. He was just more respectful of the sea than most.

"You kidding? There's already a small-craft advisory in place, and even the Casco Bay ferries are going to stop running in an hour. There won't be a boat on the water after that. Soon as I finish my coffee I'm heading home, and that'll be me done until the morning."

"Okay, just thought I'd make sure. Say, you know the captain of that water taxi that came in just now?"

"Yeah, that's Ed Oldfield. I was surprised to see him out so far on a night like this."

"He say anything to you about the woman he brought over?"

"Marianne? No, just that she seemed to want him to wait for her and take her back to Portland. He wouldn't do it. If he waited any longer he'd be stuck here overnight, and he's got a family at home on Chebeague."

Macy thanked him and returned to the Explorer, then headed back through town toward the station house. Dupree was still hunched over his desk, painstakingly typing details into the primitive-looking computer on his desk as he tried to avoid hitting two keys simultaneously with his big fingers. He looked up as Macy entered, brushing snow from her jacket.

"Anything unusual?"

"A few locals, and a water taxi. Just one passenger onboard. She said her name was Marianne Elliot."

Macy picked up on the look that crossed Dupree's face.

"You know her?"

"Yeah," he said.

Was he blushing? she wondered.

"She's a friend."

"She was in quite a hurry. Said she was late to pick up her kid. Thorson said he thought she might be trying to get back to the mainland tonight."

Dupree frowned. "Nobody's going back to Portland tonight. Maybe I'll take a run by her place later, make sure she's okay."

Despite herself, Macy felt one of her eyebrows arch.

"What?" said Dupree.

"Nothing," said Macy, trying to sound innocent. "Nothing like a concerned, active police force."

"Yeah." He sounded dubious. "Speaking of concerned and active, you mind taking a short ride out?" Dupree was worried about Marianne now. He couldn't understand why she would want to return to Portland before morning, unless there was something wrong. He'd use his own Jeep to drop in at her place as soon as he had finished his paperwork.

"No problem, but that snow is falling pretty heavily and the wind is picking up some. Soon, it's going to start to drift."

"I don't want you to make a full circuit of the island, not in this weather. Larry Amerling told me you were out by the main watchtower today. You think you can find it again?"

"It's easy enough to find: take a right on Division and straight on till morning, right?"

"That's it. Heard you ran into Carl Lubey while you were out there."

"He was charming. Still single too. Quite a catch."

"Yeah, like catching rabies. Could you swing by Lubey's place?" He pointed it out to her on the wall map. "It's a shit-hole, so you can't miss it, even in this weather. Couple of rusted-out cars in the drive and a big screw-you satellite dish in the yard. Last night, I had to roust him from the bar along with a mainland lowlife named Terry Scarfe. According to Thorson, Terry didn't come back over today, but I still don't like the fact that he and Lubey were spending time together."

Macy zipped up her jacket and got ready to go, but Dupree stopped her.

"I guess you already know it, but Carl Lubey is the brother of a man I shot. I killed him. Carl's a sleazebag, but he's harmless alone. If I go out there, I'll only rile him up, and the next thing we know we'll have him cuffed to the chair over there, smelling up the place until morning. I hate to do this to you on your first night and all, but it will put my mind at rest if I know that Carl Lubey is tucked up safe in his bed. The tree coverage should mean that the road is still okay, but you run into any problems and you just come right back, y'hear?"

Macy told him that she would. Secretly, she was pleased to be leaving the station house. The TV wasn't working properly and she was likely to be cooped up inside until morning. One last trip out would kill some time and leave her with more of her book to read. She drove carefully up Island Avenue until she left the street lamps behind, then put her headlights on full and followed the coast toward Division.

Carl Lubey was not tucked up safe in his bed, although he was starting to wish that he was. Curiously, he was thinking about Macy, just as Macy was now thinking about him, because he was staring into the innards of his truck, a truck that right now just would not start.

The cop had warned him. She said she'd seen it billowing fumes, but he just hadn't listened.

Son of a bitch.

It had been driving okay earlier in the day, but now, just when he needed it to run, the engine was turning over with a click. The battery was new, so it couldn't be that. Inside his garage, with the lamp hanging from the hood, Carl took a rag and wiped the oil from his hands. It could be the starter, he figured, but that would take time to repair and he didn't have that kind of time. He had people to meet, and if Scarfe was telling the truth, they were the kind of people who wouldn't take kindly to being kept waiting. He didn't want them to wait, either. The sooner they got what they wanted, the sooner he would get what he wanted, which was a big dead policeman.

Carl was a coward. He knew he was a coward, although sometimes, when he was liquored up, he liked to tell himself that he was just smart, and that men like him, smaller and weaker than those around them, had to find other ways to fight back when people did them a bad turn. If that meant stabbing them in the back, then so be it. If they hadn't crossed him, they wouldn't have had to worry about their backs anyway.

Carl's brother was different—strong and hard and, hell, maybe even kind of mean, but a real man, one who had stood up for his little brother time and time again. And because Ron had been a stand-up guy for Carl, when the time came, Carl had been a stand-up guy for him.

Carl still remembered the call. They'd both been out drinking in Portland, and Ron had headed off with some woman he'd picked up in Three-Dollar Dewey's. She looked kind of familiar to Carl. According to Ron, she was Jeanne Aiello, all grown up. Generations of Aiellos had lived out on Dutch until Jeanne's parents had grown tired of the isolation and had left for more "civilized" surroundings. Now little Jeanne was back in Maine, working in one of those tourist stores in the Old Port, and seemed real happy to be making Ron's acquaintance once again.

Carl left them to it, and because he was still thirsty and had a beer appetite, he took a cab out to the Great Lost Bear on Forest Avenue and got himself a big basket of wings. It wasn't Carl's favorite bar, owing to the fact that the Portland cops liked to drink there, but he was hungry and the Bear was one of the few bars that served food late at night. He was halfway through his wings when his cell phone started ringing and he heard his brother's voice when he answered the call. Ron wasn't panicked, though, or afraid. He just told Carl to get in a cab and head over to Windham, and Carl had done just that, leaving the cab about a half mile from the address his brother had given him, as he had been instructed to do. Ron was waiting at the door of the house when he got there, and waved his brother in quickly. There were cuts on his face.

The woman was lying on the bathroom floor, and her face was all torn up. The mirror above the sink was shattered and there was a big shard of it in her eye. Smaller pieces were embedded in her cheeks and her forehead. Carl looked at his brother's right hand and saw that some of the woman's hair was still caught in his nails.

"I just lost it, man," said Ron. "I don't know what happened. She brought me back here and we was drinking, fooling around. We head for the bedroom and I try to get it on and next thing she's pushing me away, calling me an animal. We started fighting, she ran to the bathroom, and then I was just pushing her against the wall and I couldn't stop."

He began to cry.

"I couldn't stop, Carlie. I couldn't stop."

It was Carl's finest moment. He told his brother to go find some rubber gloves and cleaning products, anything that could help them clear the scene. While Ron wiped everything, Carl wrapped the woman in sheets, then double-bagged her with black plastic garbage sacks, using tape to bind her tight as a fly's ass. They washed everything down, until the house was cleaner than it had ever been before, then filled a suitcase with clothes, makeup, and what little jewelry they could find. There wasn't much that could be done about the broken mirror, so Carl just removed the last pieces from the frame and put a small vanity mirror from the bedroom on the bathroom sink.

That way, he hoped, anyone who saw it would think that Jeanne had broken the bathroom mirror herself and was content to use the vanity mirror until she got around to replacing it. They put the suitcase and the body in the trunk of her car and drove down to their boat. Jeanne was loaded into the cabin and covered with a tarp, and then Carl parked her car on India Street and walked back to rejoin his brother. When they were half an hour out of port, they weighted her body with Carl's old toolbox, which they kept in the boat for emergencies, and then dumped her overboard. She was never seen again by any living person, her body descending beneath the waves, lost to the eyes of the world and watched only by the ghost of a boy, for this was his place.

Jeanne Aiello was reported missing by her parents two days later, but by then her car had already been found. The cops were suspicious, maybe because Carl and Ron had gone a little overboard with their cleaning, leading the cops to wonder why a woman seemingly intent on heading off without telling anyone where she was going would clean her house so assiduously before she left. But there was no body for them to examine, and the description of the man with whom she had left the bar was so general that half the guys in Portland could have filled the bill. It looked as if Carl and Ron had managed to get away, literally, with murder.

But the relief was only temporary. It pained Carl to see the deterioration in his brother. He stopped working, started drinking more, and began talking gibberish about the woods. That was what frightened Carl most, the stuff about the forest. His brother was spending more and more time in the woods. He liked to hunt deer, and before the cull in '99, the island had been nearly overrun with them. Nobody objected much to folks shooting them and filling up their freezers with the meat, although there was no way that Ron and Carl had a freezer big enough for all the dead meat Ron had created in the woods. But Ron wasn't even hunting anymore. He would just head out into the woods with a couple of six-packs or a bottle of sour mash, and when he returned he would be carrying on conversations that had clearly begun a long time before, and were the continuation of some ongoing argument.

"No, I tell you, I ain't done it. It weren't my fault. No, no, no. You got to let me be now, y'hear?"

He also stopped shaving and combing his hair, because doing those things meant looking in mirrors, and Ron didn't like looking in mirrors anymore, because Ron's reflection wasn't the only one he saw when he looked in the glass.

On the night that Ron died, Carl had left him to go meet up with some people down at the Rudder. Ron had seemed pretty lucid, clearer at least than he had been in months.

"Hey, little brother," he said as Carl headed for the door. His brother was sitting slumped in an easy chair, staring at the fire. "I been thinking. I forced you to do a bad thing that night with the woman. I shouldn't have made you get involved."

"You're my brother," said Carl. "I'd do anything for you."

"They're gonna make me pay," said Ron. "I have to pay for what I done. There are boundaries that you're not supposed to overstep. They won't tolerate that, so you have to pay."

"Who? Who's going to make you pay?"

But Ron didn't seem to hear him.

"But I figure that if I pay, maybe that'll be enough. Maybe they won't want no more. Maybe they'll leave you be."

But when Carl tried to get more out of him, Ron had drifted off into a boozy sleep.

He remembered sitting at a table in the Rudder, not drinking much because he was so disturbed by his brother's words.

He heard the sound of the approaching chopper, then someone came in and said that Snowman, that cop with the dumb name, had been shot, and that—

And then the guy had looked at Carl, and Carl had known.

They said later that his brother had been shooting at the houses nearby, that he was all fired up over some imaginary boundary dispute with his neighbors, but Carl never believed that was true. Ron wasn't shooting at houses when he died, and the boundaries of which he spoke had nothing to do with hedges or lawns. He was shooting at the things he imagined were speaking to him in the woods, and it was the transgression of *their* boundaries that led to his death. It was bullshit, of course. Ron's mind had just collapsed under the weight of his guilt. But since then Carl had kept well clear of the woods that surrounded his house, sticking to the roads and the main paths. Whatever had tormented his brother might have been all in his head, but Carl recalled an incident a week or two back, shortly after the fourth anniversary of Ron's death, when he was out in the yard bringing in supplies from his truck and he looked out into the forest and saw someone watching him from among the trees. Carl didn't panic, though. Instead, he laid the brown paper bags down on the ground and, never taking his eyes off the figure in the woods, removed his shotgun from its case in the back of his truck. He loaded it up with the truck shielding him, then headed for the trees.

The figure was dressed all in gray, and seemed to shimmer.

"Who are you?" asked Carl, as he drew closer.

And then the figure had exploded, shards of it spreading in all directions, into the trees, into the sky, along the ground.

And toward Carl.

Carl turned his face away and shielded himself with one

arm. He felt things striking him, felt them moving as they did so. When at last he lowered his arm, there was nothing before him but darkness and trees, but something was caught in the folds of his coat. It fluttered and beat against him, until he released it and allowed it to fly free.

It was a moth, a gray moth. Somehow, Carl had managed to disturb a whole bunch of them in the trees. That was the only excuse he could find, even as he backed toward his truck and recalled the shape that they had somehow formed: the shape of a woman.

That was all beside the point. Joe Dupree, the freak cop, had killed Carl's brother, and now there would be payback for what he had done. For the chance of revenge, Carl was prepared to risk a trip into the woods. After all, he would not be going in alone.

Carl looked at his watch, hissed in irritation, and returned to the engine of his truck.

The first boat, piloted by Scarfe, came in sight of Cray Cove shortly before nine. They could barely see the island through the wall of snow, but Scarfe knew what he was doing. Without him, they would have run aground on rocks and drowned before they came within spitting distance of land.

Despite the weather, Scarfe had enjoyed being in command of a boat again. Being on the sea was one of the things he had missed most while locked up. Scarfe's father knew about boats, and had passed on that knowledge to his son. As soon as the diesel engine began to turn over, and the vibrations commenced beneath his feet, Scarfe was at home. Under other circumstances, he would have cranked the boat faster as soon as they were out on the bay. Instead, he throttled down and kept a steady pace across the water in the face of the wind, until at last they came to the jetty. Powell tied the boat up, and, with a hint of regret, Scarfe cut the engine. He looked out on the silhouette of the island, barely visible through the falling flakes, and thought again that it was strange to see an outer island so thickly forested. Most of them boasted little more than sawgrass and burdock, but Sanctuary was different. Sanctuary had *always* been different.

The snow, thought Moloch, was a mixed blessing: the weather would keep other people indoors, and permit them to move about with greater ease, but there was now the risk of some of them getting separated and lost. And if anyone did spot them, they would have a hard time explaining why they were wandering around in a near blizzard.

Yet as soon as he set foot on the island, Moloch's fears seemed to disappear. Images flashed through his mind, pictures from his dreams and other, less familiar thoughts. He saw trails hidden from the eyes of others. He recalled the names of trees and plants. A great wave of understanding broke upon him.

I know this place.

I know it.

Moloch gestured to Dexter, Powell, Shepherd, and Scarfe, inviting them to follow him. Tell said nothing. Willard just watched them quietly.

"You stay here for now," Moloch told Tell and Willard. "Watch the boat. When we get back, we'll need to leave fast."

Then they moved away, slowly fading into the gathering whiteness.

The water taxi was within sight of the island when Leonie appeared at the boatman's shoulder. The crossing had been rough, and both she and Braun were wet and cold, their heads and shoulders sprinkled with snow.

"How do you find your way in from here?" Leonie asked.

The boatman shrugged. "The worst is past. This is easy. A child could do it. Truth is, I could put this boat in anywhere along here. Dock is just as good a place as any."

He smiled, and she smiled back. She was a good-looking woman. It was nice to see a mixed-race couple happy together, he thought. He looked over to the little parking lot by the shelter, expecting to see the shape of the police Explorer, but it wasn't there. No call for it, he supposed, now that Thorson's ferry was docked.

"You folks are looking for a place to stay, the motel's over there," he said, pointing to his right. The motel had four rooms, and backed onto a slope that led down to the small, rocky cove that gave the town its name. "If there's nobody around, call over at the bar. Jeb Burris owns both. His house is just behind it."

Leonie thanked him, then added: "Looks quiet."

"Yeah, sure doesn't look like there's anyone around."

Leonie stepped away, raised her silenced pistol, and shot the boatman in the head.

Willard watched the group of men depart. Cray Cove was a small inlet with a jetty made of rocks that jutted out a little from the shore. It was secluded and Willard could make out no lights on the shore. A pathway led up from the stony beach and he could see flashlights dancing, the only visible sign of the ascent to the road above.

During the crossing, Moloch had sat beside him and told him that he would not be joining them.

"You don't trust me," said Willard.

Moloch touched the younger man's shoulder. "I'm concerned about you, that's all. Maybe you've been forced to do too much this last week. I just want you to bring it down a couple of notches, take a breather. As for trust, it's Tell I don't trust, not you. We've never worked with him before. If things go wrong and he tries to leave without us, you take him apart, you hear?"

Willard nodded, and Moloch left him and returned to the wheelhouse.

Willard wanted to believe him. He wanted to believe him so badly. He might have stifled his doubts too, had it not been for Dexter. As Dexter had disembarked, he had glanced back at Willard and Willard had understood that as far as Dexter was concerned, it was the last time that they would look upon each other.

Dexter had even smiled at him.

The five men were making slow progress on the track, slipping on the new-fallen snow and stumbling into one another. Dexter reached the top before the others, followed closely by Powell. Moloch, Shepherd, and Scarfe were some way behind.

It was Dexter who saw the man first. He was standing at the doorway of a small, three-story tower with slit windows, one gloved hand shielding his eyes so he could better see the lights of the approaching men. Dexter's first impression was that the man was pulling a face at him, taunting him, but then Dexter spotted the heavy lids, the muted curiosity in the eyes, the slight slackness at the jaw.

"We got trouble," said Dexter.

* * *

Richie Claeson liked snow more than just about anything else in the world. He thought about waking Danny and asking him to come out with him, but then he reconsidered. Danny was small, and didn't know the woods like he did, so Richie dressed quietly, then put on his boots, his thick coat, and his hat and gloves, and headed out. He didn't tell Momma. She was asleep in front of the TV and he didn't want to wake her. Anyway, she would tell him no, and he didn't want that. He wanted to see the island in the snow, but instead of heading directly through the forest, he had stuck close by the road until he found himself upon the shore.

Richie usually felt no threat from the woods, and he was, though he would never have been able to put it in such terms, acutely sensitive to danger, a consequence of his condition that had kept him safe from harm on those occasions when he was at risk from older boys or, once, while he was in Portland with his mother and an old man had tried to entice him into an alleyway with the promise of discarded comic books. He had smelled the threat the old man posed, a stale scent of raddled discharges and unwashed clothing, and had walked away, keeping his head down, his left side to the wall, his eyes slightly to the right in case the man should choose to follow him.

The woods were different. They were safe. There was a presence in the woods, although Richie had long believed that he had no reason to be afraid of it. The woods still smelled as woods should, of pine and fallen leaves and animal spoor, but there was a stillness to them, a watchfulness that made him feel safe, as if some stronger, older being was watching over him, just as Mrs. Arbinot in the kindergarten had tried to look out for him before they took Richie away from the other children and put him in the special school in Portland. He liked the special school. He made friends there for the first time, proper friends. He even kissed a girl, Abbie, and recalled with embarrassment the feelings that she had aroused in him, and how he had half-shuffled away from her to disguise his growing discomfort.

But the woods had changed in recent times. In the past, Richie had caught glimpses of the boy, the one who stood at the water's edge staring out at the sea, the boy who left no footprints on the wet sand. Richie had tried calling to him, and waving, but the boy never looked back, and eventually Richie had given up trying to talk to him. Sometimes he saw the boy in the woods, but mostly the boy stayed by the shore and watched the waves break. The boy didn't frighten Richie, though. The boy was dead. He just didn't want to leave the island, and Richie could understand that. Richie didn't want to leave the island either.

But the Gray Girl *did* frighten Richie. He had seen her only two or three times, hanging in the air, her feet not quite touching the ground, her eyes like the backs of black beetles that had crawled into her head and nested in her sockets, but she scared Richie bad enough to make him piss his pants. The Gray Girl was angry, angry with everyone who lived because she wanted to be alive too. The boy was waiting for something, but the little Gray Girl didn't want to wait. She wanted it *now*. So Richie had begun to stay away from the Site, where the woods were thickest, and from the tall watchtower at the center of the island. He used to like the big watchtower a lot. From the top, he could see for miles and miles, and the wind would blow his hair and he could taste the sea on his tongue when he opened his mouth. But that was the Gray Girl's place now. Joe Dupree came by to check on it, and he would make sure that the door was locked, but the Gray Girl didn't like it when the door was locked so she found ways to open it again. The Gray Girl wanted the door open, because if it was open, then people might come in.

And if people came in, and they weren't too careful, then they might get to play with the Gray Girl.

She was the worst, but there were others too, and the area around the tower and the cross belonged to them. To go in there now would be like standing in front of a train. The train wouldn't mean to hit you, wouldn't have any intention of hurting you, but if you got in its way, it would kill you as it hurtled toward its destination. That was what the woods now felt like to Richie: a dark tunnel, with a train rushing through it, ready to smash anything in its path.

But the shore was still safe, and there were trees beneath which to shelter. Except tonight the snow had started to fall really heavily, heavier than Richie had ever seen it fall before, and the wind had grown very strong and had blown the snow into Richie's eyes. He had sought cover in one of the old observation towers, a little one by the road, hoping to wait out the bad weather. Then the boat had come. He could barely make it out until it got close to shore, but he heard the men as they reached land.

And suddenly, he was afraid.

He wanted to go home.

He left the shelter of the tower just as the black man appeared and saw him.

Tell's voice brought Willard back. He could no longer perceive Moloch and the others, for they had now ascended the slope, but he thought that he could still catch glimpses of their flashlight beams through the snow. There was a pain in Willard's belly. It made him want to curl up in a ball, like a little child. His eyes stung and he felt tears creep down his cheeks.

"I said, you want to stow these away?"

Willard wiped his face hurriedly as Tell handed him a stack of life jackets. He pointed to the storage chest at the stern of the little boat.

"In there."

Willard took the jackets in his arms, then knelt down to store them. Behind him, he heard Tell rummaging in his pack, then sensed the little man moving close behind him. He looked over his shoulder and into the barrel of the pistol. Tell's own gun, a Colt .45, was still in his belt. The gun in his hand was a one-shot .22, silenced to hell and back.

No noise, that was Moloch's instruction to Tell. No noise and no pain.

"You're a crazy bastard, you know that?" said Tell. "You gave us all the fucking creeps."

Willard didn't blink as the trigger was pulled.

"He's a dummy," said Dexter.

Powell looked at him.

"What did you say?"

"The guy's a dummy," repeated Dexter. "He's handicapped."

Richie stood across the road from them, but didn't move. Powell squinted against the snow and saw the man's face, except now that he looked, the man seemed younger, more a kid than an adult. But Dexter was right. The kid, or man, or whatever the hell he was, was retarded.

"What are we going to do with him?" asked Powell.

"Take him back to the boat, I guess," said Scarfe. "Let Tell keep an eye on him until we got to go, then turn him loose."

He heard a scrabbling sound behind him, and turned to see Moloch hauling himself up the last stretch of trail with the aid of a sapling.

Moloch looked at Richie, and Richie stared back.

"Bad men," said Richie.

"What did he say?" asked Powell.

Richie began to walk quickly away, but they could hear him muttering to himself.

"He recognized me," said Moloch.

"The fuck could he do that? Dex said he was a dummy."

"I don't know how. TV maybe. Stop him."

Dexter and Powell began to move after him, but the snow was thicker up here on the exposed road, and they struggled and slipped as they tried to catch up with him.

"Hey, wait up!" called Dexter, but Richie kept his head down, his face set determinedly. It was the face he wore when other boys taunted him, or tried to show him pictures of naked ladies.

It was the face he wore when he was afraid, and trying not to cry.

"Bad men," he whispered to himself. "Badmenbadmen-badmen."

Behind him, he heard the black man swear loudly as he stumbled.

Richie started to run.

Carl Lubey was beginning to panic. He had tried everything he knew and there was still no sign of life from the truck. As a last resort, he'd decided to change the battery. He was lifting the spare from the back of the garage when the radio in the truck exploded into life, almost deafening him with the last bars of

"Freebird." The radio was permanently tuned to the island's amateur station, run by Dickie Norcross out of his attic, except Dickie broadcast only between the hours of two and six, and it was now well past Dickie's good-bye time.

"And that one's going out to all the folks on the island who are battening down the hatches for a hard night ahead," said the disc jockey's voice. It sounded strangely familiar to Carl. It wasn't Dickie Norcross, not by a long shot. Dickie had a kind of high-pitched voice, and tended to limit his voice-overs to birthday greetings and obituaries. This was a woman's voice.

"Especially Carl Lubey over there in the deep, dark forest, who's having trouble with his truck. *Ain't ya, Carlie?*"

The voice was distorted, as though the woman had just put her mouth right over the mike.

"This one's for you, Carl," said the voice, and then the first bars of "Freebird" commenced. "Freebird": his brother's favorite song.

"It's all 'Freebird,' all night," continued the DJ, and Carl knew the voice, recalled it from that night in the Old Port when his brother had leaned into little Jeanne Aiello as their voices rose in harmony over the sound of some piece of southern-rock shit playing on the jukebox.

Carl Lubey grabbed a crowbar and smashed the radio with one blow, sending the dead woman's voice back into the void from which it had issued.

"Fuck!" said Dexter. The dummy was disappearing from sight. Even in his bright orange winter clothing he would soon be lost in the snow. Already he was little more than a blur among the falling snowflakes, but for some reason he was staying away from the woods. Instead, Dexter could see him silhouetted against the cliff edge some forty feet above the water, running with a strange, awkward gait, his elbows held rigid against his sides.

Dexter drew his bow from his back and notched one of the heavy Beman Camo Hunter arrows against the string. The head was triangular, with three blades extending out from the central point.

"What are you doing?"

Dexter felt Scarfe's hand on his arm, distracting him from the coldness of the arrow against his cheek.

"Get your hand off me, man."

"He's handicapped. He's no threat to us."

"I said get your hand off me."

"Do as he says." It was Moloch.

Scarfe's hand remained on the black man's arm for a second or two longer, then fell away.

Dexter aimed, then released the arrow.

Richie could no longer hear the men behind him. Maybe he was safe. Maybe they were letting him go. He thought of his mother, and began to cry. His mother often told him that he wasn't a little kid anymore, that he was a man, and that men didn't cry, but he was frightened, and he wanted to be back at home, back in his bed. He wanted to be asleep. He wanted—

Richie felt a push at his back, as if a great hand had shoved him forward, and then a searing pain tore straight through the center of his being and erupted from his chest. He staggered, and looked down. His fingertips brushed the blades as his mind tried to register what he was seeing.

It was an arrow. In him. Through him. Hurt.

Richie did a little pirouette on the tips of his toes, then fell from the cliff into the waiting sea. The circuit was completed, and so it would begin as it had begun once before, many years ago, with the loss of a boy and the arrival of men upon the island. Sanctuary's long wait was over. It was the beginning, and the end.

All over the island the power failed and the lights went out, and Sanctuary was plunged into darkness.

Carl Lubey knocked his beer from the rickety table by his easy chair and cursed the blackness. There was still a faint glow from the TV, which was always left on, but it was fading rapidly. The thick drapes were drawn on all the windows, as they always were, because Carl didn't like the thought of anybody peering inside and seeing his business. He shuffled across the carpet, barking his shin painfully against the table and then catching his foot on a cable and almost sending himself sprawling on the floor, until his right hand found the switch on the wall and gave it a few futile flicks. Nothing. Not that he'd expected anything to happen, but Carl was kind of an optimist at heart and liked to think that sometimes the easiest solution was the best. To others, especially those who'd made the mistake of trusting Carl to fix their siding or pave their driveways, Carl was a lazy, corner-cutting creep. Carl preferred "optimist" himself. It had a nicer ring to it.

Carl had gone inside to pour himself a stiff drink, and then the lights had gone out. The incident with the radio had unnerved him, but the more he thought about it, the more he figured it was one of the island assholes jerking him around. He couldn't figure out who it might be, or how they might have done it, but it was the only explanation he could come up with. Now, lost and disoriented in his own house, he vowed revenge on whoever it was.

In the kitchen he found a flashlight, but the batteries were dead. He rummaged in the drawers until he came across a pack of candles and a box of matches. He lit a candle and jammed it into the top of an empty beer bottle to keep the wax from dripping onto his hand.

Carl heard a fluttering sound against the window, then a shadow flew above him. It was a moth, excited by the light from the candle. Carl watched it until it came to rest briefly on the kitchen sink. It was a big bastard, its long body dotted with small yellow orbs. The moth had no right to be in Carl's kitchen. Hell, it had no right to be alive at all, now that winter had come. He was so rattled that he failed to connect it with the moths he had glimpsed in the forest the week before, the moths that had briefly assumed the shape of a woman.

Instead, Carl crushed the insect with the base of the empty beer bottle.

The fuse box was in the basement, along with a bunch of spare fuses. Mind, it could be something as simple as the main switch tripping. After all, Carl had wired the place up himself and sometimes, like on the odd occasion when he decided to take a proper shower, the act of turning on the water would cause every light in the place to switch off, as well as the refrigerator.

Shit, thought Carl. He had the best part of half a cow in the freezer in his basement, and he didn't want to take the chance of his winter feed turning to maggot food if the cold spell broke. He raised the candle and headed toward the basement. He had almost reached the door when he heard the noises coming from below. They were soft, hardly there at all, as though someone was moving very slowly and carefully through the accumulation of garbage and stolen goods that Carl kept stored down there. There was somebody in his basement, maybe the same somebody who had caused the switches to trip, plunging Carl into darkness so he'd be easier to subdue. Carl had no idea who that someone might be, but he wasn't taking any chances.

He drew the Browning from his belt and opened the basement door.

Macy was about a ten-minute ride from Carl Lubey's house when her engine failed. She stopped the Explorer and stepped out onto the road, the snowflakes gathering on her hair. All that was visible to her were the snow and the shapes of the trees around her. She got back into the vehicle and tried the radio, but there was no response. No static, no crackle, nothing. She turned the key in the ignition and received only a click in return, then banged her hands impotently against the wheel before resting her forehead against the plastic. She had three choices: she could stay here, which was hardly a choice at all; she could head back toward town and try to hook up with Dupree; or she could keep going toward Lubey's house and check him out, just as Dupree had asked her to do, and then use his phone if it was working or get him to tow her back to town with his truck. She got out again, took a flashlight and an emergency pack from the trunk, and began walking in the direction of Lubey's place.

Carl Lubey opened the basement door toward him, keeping away from the exposed opening. There was no other way into or out of the basement, and only two small windows in the walls, neither of which was large enough to admit anything bigger than a small child. In any case, both of those windows were firmly locked, to prevent rodents or forest mammals from making their home in Carl's basement.

There was now silence below. He wondered if it might have been his imagination, or the occasional shifting of materials that occurs in such spaces, a consequence of drafts and rot. Carl took a breath and registered, for the first time, the stink in the room. It was a dense, damp smell, like stale seawater. Something else hung behind it, something more unpleasant, a kind of stagnancy, and Carl was reminded of the time he and Ron had found a dead seal on the beach, bloated and rotten. Carl hadn't been able to eat for two days afterward because the stench of the dead seal seemed to cling to his skin and the insides of his nostrils.

It made no sense to Carl. It was snowing outside, and the days preceding had been fiercely cold. Nothing decayed in this cold. Even Carl's beef might survive a couple of days if the weather held out. But the smell was there, he was sure of it. It trickled into the hallway now and began to adhere to his clothes, but it was definitely coming from the basement. Maybe the pipes had burst down there, soaking the stacked newspapers and cardboard boxes, even his brother's old clothes, the ones Carl hadn't had the heart to get rid of.

Carl stepped through the doorway. The candle illuminated the wooden stairs leading down into the basement and cast a faint glow into the sunken room itself. He heard the first step creak beneath his feet as he moved forward, the circle of light from the candle expanding as he advanced, catching the whitewashed walls, the shelves stacked with paints and tools, the boxes piled on top of one another, the more valuable items—a couple of portable TVs, some toasters and VCRs—off to one side, draped with a tarp.

There was movement there. Carl was sure of it.

"Hey, you down there! Come out, now. I can see you. No point in hiding."

The figure retreated back into the shadows beneath the steps.

"Come on, now," Carl repeated. He tried to catch a glimpse of the shape through the slats of the stairs. "I won't hurt you, but you're making me real nervous. Come out or I don't know what I might do."

Carl moved down two more steps, and the basement door slammed closed behind him. He turned, and felt his feet slide out from under him. For a moment, he teetered on the very edge of the step, then his balance failed him and he tumbled down the remaining stairs.

As he fell, his thought was: Hands. I felt hands on my legs.

Scarfe stared hard at Dexter but kept his mouth closed until the big man spoke to him.

"You got something to say?" asked Dexter.

"We could have taken him alive."

"You think? I could barely see the fucking guy to take the shot. If I hadn't taken it, we'd have lost him."

"You didn't have to kill him."

Dexter looked to Moloch to intervene, but Moloch was already moving past them, following the road as it sloped down, the road at his right and the sound of the sea to his left.

"Listen," said Dexter to Scarfe. "I got six more arrows. You keep fucking with me and one of them might just have your name on it."

"You're forgetting something."

"What's that?"

Scarfe was red with cold and righteous indignation. It made him forget how much Dexter frightened him. "I'm not a dummy running away from you," he said. "You'll find me a little harder to kill."

Dexter sprang for Scarfe, but the smaller man was too fast for him. He slipped past Dexter, drawing his gun as he did so. Within seconds, Dexter was staring down the barrel of the Glock. The gun was shaking in Scarfe's hand.

"You done fucked up now," said Dexter.

"You're the one with a gun aimed at him."

"Then you better use it, pussy boy, or else I'm going to kill you."

Scarfe heard movement behind him, and the sound of a hammer cocking.

"Let it go," said Moloch. "Both of you, let it go."

Scarfe lowered his gun. Dexter made a move for him, but Powell reached out and held him back by extending his forearm in front of his chest.

"I won't forget that," said Dexter.

Scarfe, his burst of adrenaline receding, backed away. Shepherd, who had stayed quiet throughout, followed Moloch to the edge of the forest.

"He should be here," he said. "Lubey should be here."

"It's the weather," said Moloch. "It's just delayed him."

He called to Scarfe, but Scarfe wasn't looking at him. Instead, he was staring down at the sea below.

"Hey," he said softly, yet there was something in his tone that made Moloch and the others approach him, even causing Dexter to forget his animosity in order to follow his gaze.

"Hey," repeated Scarfe. "The guy, he's still alive."

* * *

Carl Lubey lay on his back among the newspapers and the fallen boxes, slowly coming to. His head ached. He didn't know how long he had been out, but he guessed it had been no more than a minute or two. There was light coming from somewhere close by, and an acrid smell.

Burning.

He turned his head and saw the flames licking at the newspapers beneath the basement stairs. Carl tried to raise himself, but there was a weight across his chest and he couldn't feel his legs. He reached out and encountered no obstacle, merely a coldness in the air that chilled his fingers despite the growing heat. The flames were licking against the back wall, devouring paper and clothing and old suitcases. Soon they would reach the shelves of paints and spirits.

Carl saw more flames flicker in the darkness to his left. He couldn't figure out how the fire had spread over there, because it was as far away as you could get from the conflagration over by the far wall, yet he could clearly discern flares of light close to the floor. They were slowly moving toward him, but they weren't increasing in size and he could feel no warmth. Instead, they seemed to hang in midair, like sparks carried on a breeze.

And suddenly Carl understood that what he was looking at was not fire but the reflection of fire, caught in shards of mirror that were now drawing closer and closer to him, the smell of dead fish and rotting seaweed growing stronger, filling his nostrils with the stench of decay. A woman's ruined face emerged from the shadows and Carl opened his mouth as the flames reached the paint and turpentine on the shelves, and his final agony was lost in a great roar.

CHAPTER THIRTEEN

Dupree leaned back in his chair and stretched. Chair and bones alike made cracking noises, so he stopped in midextension and carefully eased himself back toward the desk. If he broke the chair, he would have to requisition another and that would mean dealing with the jibes, because the wiseasses in supplies would assume—correctly—that his great bulk had taken out the item of furniture in question. In the end, it would be easier for everyone if he just bought his own damn chair.

He checked his watch and shuffled his completed paperwork to one side of the desk. None of it had been very urgent, but he had allowed untyped reports to pile up these last few weeks and the blizzard had given him an excuse to remain at the station house and catch up on the mundane details of speeding offenses, DUIs, and minor fender benders. The reports had also allowed him to forget, for a while, his worries about the island. The time spent immersed in the routines of day-to-day life had enabled him to put those concerns into perspective. When

Macy returned, he would take a drive over to Marianne's house and make sure she was okay. He wanted to know why she had been in such a rush to get back to Portland, and enough time had elapsed since the arrival of the water taxi to make it look as if he wasn't checking up on her too closely. It might have been something to do with Danny, but if Danny was really sick, then Marianne would have been in touch with him to arrange emergency transportation. All in all, it was a puzzler.

He heard the main station door open and footsteps in the reception area. Dupree had asked headquarters to consider putting in a counter to section off the office from the public area, but so far nothing had been done. It wasn't a big deal at this time of year, but during the summer, when the incidence of petty thefts, lost children, and stolen bicycles took a sudden sharp rise, there could be up to a half dozen people crowding around the office door.

He left his desk and stepped out into reception. To his right, a pretty black woman with an Afro was running the fingers of her left hand along the side of Engine 14. She wore a hooded waterproof jacket and blue jeans tucked into shin-high boots. The fake fur lining of her hood was spangled with melting snow.

"Can I help you, ma'am?"

The woman looked at him, and her eyes widened.

"My, aren't you the big one?" said Leonie.

Dupree didn't react. "Like I said, can I help you with something, ma'am?"

"Sure, baby, you can help me," she said. She turned away from the engine and he saw the silenced pistol in her hand. "You can help me by taking the thumb and middle finger of your left hand and lifting that gun from your holster. You think you can do that?"

Dupree caught movement to her right as a man appeared from the shadows behind the fire trucks. He was redhaired and wrapped up tightly against the cold in a padded blue coat, but Dupree could see that he was a big man even without the padding. He too had a gun in his hand, the silencer like a swollen tumor at its muzzle, and it was also pointing in Dupree's direction.

"Now," said Braun. "Do it."

Slowly, Dupree moved his hand to his holster, flipped the clasp, and drew the gun out using his thumb and middle finger, as he had been told. The two strangers didn't tense as he performed the action and he felt his heart sink. He had only read about people like this in newspapers and internal memoranda.

They were killers. Real, stone-cold killers.

"Lay it down on the floor, then kick it toward me," said the man.

Dupree did as he was told. The man stopped the gun with his foot as it reached him. Beside him, the woman closed the door to the station house and turned the lock.

"Who are you?" asked Dupree.

"Doesn't matter," said Braun. "Tell me where your partner is at."

"I don't know."

"Don't fuck with me."

"She's out on patrol. I don't know where she is exactly."

"Call her."

The man and woman moved in unison, keeping the same distance from each other as they advanced on Dupree in a ten-to-two position.

"She's out of radio contact."

Braun fired his gun, aiming to Dupree's left. The shot blew a hole in the computer screen on the desk behind him.

"Why would you think I'm fucking with you, Andre? I want you to call her and bring her in."

Dupree didn't know if the radio was still out, but he had no plans to use it even if it was functioning again. Macy would be no match for these people if he brought her back here. The way things were looking, he was no match for them himself.

"I can't do that," said Dupree.

"You mean you won't do it."

"Comes down to the same thing. Why are you doing this?"

Braun smiled regretfully.

"You shouldn't have fucked his wife," he said.

He raised his gun and sighted down the barrel.

"You really shouldn't have fucked his wife."

Then, without warning, the lights went out.

Doug Newton was sitting downstairs in his favorite chair when the power died. His first reaction was that of most people on the island: he reached for a flashlight so he could check the fuse box. When the flashlight wouldn't work, he went scouting for candles, eventually finding a pack of tea lights behind the spare bulbs in the kitchen cabinet. He dropped a tea light in an ashtray, lit it, then took a second candle and placed it on a saucer. His mother would be frightened if she woke and found that her TV wasn't working. She liked the light from the tube, found it comforting. Her greatest fear, Doug believed, was that she might be alone when she died, and she would rather die with Letterman than with nobody at all.

Doug had just begun to climb the stairs when the candles flickered slightly and he felt the blast of cold air: a window was open. At the same instant a shuffling sound came from above, then a tapping that sounded like small bare feet running on boards.

Finally, he heard his mother cry out.

Doug knew that the cops, with the possible exception of Joe Dupree, hadn't believed him when he'd told them about the little girl. Hell, Doug wasn't too sure that he believed it himself, but he'd seen it and he was pretty certain his mother had seen it too, although she later convinced herself that it was just a dream. Ever since then, as he had admitted to Dupree, Doug had kept a pistol by his bedside and a loaded shotgun beside the hat stand in the hallway. He put the two tea lights down on the hall table and picked up the shotgun. Light filtered through the small square window at the first landing as he ascended the stairs, but he didn't really need it. Doug knew this house: he'd been born here, lived here, and would die here, if he had his way.

His mother's room was the second on the right. The door was slightly ajar, as it always was, and Doug thought that he could see shadows moving against the wall. From inside came the sounds of thrashing, and what might have been his mother softly whimpering.

Doug hit the door at a run, the shotgun at his shoulder.

The sheets had been thrown back from his mother's bed and lay piled on the floor. Snow was blowing in through the open window, the flakes billowing and colliding with one another before falling gently on the carpet. The Gray Girl crouched over Doug's mother, her mouth pressed against the old woman's lips, while his mother's thin arms and skeletal hands pushed at her, trying to force her away. Her hands caught in the folds of the Gray Girl's gown, which appeared to move independently of the limbs it concealed. It seemed to be part of the girl, as though her body had fused with the shroud in which she had been interred, creating a new skin that hung over her arms like wings.

As Doug entered, the Gray Girl disengaged herself from his mother and swiveled her head in the direction of the intruder. He saw then that she was old, desperately old, a child in form only. Her hair, blond from a distance, was now clearly silver-white. Her cheeks were sunken and Doug perceived bone protruding through the parched skin below her eyes, which were entirely black. Her mouth was strangely rounded and Doug was reminded of a lamprey, a creature designed by nature to adhere to another creature and draw the life from it. Beneath the girl, he saw his mother's face, her lips trembling and tears falling from her face. Her breathing was barely audible, and as Doug moved toward the bed, the light faded from her eyes and he heard the rattle in her throat as she died.

The Gray Girl hissed at Doug, and he saw the rage in her black eyes at what Doug had done, the distraction of his presence depriving her of that which she sought. Her hand reached out, her fingers little more than bone wrapped in tattered parchment.

And Doug fired.

The force of the blast blew the Gray Girl from the bed and tossed her against the wall. She rolled when she hit the floor, then rose up again and stood before him, framed by the window. The shot had torn holes through her gown and the skin beneath, but no blood came, and there was only a smear of gray tissue where she had struck the wall. She stood and regarded Doug with a malevolence that made him want to run and hide, to curl himself up into a ball in a closet until she went away. For an instant, Doug pictured himself cocooned, listening in the darkness, then hearing the pad of those feet as they approached and halted before his hiding place, the door being drawn slowly open as—

Doug fired again, and the gray child disintegrated into a cloud of moths.

The room was filled with snowflakes and insects and broken glass, and the sound of Doug Newton crying for his dead mother, and for himself.

Nancy Tooker was descending warily to the kitchen to get some food for her sister and the dogs when the lights went out. She was a big woman, as Officer Berman had not failed to notice, and once she missed her step, there was no way that she could keep her balance. She tumbled awkwardly down the stairs, striking the slate floor hard with her head and coming to rest with a sigh. Her sister cried out her name, then used both the wall and the stair rail to support herself as she descended to Nancy's side. After a moment's hesitation, the dogs followed.

There was blood flowing from a wound in Nancy's head. A shard of bone had pushed through the skin of her left arm and her left ankle was clearly broken. Her breathing was very shallow and Linda feared that her sister had done herself some internal damage that only a hospital could ascertain. She went to dial the station house number, but the line was dead. She switched the phone off, powered it up, then tried again, but there was still no tone.

Linda ran to the living room, where she removed the cushions from the armchairs and couches, and did her best to make her sister comfortable. She was afraid to move her, and wasn't sure that she could have even if she'd wanted to, for Linda was sixty or seventy pounds lighter than her sister. Instead, she gingerly raised Nancy's head and slipped a cushion beneath it, then tried to do the same for her arm and ankle. During the whole operation, Nancy moaned softly only once, when Linda placed a pair of cushions beneath her leg. That worried Linda more than anything else, because moving that leg should have hurt Nancy like a bitch. She went to the hall closet and removed all the coats she could find, then laid them across her sister to keep her warm. Their nearest neighbors were the Newtons, just on the other side of Fern Avenue. If she could get to them, she could use their phone, assuming that the problem with the phones hadn't affected the whole island. She didn't want to think about what might happen to Nancy if that were the case. Someone would just have to drive over to Joe Dupree and tell him what had happened so he could call for help from the mainland.

She leaned in close to her sister, stroked her hair from her eyes, and whispered to her.

"Nancy, I'm going to go for help. I won't be gone but five minutes."

Linda kissed her sister's brow. It was clammy and hot. She stood and shrugged on her own overcoat. At her feet, the dogs began to turn in circles, alternately barking and whining.

"No, you dumb mutts, this isn't a walk."

But the dogs weren't following her to the door. Instead, they were moving back from it. Max, the German shepherd, went down on his front paws, his tail between his legs, and began to growl. Something of their fear returned to Linda as she looked back at them.

"The hell is wrong with you both?" she asked.

She opened the front door, and the Gray Girl pounced.

For a moment, there was confusion in the station house. The blinds had been drawn in Dupree's office and the heavy cloud cover meant that there was no moonlight. With the loss of the street lamps, the small station house was suddenly plunged into darkness. The suppressed guns spat softly, but Dupree was already moving. Braun and Leonie heard a door opening in the far-right-hand corner of the office. Both fired toward the sound.

"Go around," said Leonie. "Don't let him get into the woods."

Braun ran into the street, then hung a left and made for the rear of the station. Silently, Leonie advanced toward the back room. Her night vision was already improving and she could see the shape of the doorway ahead of her. She stopped to the right of the frame and listened. There was no sound from within. Leonie crouched down and risked a glance inside. She saw a big water tank with a small generator behind it. Oilskins were hanging from hooks on the wall. There were two lockers, one of them open. Beyond them, the back door stood ajar and snow was already beginning to cover the floor.

Leonie moved slowly into the room. To her right was a narrow gap between the tank and the wall. The open mouth of a pipe was visible in the gap. Leonie paused for a moment and the pipe belched fire. She heard the bellow of the shotgun as her being ignited in pain, and then a voice was calling her name. Braun. It was Braun. She tried to speak, but no words would form. She felt herself sliding down the wall.

"Bra—"

There was blood in her mouth.

"Br—"

The monstrous form of the giant emerged from the shadows in the corner of the room, the very darkness come to life. There came the sound of another load being jacked, but already she knew that he would have no call for it. Leonie's fingers brushed the gun upon the floor beside her, and she was no longer dying in an alien place. She was a young girl walking across a patch of waste ground, the revolver like a warm hand upon her belly, spreading tendrils of heat through her body and filling her with pleasure and power. She felt a great pressure build inside her, pain and remembrance intertwining like lovers in her mind. Her lips parted in a kind of ecstasy, and her eyes closed as the life left her body, her final breath briefly catching in her throat before at last it found its release.

Braun was almost at the corner when he heard the shotgun blast. Ahead of him, he could see the open back door of the station house. There were no footprints in the snow.

"Leonie," he cried out instinctively. There was no reply.

Braun looked toward the forest. The big cop could be anywhere inside the station house. If he approached the doorway, Braun would make an easy target. He retreated instead, making his way in a wide arc into the trees at the back of the station. He moved as quietly as he could, the snow muffling his footfalls. The doorway was empty, but it was dark inside and he could see no movement within. Then the reinforced steel door closed suddenly, propelled shut by the force of Dupree's shoe, and Braun swore loudly. He couldn't leave the cop alive in there. He would call for help, and next thing he knew there would be a blue army arriving on the island. Braun prepared to move just as a noise came from close by. He spun rapidly, his back to the station house. There was something big in the trees: a deer, perhaps, or maybe the rookie had come back and was already behind him.

The sound came again but this time it was far to his right.

His first thought was that, whatever it was, it was moving quickly, but that was swiftly followed by the realization that nothing could move that fast through the woods. He would have heard branches rustling, twigs snapping, even in the snow. Now there was more than one and the disturbances seemed to be coming from above his head, as though some great bird were flying unseen through the trees.

Braun rose and started moving backward, trying to keep both the woods and the station house in sight, his gun panning across the trees. There were figures moving in the darkness. They were gray, seemingly iridescent, like moonlight shining on the fur of animals, and they glided across the snow or flitted through the gaps between the branches of the evergreens. Then one of the shapes seemed to halt and he caught a glimpse of gray skin and a reflection of himself in a dark pupil.

And teeth. Rotting yellow teeth.

"What the hell?"

The gray shape curled in on itself, like paper crumpled in a fist, then moved swiftly toward him. Braun started firing, but the thing kept on coming. Braun staggered out of the cover of the woods and turned to see Joe Dupree leaning against the wall of the station, the shotgun at his shoulder. He dove to the ground as the shotgun bucked in Dupree's hands. Bark and splinters exploded from the tree trunk above Braun's head. He heard a second shot, and felt a pull at his left arm. He looked down to see blood above his elbow and part of his forearm reduced to red meat by the blast. A searing white heat began to burn its way through his upper body.

Braun staggered into the forest, and the gray shapes followed.

* * *

Linda Tooker wasn't a particularly fast mover. Even during rush hour in the diner (which never numbered more than a dozen people, yet still put the sisters under pressure) she served at a slower pace than her sister cooked, which meant lukewarm sandwiches and cool soup for everyone. Yet in the instant after she registered the approaching figure—its tattered skin, its black eyes, its mouth like a sucking wound—she reacted faster than she had since high school. She slammed the door in the Gray Girl's face and felt the wood strike her, but the gap wouldn't close. She looked to her right and saw the child's fingers caught between the door and the frame. The nails were sharp and yellowed and there was no flesh on the bones. They looked like twigs wrapped in burnt paper, delicate enough to be snapped off by a heavy door.

Except the fingers weren't snapping.

They were gripping.

Linda felt her feet begin to slide on the floor as the door was pushed inward. That's not possible, she thought. No child could be so strong. There must be someone else out there, someone helping her. Then a second hand materialized in the growing breach, this time braced against the frame, and the Gray Girl's face appeared, her black eyes focused not on Linda but on her sister.

"No!" shouted Linda. She jammed her right foot against the last stair, placed her forearm against the door, and swung her fisted right hand with all her force into the child's face. She heard bone crack as the blow struck, and the child's head rocked slightly. Then it was back in the opening again, the gray skin open across the nose to reveal the dirty bone beneath. The punch appeared only to have angered her, increasing her strength, for she pushed with renewed force, Linda's legs giving way, the gap now almost big enough to permit the child's whole body to enter. Linda heard herself sob as her strength failed and the door opened wide.

A dark blur shot by her from the hallway and she felt the dog's fur brush against her shoulder as Max leaped and struck the Gray Girl, his jaws tearing at her throat as his weight knocked her away from the doorway. Linda slammed the door shut behind them, locking and bolting it, then sliding down its length until she came to rest on the floor. The collie, Claude, began to scratch at the door, trying to reach its companion. From outside she heard scuffling noises in the snow, and Max's growls.

Then the dog howled sharply once, and all was quiet.

CHAPTER FOURTEEN

The five men stood on the edge of the shallow cliff, the stony beach some forty feet below them, and stared at the figure that stood amid the waves. Its features could not be distinguished, but there was no mistaking the arrow that pierced its torso. It remained still, despite the force of the water rolling in from behind. To its right was a rocky outcrop, blocking the pierced man from the view of Tell and Willard, on the boat.

"No way," said Dexter. "No fucking way. I've taken a black bear with one of those arrows. There's no way he can still be alive."

Moloch regarded the sea in silence, then turned to Shepherd.

"Go down there and finish him."

Shepherd shook his gray head once.

"Not me," he said. "No."

"I don't think you heard me correctly. You seem to have turned an order into a request."

Shepherd remained impassive. He had been watching

Moloch carefully throughout the boat journey, growing more and more troubled by what he was seeing, and in the short time since their arrival on the island, his concerns had only increased. He had seen Moloch's eyes glaze over when nobody was looking, his lips moving, forming unspoken words. During the ascent of the slope, Moloch had slipped more times than any of the others and his eyes seemed to be focused less on the climb than on the thin scrub and brush that had found purchase among the rocks. When they had reached the top, it had taken Dexter to alert him to the presence of the retarded man. Moloch had not been looking at the tower, or at the man in the bright orange vest. His gaze was fixed on the woods, and his lips were moving again. This time, Shepherd could distinguish words and phrases.

We move on.

Did they tell you to keep watch for me?

I told you I'd return.

The last was repeated, again and again, over and over like a mantra.

I told you I'd return. I told you I'd return. I told you—

"Like I just told you, not me," Shepherd said. He didn't break eye contact with Moloch, but he was aware of the gun in the other man's hand. Throughout their confrontation, Shepherd's own hand rested lazily against the folding stock of the Mossberg Persuader that hung from a leather strap on his shoulder. He had jacked a load as soon as they'd landed and his finger was inches from the trigger. Shepherd did not know what would happen if he was forced to kill Moloch. He guessed that he would have to take out Dexter too. Powell could go either way, he figured. Scarfe didn't concern him. Scarfe just wanted to get out of this alive.

Moloch considered the other man carefully, then seemed to reach a decision.

"This once," he said.

Shepherd nodded, and Moloch turned to Powell. Dexter, Shepherd noticed, had notched another arrow on his bow during the standoff. Shepherd wondered if it had been meant for him. We may yet find out, he thought.

"You do it, then follow," Moloch told Powell.

"Shit," said Powell, gesturing at Dexter, "it was this asshole couldn't kill him, and now I got to go down there?"

Dexter didn't react to the taunt. In the space of a couple of minutes, four white men had managed to get in his face, each one in a different way: Scarfe had laid a hand on him; Powell had insulted him; Shepherd had almost forced Dexter to kill him; and a retarded man with an arrow through his chest simply refused to die. Faced with so many possible targets, Dexter's wrath had simply diffused, briefly leaving him more puzzled than angry.

"Just do it," Moloch told Powell. "And quietly."

Powell sighed theatrically and removed his gun from its holster. He rummaged in the pockets of his jacket until he found the suppressor, then attached it to the muzzle. Moloch's insistence on silence puzzled him. There was nobody out here to hear a shot, and anyway, even if someone was outside, the wind and snow would muffle any noise. Still, Powell wasn't about to argue with Moloch. Like Shepherd, he found Moloch's behavior peculiar, but he wasn't going to risk taking a bullet in order to point it out.

"How will I find you when I'm done?"

"There's a path through the forest. You'll pick it up behind the tower. Stay on it and it will lead you straight to us. For now, we move on."

When he said the words, he looked puzzled.

We move on.

Shepherd said nothing, but his finger found the trigger guard of the Mossberg and remained there.

"We're not waiting for Carl Lubey?" asked Scarfe.

"He's not here and I want to get off the road and out of sight," said Moloch. "In case you hadn't noticed, we're on a tight schedule. We'll make for his place and take it from there."

"There's a snowstorm blowing," said Scarfe. "And you don't know the island."

"You're wrong," said Moloch. "I know this island very well."

Scarfe shook his head in disbelief and looked to the other men for support, but they were already preparing to follow their leader. Powell, meanwhile, shot Dexter a look of disgust, then began to descend the rocks, toward the beach. Scarfe watched him go until Dexter grasped his arm.

"By my reckoning, pussy," he said, "you got no lives left."

Dexter released him and spit once into the snow by Scarfe's foot. Scarfe shot one last look at the figure that stood among the waves before adjusting his pack on his shoulder and following Moloch, Shepherd, and Dexter across the white road that skirted the woods. He expected Moloch to stop and look at a map or check a compass, but instead he moved purposefully into the trees. Within minutes, the four men were heading for the center of the island on an old trail that wound its way through the forest. While they walked, Scarfe unfolded his map from his pocket and tried to read it, hampered by darkness and snow and wind. It was a struggle, but he eventually confirmed what he had suspected from the moment they had found the trail.

It wasn't detailed on the map.

Somehow, Moloch had found an unmarked path.

* * *

Moloch drifted. Sometimes he was beside Dexter, moving through a white forest, the snow melting on his face and hair. At other times there was no snow, just a harsh wind and frost upon the ground, and there were other men around him, dressed in furs and hand-stitched hides. Eventually, the two worlds began to coexist, like transparencies laid one upon the other, and he was both Moloch and someone else, a man at once known and unknown. Moloch was confused but not frightened by the sensation, for what he felt more than anything else was a sense of belonging, a feeling of returning. This was not home. This was not a place of solace or comfort. There was no shelter for him here, but it was the beginning. Here Moloch, or whatever he truly was, had flamed into being. Whatever else might happen here, he would at last reach an understanding of himself, and those torn pictures that had tormented him in so many dreams would reform themselves, enabling him to see himself as he truly was.

He was coming to recognize that all this was meant to be. His wife was always going to flee here, and he was always going to follow. Men would come with him, for men had come with him before, because that was the way it had always been. It had been taken out of his hands and all that he could do was follow the path to its end, and to the final revelation that awaited him.

It took Powell only minutes to half climb, half slide his way down the slope to the rocky beach. When he reached the bottom, he was breathing heavily, and his hands stung from the cold. His finger was almost numb as he inserted it beneath the trigger guard. He advanced to the shoreline and raised the gun, resting its barrel against his forearm.

The man with the arrow through his torso stood in the water. The sea was just below the level of his chest, but the waves that billowed against him had no effect. He remained entirely still, his orange jacket glowing luminously in the faint light that somehow contrived to penetrate the dense clouds above. Powell could even see the point of the arrow, gleaming, just above the water.

He's dead, thought Powell. He's dead, but he's just too dumb to realize it. He's like a dinosaur, waiting for the message to penetrate to his brain. Well, I'll help it along. I've got an express delivery for him, going straight to his head.

Powell sighted, then squeezed off two shots in quick succession and watched in satisfaction as twin puffs of red sprang from the breast of the figure among the waves.

The man didn't fall.

Powell lowered the gun and waited. It appeared to him that the injured man had drawn closer to the shore. It looked like he had moved forward a clear five feet or more, as the water was now approaching the level of his navel. Powell took aim again and emptied the clip into the injured man. He thought he saw him buck slightly at the impact of the bullets, but that was the only sign Powell got that he had struck home.

He ejected the empty clip, replaced it, then advanced into the sea. The cold was intense, but he shrugged it away. Instead he concentrated on the head of the man, moving toward him steadily despite the waves, and with every step he took he fired a shot. The last one struck the top of the guy's head when Powell was barely five feet away. His chin lay against his chest, and no movement came from him. Powell could see the wounds left by the bullets, could even see something white glistening through a hole in the man's skull.

He's dead now, Powell told himself. There's something

holding him in place—soft sand, maybe, or rocks, or even the remains of a boat—but he's dead for sure. Whatever is anchoring him there, it sure as hell isn't free will.

At that moment, Powell became aware of a presence to his rear. He looked back to see a boy watching him from the shore. The boy's clothing looked dated, and the waves worshiped at his bare feet. His skin was pale and he held his hand to his throat, as if remembering some ancient hurt. Powell was about to speak to him when the dead man in the sea raised his head, a sharp clicking noise in his throat alerting the gunman to the movement. Powell slowly turned to face him, then rocked back on his heels, trying to steady himself against the twin impacts of shock and water. It was the dummy, but not the dummy. The distortion in his face—the drooping mouth, the too-wide eyes, the sheer strangeness of his features' composition—was now gone, and the man before him was, well, handsome, and his eyes gleamed with newfound intelligence.

Powell fumbled for a new clip, but the coldness and the damp caused his fingers to betray him and the clip slipped from his grasp and dropped into the sea with a soft splash. He looked down to follow its progress, then raised his eyes in time to see a huge wave rising up behind the dead man who stood before him. It lifted him off his feet and propelled him at speed toward Powell, his body riding the crest, carried forward like a piece of driftwood before it slammed into the gunman. Powell screamed as he felt the point of the arrow enter his chest, the dead man's arms enveloping him, his face pressed hard against Powell's, his mouth twisted into a smile.

The wave broke over them and they disappeared beneath the sea.

* * *

Carl Lubey's home was already engulfed in flames by the time Macy reached it. She had seen the smoke rising and had smelled it on the wind, which caused her to speed up her progress toward the house. She made a couple of halfhearted efforts to get close to the front door, then gave up as the heat forced her back. Her main concern was the possibility that the fire might reach the forest, but Lubey had cleared his land of trees in order to allow space for his garden, thereby creating a natural firebreak. With luck, the break, combined with the heavily falling snow, would be enough to contain the conflagration. But somebody needed to be told about it, just in case.

Macy took the radio from her belt and tried, for the third time since she'd left her vehicle, to raise someone on the system. On the first two occasions, the radio had been dead, clicking emptily just like the ignition in the car. Now, as she stood within sight of Lubey's burning home, she could hear static. She brought the handset close to her mouth and spoke.

"This is Macy. Do you read me? Over."

She tried again, using her call sign. "This is six-nine-one. Over."

Static, nothing more. She was about to replace the handset when its tone changed. Slowly, she raised the radio to her ear and listened.

It wasn't static now. Perhaps it had never been. It seemed to her that what she was hearing was an irregular hissing sound, like someone constantly adjusting escaping gas. She listened harder, and thought she distinguished patterns and pauses, a kind of cadence.

Not static, and not hissing.

But whispers.

* * *

At the edge of the forest, Moloch and his men watched the sky glow above the tips of the trees. Their flashlights were dead and now, as they paused before the distant conflagration, Dexter took the opportunity to change the batteries, using the spares in his pack. Nothing happened. The flashlight remained dark.

"Those batteries were fresh from the store," said Dexter. Scarfe tried changing the batteries in his own flashlight, and found that it too remained dead.

"Bad batch," he said. "Looks like we're shit out of luck."

He took his Zippo from the pocket of his jacket, lit it, then held it close to the map. His finger pointed to details.

"I figure we're here. Best I can reckon it, Carl's house is over there."

He raised his hand and pointed toward the flames.

"Since his place is the only one in that section of the island, that means—"

Dexter finished the sentence for him.

"That either we got a forest fire, which don't seem likely, or right now Lubey's house is just about the warmest place to be on this island. Explains why he didn't make it to the rendezvous. A man's likely to be distracted if his house is burning down around his ears."

"People will come," said Scarfe. "The cops run the fire department. Dupree will be here soon."

"I don't think so," said Moloch, interrupting for the first time. He regarded Scarfe for a moment, until the smaller man's mouth gaped in understanding and he looked away.

Moloch traced his finger across the woods on the map.

"We keep going, then take a look at what's going on from cover. We need Lubey's truck if we're going to get out of here ahead of the cops. The fire will be our marker."

* * *

Dupree was looking to the east, where a faint red glow hovered above the trees. Larry Amerling stood beside him. The old postmaster's house was nearest the station and he had heard the gunfire. Dupree had almost turned his gun on him, for Braun had headed into the forest only moments before and Dupree had been about to follow him when the postmaster had intervened. Amerling took a look at the body of the woman in the generator room. He emerged pale and gulping cold air.

"We need to get some men over to that fire," said Dupree, "but there's at least one armed man out there, and probably more."

"Why do you say that?"

"Something he told me before the lights went out. I want you to go and get Frank Macomber and as many of the fire crew as you can round up. The phones are out, so you'll have to do it door-to-door. Make sure Frank brings a gun. Then I want you to come back here and try to contact someone on the radio. If you don't get any results within the next half hour, then start sending up distress flares from the dock. We need to keep people indoors and off the streets as well."

Already Dupree could see some of those who lived off Island Avenue approaching the station house to inquire about the power cuts. Among them was big Earl Kruhm, who had a good head on his shoulders.

"Earl can take care of that," said Amerling. "Nobody's going to argue with him."

"Talk to him," said Dupree. "Make sure he understands that folks could be in danger if they don't stay indoors. It shouldn't be too hard to convince them, what with the blizzard and all. And, Larry, tell Frank and the firemen to stay out of the forest as much as they can, you hear? Make sure they keep to the trails."

Amerling nodded and went to get his car. He came back minutes later, just as Dupree was filling his pockets with shotgun shells.

"Joe, my car won't start. It's dead."

Dupree looked at him, almost in irritation, then took the keys to Engine 14 from a hook in his office and tried to start the truck. It turned over with a click.

"No radios, no phones, no cars, no power," he said.

"No help," said Amerling.

"It's begun, hasn't it?"

"I guess so."

"I felt it out at the Site, but I didn't tell you. I don't know why. I guess I didn't want to worry you."

Amerling managed a twisted smile. "Wouldn't have made a difference anyway, but thanks for sparing my feelings."

"Macy's out there," said Dupree. "She was headed for Carl Lubey's place before that fire started."

He felt a rush of concern for the young woman. He hoped that she hadn't taken it into her head to do something stupid when she'd seen the fire. At least she didn't seem like the type for futile heroics. He put out of his mind the terrible possibility that the fire and Macy might be connected, and that she might be hurt, or worse.

"We stick to the plan," he told Amerling. "Go door-to-door. They're going to have to head for that fire on foot and do what they can once they get there."

He hefted the shotgun onto his shoulder and started for the door.

"Where are you going?"

"I'm going after the dead woman's partner. After that, I'm heading for Marianne Elliot's place. I think she's in serious trouble."

Amerling watched him go, but he didn't say what was on his mind.

I think we're all in serious trouble.

Time melted.

Scarfe felt it more acutely than the rest. They should have been at Lubey's house by now, but instead they were still walking through the woods, and the glow of the fire was no longer always visible to them. Even Moloch seemed to realize it. He paused and stared around him, momentarily confused.

"We're lost," said Scarfe.

"No," said Moloch. "We're still on the trail."

"Then the path is going in circles."

"Powell should have caught up by now," said Dexter.

Moloch nodded. "Head back down the trail, see if he's on his way."

Dexter left at speed and Moloch drew the map from inside his jacket. Scarfe, after a moment's hesitation, joined him in examining it, while Shepherd leaned against a tree and said nothing.

"We got on the trail about here," said Scarfe, indicating with a finger, "and Lubey's place is here. That's fifteen minutes on a good day, twenty or more in weather like this."

"It has to be close. Maybe we passed it."

But when they looked up, the light from the fire was still ahead of them.

"Makes no sense," said Scarfe. He looked to Shepherd for support, but Shepherd was not looking at him. He was staring into the forest, his hands shielding his eyes. Moloch called his name.

"I thought I saw something," said Shepherd. "Out there."

He pointed into the depths of the woods. Scarfe squinted, but could see nothing. The snow was blowing in his face, making it difficult to distinguish even the shapes of the more distant trees. He could smell smoke, though.

"It's the fire," he said. "Maybe you saw smoke."

No, thought Shepherd, not smoke. He was about to say more when Dexter returned from his brief reconnaissance.

"There's no sign of him," he told Moloch.

Moloch kicked at the newly fallen snow. "If he's lost, he'll find his way back to the boat."

"If he's lost," echoed Dexter.

"You think a dummy with an arrow through him took him? Fuck him. If he got washed away, so much more money for the rest of you. We keep going."

They shouldered their weapons and followed Moloch deeper into the forest.

CHAPTER FIFTEEN

Marianne was still shaken by her encounter with the new female cop. She had been afraid that the woman would make her follow her to the station house, that something in her face or behavior had revealed the truth of her situation. She could see it in the cop's face. Why else would she have come after her?

She knows I'm running. She knows I've been bad. She'll make me go with her and I'll break down and tell them everything and they'll take Danny away and I'll go to jail for stealing the money and—

Marianne forced herself to stay calm. She fumbled with the car key a couple of times before she managed to fit it into the ignition, and watched in the mirror as the cop seemed to pause and consider her once again. Then the key clicked into place and the engine purred into life. Marianne was maybe a little too heavy on the gas as she drove away, but the cop appeared content to let her go. She relaxed a little when she saw the Explorer move down toward the ferry, until the enormity of the situation she was dealing with came back to her, and she gripped the wheel so tightly that the veins stood out on her hands, the knuckles blanching beneath the skin.

She had been so distracted these last few days that she hadn't bothered to watch anything on TV except light comedies, and her absence from the market meant that she hadn't picked up a newspaper since the previous weekend. Something terrible had happened and now *he* was free, because he would not allow others to punish her on his behalf. No, he would want to do it himself. If they were in Maine, then he was with them. They had found her, and Moloch was probably already on his way to the island. Maybe he even had men here already, waiting for her. She would get back to Bonnie's and find Danny crying, in the grip of strangers, and Bonnie and Richie hurt or dead. There would be nothing for her to do but comfort her son while they sat and waited for Moloch to come. She thought again of her sister, Patricia, and her useless husband, whom she suspected of cheating on her yet with whom she continued to stay because, despite it all, she loved him and felt that there was still something worthwhile and decent within him. Perhaps she was right, for when she had told them both of her plan to run, and reminded them that if she ran, then they would have to run too, they had accepted it with equanimity, and Bill had held his wife's hand and told his sister-in-law that they would support her in any way they could. True, Bill had lost his job, and there was nothing to keep them where they were, but Marianne could still not disguise her surprise at his reaction. The memory of it made her ashamed, for she knew in the quiet dark places of her heart that they were both dead, and that they had died because of her. Yet part of her suspected that they were not the reason that Moloch had found her. Bill didn't know her exact location, and Patricia would never tell.

Marianne wiped away mucus and tears with the heel of her hand.

Patricia would never tell. She would die before she told.

Jesus, Pat, I'm sorry, I'm so sorry. I was so scared of him. I thought I had no other choice. He hurt me, and he was starting to hurt Danny. I should have killed him, but I'd have gone to jail and I'd never have seen Danny grow up. But now, if I could go back, I would murder him. I would take a knife to him in his sleep and stab him until the blood dripped through the mattress to the floor beneath. I would cut him again and again for all that he had done to us. I would tear him apart with the blade until his face was unrecognizable. I would do all of this to protect Danny, except—

Except that sometimes when she awoke in their bed during those final months, the room rich with darkness or the first dawn light seeping through the drapes, she would turn to him and find him awake, staring lazily at her, as if daring her to take him on, as though guessing the thoughts that were in her head and inviting her to test her strength against him. Then, when she did not respond, he would draw her to him and, without tenderness, work himself inside her, his hands pinning her arms to the bed. No words would be exchanged, no intimacies spoken. It was simply his way of letting her know that he could do with her as he wished, that she was alive by his grace alone, and that such grace was not without its limits.

Had she stayed with him she would have been dead within the year, of that she was certain. He might have let Danny live, but what life would he have had with such a man? So they ran, and in doing so contaminated every life that they touched, and now Patricia and Bill were dead because of them.

Then there was Karen. They had stayed in touch and Marianne had recently sent her a photo of Danny on his last birthday, a smear of chocolate cake across his face and a cardboard crown on his head, his name spelled out on it in colored letters. She had sent the photograph from Boston during a shopping trip, her first foray out of Maine since they'd arrived there, sunglasses permanently perched on her nose to hide her eyes, her hair tied up tight in a bun, her face unadorned by makeup and therefore, she thought, unremarkable. She had called Karen a little later that evening from a telephone at South Station before catching her bus back north. The number that Karen had given her was a private, unlisted second line. Only a handful of people, family and friends mostly, had the number. If she was away from the phone, the call was automatically redirected to her private cell. Day or night, Karen would answer a call that came through on one of those phones.

But when Marianne had called earlier, there had been no reply. Did Karen tell? she wondered. Probably, but not willingly. Marianne felt no bitterness, no anger, that Karen had revealed their location to Moloch. Instead, there was only the same terrible guilt that she felt over her sister and Bill. Her stupidity and her selfishness had exposed them to terrible harm, and they had paid the ultimate price for their affection for her. She hoped only that Karen had told all that she knew early on and had spared herself some pain at the end.

Now Bonnie's house was coming into view. Marianne braked and killed the lights, but the house was quiet as she approached, only her friend's rust-bucket Plymouth in the drive. Through the living room window she could see Bonnie snoozing in front of the television. She pulled up hard outside the window, the gravel beneath the wheels making a sound like the breaking of waves, then she ran to the door and knocked hard. It took Bonnie a couple of seconds to get to the door.

"Where's Danny?" she said when she was facing the older woman.

Bonnie stepped back to let her in. "He's in bed. You can leave him there if you like. Hey, honey—" She reached for Marianne, but Marianne pulled away from her and headed for the stairs. "What's the matter?"

She took the steps two at a time, Bonnie close behind. Marianne pushed the bedroom door hard and saw one empty bed in the twin-bed room. In the other, Danny lay sleeping. She sagged back against the wall, put her hands on her knees, and lowered her head in relief.

"Aw, hell," said Bonnie. "Richie must have sneaked out. I don't believe that boy. I'll have to call Joe and get him to keep an eye out for him."

Marianne laid a hand on her wrist.

"I need to get Danny out of here before you call anyone, Bonnie."

"But Richie is out there."

"He's always out there, Bon. I need to get Danny away from here."

"Why? Have I done something wrong?"

"Bonnie, I can't explain it all, not now, but there are men coming and they're going to make trouble for Danny and me. I need to get us both away from the house, then find a way off the island."

Bonnie looked distraught. "Honey, you're making no sense. What men? If you're in trouble, we have to call the police."

Marianne shook her head. She wanted to grab Bonnie and force her to understand. She wanted to strike out at someone and ease some of her rage and fear. Most of all, she wanted to take Danny in her arms and get him away from here. They were coming. Moloch and his men were coming. For all she knew, they were already moving purposefully toward her home, trying to smell her out.

"No, no police. I did something bad a few years ago. I had to do it. I had to get Danny away and keep us both safe. Now I have to move again. Bonnie, please, help me get him dressed."

Bonnie reached out and took her by the shoulders. "Look," she said. "If there's one thing I know about, it's men, men gone bad or men who were bad to begin with. If these people have tracked you down once, then they can do it again. You can't run away for the rest of your life. You need to talk to Joe. You need to trust him."

"Bonnie, I broke the law. I took money that didn't belong to me. If I can get off the island with Danny, I can make this okay."

"Honey, you can't get off the island. It's snowing hard, in case you haven't noticed. They've taken all the boats off the water. It was on the news. No taxi is going to come all the way out here now, and nobody on the island is going to take a boat out in this weather. It's too risky."

Marianne almost gave up then. It was all too much. She should stop running. She should tell Joe everything. Better still, she should just lie down in front of her house, Danny in her arms, and wait for them to find her. Then it would all be over and they could rest at last, together.

"Bonnie," she said, and this time the tone in her voice made the older woman flinch. "I have to go."

Tell stared down the barrel of the gun at Willard. The sound of the hammer clicking emptily still seemed to hang in the air.

Tell felt it echoing through his brain. Looking into Willard's eyes, he knew that it sounded his death knell as surely as if it were he that was looking into the muzzle of the gun and the weapon was about to discharge a shot straight into his brain. He swallowed, then swiped the barrel wildly at Willard. Willard dodged it easily and something flashed in his hand. Tell experienced a fierce pain in his belly as the blade entered. Willard rose, forcing the blade up as he did so, and the tearing began. Tell could smell Willard's breath against his face. It smelled sweet, like cheap perfume.

"I could see it in your eyes," Willard whispered. "I could smell what you were planning to do before we ever left the dock. It was seeping through your pores with your sweat. You should never have let that gun out of your sight."

Tell shuddered against the blade, his hands clutching tightly at Willard's shoulders.

"He told you to do this, didn't he? He told you to kill me."

Tell tried to speak, but only blood came from his mouth.

"Good-bye," said Willard, as Tell died against him.

Marianne had Danny, bleary-eyed and irascible at being woken from his sleep, dressed within five minutes. She left Bonnie standing at her front door, looking anxiously after her as she headed for their house. They would need clothes, toiletries. Most of all, they would need the money. She strapped Danny into his seat and glanced at her watch. There wasn't much time left. She started the car and hit the headlights. Behind her, Danny had already dozed off to sleep again.

God, Danny, I'm sorry for this. I'm so sorry.

* * *

As soon as Marianne was gone from sight, Bonnie Claeson went straight to the liquor cabinet and poured herself a vodka. She looked at it, then on impulse walked to the kitchen and poured the drink down the sink.

She was worried about Marianne and Danny, but more than that, she was worried about Richie. He probably hadn't gone far, and nothing had ever happened to him during his wanderings on the island. He knew it well and usually stayed close to the roads and trails. But the weather was turning real bad and that was a factor her son wouldn't have taken into account on his latest nocturnal ramble. No, she had to call Joe, for all of their sakes.

She walked into the hallway, picked up the phone, and began to dial, then stopped. There was no dial tone. She replaced the receiver and tried again, but it remained silent.

No, not quite silent. She could hear faint noises. It was like holding a shell to one's ear and hearing, if only ever so faintly, the sound of the sea.

Then she heard Richie's voice.

Momma! Momma! Bad men. Badmenbadmenbadmenbad-menbad—

"Richie!" she called.

A high-pitched wailing tone, a kind of electronic scream, almost shredded her eardrum and she thrust the phone away. When it had receded, she brought the receiver back to her ear.

"Richie?" She was crying now, and felt the certainty of his loss like a great darkness that covered her, wrapping itself around her body and head, suffocating her in its depths. Then the darkness became real as the lights went out and the TV died and the buzz of the refrigerator stopped, like the life of an insect suddenly cut short.

And in the midst of her sorrow and pain, she heard a sound

like a sudden exhalation of breath, as though a great many souls had found at last the release that they had sought for so long.

Marianne was barely on the road when the engine of her car failed.

"No!" she cried. "Not now."

She tried to start it again, but the car was dead. She could go back to Bonnie and ask to borrow her Plymouth, but by now Bonnie would have called the police and she would argue with her again, or insist that she needed to find Richie first, and there would be more delays, and Joe would come, and then there would be no way out.

She opened her door, then Danny's, and began pulling him from his car seat.

"No, Mommy, I'm tired."

"I'm sorry, Danny, really I am."

She held him in her arms and started to run.

It was Shepherd who went astray first. He was bringing up the rear, the bulk of Dexter like a great black bear before him. The shapes in the forest had unnerved him. Scarfe might have been right: it could have been smoke from the fire, or even shadows cast by it from the topmost trees. He had glimpsed them only briefly, but it had seemed to him that they were moving *against* the wind, walking parallel to their own group. He tried to tell Dexter as they walked, but Dexter was only mildly concerned.

"Could be locals on their way to help at the fire," he said. "We can take care of them at the house, or avoid them. Doesn't matter."

Shepherd didn't think it would be that simple. They *looked* almost like men, but Shepherd could have sworn that they were wearing furs, and even out here people had probably given up on furs a long time ago.

As they continued along the trail, Shepherd spent more and more time looking behind him, or to either side, and less time trying to keep Dexter in sight. The snow grew thicker and the bear shape ahead grew fainter, distinguishable only from the trunks of the trees by its movement. Shepherd stumbled on a hidden stone and landed on his hands and knees in the snow. When he stood up, there was no one in front of him, and the trail was gone.

"Shit," he said. He put his hands to his mouth and whistled, then waited. There was no response. He whistled again, then tried calling. He didn't care about the barely glimpsed figures now. He had a gun and anybody who was out here with them would have to be crazier than—

Than Moloch, he heard himself finish. Because Moloch was crazy. They all knew it, even if none of them had the guts to say it out loud. This obsession with the woman had led them into alien territory during just about the worst snowstorm that Shepherd had ever encountered. What they had here was a full-on blizzard, with Shepherd now stuck on his lonesome in the heart of it, and he was one hundred percent pissed at this turn of events. He had come for the promise of easy money, the lure of $100,000 for a couple of days' work. That money could buy him a lot: a small house somewhere cheap and quiet, maybe a share in a business. Like Dexter and Braun, Shepherd was tired. He'd done time, and as you got older, jail time aged you faster. Even as the years inside passed slowly, infinitesimally slowly, the aging process seemed to accelerate. Dexter had seen young men come out old from a nickel stretch, and older men come out dying after a dime. Shepherd wasn't sure that he could survive another spell inside. This was to have been his final gamble; Dexter's and Braun's too, he guessed, except that Dexter had changed since they'd last met. Now he spent his spare time staring into space or watching those damn DVDs in which everybody went down in a blaze of glory at the end. Dexter had given up hope, and now Shepherd wasn't sure that he was any saner than Moloch. His was just a better organized form of insanity.

Shepherd looked at the compass on his watch. If he headed northwest, back the way they had come, he could find the road and then follow it to the boat. The way things were going, that boat was going to be a regular hot spot for lost men. He made one last effort to summon the others, then turned around and headed back toward the sea.

Dexter noticed Shepherd's absence first, but the wind had found renewed force and was now howling into their faces. When he opened his mouth to speak, snowflakes began to colonize it like bugs on a summer's day.

"Hey!" he shouted. Moloch and Scarfe paused.

"Shepherd ain't back there."

Moloch, buffeted by the wind, the snow thick around his boots, joined Dexter. "How long?"

"I don't know. I checked just now and he was gone."

Scarfe joined them, placed his fingers to his lips, and whistled. The sound was loud and shrill, even allowing for the dampening effect of the falling snow. There was no reply. Dexter leaned close to Moloch's ear.

"This is turning to shit."

"What do you suggest we do?"

"Go back."

"No."

"We're down to three men and we got no means of communication. I say we head back to the boat and wait this thing out."

"Then what? You think they won't clear the roads come morning?"

"First light, man. First light and we can do this thing, be gone before the people on the island start making breakfast."

"She knows we're here. First light, *she'll* be gone. Worse, maybe she'll figure that the best thing to do is to come clean with the cops. She does that, my friend, and we are royally fucked. We go on."

"Listen—"

Moloch shoved him hard.

"We go on! The bitch is running now. We don't have much time."

It didn't take Shepherd long to figure out that he was lost. After all, the forest should have been thinning out by now. Instead, it seemed to him thicker than ever, even though he was still heading northwest according to the compass. He was forced to push low foliage back from his face. His gloves were sticky with sap and his cheeks were scarred by errant branches. The only consolation was that the snow was not as heavy on the ground, the great trees above and around him sheltering him from the worst of it.

He leaned against a tree trunk, took out his Zippo and lit up, keeping the cigarette shielded in his palm. He took a long drag, closed his eyes, then released the smoke through his nostrils.

When he opened his eyes, there were three men moving through the forest about fifty feet ahead of him. Shepherd whistled loudly but they didn't respond, so he flicked the butt into the snow and started to go after them. He had closed the gap by about twenty feet when the man bringing up the rear turned around.

It wasn't Dexter.

First of all, Dex had been wearing a black jacket and green combat pants. This guy was wearing some kind of hooded arrangement made from skins and fur. His face wasn't visible beneath the hood. When he stopped, the other men paused too, and all three of them stared back at Shepherd.

Then the man bringing up the rear raised his weapon, and even through the snow Shepherd could see that it was an old, old gun, a muzzle loader.

Shepherd dived for cover as the gun flashed and smoke rose and a noise like cannon fire echoed through the forest. When Shepherd looked up, the men were spreading out. He could see the one who had fired at him reloading as he moved, his hand ascending and descending as he pressed the ball down.

Shepherd aimed his own weapon and fired two shots. He didn't give a damn about the need for silence or for concealment of their presence. Right now, his need was to survive. Shepherd saw one of the men rise and he fired again, the shot tearing through the layer of furs, and watched with satisfaction as he went down.

And rose again.

"No way," said Shepherd. "That's not possible."

They were surrounding him. He could see one of them trying to flank him, to get behind him and cut off his retreat. Shepherd retreated, firing as he went, using the trees for cover.

Twice he heard the great eruptions of the muzzle loaders, and one shot came so close that he felt its heat against his cheek as it passed.

He had been backing away for about a hundred feet when he found himself in the clearing. To his rear were a number of rough-hewn houses built from tree trunks. There were six or seven in all. In the doorway of one he spied a woman's body, naked from the waist down. There was blood on her face and neck. Other bodies lay nearby, in various states of undress and mutilation. He could smell burning.

"No," he said aloud, remembering the layout of the island from Moloch's map. "I was going toward the boat. This is—"

The south. I could not have gone so far astray.

The image faded, and now he was surrounded only by broken rocks and old graves and a huge stone cross that cast its shadow on him.

He registered the shot at almost the same instant as his belly exploded in agony. His dropped his shotgun and fell to his knees, clutching his stomach. His body began to burn, as though wreathed in flame. The pain was too much. He took his hands away to examine the wound, but his jacket was intact.

But I feel pain. I feel *pain.*

He heard snow crunching beneath approaching footsteps and looked up to see the three figures closing in on him, their heads low and hooded, their weapons held at port arms. Two of them paused while the third moved forward, so close now to Shepherd that the wounded man could smell the stink of dead animals that rose from the hunter. He tried to crawl away and felt a hand grip his leg, pulling him back. Shepherd searched inside his jacket and found the butt of his Colt. He twisted and raised the weapon, aiming it at the man who was dragging him backward, then emptied five shots into him.

The hunter released him and lowered the hood of furs from his head.

"Aw fuck," said Shepherd, as he saw at last what had come for him. His disintegrating mind registered pale, withered skin, and blue lips, and eyes that burned cold red with a fearsome, implacable fury. Here were the true hunters, not bound by time or space, traversing the centuries in their quest for vengeance, seeking final reparation for old sins.

Shepherd started to cry. They should never have come here. It was a mistake, a terrible mistake.

"Aw fuck aw fuck aw fuck aw fuck . . ."

He placed the barrel of the gun against his skull.

"Aw fuck aw fuck aw—"

And fired.

Moloch and his men heard the sound of the shotgun blasts and the final shot as Shepherd turned his gun upon himself. Dexter and Moloch exchanged a glance, but said nothing.

Willard, moving along the road, skirting the outer reaches of the forest, paused as he too heard the shots, then began to run faster. He wanted answers, and dead men could tell him nothing. He also wanted to believe in Moloch, to be reassured that Tell had acted on the wishes of Dexter and Shepherd and not those of Moloch himself. If Moloch was in trouble, then he would need Willard's help. Willard would show his loyalty, and Moloch would reward it with his love.

And Sharon Macy, trying to warm herself before the flames rising from Lubey's house, heard them as well. They sounded some way off. She stared into the forest, its outer reaches now lit by the fire, and tried to discern movement within, but there was nothing. Keeping away from the flames, she circled the house and retreated into the shadows.

Moloch had grown quieter. Dexter watched him as they progressed toward the fire, but didn't say what was on his mind. They had lost two men already. Maybe Moloch was right. Perhaps Powell had just given up and headed back to the boat, and Shepherd had done the same, but Dexter didn't think so. That wasn't like either man. They had been approached because Dexter knew that they would stand firm. For Shepherd it was primarily about the money, for Powell the promise of a little action. But they had also come because there were few opportunities for men like them to strike back at all that they hated; to break a prisoner loose, to hunt down a betrayer, to kill a cop. Their discipline was almost military. They were not the kind of men to turn back at the first sign of trouble.

Moloch swiped at something unseen in the air, as though swatting away a fly. No, thought Dexter, not a fly.

More like unwanted company.

There were voices in Moloch's head. They were whispering to him, saying things in a mocking, familiar tone, but he couldn't understand the words. And each time he felt his footing slip, and reached out to grasp a tree or a rock for support, he seemed to endure a kind of mental flash.

Blood.

Men among the trees.

A woman beneath him, dying as blade and man moved in unison.

And darkness; the sensation of being trapped in a mine, or a tunnel network, or a honeycomb.

He felt a hand on his shoulder and thought:

Gray. They're gray.

"You okay?"

It was Dexter.

"I'm good," he said. "I'm—"

They're gray, and they carry lights.

"—real good."

Braun was leaving a trail of blood on the snow. There was nothing he could do to stop it. He'd tried to stem the flow, but the cop's shot had torn up his arm badly. Despite the cold, he was sweating and feverish. He wanted to rest, to lie back against a rock and let sleep come, but Dupree was following him. He had caught a glimpse of him through the trees, and had considered waiting for him in the darkness in the hope of ambushing him, but he was afraid that if he stopped to rest he might lose consciousness and become an easy target.

And he wasn't running only from Dupree. When he paused briefly to catch his breath and examine his copy of the crude map while leaning against a big fir, the snow thick on his shoulders and bright red hair, he heard a whispering and saw the gray shapes moving along the ground, trying to get ahead of him and cut off his escape. He was delirious with pain, he told himself. His mind was playing tricks on him, forcing him to believe that figures were crawling along the ground, clutching at roots and stones with emaciated hands as they pulled themselves across the earth.

Braun checked the compass attachment on his watch. All he knew was that if he continued due east, he would reach the heart of the island, and from there a trail, hacked through the forest for tourists, would lead him close by Lubey's house. He broke through a bank of evergreens and found himself in a clearing filled with dead trees, most of them little more than white staves, their branches long since decayed. Some had fallen sideways, to be supported here and there by their stronger fellows, creating archways over the trail. Braun tested the black ground on either side of the causeway and felt his foot begin to sink. It was beaver bog, he figured, or something similar. He began moving, anxious to get back under the cover of the trees again. Out here, he was a sitting duck for the cop.

Braun was halfway across the bog when he realized that the gray figures were no longer shadowing him. When he looked back, he thought he glimpsed a single pale shape moving across the snow, like a crazed hound chained to a post walking over and over the same ground. Braun raised his gun and fired off a shot. He didn't care about the cop now, didn't care about Moloch or the woman or the money. Braun just didn't want to die out here, among these things.

He became aware of new movement around him. The surface of the marsh rippled, the forms of what swam beneath visible briefly when they broke the surface. Braun fired down at one and something gushed darkly, then fell away. He heard a slithering sound behind him and spun just in time to see a dark body sliding back into the bog, blackened, withered feet glimpsed beneath the wetness of its shroud, its hips still round, a halo of white hair pooling briefly on the surface of the bog before sinking back into its depths.

It's a woman, thought Braun.

No, it *was* a woman.

Then a voice spoke, and he turned to see Dupree using a tree for cover, his shotgun pointing directly at Braun.

"I said, 'Drop it.'"

Braun started to giggle.

Dupree couldn't figure out what the gunman was doing. He had seen him pause in the middle of the trail, then begin firing wildly at the trees and the bog. Maybe he was hallucinating from the pain of his wound. If so, his unpredictability would make him even more dangerous. He made his move when the man turned quickly, seemingly distracted by something on the ground behind him. Dupree took up a position against the biggest fir he could find, then shouted a warning.

The man turned.

Dupree gave him a second warning.

The man laughed, then raised his gun and fired in the policeman's direction.

Dupree pulled the trigger and blew him into the marsh.

Braun's lower body took the force of the blast, and he fell backward, his feet slipping from beneath him. The trees tilted crazily and he was lost for a moment in snowflakes, suspended between the path and the blackness below. Then his back hit the water and his head disappeared into the murk. He tasted rot and decay, and even as the pain began to separate body from mind, death from life, he attempted to raise himself up. His face cleared the surface and he spit mud and vegetation from his mouth. He tried to open his eyes, but his vision was blurred. He could see the shape of the cop, Dupree, the gun held to his shoulder as he approached him along the path, and he could sense movement in the marsh to his right and left as the black beings converged upon him.

The cop was right above him now. Braun was dying. He could feel it as a gathering darkness, punctured by slivers of red, like wounds in burnt skin. It was coming slowly, too slowly. The things in the bog were faster. They would get to him first, and Braun didn't want that. He didn't want to go that way.

With a last surge of effort, Braun raised his gun from the water and died in the shotgun's merciful roar.

Moloch cleared the trees first and stood looking at the remains of Carl Lubey's burning house. The garage door was open and he could see the truck inside, the hood gaping, the shape of the cab behind it making it seem like the flaming skull of some great bird. Scarfe and Dexter took up positions at either side of him. Nobody spoke for a moment.

"Looks like our ride's gone," said Dexter.

Scarfe shielded his face from the heat of the flames and thought about running. He'd take his chances with the Russians back in Boston. They were brutal, but at least they weren't crazy. It was supposed to be simple: Scarfe would do the groundwork, set them up with Carl Lubey, and take off. Then Scarfe found himself pushed into the role of boatman and now there were cops being killed, and handicapped men shot with arrows, and his buddy Carl's place was burning like a bonfire at Halloween, with Carl, he felt sure, burning right along with it. Scarfe didn't hold out much hope for the woman they were hunting either, nor her boy. The money wasn't going to be enough for Moloch. Whatever she'd done to him, Scarfe figured it must have been pretty bad.

There was a rustle of bushes to Scarfe's right and a female cop appeared. Her gun was in her hand. Scarfe looked at her, then Moloch and Dexter followed his lead.

Scarfe recognized Macy at the same instant that she recognized him.

"Aw, this is just great," said Scarfe.

Dexter didn't even wait for the cop to speak. He just started shooting.

I was too slow, thought Macy, dumb and slow, but the black man had moved so fast, forcing her to run. Then the others had joined in, and the forest around her was now alive with falling branches, shredded leaves, and the hiss of bullets melting snow. Macy hit a rock with her foot and went tumbling down the slope at the rear of Carl Lubey's property, wrenching her ankle painfully before at last coming to rest among a pile of trash and discarded metal. She was in Lubey's private dump, and it stank. Macy got to her feet, but her ankle almost instantly collapsed beneath her weight, so she leaned against a tree for support. Above her, she heard the men moving, but the trees on the slope shielded her from the light of the fire.

There was another blast of gunfire. Macy pressed her face hard into the tree and drew her body in as close as she could to the trunk. A bullet blew bark inches from her face and she closed her eyes a second too late to avoid being momentarily blinded by a spray of wood and sap. It got into her mouth and she coughed, trying desperately to mask the sound with the sleeve of her jacket.

But the men heard her.

A thrashing came from the trees above as one of them began to descend.

Macy, hurt and afraid, headed into the forest.

* * *

They sent Scarfe.

According to Moloch's map and the late Carl Lubey's directions, they were pretty close to his wife's house. Scarfe could take care of the cop while they got the woman. They would wait for Scarfe at her house, then find a car and head back to the boat.

It sounded simple.

Even Scarfe thought it sounded easy, except he had no intention of coming back to the woman's house. Scarfe wasn't really a killer. He'd never killed anybody, but he was pretty certain that he could do it if he had to. The cop knew who he was. If she got away, Scarfe would be in serious shit. Maine didn't have the death penalty, but he'd die behind bars as an accomplice to murder if the cop lived to tell what she'd seen. Scarfe was a weak man and a coward, but he was quite capable, under those circumstances, of killing a cop.

The ground was now rising beneath Macy's feet, the slope gradually becoming more pronounced so that she could feel the effort of the climb in her right leg. She was trying to keep her weight off her left foot, although the pain was not as intense now. It was a pretty bad sprain, but at least the ankle wasn't broken. That said, her pursuer was gaining on her. She couldn't see well enough in the snow to pick him out but she could hear him. There was only one, but uninjured and perhaps better armed than she was.

Ahead of her, a tall structure blotted out the descending snow: the island's main observation tower, the one she had explored during her introductory tour earlier that day. Watching for rocks and stray roots, she made her way toward it.

The rusted iron door stood partially open. She had slipped the bolt earlier, she recalled, and had wrapped the chain around it. Someone had been there since then. From behind came the sounds of her pursuer. She couldn't keep running. Her ankle hurt too badly. After a moment's hesitation, she entered the tower, feeling broken glass crunch beneath her feet. There was no bolt on the inside of the door. To her right, the flight of concrete steps led up to the second level. She followed them, then stopped.

A moth was bouncing against one of the windows. She looked up and in the faint light saw more of the insects fluttering around the room. One of them brushed against her face and she slapped it away, feeling it against her palm and then instinctively rubbing her hand against her leg as if she risked contamination from its touch.

A noise came from somewhere above her. It sounded like boards creaking beneath the weight of a footfall. Macy's bowels churned. She shouldn't have come in here. The realization hit her with the force of a fist. Everything about the place felt wrong. She was like a rat caught in a maze with no prize at the end of it, or an insect teetering on the edge of a jar of sugared water.

The sound came again, clearer now. She imagined that she heard someone crying. It sounded like a little girl.

"Hey?" called Macy softly. "Hey, are you okay?"

Scarfe saw a gray shape in the shadows, moving close to the ground. He raised his gun, then pivoted swiftly to his right as he registered a second presence in the trees, then a third behind him, the shapes in a state of constant movement, circling him from the shelter of the forest.

"Who's there?" he whispered, more to himself than to anyone else. Then, louder: "Who's there?"

The sound of the wind in the trees was almost deafening. A mist appeared to rise before him and he thought that he could discern figures and, for a second, even faces. Then the figures spread out, moving faster, trying to surround him.

Scarfe ran, the ground rising before him, until he came to the clearing, and the tower.

Macy walked across the floor and stood at the base of the next flight of steps. All was darkness above, but she could see, faintly, the edges of the wooden floor. She reached out a hand to steady herself against the wall, then recoiled instantly as she felt movement on her skin. There were more moths up here. As she looked closer, she saw that they entirely covered the wall beside the ascending stairs. Macy took a step back and a figure passed across the top of the steps. She had a fleeting image of something small and gray, with white-blond hair. A tattered gown seemed to hang from it, as though she were shedding a skin.

It was a girl, a little girl dressed in gray.

The crying came again.

"Honey, come on down," said Macy. "You don't have to be afraid."

"No, you come up."

But Macy didn't move. The voice was not that of a child. It was older. It sounded sick. There was desire in that voice, despite the tears, and hunger. Macy stood still, undecided, and again the image of a honey pot came to her.

Then her decision was made for her. There came a gunshot, followed by a second. Moments later she heard the door beneath her slam closed, and then there was silence.

* * *

Willard was unusual in many ways, not the least of which was his total lack of imagination. He didn't read books, didn't like movies, didn't even watch much TV. He didn't need to live in a fantasy world created by others. Instead, Willard moved through this world and carved his own reality from it.

Yet even Willard felt that there was something wrong with this island. There was a buzzing in his head, like an out-of-tune radio. He thought that he sensed movement around him but when he looked closer there was nothing. Willard felt as if he were the subject of a conversation that he couldn't quite hear, or the punch line of a joke that had not yet been told.

He considered his options. He could go back to the boat and return to the mainland, but he didn't know much about boats, and even if he could get it started, he didn't think he could even *find* the mainland in this weather. But he also had scores to settle and questions to be answered. When Willard had all the information at his disposal, he would then decide what moves to make against the others.

Macy went down the stairs as quietly as she could, carefully placing each foot so that she did not slip. She listened carefully, and once or twice she believed she heard heavy breathing, the sound of a man recovering from sudden, unaccustomed exertion. She kept her back against the wall, trying to listen to both what was below her and what was above.

A shadow moved across the Plexiglas of the window and Macy, puzzled, found her attention distracted. The shadow came again, and Macy was aware of a darkness hovering beyond the window, out of sight yet still capable of stealing what little light she had. The gun in her hand made a regular arc, first pointing down toward the unknown man below, then swinging up toward the shadows above, and the child who was not a child. The darkness in the stairway was almost liquid, pouring from the walls and oozing down the stairs. She was halfway down when she heard a soft hiss and the Gray Girl's hand emerged from the shadows and pushed her.

Macy lost her footing and stumbled down the last of the concrete steps.

The porch light was out and the house was in complete darkness as Marianne at last reached her home. Even the night-lights that came on automatically as the day faded were out.

They're here. They've cut off the power and they're here.

But then she looked to her right, where Jack's house lay, and saw that it too was dark. That never happened, for the old man stayed awake until the wee hours, working in his studio. She saw him, sometimes, when she couldn't sleep during the warm summer months and sat outside on her porch, watching him working on his terrible paintings. It was a power failure, that was all, although it didn't explain her car dying. Coincidence, she decided. After all, what other reason could there be?

She found her keys, opened the door, then slammed it closed behind her with the heel of her shoe. She carried Danny upstairs and laid him on his bed, then took two bags from her closet and began thrusting clothes into them, her own first, then Danny's. She grabbed some toys and books and placed them in his bag, then zipped it closed.

Finally, she pulled down the attic stairs and headed up. Her flashlight wasn't working, and she was almost certain that she'd filled her bag with a selection of mismatched clothing, but it didn't matter. What mattered was the knapsack that lay hidden under piles of trash and junk at the rear of the attic. She stepped carefully, one hand raised ahead of her so that she would not bump her head on the eaves. Kneeling down, she began tossing bags and boxes away until beneath her fingers she felt the canvas straps on the bag. She dragged it out, hauled it to the edge of the attic door, then tipped it down into the hallway.

It landed with the kind of sound that only three quarters of a million dollars can make.

Scarfe too had seen the shadows outside. Panicked, he held his gun in a double-handed grip and tried to catch the figures as they moved beyond the windows.

Two noises came together: a loud scuffling from the staircase across from him, and a rattle as something thrust itself against the door from outside. Torn between the two threats, Scarfe retreated against the wall just as Macy's voice called out: "Police! Drop your weapon."

And then the door flew open, and the man in her sights turned to stare at what lay beyond. He raised his weapon and fired. Macy, aware only of the gun and the threat that it posed, fired at the same time, and watched the man buck against the wall, then slide down, the gun falling from his hand.

Macy advanced toward Scarfe and kicked his gun away with her foot. The doorway was empty. Only snow was entering. The shot had taken him clean in the chest and he was bleeding from the mouth. She tried to open his jacket but his hand gripped hers as he tried to speak.

"Tell me," said Macy. "Tell me why you're here."

"Elliot," Scarfe whispered. *"Moloch!"*

He was staring straight at her, pulling her closer, and then his gaze shifted to a point over her shoulder and his grip tightened. She was already turning when she felt a presence close by, flitting mothlike in the shadows.

The Gray Girl hung in the air behind her, moving swiftly back and forth, trying to find some means of access to the dying man. Macy could see her eyes, jet black within her wrinkled skin, and the edges of her teeth almost hidden beneath the lips of her rounded mouth.

She raised her gun as Scarfe began to spasm beside her. His nails dug into her painfully. The Gray Girl darted forward, then retreated again as Macy shielded the dying man's body from her. Scarfe coughed once, and his fingers relaxed their grip as the life passed from him. Macy watched as the child's features contorted with rage, her head and arms trembling with the depth of her anger, and then she seemed to sink back into the shadows in the corner. Seconds later, a flight of moths burst from the darkness and disappeared into the night, forming a mist that moved against the direction of the wind, heading deeper and deeper into the forest, making for the very heart of the island.

CHAPTER SIXTEEN

Dexter and Moloch left Carl Lubey's burning house behind them, traveling southwest until they came to a road, banks of firs standing like temple columns at either side.

"You want the map?" asked Dexter.

"I know where we're going," said Moloch. He sounded distracted, almost distant. "We need to spread out, take them from every angle."

Dexter stared at him.

"Spread out how? There's just you and me."

Moloch acted like a man suddenly awakened from a strange dream. Once again, the sensation of worlds overlapping came to him, but it was accompanied by an uncomfortable feeling of separation. Moments earlier, he had been surrounded by men, men willing to act at his command. He had strength and authority. Now there was only Dexter, and Moloch himself was weakening. Increasingly, he was troubled by the sense that he was less alive here than he was in the past, that each time he flipped between worlds he left more of himself behind in an earlier life.

"They haven't come back yet?" he asked.

"Who, Shepherd and Scarfe? No, they ain't back yet."

Moloch nodded, then pointed. "Her house is just over that rise. Shouldn't take us more than—"

He glanced at his watch. It had stopped.

"You know what time it is?"

Dexter wore a Seiko digital. No numerals showed on its face.

"I don't know. It's not working right."

"It doesn't matter," said Moloch, but again Dexter detected a wavering note in his voice. Don't fall apart on me now, man, he thought, not after all this time.

The wind was dying down now, the snow falling a little less thickly. They leaped a small ditch that ran along the side of the road, now almost entirely filled with snow, and stepped out onto the trail. In doing so, they almost ran into the woman. She let out a little yelp of surprise, then saw their guns and started to back away.

"Now, where are you going?" said Dexter. He advanced upon her, gripped her by the hair, and dragged her back to Moloch.

Bonnie Claeson had given up on the phone, on her car, and on Joe Dupree. She had given up on everything. Something had broken inside her when she'd heard her son's voice echoing down a dead telephone line, and so she had retreated into a beautiful illusion. Richie, her sad, troubled, loving son, was out in the snow alone, probably tired and afraid. She had to find him and bring him home. She wore only an open coat over her sweater and jeans, and her clothing was now crusted white with flakes. Her cheap boots had not protected her feet, yet she did not feel the cold. She was lost to herself, and now she only wished for her son to appear out of the darkness, his orange jacket bright against the snow, his face filled with relief and affection as his mother came for him and drew him to her.

"I'm searching for my boy," she said. "Have you seen him?"

She looked first at Dexter, then at Moloch, examining their faces. They seemed familiar to her. Briefly, her clouded mind was illuminated by a flash of clarity. She shook her head and moved away from the two men, never allowing her eyes to leave their faces.

They were Richie's bad men, the men from the TV. She heard her son's voice crying out its last words to her.

Momma! Momma! Bad men. Badmenbadmenbadmenbad-menbad—

Dexter saw the recognition in her eyes.

"Shit," he said, "now we're gonna—"

The gunshot came from so close to his head that he recoiled in shock, his ears ringing. The woman crumpled to the ground and began to bleed on the snow. Beside him, Moloch holstered his gun.

"We could have taken her with us," said Dexter. "She could have helped us."

"You going soft on me, Dex?" came the reply, and Dexter was sure now that Moloch was mad. In the unspoken threat he heard the death sentence being passed on Willard, the abandonment of Powell, Shepherd, and Scarfe to their fates, and the single-minded obsession that had brought them to this place. It was no longer about money, or a woman, or a child. Moloch might once have thought that it was, but it wasn't. He had come here for some unknowable reason of his own, and those who stood alongside him were expendable.

We're going to die here, Dexter realized. I think I always knew, and just hoped that it wouldn't be true, but it will end here. I have no choice now but to follow it to its conclusion, and to embrace it when it comes.

"No," said Dexter. "I ain't going soft."

He walked over to where the woman lay and looked down on her. She was lying very still. Her eyes blinked and he saw her chest rise and fall, blood spreading from the wound on her left breast. Her lips formed a word.

"Richie," she whispered, for the boy was beside her now. He had always appeared wondrous to her, always kind, but now he seemed transformed, his features perfectly sculpted and his eyes alive with an intelligence that he had never known in life.

"Richie," she repeated. He reached out his hand to her and took it in his own, and he drew her to him and carried her away so that she would not feel the pain of the final bullet.

Marianne was on her doorstep when she heard the shots. They came from close by. Two overnight bags, crammed full of clothing, lay by her feet, and the knapsack hung over her shoulder. Danny sat on top of one of the bags, still drowsy. When he heard the shots, he looked up briefly, then resumed his previous position, his head cupped in his hands, his eyes nearly closed.

"Come on, Danny, we have to go."

"Where?" There was that whining tone to his voice, and for the first time she lost her temper with him.

"We're going to Jack's. Now get up, Danny! I mean it! You get up or I'm going to give you such a spanking that you won't be able to sit for a week. Do you hear me? Get up!"

The boy started to cry, but at least he was on his feet. Marianne took a bag in each hand, then gave him a little swipe with one of them, propelling him toward the door. She pulled it closed behind her with her toe, then urged him on down the path to Jack's house. Once they got to Jack's, she could convince the old man to take them off Dutch. Even if they got only as far as one of the neighboring islands, it would be enough. All that mattered was that they get away from here. The weight of the gun in her coat pocket slapped painfully against her leg as she walked, but she didn't care. It had been in the knapsack with the money. She had cleaned and oiled it only twice in the years since she had fled, following instructions from a gun magazine, and had never fired it, not even on a range. She would use it, though, if she was forced to do so. This time there would be no fear. She would take his dare. She was stronger than he had ever suspected, stronger than even she had known. She would kill him, if she had to, and some secret part of her hoped that she would be given that opportunity.

From the top of the rise, Moloch and Dexter watched them leave the house, but they were not the only ones. Far to their right, almost at the edge of Jack's property, a pretty man with blond hair stood among the trees and admired once again the shape of the woman's legs, the swell of her breasts beneath her open coat, the way her jeans hugged her groin. In her way, she was to blame for all that had happened to him, for his rejection and abandonment by the man he admired so much. She had deceived him, betrayed his beloved Moloch, and he would make her pay. He vaguely recalled Moloch's warning that she was not to be harmed, but he had the hunger upon him now. He would first make her tell him where the money was, and then he would finish her.

After all, Willard had needs too.

* * *

Jack heard the banging on his kitchen door as he dozed in his armchair. He had tried to paint, but nothing came. Instead, he found himself drawn again and again to the painting with the two figures burned upon it, his fingers tracing their contours as he tried to understand how they had come to be. Then the lights had gone out and the heat with them. The small fire faded in the grate and he noticed only when the cold began to tell on his bones. There was no wood left by the fireplace, so he grabbed his coat and opened the door, preparing to risk the cold in order to replenish his stock from the store of firewood in the shed.

But as he stood at the door, he became aware of a presence beyond the house.

No, not a single presence, but many presences.

"Who's there?" he called, but he expected no reply. Instead, he thought he saw a shadow move against the wind, gray upon the white ground, like a cobweb blown, or an old cloak discarded. There were more shadows to his left and right. They seemed to be circling the house, waiting.

"Go away," he said, softly. "Please go away."

He closed and locked the door then, and checked all the windows. He took a blanket from his bed, wrapped it around his shoulders, and sat as close as he could to the dying embers of the fire. He thought that he might have slept for a time, for he dreamed of shadows moving closer to the great picture window, and faces pressed against the glass, their skin gray and withered, their lips thin and bloodless, their eyes black and hungry. They tapped at the glass with their long nails, the tapping growing harder until at last the glass exploded inward and they descended upon him and began to devour him.

Jack's eyes flicked open. He could still hear the banging and for a moment he found himself unable to distinguish between dream and reality. Then he heard Marianne Elliot calling his name and he struggled to his feet, his joints stiff from sitting slumped against the chair. He walked to the kitchen door and saw the faces of Marianne and Danny, the woman scared and panicky, the boy drowsy and his face streaked with tears. He opened the door.

"Come in," he said. "What's wrong?"

She dropped the bags she was holding, then knelt down and hugged the boy close to her.

"I'm sorry for shouting at you, Danny. I'm so sorry."

The boy began to cry again, but at least he hugged her back. Marianne, the boy's head cradled against her neck, looked imploringly at Jack.

"We need to get off the island."

"There's no way you can get away from here until this snow thins out some more," he said.

"We can't wait that long."

Jack said nothing. She understood that he wanted more from her.

"Danny," she said, "go inside and lie down for few minutes."

The boy did not need to be told twice. He passed by the old man and headed for the couch, where he instantly fell asleep.

"I've told some lies," she said when she saw her son curl up with his eyes closed. "My husband isn't dead. He was put in prison. I betrayed him to the police so that Danny and I could get away from him. And . . . I took money from him. A lot of money."

She opened the knapsack and showed Jack the wads of notes. His mouth opened slightly in surprise, then closed with a snap.

"I'm not sure how he got it all, but I can guess, and so can you. Now he's here on the island and he's brought men with him. They're close. I heard shots."

She reached out and took the painter's hand.

"My car is dead, but you have a boat. I need you to get us away from here, even just to one of the other islands. If we don't leave, they'll find us and they'll kill me and take Danny away."

She paused.

"Or they may kill Danny too. My husband, he never had any love for Danny."

The old man looked back at the swing door of the kitchen, beyond which the boy lay sleeping.

"You told Joe Dupree any of this?"

Marianne shook her head.

"He'll help you, you know that. He's different."

"I was afraid, afraid that they'd put me in jail or take Danny from me."

"I don't know enough about the law to say one way or the other, but it seems to me that they'd be a little more sympathetic than that."

"Just take us off the island, please. I'll think about telling someone once we're away from here."

Jack bit his lip, then nodded. "Okay, we can try. This all your stuff?"

"It's all that I had time to pack."

Jack took a bag in each hand, then kicked the knapsack and said: "You'd best look after that yourself."

They entered the living room, Jack leading. Marianne was so close behind him when the shot came that Jack's blood hit her in the face before he fell to the floor. There was a wound at his shoulder. He clutched it with his hand, his teeth clenched as he trembled and began to go into shock. Danny awoke and started crying loudly, but she could not go to him. She could not move.

All that she could do was stare impotently at her husband, even as Dexter frisked her and took the gun from her coat. He raised it so that Moloch could see it.

Moloch grinned.

"Is that a gun in your pocket, or are you just not happy to see me?" Moloch asked.

He stepped closer to her and struck her hard with his right hand, sending her sprawling on a rug. She lay still for a moment, then crawled across the floor to Danny and gathered him in her arms.

"You'd better make that last," said Moloch. "You don't have much time left together."

Moloch stared at his reflection in the painting, his face seeming to hang suspended above the dark waves that the old man had painted, the twin arms of the outcrops like horns erupting from his head, almost touching above his hair. He moved on to the next, a watercolor filled with blues and greens, before returning to the first. The waves in this version were very dark, almost black, white peaks breaking through, like the pale bodies of drowning men. A sliver of moonlight cast a weak silver glow across the skies above. There were no stars.

"I like this one," he said.

Jack, seated on the floor, his hands bound before him with a length of clothesline, peered up at the intruder. He was deathly pale, apart from a smear of blood across his cheek. In the murk of the room, the blood appeared black against the pallor of his face, creating a strange resemblance between the artist and the work of art before which Moloch now stood.

"You go away and you can have it for free," said Jack.

Moloch's mouth twitched, the only sign he gave that he might be enjoying the joke.

"Something I've learned," he said. "You get nothing for free in this life. Although I can say, with some certainty, that if you fuck with me, money is never likely to be a worry for you again."

Dexter stood behind the couch. The appearance of the woman and the money seemed to have concentrated Moloch's mind some. He was no longer rambling. Dexter began to experience a faint hope that they might somehow get out of this alive. His hand rested on the back of Danny's neck in what might have been almost a protective way, were it not for the fact that the tips of his fingers were digging painfully into the boy's skin, almost cupping his spine.

"Make him stop," said Marianne. "He's your son. Make him stop hurting him."

Moloch walked toward the boy, who attempted to shrink back but found himself anchored to the spot by the force of Dexter's hand. Moloch reached out and touched the back of his hand to the boy's cheek.

"You're cold," he said. "If you're not careful, you'll catch your death."

He glanced at Marianne.

"He doesn't look much like me. You sure he's mine? Maybe he's something that you and that dyke bitch cooked up between you with a turkey baster. She's dead, by the way, but I suspect you knew that already."

Marianne's eyes blinked closed. She bit her lip to try to keep from crying.

"Actually, I got to tell you that a lot of people are dead

because of you. Your sister, her husband, fuck knows how many people on this island, all because you were a greedy bitch who screwed over her own husband. You try that out for size, see how it fits on your conscience."

He turned to Dexter.

"How long have we been here?"

"Ten, fifteen minutes, maybe."

"We can't afford to wait any longer for the others, but now that we have a boat a little closer to home"—Moloch kicked Jack's leg, causing the old man to flinch—"it looks like I have some time to kill, in a manner of speaking."

He reached out to Marianne, lifted her up by the arm, and started to guide her toward the bedroom. Danny tried to hold on to her, but Dexter's hand kept him rooted to the couch.

"I've been waiting a long time to see you again," he whispered. He grabbed her left breast and squeezed it painfully. "Look upon this as a conjugal visit."

Marianne tried to pull away from him. Instead he thrust her forward, sending her staggering into the hallway.

"There was a time," said Moloch, "when you used to beg me for what I'm about to give you." He pushed her against the wall, the length of his body pressed hard against her, and clasped her cheeks in his hands, forcing her mouth into the shape of a kiss. He composed his own features into an expression of sadness.

"Maybe you've just forgotten the good times," he said. "You know, I can promise you that in all the years we've spent apart, I've never been with another woman."

He forced his mouth over hers. She struggled, making small moans of disgust against his lips. Then her body began to relax, her mouth now working along with his. His hand relaxed its grip upon her cheeks.

Marianne bit him hard in one single movement of her jaws, almost severing his bottom lip, her teeth meeting where they cut through the flesh. Moloch howled. He hit her across the side of the head with his fist and she tumbled to her right, falling against a small table and sending a bowl of fresh-cut flowers crashing to the ground.

Danny screamed.

Moloch held his hand to his wounded mouth, cupping the blood that was pouring from the cut. He stared at himself in the hall mirror, then looked down at Marianne. His words were distorted as he tried to talk without moving his ruined lip, but she understood. They all did.

"I'm going to cut you for that," he said. "After I've fucked you, I'm going to cut you to pieces. And then I'm going to start on the boy."

He took his knife from his belt, flicked the blade open, then advanced on her. He caught her by the hair and began to drag her down the hallway, Danny screaming all the time, Jack struggling against his bonds.

Then the sliding doors exploded and blood shot from Dexter's chest. He tried to turn, and a second shot sent him sprawling into the fireplace. He rolled away from the red glow of the ashes. A third shot hit him in the small of the back, and he finally lay still.

Willard entered through the ruined glass, shards crunching beneath his feet.

"Y'all look surprised to see me," he said.

Joe Dupree was almost within sight of Jack's house when he heard the shots and the shattering of glass. Marianne's house had been empty. He figured that she must have taken Danny over to Jack's. He was approaching the house from the west, so the big windows were on the opposite side and he could not see what was transpiring inside.

He tightened his grip on the shotgun and began to circle the house.

Moloch smiled at Willard.

"I knew you'd make it," he said.

Willard looked confused.

"You told them to kill me."

Moloch shook his head. "No, that was Dexter's decision, and he didn't tell me about it until we were in trouble. I wanted to kill him for it, but by then I needed all the help I could get. There's something on this damn island, something that wants us all dead, and we need to stick together if we're going to get off it alive."

Willard looked at the older man, and Moloch could see that he wanted to believe him. Whatever love Willard had for anything in this world, he had for Moloch.

"You hadn't killed Dexter, I'd have killed him myself once we got to land. I won't shed tears for him."

Despite the agony of his lip, Moloch tried to seem compassionate and concerned about Willard's own pain. It appeared to work. The gun, trained on Moloch, wavered, then fell.

"Thank you, Willard," said Moloch.

Willard nodded.

"Where we at?" he asked.

Moloch shook Marianne hard, by the hair. "My wife and I were about to make love, but now I've decided to go straight to the afterglow."

"What happened to your mouth?"

Moloch smiled, his teeth red. "Love bite," he said, then looked to Jack. "You got a first-aid kit?"

"In the kitchen, under the sink."

Moloch inclined his head toward the kitchen. "Go in, see what you can find for my mouth," he told Willard.

Willard took one last look at Dexter, lying unmoving on the floor, then headed for the kitchen, tucking his gun into his belt. The only sign of doubt he exhibited was his reluctance to turn away from Moloch. He was still looking back at him as the kitchen door swung closed on its hinges, hiding him from the view of those in the living room, and Joe Dupree's great hand closed around his throat. Willard tried to reach for his gun, but the giant's left hand plucked it from its belt and laid it gently on the top of the refrigerator.

Willard's feet began to rise from the ground. He tried to make a sound, but Dupree's grip was too strong. He kicked out with his feet, hoping to hit the walls or the door and alert Moloch, but the giant held him in the very center of the large kitchen, away from anything that might allow Willard to give his presence away. Willard stretched for the giant's face, but his arms were too short. Instead, he dug his nails into Dupree's hand, tearing and gouging, even as he felt his eyes bulging from his face, his lungs burning. Spittle shot from his mouth, and he began to shudder.

Then the giant's grip tightened, and the small bones in Willard's neck started to snap.

Outside, Moloch's head turned sharply toward the kitchen.

"Willard?" he called. "You okay in there?"

He discarded his knife. Keeping a grip on Marianne's hair, he drew his own gun. He pressed it hard against her temple, moving her slowly toward the living room. He saw Jack look to his right, the boy too. Moloch risked a look around the corner.

The female cop was standing at the ruined window. Her gun was raised. She fired. The glass on the painting closest to Moloch's head shattered.

At the same instant, Dupree emerged from the kitchen, his great bulk filling the doorway as he crouched slightly to enter the room. Moloch instantly drew Marianne up to her full height and forced her against him, using her body as a shield, the barrel of the gun now pushed hard into the soft flesh beneath her chin. Only Dupree could see him. Macy stood uncertainly at the window. Moloch adjusted his line of sight so that he could see the hall mirror and Macy's reflection in its surface.

"Peekaboo," he said. "I see you. You stay right there, missy."

Dupree remained still, the shotgun pointed at Moloch. The two men confronted each other for the first time, brought together by forces neither fully understood, and bound together by circumstances barely recognized: their shared knowledge of the woman who stood between them; their links to the island and its strange, bloody heritage; and finally, their own curiously similar situations, for they were both men out of place in the world and only Sanctuary could hold out to them a promise of belonging.

"Let her go," said Dupree. "It's over."

"You think?" said Moloch. "I reckon it's just beginning."

"Your people are all dead, and you'll never be allowed to leave this place. Let her go."

"Uh, no. I don't think that's going to happen. My wife and I have just been reunited after a long absence. We've got a lot of catching up to do."

Moloch jerked Marianne's head back and, despite the pain that it caused him, kissed her cheek, leaving a bloody smear on her skin.

"I bet she didn't tell you about me. I'm shocked. People got to be honest right from the start, otherwise what hope is there for two lovers in this world?"

Marianne kept her eyes away from Dupree, afraid to look at his face. To her left, she could see Macy, her gun moving as she waited for Moloch to make himself a target for her.

"Yeah, I know all about you and my wife. I don't like a man who milks through another man's fence, no matter what he's been told, but I'm inclined to forgive you. After all, she used you."

Dupree couldn't hide his confusion.

"What did you think, that she was *attracted* to you, you fucking freak? This isn't beauty and the beast. This is real life. She took us both for a ride, but hey, don't beat yourself up over it. She's smarter than I gave her credit for, and there's no denying that she's a looker. Not for too much longer, maybe, but right now most men would give a lot to split this particular piece of white oak. She used you, used you as a lookout, an early-warning system so she could take off with my money when the time came."

Marianne tried to speak, but the gun pressed so hard into her skin that she felt sure it would push through into her mouth. Now, at last, she allowed herself to stare into Dupree's face as she tried to communicate with him, to express her shame, her regret, her fear, and her feelings for him.

They're lies. He's telling lies. I never wanted to hurt anyone, least of all you.

"She'll try to deny it, but it was there in her head. I know her. Hell, I was married to her for long enough, and she still fucked me over. Maybe she even thought that you might protect her if things went wrong. Well, she was right about that much at least, because here you are."

In the mirror, Moloch saw Macy attempt to move off, making for the front door to cut off another line of escape. "Missy, I said I could see you. You move another fucking inch and I'll blow my bitch wife's brains all over the ceiling."

Macy stopped.

"Put the shotgun down," Moloch told Dupree. "You can get rid of the Smith on your belt as well. I won't even waste my time counting to three."

Dupree, against all his instincts, did as he was told, laying the shotgun down gently on the floor, followed by his Smith & Wesson.

"You too, missy," said Moloch. He kept his back to the wall so that he could see Macy clearly. She didn't move.

"You think I'm fucking with you? Do it!"

Macy began to lower the gun slowly as Moloch's attention flicked back to Dupree.

"Look at you," he said. "You're a freak, a giant pretending to be a knight in shining armor. But you don't read your fairy stories, Mr. Giant."

The gun moved suddenly from Marianne's face, its barrel now pointing at Dupree.

"At the end of the story, the giant always dies."

He pulled the trigger, and the policeman's throat blossomed like a new flower.

It seemed to happen slowly for Joe Dupree. He thought that he could almost see the bullet as it moved, tearing a path through the cold air. It entered his skin in tiny increments, fractions of inches, ripping through flesh and bone, exiting just to the right of his spine. He fell backward through the kitchen door, coming to rest close to Willard's body. He tried to breathe, but already his throat was flooding with blood. The kitchen door was held open by his feet and he saw Marianne spin and strike at Moloch's injured mouth, then throw herself against him in an effort to dislodge his gun. He saw Macy moving through the living room, her gun extended, her face turning in horror toward him. He watched Moloch push Marianne away, then run for the door, firing as he did so, his wife scrambling for the cover of the corner as the bullets sent plaster and paint flying from the walls.

Then he was gone, Macy uncertain whether to follow him or tend to her wounded comrade. She ran to Dupree, limping slightly, favoring her right foot.

"Stay with me, Joe," she began. "We'll get help."

He reached out, took her shirt in his hand, then pushed her away.

Still she paused. He could not speak, but he pointed his hand in the direction of the fleeing man. She nodded and headed after Moloch, stopping just once to look back at the dying policeman.

Marianne came to him. She was crying. The boy was behind her, staring at the two men on the kitchen floor.

"I'm sorry," she said. "I'm so sorry."

She tried to remove her coat in order to lay it on him, but he gripped her hand and brought it instead to his lips.

"No," she whispered. "We have to keep you warm."

But then she registered the blood spreading behind his head, flowing from the exit wound hidden from them, and she knew.

"No," she repeated, softer now. "Don't do this."

The giant coughed and began to spasm. She tried to hold

him down but his great weight was too much for her. His body jerked as he clawed at the floor, an irregular clicking noise emerging from the back of his throat.

Then the spasming stopped, and Joe Dupree's eyes widened as he died, as though in sudden understanding of the nature of this world.

CHAPTER SEVENTEEN

Moloch ran.

He was conscious of movement around him—branches whipping in the wind, dead leaves pirouetting, and the shapes that lingered at the limits of his perception, not caring now whether he noticed them or not, merely content to shadow his progress through the forest. There was blood on his shirt and face; he could feel it cooling upon him in the night air. His lip ached, the pain like needles in his mouth each time he drew a breath. He heard the sounds of pursuit coming from behind and knew that the female cop was coming after him. He thought of all that he wanted to do to the woman, all of the hurt that he desired to inflict on her and on his wife. At least he'd put an end to the big cop. That was something.

His head struck a broken branch, almost severed by the actions of the storm, and he cried out as he fell back against the tree. When the pain in his mouth and head had subsided, he took a breath and stumbled along a narrow pathway that wound through a patch of marshland, until finally he found himself in a clearing in the middle of the forest. Low stones lay half buried in the ground and a simple stone cross stood at its center. He moved slowly forward until he was facing the monument. It was still possible to read the names on it, and he found his hand reaching out to trace the letters, his bloodied finger outstretched. He touched the stone and—

Men. Forest. Shooting. Women.

Woman.

The fillings in his mouth tingled and he was suddenly light-headed. He staggered back as the ground began to crumble under his feet. Visions of suffering and death assailed him. He felt flesh beneath his fingers, and smelled powder on the air. A noise came from below as the earth gave way beneath him, and Moloch tumbled into blackness.

Marianne turned Danny away from Joe Dupree's body, hiding his face in the folds of her jacket just as days—years?—before she had allowed him to shield himself from the reality of a bird's death. Willard's body lay in a corner, partly concealed by the breakfast counter. Danny wouldn't stop crying. He was holding on to her so tightly that his nails were drawing blood. Behind them, Jack had raised himself and now stood at the kitchen door. She found a knife in a drawer and used it to cut the bindings on his hands, then gently removed Danny's fingers from her legs.

"I want you to stay here with Jack, okay?"

Danny let out a loud wail and tried to claw his way back to her, but she kept him at arm's length and pushed him into the old man's arms. Jack held him as firmly as he could, folding his uninjured arm across Danny's chest. Marianne picked up

Dupree's gun from the floor, then headed for the front door.

"I'll be back before you know it, Danny. You look after Jack for me."

But Danny could only cry, and in the confusion and shock of the moment, none of them noticed that Dexter's body was gone.

Moloch fell for what seemed like a long, long time, yet the distance could have been only twenty feet, for when he hit the bottom he could still see a ragged hole above him, loose earth spilling down from the edges, snowflakes joining it in its descent. Dim light filtered down, bathing him in a patina of gray, like one who was already fading from this world. The impact made him gag, and he lay for a moment tasting bile and blood in his mouth.

Moloch smelled damp earth. He reached out a hand blindly and felt it brush against ragged hair.

Woman. A woman's hair.

He instantly drew his hand back, forcing the fear from himself. The cop was coming. If he stayed here and waited to be found, he would be trapped like an animal. He needed to find a way out. He needed to know what was around him.

He advanced into the shadows, grateful now for the improvements forced upon his vision by hours of struggling through the snowstorm without flashlights. He discovered that he had been touching the exposed roots of vegetation. Moloch released a spluttering laugh of relief, then heard it die in his mouth as he began to take in his surroundings.

He was in a semicircular hollow of earth and stone, about fifteen feet in diameter. At its extremities were openings, large enough for a man to crawl through on his belly. Moloch approached the widest of the entrances and carefully reached inside, disturbing some beetles as he felt the ends of more tree roots dangling from the top of the tunnel. He listened. From beyond he could hear the sound of flowing water. He glanced back toward the hole through which he had fallen, then took another look at the walls of earth and stone that descended from it. There was no way that he could climb them. Either he stayed here and waited to be found or he took his chances in one of the tunnels. Moloch had no fear of enclosed spaces—even prison had not troubled him in that way—but he still felt uneasy about committing himself to the hole before him. He might have trouble squeezing through if it narrowed significantly farther on, and he had no idea how, or for what purpose, the tunnels had been constructed. Still, there was the sound of water, which could mean that the tunnel led to the bank of a river or stream, and he thought that he could make out a faint light ahead.

He made his decision.

He got down on his knees and entered the hole.

Twenty feet above, Macy entered the clearing. She was still feeling the shock of Dupree's death and of her own actions in the tower. Until tonight, she had never fired her gun in the line of duty, and had barely had cause to draw it from its holster. Now a man had died at her hands and another was fleeing from her, and Joe Dupree was dead because she hadn't been fast enough.

Joe Dupree was dead because of her.

Her foot struck stone. She looked down at the monument protruding from the ground, at the others surrounding it, and at the raised stone cross at the center of the little cemetery. She was reluctant to enter the clearing. Her quarry was still armed, and she was unwilling to risk exposing herself. She crouched down low and tried to scan the forest.

There was blood on the snow by the cross.

She swallowed, then headed toward the middle of the site. She was almost upon it when her foot treaded air and she stumbled, her leg disappearing into the hole. She fell backward, then scuttled away from the gap, anticipating gunfire from below, but no sound came. She counted to five, then inched forward again. The opening was new. She could see damp earth, and the tree roots were moist when she touched her fingers to them. She risked a quick glance below, barely allowing the top of her head to appear over the rim of the hole in order to provide the smallest possible target. She could see nothing but fallen earth, broken branches, and a light dusting of snow down below.

Joe Dupree's killer was down there. He had to be.

She was about to descend when a hand gripped her shoulder. She looked up to see Marianne Elliot behind her.

"Don't," said Marianne. "You have to get out of here. We both have to get out of here. Now."

Even in the falling snow, the trail left by Moloch and Macy had been easy for Marianne to discern. They were heading toward the Site. Marianne followed them carefully, checking the woods ahead and always trying to use trees for cover, but could not see either of them. They were too far ahead.

She was almost at the clearing when something brushed by her feet. She looked down and saw a gray shape moving swiftly past her, tattered clothing hanging on mummified skin, wisps of hair protruding from beneath the folds of its shroud. It appeared to float slightly above the ground, leaving no trace of its passage, while its thin hands used rocks and tree trunks to pull itself along, like a diver exploring the seabed. Marianne shrank from it and her legs touched another shape as it swept by her, seemingly oblivious to her presence.

She raised her head and saw that she was surrounded. Pale forms moved across the forest floor, some as big as men, others as small as children. She caught indistinct glimpses of faces lost in the folds of gowns and shrouds, flashes of torn feet, broken skin, and large, dark eyes. Rooted to the spot, she tried to scream, but no sound came.

Then a voice spoke, and it was her voice, yet it did not come from her.

"Leave," the voice said, and Marianne thought that she felt a hand brush against her skin and she saw—

A man descending upon her, Moloch, yet not Moloch, and she felt him enter her, and the blade beginning its work, cutting and tearing at her. She was dying, and others were dying around her.

The voice came again, a soft woman's voice.

"Leave."

And the gray shapes continued to weave around her, disappearing beneath rocks and under tree trunks, descending through all the dark, hollow places and into the world below.

The last to sink away was a woman. Marianne could see the swell of breasts beneath her clothing, and stray strands of hair brushing the snow. Before she descended, the woman stared back at her, and Marianne looked into her own face. It was a face ruined by old wounds, its nose broken and its cheekbones shattered, its eyes a deep black, as though colonized by some terrible cancer, but it was still a face that closely resembled her own.

Then the woman found a gap between the roots of a great beech tree, and was gone.

* * *

Dexter had made it to the edge of the old man's yard, half stumbling, half crawling until he reached the treeline. He had jammed wads of bills, now soaked with red, into the waistband of his pants. Ahead of him he could see a narrow pathway leading from the cliff edge to the shore. The boat would be down there. If he could get to it, he would take his chances on the sea. If he stayed on the island, he would be found, or he would die.

He leaned against a tree trunk to catch his breath, but when he tried to rise again he found that he could not. His body had taken too many shots. He had lost too much blood. He was weakening.

Dexter slid down the bark until he came to rest on the ground. The blizzard was easing, he noticed. The snow was falling more gently now. He stretched his legs out before him and removed the money from his pants. The bills were smeared so thickly with his blood that he could barely read the denominations. He removed the band from one of the wads, spread the notes in his hand, and watched the wind spirit them away, some carried up into the air, others dancing across the snow.

Dexter noticed other shapes moving among the discarded bills. One came to rest on his leg. He reached down and gently touched the moth's wings. It fluttered against his fingers, then took flight. He watched it, following its progress until it came to rest upon a small girl who stood among the trees, watching him. Dexter could see her long, pale hair, but her face was lost in shadow. She looked almost like a moth herself, Dexter thought. A cloak hung over her shoulders, so that when she extended her arms, they took on the appearance of wings.

"Hey," said Dexter. "You think you could help me?"

He swallowed.

"I want to get down to the water. I have money. You could buy yourself something nice."

He extended one of the remaining wads of bills toward her. The girl moved forward.

"That's it," said Dexter. "Come on now. You help me get out of here and I'll—"

The Gray Girl's feet were not touching the ground. She floated toward Dexter, her arms wide and her dark eyes gleaming, her skin wrinkled and decayed. Dexter opened his mouth to scream and the Gray Girl's lips closed on his. Her hands gripped his head and her knees pinned his arms to the trunk of the tree. Blood poured from the meeting of their mouths as Dexter shook, the life slowly being drawn from him and into the Gray Girl, a life taken in return for the life stolen from her.

And then the Gray Girl drew back from the dead man, her dark eyes closing briefly in ecstasy, moths falling dead around her as she followed her companions at last into the depths.

Moloch was ten feet into the tunnel now, and rather than narrowing, it seemed to have increased in size. He paused and listened. If the cop decided to come down after him, he would be in real trouble, but he didn't believe that she would. It was a considerable drop down. Moloch was surprised that he hadn't injured himself in the fall. No, she would wait, maybe look for a rope. She would not risk being trapped beneath the earth with him. He moved on.

He had progressed five or six feet more when he thought that he heard movement behind him. He stopped, and found only silence.

Jittery. I'm getting jittery.

Then he heard it again, clearer now. For a second, he thought it was falling earth, and panic hit him as he imagined the tunnel collapsing around him, trapping him. He listened harder and realized that what he was hearing was scraping, the slow movement of earth beneath nails and hands, the same sounds that he himself had probably been making since he had begun moving through the tunnel. He tried to turn his head, but the tunnel was still too narrow to allow him to see clearly behind him.

The cop. It had to be the cop. She had come down after all. Maybe she had brought rope with her, or had found some among the detritus of the forest.

Shit.

He started to pull himself forward again, faster now. He was certain that he could hear water. Hell, he could even smell it. Cool air was coming through the tunnel. He felt it on his face, took a deep breath—

And then it was gone. Moloch stopped again. The airflow had ceased. He had heard no sounds of collapse. Something had deliberately blocked the tunnel.

The sounds from behind were drawing closer, and now another smell had taken the place of the river and the forest, a stench like old meat left to boil in a pot for too long, of offal and waste. He found himself retching from it. Light filtered through the tunnel. It was silver, almost gray. He was grateful for it, even if he could not identify its source. He didn't want to be trapped down here in the darkness with—

With what?

He tried to turn his head again and found that he now had enough space to peer behind him. The tunnel wall curved slightly but he could still hear the sound. It was closer now, he thought. If it was the cop, she would give him some warning.

If it was the cop.

"Who's there?" he called out.

The sound stopped, but he sensed that his pursuer was at the very edge of the tunnel wall, barely out of sight.

"I got a gun," he said. "You better back out now. I hear you following me, I'll use it."

The light seemed to grow stronger around him. There were gray-white worms emerging from the earth of the tunnel wall, coiling around it, probing . . .

Then Moloch saw the nails on the ends of the pale fingers, and the wounds on the back of the hand, wounds that would never heal. There was movement everywhere now, above and below. Earth dropped onto his head from above as something scrabbled across one of the higher tunnels. It was like a honeycomb, teeming with dark life.

Moloch heard himself sobbing with fear, even as he turned and found himself gilded in silvery light.

And in the final seconds of life granted to him, he saw the woman's face, her skin gray parchment, her hair a handful of strands clinging to the skull, the roots of her teeth exposed by the retreating gums and the parted lips. He could make out the cuts in her face, the damage inflicted by fist and knife. The lamp in her hands radiated dimly, for in the darkest places even the dead need light.

He smelled her breath, fetid and rank, and he heard her voice—*"Know me, husband"*—as the light died and he was enveloped in darkness.

"He's down there," said Macy. "There's nowhere he can go."

But Marianne was pulling her back.

"You don't understand," she said. "There's something else down there too."

Macy looked at her. She remembered the tower, and the floating child, and the look on Scarfe's face as he stared out into the forest and saw what was pursuing him.

Macy began to run. A rumbling sound came from the ground below her, and she felt the earth begin to give way beneath her. She increased her speed, Marianne beside her, the two women racing as the ground around the Site collapsed, taking the stones and the cross and the remnants of the settlement with it, smothering Moloch's final cries in the thunder of its destruction.

CHAPTER EIGHTEEN

Barron sat in the SUV over by the Portland Marine Company, an empty coffee container from the 7-Eleven on Congress in the cup holder by his right hand, the radio playing some Cheap Trick for the night owls. Once or twice prowl cars had passed his way, but he'd hunched down low in his seat and the cops hadn't even slowed, the SUV just another vehicle parked in the lot. The snow was still falling, although the wind had died down some. The SUV was warm, the heat on full blast, but he had kept his gloves and coat on just the same.

Barron had spent most of his evening trying to reach a decision about Parker, the private detective who was nosing around. People listened when Parker spoke, and it was only a matter of time before somebody with real authority started paying attention to his noises about a sexual predator at work in the area, possibly a predator in a uniform.

The men in Boston were his only option. He was their tame cop, in so deep with them now that he could never escape. If they heard he was under threat, then they might be prepared to deal with his problem for him. The Russians didn't give a rat's ass about reputation, or influence. They were in it for the money, and anything that threatened their sources of income, or their carefully cultivated contacts, would be annihilated without a moment's thought. He had once hoped that they might let him go, but it had been a faint hope. If that was the case, he might just have to resign himself to the fact and take advantage of the situation.

He glanced again at the dashboard clock: almost midnight. All was quiet. If Scarfe's buddies did come back to the port, it looked like they would be able to do so without interference. Barron had even spotted one or two ships, dense with lights, braving the bay as the snow began to ease and the wind faded from a howl to a whisper. The streets were deserted and Scarfe's battered Grand Am was parked not ten feet from where he sat, along with two vans. They had wheels. They were free and clear once they got back to Portland. Barron had done all that he could be expected to do. He had waited, he had kept an ear to traffic on the two police bands. He had his cell phone ready, the number he had been given by the men in Boston written on a napkin and not stored in the phone's memory just in case any of this came back to bite him on the ass.

Then his scanner burst into life, and next thing Barron knew there was a chopper being readied for a run to Dutch, the Coast Guard was moving in, and there were enough armed police heading for the water to mount an invasion. Barron started his engine and drove.

It had all turned to shit, just as he had expected.

Barron ditched the SUV at Hoyt's Pond, then retrieved his own car and headed home. He spent the next two hours pacing his apartment floor, wondering if he should run, fearing that his colleagues were already coming for him, sold out by Scarfe to save himself. After a while, he just had to know. He returned to Commercial and contrived to bump into one of the detectives from headquarters, who gave him the lowdown on the situation. Dupree was dead, killed by persons yet to be identified. Some, maybe all, of those responsible were also dead, but they were still searching the island. Macy had blooded herself: Terry Scarfe, who appeared to be tied in with those involved, had died at her hands. Barron was particularly happy to receive this last piece of information. If he had survived, Scarfe would have fed him to the department like fish bait.

Barron returned to his apartment relieved and began to feel the old urge gnawing at him, brought on in part by his relief at what he had learned about the events on Dutch. His appetites had forced him to risk his job and jail time for men he didn't know, yet he was still unable to control his urges. Lipski, the little Polack who acted as Boston's representative in Maine, had promised him some payback if he did as he was told, even as he was blackmailing him in another's name. Barron felt saliva flooding his mouth and the welcome ache building at his groin. He made the call.

"Yeah, it's me. Something went wrong, and the cops moved on the island."

He gave Lipski a summary of what little he knew. "Now I want what's coming to me."

He sighed when he heard the other man's reply.

"Yeah, I know I still got to pay, but you promised me something fresh, with a little off the top for my time."

Barron grinned.

"Man, you crack me up, you really do. I'll be waiting."

* * *

Barron's apartment lay off Forest, close to the university. It took up the entire top floor of the building, the rooms below rented out to students, and nurses from Maine Medical. They paid their rent to Barron although they didn't know it. He used an agency. To them, he was just another tenant. Barron didn't want them bothering him with their shit.

He took a beer from the fridge, walked to the bathroom, and lit some candles, then ran a bath, testing the water with his fingers to make sure the temperature was okay. He wanted it just a little too hot, so that it would have cooled down just enough by the time the package arrived. He stripped, put on a robe, then turned some music on low. He was just heading back to the kitchen for another beer when there was a knock at his door. There had been no buzzer, no voice over his intercom. He went to his bedside table and took out his gun, keeping it to his side and slightly behind his back as he approached the door. He looked out of the peephole, then relaxed and opened the door.

There was a boy standing before him, fifteen or sixteen at most, just the age Barron liked. He had dark hair and pale skin, with reddish-purple smudges beneath his eyes. Truth be told, Barron thought he looked kind of ill, and for a moment he was worried that maybe the kid had the virus, but Lipski had assured him that he was clean, and that was one thing about Lipski: he didn't lie about shit like that.

"How'd you get up? I leave the door open? I must have left the door open." Barron heard himself babbling, but hell, the kid had something. He was almost otherworldly. Barron felt certain that tonight was going to be special. He stepped aside to let the kid enter, noticing his faded, crude trousers, his rough cotton shirt, his bare feet. Bare feet? The hell was Lipski thinking, on a night like this?

"You leave your shoes at the front door?" Barron asked.

The boy nodded. He smelled clean, like the sea.

"Yeah, bet they got real wet. Maybe tomorrow we'll head out, buy you some sneakers."

The boy didn't reply. Instead, he looked toward the bathroom. Steam was rising from the tub.

"You like the water?"

The boy spoke for the first time.

"Yes," he said.

He followed the older man into the bathroom, his thumbs rubbing against his fingers, tracing the grooves that the waves had worn into his skin like an old song waiting for the touch of the Victrola needle to bring it alive.

"I like the water very much."

Lipski arrived forty minutes later and tried the buzzer. There was no reply. He tried twice more, then tested the door with his hand. It opened at his touch. He gestured to the boy waiting in the car, and the young man stepped out. He wore jeans, a white T-shirt, and a black leather jacket. He was shivering as he followed Lipski into the house.

The door to Barron's apartment was open when they reached it. Lipski knocked once, then again, harder this time. The door unlatched beneath the pressure of his hand. Inside there was water on the floor; just a little, as if someone had left the shower or the bath without properly drying off first. To Lipski's left, the bathroom door stood half open and he heard the sound of the tap dripping. The only light came from there.

"Barron?" he called. "Barron, man, you in there? It's Lipski."

He walked to the bathroom door and pushed it open. He took in the naked man, his knees above the surface of the water, his head below it, eyes and mouth open, one arm dangling over the edge of the tub; registered too the faint tang of saltwater that hung in the air.

He turned to the boy, who had remained standing at the door.

"Let's go," he said.

"Don't I get my money?" said the boy.

"I'll give you your money," said Lipski. "Forget you were ever here. Just forget you were ever here . . ."

Lipski led the boy down the stairs and out into the street, then stopped as two uniformed policemen advanced toward him, a plainclothes detective walking close beside them. Behind the cops, he saw the private detective named Charlie Parker leaning against a Mustang. Parker's face was expressionless as the uniforms separated Lipski from the boy. Only when Lipski was cuffed did Parker step away from the car and join the cops.

"What's this about?" said Lipski.

"I think you know what this is about," said Parker.

"No," said Lipski. "I don't."

Parker leaned in close to Lipski's face.

"It's about Barron," he said. "It's about children."

EPILOGUE

> The best way to suppose what may come, is to remember what is past.
>
> —George Halifax (1633–1695)

Marianne looked out of the window to where the boy sat on the small wooden bench at the end of the garden. From that seat, it was possible to peer through the branches of the evergreens and catch glimpses of the sea beyond. She stood at the sink, her hands immersed in soapy water, and waited for him to move, but he did not.

He has not cried, she thought. He has not wept since the night Joe Dupree died. He has not asked that we leave this place, and for the present we cannot. They are still trying to work out what happened here. Men are dead, and the reporters have washed over the island like a flood, questioning anyone who will stand still long enough to talk to them. Two weeks have gone by, and still they ask questions.

So many had died because of her: Bonnie Claeson was dead, and Richie too. His body had been washed ashore the night after the blizzard, the body of another man joined with it, both impaled upon a single arrow. Joe Dupree, the man who had shared her bed, had been laid to rest the week before. She had wept by his grave, haunted by the thought that he had died believing that he had been used and that she had felt nothing at all for him. The police were unwilling to let her leave the state until they had finished their investigation, and so the bodies of Patricia and Bill remained on ice in a morgue until she could officially identify them. She had read of the discovery of Karen Meyer's body in the newspapers. Marianne had brought death upon them all, and for that she could never forgive herself.

They had found her husband's body two days before, buried in the remains of a network of tunnels beneath the site. It appeared that he had died in the collapse. The searchers discovered dirt in his mouth; dirt, and human remains. There were finger bones lodged in his throat.

Throughout the days that followed, Sharon Macy had been her ally, her protector, the two women united by their experiences. The investigators had taken away the money, but she had been told quietly that no charges would be filed against her. The states of Maine and Virginia proved remarkably sympathetic to her plight, perhaps recognizing that a battered wife, fleeing her husband to save herself and her child, would sway even the most hard-hearted of jurors.

But Danny concerned her most of all. He had suffered through a terrible ordeal, and had seen men die in front of him. She felt that she needed to get him away from the island and the memories it held for him in the hope that time and distance might fade them. They were seated at the breakfast table, and he was merely toying with his Cheerios when she'd brought the subject up for the first time.

"I don't want to leave," Danny replied. "I want to stay here."

"But after all that has happened—"

"It doesn't matter. The bad men are dead."

"We may have to leave. People here may not want us to stay after what happened."

"They won't make us leave," he said.

And now it was she who seemed to be the younger one, the child, and he the older one, the one offering reassurance.

"How do you know?"

"He told me."

"Who told you?"

"Joe. He told me it would be okay."

She let it rest then, not wishing to return either of them to the vision of the dying policeman on the floor, the ragged wound in his throat and his blood spilling across the tiles. It came to her at night, unbidden, just as she supposed that it came to Danny too. She would not allow it to torment her son's waking moments as well.

But then Larry Amerling came to her, and he and Jack sat with her in her living room. Amerling told her that nobody on the island blamed her for what had happened, at least nobody who mattered, and that she couldn't be held responsible for the actions of her husband. The deaths of Bonnie and Richie and Joe would remain with them always, and nobody who knew them would ever forget them, but they would not be brought back by forcing Marianne and Danny to leave.

"Joe cared for you, and I know Bonnie and Richie did too," said Amerling. "Of all people, they would want you to stay."

She cried and told them that she would think about it, but

Jack, his right arm still in a sling, took her hand, and hushed her and told her that there was nothing to think about. Then Larry Amerling said something very strange.

"Maybe I'm just getting fatalistic in my old age, but I think that what happened was meant to happen," he said. "Strange as it sounds, you and Danny were brought here for a reason, your husband too. There are things about that night that I don't understand, and that I don't want to understand. I've spoken to Officer Macy, to Linda Tooker and her sister, to old Doug Newton, and others too. A lot of people on this island have tales to tell about what they saw that night. You didn't cause any of that. It was here, waiting. My guess is that it had been waiting for a long time for the chance to emerge. The island feels different now because of it. It's been purged of something that's troubled it, and it's at peace. You should stay. You're part of us. Sometimes I think you were always part of us."

Now, as she stood watching her son, she wondered at the change that had come over him in recent days. He was quieter, more subdued, and that was to be expected. But rather than his confidence being shaken, or his becoming fearful of the world beyond the island, he seemed to have grown in assurance as a consequence of the events that had occurred. The night sounds that scared her did not trouble him, and he no longer even required his night-light to be left on, the little rocket that she had bought for him at Abacus in the Old Port for his last birthday. In truth, he now appeared happier in the darkness.

As she watched him, a shadow passed over him.

It must be clouds, she thought, straining to look up at the winter sky. Maybe it's just the play of light, but there's nothing out there, nothing that I can see. The sky is empty of clouds ıd the yard is clear but for my son on his bench and the ıadow that stretches across him like a sentinel.

ɛated on his bench, the boy stared straight ahead. He did not ɔok behind him, even as he saw the shadow grow and felt the ɾesence at his shoulder.

"Listen," said the giant's voice. *"My father told me these ɔings, and now I will tell you. It is important that we remember, that the nature of the island may be understood. The first one ɔho came was named Thomas Lunt, and he brought with him his ɔife, Katie, and their children, Erik and Johann. That was in the ɔring of 1691. With them came the Leggits, Robert and Marie. Marie was pregnant at the time, and would later give birth to a ɔy, William. Others came in the weeks that followed. These are ɔeir names. You must remember them, Danny. It's very important ɔat you remember."*

And the boy listened, and he remembered all that he was ɔld.

ACKNOWLEDGMENTS

While Sanctuary is an entirely fictitious island, elements of its history and geography are based loosely on Peaks Island, which lies in Casco Bay, close to Portland, Maine. Without exception, the people I met on the island were wonderful. You should visit. You'd like it.

I am particularly grateful to Officers Christopher Hawley and Bob Morton of the Portland Police Department, who carry out their duties on Peaks Island and who were kind and patient enough to answer my endless questions about the island and their work. My thanks also to Captain Russell Gauvin of the Portland Police Department, who was once again generous enough to facilitate my research, and to Sarah Yeates, a font of knowledge. *Peaks Island: An Affectionate History* by John K. Moulton (1993); *Islands of Maine* by Bill Caldwell (Down East Books, 1981); *The Maine Coast Guide* by Curtis Rindlaub (Casco Bay, 2000); *Maine: The Pine Tree State from Prehistory to the Present,* edited by Richard W. Judd, Edwin A. Churchill, and Joel. W. Eastman (University of Maine Press, 1995); and *The Handbook of Acromegaly,* edited by John Wass (BioScientifica, 2001) were also useful to me. All mistakes are, as ever, my own.

On a personal note, my thanks go out, as always, to my wonderful editor at Atria Books, Emily Bestler; her associat[e] editor Sarah Branham; and to Louise Burke, Judith Curr, and all at Pocket and Atria for their faith in me, and for their constant kindness and support; to my editor at Hodder & Stoughton, Sue Fletcher; to Megan Underwood and the folk at Goldberg McDuffie Communications; and to my agent and friend, Darley Anderson, and his staff, for all that they have done for me; and, finally, thanks to the many booksellers and critics who have been generous enough to support my work.

Atria Books
Proudly Presents

THE BLACK ANGEL

John Connolly

Available in hardcover June 2005
from Atria Books

Turn this page for a preview of
The Black Angel . . .

The woman was seated by a window on the right side of the bus. In one day, she was passing through more states than she had previously visited in her entire life. The bus pulled into South Station in Boston. Now, with thirty minutes to spare, she wandered down to the Amtrak concourse and bought herself a cup of coffee and a Danish. Both were expensive, and she looked with dismay at the little wad of bills in her purse, adorned by a smattering of change, but she was hungry, even after the muffin the man from the garage had so kindly bought for her. She took a seat and watched the people go by, the businessmen in their suits, the harried mothers with their children. She watched the arrivals and departures change, the names clicking rapidly across the big board above her head. The trains on the platform were silver and sleek. A young black woman took a seat beside her and opened a newspaper. Her suit was neatly tailored, and her hair was cut very short. A brown leather attaché case stood at her feet, and she wore a small matching purse upon her shoulder. A diamond engagement ring gleamed upon her left hand.

I have a daughter your age, thought the old woman, but she will never be like you. She will never wear a tailored suit, or read what you read, and no man will ever give her a ring like the one that you wear. She is a lost soul, a troubled soul, but I love her, and she is mine. The man who had her upon me is gone now. He is dead, and he is no loss to the world. They would call what he did to me rape, I suppose, for I surrendered to him out of fear. We were all afraid of him, and of what he could do. We believed that he had killed my sister, for she went away with him and did not return home alive, and when he came back to us he took me in her place.

But he died for what he did, and he died badly. They asked us if we wanted them to rebuild his face, if we wanted to leave the casket open for a viewing. We told them to leave him as he was found, and to bury him in a pine box with ropes for handles. They marked his grave with a wooden cross, but on the night he was buried I went to the place where he lay and I took the cross away, and I burned it in the hope that he would be forgotten. But I gave birth to his child, and I loved her even though there was something of him in her. Perhaps she never had a chance, cursed with a father like that. He tainted her, polluting her from the moment she was born, the seed of her own destruction contained within his own. She was always a sad child, an angry child, yet how could she leave us for that other life? How could she find peace in such a city, among men who would use her for money, who would feed her drugs and alcohol to keep her pliant? How could we have let that happen to her?

And the boy—no, the man, for that is what he is now—tried to look out for her, but he gave up on her, and now she is gone. My daughter is gone, and nobody yet cares enough about her to seek her out, nobody except me. But I will make them care. She is mine, and I will bring her back. He will help me, for she is blood to him, and he owes her a blood debt.

He killed her father. Now he will bring her back to this life, and to me.

The guests were scattered through the living room and the kitchen. Some had found their way outside and were sitting beneath the bare trees in our yard, wearing their coats and enjoying the open air as they drank beer and wine and ate hot food from paper plates. Angel and Louis, as always, were slightly apart from the rest, occupying a stone bench that looked out over the marshes. Our Lab retriever, Walter, lay at their feet, Angel's fingers gently stroking his head. I went over to join them, checking as I went that nobody lacked for food and drink. . . .

A man touched me on the arm, and I found Walter Cole standing beside me. He was retired now, but he had taught me much of what I knew when I was a cop. Our bad days were behind us now, and he had come to an accommodation with what I was, and with what I was capable of doing. I left Angel and Louis . . . and walked back to the house with Walter.

"About that dog," he said.

"He's a good dog," I said. "Not smart, but loyal."

"I'm not looking to give him a job. You called him Walter."

"I like the name."

"You named your *dog* after me?"

"I thought you'd be flattered. Anyway, nobody needs to know. It's not as if he looks like you. He has more hair, for a start."

"Oh, that's very funny. Even the dog is funnier than you."

We entered the kitchen, and Walter retrieved a bottle of Sebago ale from the fridge. I didn't offer him a glass. I knew that he preferred to drink it by the neck when he could, which meant anytime he was out of his wife's sight. Outside, I saw Rachel talking with Pam. Her sister was smaller than Rachel, and spikier, which was saying something. Whenever I hugged her, I expected to be pierced by spines. Sam was asleep in an upstairs room. Rachel's mother was keeping an eye on her.

Walter saw me follow Rachel's progress through the garden.

"How are you two doing?" asked Walter.

"Three of us," I reminded him. "We're doing okay, I guess."

"It's hard, when there's a new baby in a house."

"I know. I remember."

Walter's hand rose slightly. He seemed on the verge of touching my shoulder, until his hand slowly fell away.

"I'm sorry," he said, instead. "It's not that I forget them. I don't know what it is exactly. Sometimes it seems like another life, another time. Does that make sense?"

"Yes," I said. "I know just what you mean."

There was a breeze blowing, and it caused the rope swing on the oak tree to move in a slow arc, as though an unseen child were playing upon it. I could see the channels shining in the marshes beyond, intersecting in places as they carved their paths through the reeds, the waters of one intermingling with those of another, each changed irrevocably by the meeting. Lives were like that: when their paths crossed, they emerged changed forever by the encounter, sometimes in small, almost invisible ways, and other times so profoundly that nothing that followed could ever be the same again. The residue of other lives infects us, and we in turn pass it on to those whom we later meet.

"I think she worries," I said.

"About what?"

"About us. About me. She's risked so much, and she's been hurt for it. She doesn't want to be afraid anymore, but she is. She's afraid for us, and she's afraid for Sam."

"You've talked about it?"

"No, not really."

"Maybe it's time, before things get worse."

Right now, I found it hard to imagine how much worse circumstances could get. I hated these unspoken tensions between Rachel and me. I loved her, and I needed her, but I was angry too. The burden of blame slipped too easily onto my shoulders these days. I was tired of carrying it. . . .

I won't bring harm upon you and our daughter, not by my choosing, yet still it comes. That's what I'm afraid of. It has found me before, and it will find me again. I am a danger to you, and to our child, and I think you know that.

We are coming apart.

I love you, but we are coming apart.

The day drew on. People left, and others, who were unable to make the ceremony, took their places. As the light faded, Angel and Louis were no longer speaking and were more obviously maintaining their distance from all that was taking place around them than before. Both kept their eyes fixed on the road that wound from Route 1 to the coast. Between them lay a cell phone. Arno had called them earlier that day, as soon as he had seen the woman safely onto the Greyhound bus to Boston.

"She didn't leave a name," he told Louis, his voice crackling slightly over the connection.

"I know who she is," said Louis. "You did right to call."

Now there were lights on the road. I joined them where they sat, leaning slightly on the back of the bench. Together we watched the cab cross the bridge over the marsh, the sunlight gleaming on the waters, the car's progress reflected in their depths. There was a tugging at my stomach, and my head felt as though hands were pressed hard against my temples. I could see Rachel standing unmoving among the guests. She too was watching the approaching car. Louis rose as it turned into the driveway of the house.

"This isn't about you," he said. "You got no reason to be concerned."

And I wondered at what he had brought to my house.

I followed them through the open gate at the end of the yard. Angel stayed back as Louis walked to the cab and opened the door. A woman emerged, a large, multicolored bag clasped in her hands. She was smaller than Louis by perhaps eighteen inches, and probably no more than a decade or so older than he, although her face bore the marks of a difficult life, and she wore her worries like a veil across her features. I imagined that she had been beautiful when she was younger. There was little of that physical beauty left now, but there was an inner strength to her that shone brightly from her eyes. I could see some bruising to her face. It looked very recent.

She stood close to Louis and gazed up at him with something almost like love, then slapped him hard across the left cheek with her right hand.

"She's gone," she said. "You were supposed to look out for her, but now she's gone."

And she began to cry as he took her in his arms, and his body shook with the force of her sobs.

This is the story of Alice, who fell down a rabbit hole and never came back.

Martha was Louis's aunt. A man named Deeber, now dead, had fathered a child upon her, a girl. They called her Alice, and they loved her, but she was never a happy child. She rebeled against the company of women and turned instead to men. They told her that she was beautiful, for she was, but she was young and angry. Something gnawed deep inside her, its hunger exacerbated by the actions of the women who had loved her and cared for her. They had told her that her father was dead, but it was only through others that she learned of the kind of man he was, and the manner in which he had left this world. Nobody knew who was responsible for his death, but there were rumors, hints that the neatly dressed black women in the house with the pretty garden had colluded in his killing along with her cousin, the boy called Louis.

Alice rebeled against them and all that they represented: love, security, the bonds of family. She was drawn to a bad crowd and left the safety of her mother's home. She drank, smoked some dope, became a casual user of harder drugs, and then an addict. She drifted from the places that she knew and went to live in a tin-roofed shack at the edge of a dark forest, where men paid to take turns with her. She was paid in narcotics, although their value was far less than what the johns had paid to sleep with her, and so the bonds around her tightened. Slowly she began to lose herself, the combination of sex and drugs acting like a cancer, eating away at all that she truly was, so that she became at last their creature even as she tried to convince herself that this was only a temporary aberration, a fleeting thing to help her deal with the sense of hurt and betrayal that she felt.

It was early one Sunday morning, and she was lying on a bare cot, naked but for a pair of cheap plastic shoes. She stank of men, and the hunger was upon her. Her head hurt, and the bones in her arms and legs ached. Two other women slept nearby, their quarters separated from hers by blankets hung over ropes. A small window allowed the morning light to seep into her room, sullied by the dirt upon its pane and the cobwebs, freckled with leaves and dead bugs, that hung at its corners. She pulled the blanket aside and saw that the door of the hut was open. Lowe stood in its frame, his giant shoulders almost brushing either side of the doorway. He was shirtless, his feet bare, and sweat glistened upon his shaved head and trickled slowly down between his shoulder blades. His back was pale and hairy. He had a cigarette in his right hand and was talking to another man, who stood outside. Alice figured it was Wallace, the little "high yellow" man who ran his hookers and his small-time narcotics trade from out of this hut in the woods, with a little illicit whiskey for those of more conservative tastes. A laugh came, and then she saw Wallace as he moved across the large window at the front of the hut, zipping up his fly and rubbing his fingers upon his jeans. His shirt was open and hung loose upon his pigeon chest and his little belly. He was an ugly man and rarely bathed. Sometimes he asked her to do things for him, and it was all she could do not to choke on the taste of him. But she needed him now. She needed what he had, even if it meant adding to her debt, a debt that would never be paid.

She put on a T-shirt and skirt to cover her nakedness, then lit a cigarette and prepared to pull the blanket fully across. Sundays were quiet. Some of the men who used this place would already be preparing for church, and they would sit in the pews and pretend to listen to the sermon, even as they thought of her. There were others who had not darkened a church door in many years, but even for them Sundays were different. If she could work up the energy, she might go to the mall, pick up some new clothes with the little money that she had, maybe some cosmetics too. She had been meaning to do it for a couple of weeks, but there were other distractions here. Still, even Wallace had recently commented on the state of her dresses and her underwear, although the men who came here weren't too particular. Some even liked the squalor of it, for it added a certain spice to their sense of transgression, but Wallace generally preferred to pretend that his women were clean even if their surroundings were not. If she went out early she could get her business done, then come back and relax for the afternoon. There might be some work for her in the evening, but it would not be as demanding as the night before, not by any means. Fridays and Saturdays were always the worst, with the threat of alcohol-fueled violence ever present. True, Lowe and Wallace protected the women, but they couldn't stay with them behind that curtain while the men were being serviced, and it didn't take more than a split second for a man's fist to reach a woman's face.

There came the sound of a car approaching. She could see it through the doorway as it turned. Unlike most of the cars that came to this place, this one was new. It looked like one of those German cars, and the chrome on its wheels was spotless. The engine growled briefly as it came to a stop. She saw doors opening, front and back. Wallace said something that she could not hear, and Lowe tossed his cigarette on the ground, his other hand already reaching behind his back to where the butt of the big Colt emerged from his jeans. Before he could grasp it, his shoulders exploded in a red cloud that billowed briefly in the sunlight, then fell wetly to the floor. Somehow he remained standing, and she saw his hands clutch at the door frame, holding himself upright. Footsteps crunched on the gravel outside, then the second shot came and part of Lowe's head disappeared. His hands relinquished their grip, and he fell to the ground.

Alice stood frozen, rooted to the spot. Outside, she could hear Wallace pleading for his life. He was backing toward the hut, and she could see his body grow larger and larger as he neared the window. There were more shots, and the glass shattered into thousands of pieces, the remaining shards in the frames edged with blood. Now she could hear the other girls responding. To her right, Rowlene was screaming repeatedly. She was a big girl, and Alice could almost picture her on her bed, her sheet pulled up to her chest, her eyes drowsy and flecked with red as she tried to make herself small in the corner of her bunk. To her left, she could hear Pria, who was half Asian, strike the wall as she struggled to clear her head and find her clothes. Pria had partied with two johns the night before, and they had shared some of their buy with her. She was probably still high.

The figure of a man appeared in the door frame. Alice briefly glimpsed his face as he entered, and the sight gave her the impetus she needed. She allowed the blanket to fall gently, then climbed on her bunk and pushed at the window. At first it would not move, even as she heard the man moving through the hut, coming closer to the whores' quarters. She hit the frame with the base of her palm, and it swung out with barely a sound. Alice pulled herself up and squeezed herself through the gap, even as the next shot came from the stall beside her own and splinters burst from the wall. Rowena was gone. She uld be next. Behind her, a hand grasped the blanket and lled it to the floor as gravity took hold and Alice tumbled to ground. She felt something snap in her hand as she fell kwardly, and then she was running for the cover of the trees, len branches snapping beneath her feet as she ducked and aved into the forest. The shotgun roared again, and an alder integrated barely inches from her right foot.

She kept running, even though her feet were cut by stones d her clothing torn by briars and thorns. She did not stop til the pain in her side was so great that she felt as though were being ripped in half. She lay against a tree and ought that she heard, distantly, the sounds of men. She knew face of the man at the door. He was one of those who had ken Pria the night before. She did not know why he had urned, or what had led him to do what he did. All she knew s that she had to get away from this place, for they knew o she was. They had seen her, and they would find her. Alice led her mother from a phone at a gas station, the pumps ked and the station closed, for it was still early on Sunday orning. Her mother came with clothing, and what money had, and Alice left that afternoon and did not ever return the state in which she was born. She called in the years that lowed, mostly with requests for money. She called weekly at st, and sometimes more often than that. It was Alice's one failing concession to her mother, and even at her lowest she vays tried to keep the older woman from worrying more an she already did. There were other small kindnesses too: thday gifts that arrived early, or more often late, but arrived netheless; cards at Christmas, a little cash included in the rly years, but later only a signature and a scrawled greeting; d, very occasionally, a letter, the quality of the script and the lor of the ink varying in accordance with the lengthy process of the missive's completion. Her mother cherished them a but mostly she was grateful for the calls. They let her kno that her daughter was still alive.

Then the calls ceased.

Martha sat on the couch in my office, Louis standing to o side of her, Angel seated quietly in my chair. I was by the fi place. Rachel had looked in on us briefly, then left.

"You should have looked out for her," Martha again to Louis.

"I tried," he said. He looked old and tired. "She didn't wa help, not the kind I could offer her."

Martha's eyes ignited.

"How can you say that? She was lost. She was a lost soul. S needed someone to bring her back. That should have been you

This time, Louis said nothing.

"You went to Hunts Point?" I asked.

"Last time we spoke, she said that was where she was at, that was where I went."

"Is that where you got hurt?"

She lowered her head.

"A man hit me."

"What was his name?" asked Louis.

"Why?" she said. "You gonna do for him like you done f others? You think that will find your cousin? You just want feel like a big man, now it's too late to do what a good ma would have done. Well, that don't wash with me."

I intervened. The recriminations would get us nowhere.

"Why did you go to him?"

"Because Alice done told me she was working for him no The other one, the one she was with before, he died. She sa this new one was gonna take care of her, that he was going to find wealthy men for her. Wealthy men! What man would want her after all she'd done? What man . . . ?"

She started to cry again.

I went to her and handed her a clean tissue, then slowly knelt down before her.

"We'll need his name, if we're to start looking for her," I said quietly.

"G-Mack," she said at last. "He calls himself G-Mack. There was a young white girl too. She said she remembered Alice, but she was calling herself LaShan on the street. She didn't know where she'd gone to."

"G-Mack," said Louis.

"Ring any bells?"

"No. Last I heard she was with a pimp called Free Billy."

"Looks like things changed."

Louis stood and helped Martha from her chair.

"We need to get you something to eat. You need to rest up now."

She took his hand and gripped it tightly in her own.

"You find her for me. She's in trouble. I can feel it. You have to find her and bring her back to me."

The fat man stood at the lip of the bathtub. His name was Brightwell, and he was very, very old, far older than he seemed. Sometimes he acted like a man who had recently woken from a deep sleep, but the Mexican, whose name was Garcia, knew better than to question him about his origins. He recognized only that Brightwell was a thing to be obeyed, and to be feared. He had seen what the man had done to the woman, had watched through the glass as the fat man's mouth closed on hers. It had seemed to him that some grave knowledge had shown itself in the woman's eyes at that moment, even as she weakened and died, as though she realized what was about to occur as her body failed her at last. How many others had he taken in this way? Garcia wondered, his lips against theirs as he waited for their essence to pass from them. And even if what Garcia suspected of Brightwell was not true, what kind of man would believe such a thing of himself?

The stench was terrible as the chemicals worked on the remains, but Brightwell made no attempt to cover his face. The Mexican stood behind him now, the lower half of his face concealed by a white mask.

"What will you do now?" said Garcia.

Brightwell spit into the tub, then turned his back on the disintegrating body. "I will find the other one, and I will kill her."

"Before she died, this one spoke of a man. She thought he might come for her."

"I know. I heard her call his name."

"She was supposed to be alone. Nobody cared."

"We were misinformed, but perhaps nobody cares anyway."

Brightwell swept by him, leaving him with the decaying body of the girl. Garcia did not follow him. Brightwell was wrong, but Garcia did not have the courage to confront him further on the issue. No woman, as death approached, would cry out over and over again a name that meant nothing to her.

Someone did care.

And he would come.